The Patron Saint of Lost Comfort Lake

the PATRON SAINT *of* LOST COMFORT LAKE

RACHEL L. COYNE

New Rivers Press

American Fiction Series

First Edition
Library of Congress Control Number: 2013950958
ISBN: 978-0-89823-316-2
eISBN: 978-0-89823-317-9
American Fiction Series

Cover and interior design by Jamie Hohnadel Trosen
Author photo by Gerald Carlson

The publication of *The Patron Saint of Lost Comfort Lake* is made possible
by the generous support of Minnesota State University Moorhead,
The McKnight Foundation, the Dawson Family Endowment, Northern Lights
Library Network, and other contributors to New Rivers Press.

For copyright permission, please contact Frederick T. Courtright
at 570-839-7477 or permdude@eclipse.net.

New Rivers Press is a nonprofit literary press associated with
Minnesota State University Moorhead.

Alan Davis, Co-Director and Senior Editor
Suzzanne Kelley, Co-Director and Managing Editor
Wayne Gudmundson, Consultant
Allen Sheets, Art Director
Thom Tammaro, Poetry Editor
Kevin Carollo, MVP Poetry Coordinator
Vincent Reusch, MVP Prose Coordinator

Publishing Interns:
David Binkard, Katelin Hansen, Jan Hough, Kjersti Maday, Richard Natale,
Emily Nelson, Daniel Shudlick, Lauren Stanislawski, Michele F. Valenti

The Patron Saint of Lost Comfort Lake Book Team:
Benjamin Friesen, Särah Nour, Telia Rattliff-Cross, Nayt Rundquist

Printed in the USA

New Rivers Press books are distributed nationally by
Consortium Book Sales and Distribution.

New Rivers Press
c/MSUM
1104 7th Avenue South
Moorhead, MN 56563

For J.R.

I ACCEPT THE THINGS I CANNOT CHANGE.
—Serenity Prayer

1

Underneath, in the ground where we're buried, I assumed the three lakes around my home, Big Comfort, Little Comfort, and Lost Comfort, were all really connected—all one pool of black, subterranean cool. Above, they were as separate from each other as the moon from its reflection in their waters.

I always associated Big Comfort with the town where I went to school and where I worked at the Red Owl until I was sixteen. Little Comfort reminded me of my mother. I was baptized there with a placard around my neck announcing my sins—disrespectful to parents. But Lost Comfort always called to mind my father, Pitch, and his regular bar nestled on its far bank, the only thing that remained of a duck-hunting lodge and estate, once grand.

I drove the long, slow loop around Lost Comfort Lake—such as it was, shallow and weedy—until I reached the fork in the road. The reeds and cattails went on for miles along the ditch until some invisible border was breached, and then lake water surged from underground, overcoming the reeds, forming a true lake that stretched to a pine-ridged far bank. Left would take me home to the house—such as it was—where I'd grown up.

I stopped the car and rested my head against the wheel.

Inside the car was silent, bright, filled with light. I couldn't hear the wind moving outside, though it flattened the reeds and pushed the clouds across the sky. Without the sound, I felt disconnected, miles away from where I really was. The whole world moved on one breath. I stayed seated, fixed. It was disorienting. I closed my eyes and listened to the sound of my own breath filling the car. Visiting day with Pitch usually left me feeling like this.

When I opened my eyes again, I found myself staring at my own hands, clenched white on the steering wheel. One at a time, I pried my fingers loose and let my hands fall uselessly down. The knuckles ached. I watched them sit limply in my lap. My hands seemed utterly separate from me, odd and severed things.

I flexed my fingers and swallowed hard. Only then, I eased back into motion, squinting out through the bright sun at the uberous, undulating green all around me. I turned right, not left towards home.

The right turn pulled me away from the reeds into the thick stand of pines that circled the lake. The carpet of pine needles softened the noise of the gravel crunching under the car. The sunlight filtering into the car turned slightly cool and green. Once I made the decision to take the right turn, I felt light, as if I were being deposited on my destination's doorstep by a current of subterranean water, totally outside myself, hidden in my own rocky earth.

The Lost Comfort Bar itself was a low, log structure with a dirt parking lot and shuttered windows. The last time Pitch brought me here, I was maybe ten. I remembered it was hunting season, with all the newly-killed deer hung suspended in the trees around the parking lot. I remembered watching Pitch's back disappear into the light of the bar and the feeling of being left alone among the butchered and the dead in the dark. It wasn't a feeling you forget.

I remembered how the deer spun slowly on their ropes, their tongues hanging from their mouths like obscene members. Their antlers clicked eerily against the branches that creaked with the heavy weight of the carcasses. The animals' stomachs had been slit and the guts torn out. The old guys stuffed sticks in there to hold the cavity open. The deer drained better that way.

Even though I had known they were dead, I didn't want their blank, flat eyes to see me. Still, I knew better than to follow Pitch into the bar. When his back disappeared completely, I locked the car doors and slid down in the seat as far as I could. Old Lee Ring, the bar's owner, terrified me. I didn't want him to find me in the car. He almost had once.

The noise from the bar ought to have been reassuring. But something about the heavy tree limbs always dampened it to a low murmur, sometimes broken by a harsh laugh. It was like the noise Pitch made in his sleep when he drank too much—guttural and threatening.

Worse, the lake below would echo back the sound, and the trees collected it under their boughs. It didn't always seem as if the voices came from the bar. The murmur was both steady and all around me, seeming to come from the old cabins, the trees, and the deer themselves. Above the murmur floated Patsy Cline's voice from the juke box. Pitch's bar was the type of bar that played Patsy Cline, even then.

Still sitting in my car outside the bar, I checked my cell phone. My ex-husband had my daughter, Reine, for the day, but hadn't left any messages. I tucked the phone under the seat. They wouldn't be back from St. Paul until late. The little bit of wind I noticed earlier kicked up a small cloud of dry August dust from the parking lot. The bar's open sign wasn't lit, but the door was open. There were a few cars in the lot, including Ardell Ring's pick-up with a rusting box and volunteer fireman plates. Ardell was Lee's son. I glanced up at the trees. The deer were gone. Lee was gone and Pitch was in prison, but other than that, not a damn thing had changed since I was ten years old.

A rdell Ring was at the end of the long, wood bar. He was looking at the clock and listening to the police radio. He wasn't the twenty-year-old in my memory anymore. Now he was a man who badly needed a haircut and who showed all of his forty-five years.

Especially around his eyes. He was still tall and still lean, but the muscles in his chest and shoulders weren't strung as tight as new barbed wire anymore. The hard expression on his face had the permanent set of a surveyor's marker. I guess growing up in a bar and being Lee Ring's son will do that to you.

The wooden bar was dark and grimy with smoke. The rafters above seemed to swallow the long room whole, like a biblical whale. And the smell reminded you of being inside a fish. The bar, the chairs, the tables were all pitted with use. It wasn't a cheery place. I wouldn't have been surprised to learn that the old man's corpse had been crammed beneath the floorboards, next to his old man, like some grim Edgar Allan Poe tale.

Ardell was washing down the bar counter. An old man sat, his elbow on the bar, and a lumpy pair—man and woman—sat in a booth. The male half of the booth couple was asleep, and she was looking deeply stoned; her face expressionless and her eyes watery.

When I entered, Ardell's eyes flicked from the clock to me. On the radio, the county dispatcher hummed on, then off. There was a 911 call for a domestic on Ferber Road. Ardell was listening for the fire calls.

The old man at the bar rolled his head back and started to talk. "Do you think Larson will bother to show up?"

"Shut the fuck up, Jack," Ardell said.

"Fuck you back," the old man replied. He spat a little through his loose teeth when he talked.

Ardell met me farther down the bar, still keeping a close eye on the old man. Behind him were three long rows of bottles and a stained mirror covered with beer posters. Most featured an animal, a fish, or a mountain. The tape at the corners was yellowed. Ardell took my twenty without greeting. The ancient metal register behind the counter still had push-button keys and chimed slightly when it opened. He slammed it closed. He put a glass on the bar.

I'd been coming here after visiting day since I moved back home. I'd never taken a drink at the bar. "I'll take it with me," I said.

He knew this. Ardell shrugged and pulled a bottle from under the bar. I reached for the gin.

"How's your father?" he asked, his hand still wrapped around the neck of my bottle.

Though I'd been coming here for months, I hadn't been sure until now that Ardell remembered me. I'd left home at sixteen. Coming here was easier than buying a bottle in town where everyone knew my mom.

I nodded, meaning anything or nothing. Visiting day wasn't a good day to ask me about Pitch.

Ardell still didn't hand over the bottle.

I realized that my throat had constricted too painfully to talk. Pitch was five years sober in prison, with two years left on his sentence for manslaughter but only a few more months to live. He had cancer and it was eating him alive as fast as it could. I hadn't even told my mother yet.

I nodded stupidly at him again, which could have meant anything, and I turned to go.

He followed me to the door. "You paid for this, remember?" He held out the bottle.

I took it and placed it in my purse, relieved and angry. I wouldn't come here again. I pulled on the zipper too hard and my keys fell from my hand. I swore.

Ardell almost smiled. He bent, gathered up my keys, and handed them to me.

"I didn't mean to upset you, Janey."

For a moment, he touched my hand.

When I was a child, if it wasn't too dark, I'd poke around the old grounds and cabins while Pitch drank. It was too boring to sit in the car for hours. One cabin was stacked to the ceiling with flavored pop. I'd sit in there and drink from the hot orange bottles. Or go swimming down at the old dock. If Ardell caught me nosing around, I'd just run away. It didn't seem like the best option today.

Right next to the door was the jukebox I remembered playing "Walking After Midnight" on an endless loop through my childhood. Since I'd started coming back here, I'd noticed that it had been busted. The front glass was cracked and shattered, as if it had been hit by a blunt object. Inside, the old paper strips naming the songs hung broken and limp. They were dusty, reflecting a long-standing condition of neglect. "How come you never get this fixed?" I asked. "It's practically an antique."

Ardell looked the machine over. "I broke it myself," he said at last. "When I sobered up about four years ago. All the drunks want to play country music. No one can stay sober listening to that shit."

Whatever I had expected him to say, it wasn't that. His eyes were as dark as the room. I didn't think he was joking.

"Do you want me to fix it, Janey?" he asked.

I shook my head, irritated."Goodbye, Ardell," I said firmly.

"See you next month," he said.

When I sat down in the car again, an almost painful pinch reminded me of the medallion in my pocket—Pitch's five-year sobriety medal. I pulled it out and turned the little bit of metal over in my hand. He'd reached his milestone a few weeks ago, but waited to have the little ceremony with me on visiting day. Maybe ceremony is a strong word.

His prison drug counselor gave him the medal and they recited the Serenity Prayer. That was it. His sunken eyes and grey face looked frightened and pale. His voice faltered when he read, "I accept the things I cannot change," off the little paper card.

Pitch had made special efforts to dress up for me. Even the blanket they draped over his ruined legs had been folded crisp across the top. His sparse hair had been combed. It had made my eyes burn. The prayer had made my chest hurt, like someone had pushed me. Hard. When it was over, the counselor had left us alone. He pressed the medallion into my hand and neither of us could talk much.

I put the little medallion on the dashboard and let my eyes wander past the parking lot to the blue-green lake. I reached into my glove compartment and pulled out a juice glass wrapped in a plastic bag. The crinkling noise filled the car when I unwrapped it. There was a winking, smiling woman painted on the glass's front and the words, Welcome to Cabo. The woman wore a bright red skirt. I poured the gin just up to her hem.

I have rules when I drink. When you have a father like mine, you have to. Rule number one was never fill the glass past the skirt's hem. Rule number two was never get drunk in front of your kid. Rules number three and four didn't seem to apply anymore. At least not since my husband had left and I'd quit practicing law.

I drained my glass and stared at the old lodging house behind the bar. It had boarded windows and a mossy roof sinking in like sand being drawn down an hourglass. Lee Ring had lived there until he died, among the rats and broken floorboards. Ardell had sealed the place up.

Thinking about Ardell seemed to conjure him up. I swore softly and refilled my glass. He leaned in my open window.

"I didn't hear you leave," he said. "Everything okay, Janey?"

I nodded and placed my glass between my legs so it wouldn't spill. I started up the car and reached to put the car in reverse.

"Ardell," I said, my voice tight with anger. "Only Pitch called me Janey."

Ardell nodded. "I'll remember that."

If there are rules for living with Windy, my mother, I've yet to learn what the hell they are. When I pulled into Windy's driveway, I found her sitting on the steps of the front porch, leaning a little to one side. She was in her robe and nightgown. It was after 2 p.m.

I felt myself frown, my eyes scanning the yard and porch. For a moment I thought she'd just locked herself out. But the door behind her hung open.

When I opened the car door, her head snapped up and she saw me. She let out a cry that seemed to rip the air between us. I felt myself go numb with apprehension. Thinking of my daughter, I crossed the yard in a few steps, as if I were on casters. The look on her face reminded me of the night Pitch had his accident. I grabbed her. "What's wrong?" I demanded. "Did Denny call? Is Reine okay?"

Windy leaned heavily into me and I felt myself wobble under her weight. She gulped a little like she couldn't breathe. Her eyes bulged. "Tell me," I said more loudly, shaking her, the way my voice shook. "What's going on?"

She was a steady weight dragging me into deeper and deeper water. She collapsed against me in slow motion. "There's a girl," she said so hoarsely it was hard to hear. "A girl down by the lake at the pines."

Direction was all I'd needed. I pried Windy's fingers from my arm and I let her fall as I ran. I pictured my daughter—*something was wrong*—and I ran towards that image as fast as I could.

Windy crumbled behind me, down onto the cement sidewalk, like a house falling in on itself. "Call 911!" I screamed back at her, but knew she was beyond understanding.

There wasn't far to go and I flew. There was the shed, then a stand of pines just along the steep drop-off into the lake. And there she was.

It was not my daughter. I heard myself cry out with physical shock, like a blow. It was a noise of something being suddenly, cruelly compressed. My heart spasmed painfully in my chest. The girl, *who was not my daughter*, lay still, just in the water along the shore. She was pale like a bit of late-melting snow, sheltered from the sun by the pines and the bank. She was very young. Maybe fifteen. And she was unmistakably dead.

3

She was as cold as the lake, as a silver fish, barely glinting from the bottom. Her mouth hung open in surprise and her eyes were fixed on the sky. Windy stumbled down the incline, her face hot, red, and teary.

"Should we take her up to the house?" she quavered.

I stared at her, then the girl. Windy was reaching for me again. I shook her off quickly, needing to free myself. "I need to call 911," I said. "We have to call the police."

"I already did," she said. "I told them she looks . . ." Windy couldn't say the word. She reached for me again.

"Come up to the house with me," I said more sharply than I intended. She started at the tone of my voice. "We'll need to flag the police down at the driveway."

Chastised, she followed me meekly back up the hill and all the way down the driveway. We stood there at the mouth of the road and waited. Windy stood beside me, hugging herself to hold the loose ends of her robe closed, swaying slightly.

Then in the distance I heard the sirens coming, an aching almost-human wail. It grew sharper, more mechanical as it neared. I glanced at Windy, the noise of the sirens cutting through the deep fog in my brain. She was holding herself so tightly that she'd scratched angry red welts down her bare, freckled arms. Her eyes were fixed on the road where the police would soon appear. I felt a tinge of guilt and reached over to wrap her in my arms. Windy was small and shorter than me; I could tuck her head under my chin.

But the gesture made her start in surprise. She pushed me away from her, hard enough that I stumbled. "Leave me alone," she said, her voice breaking completely.

Just then the police squad car materialized in the distance down the road. Windy turned and ran back up towards the house.

The fire department's rescue squad arrived just behind the police in a big grass rig that hardly fit up Windy's dirt driveway. The two other trucks followed and the sheriff's deputy arrived next. There were maybe a dozen firefighters—all local guys and most of them fathers. I'd gone to school with some of them, and recognized others as friends of Pitch. One firefighter knelt beside the girl in the water and felt for a pulse in her blue-white wrist. I shivered when he touched her. No one said anything. There wasn't the usual rush of a rescue scene. The fireman's eyes met the local cop's. He stepped away. Her hand slipped back into the green water.

"Pull her out," he said. They did. I couldn't watch.

When they had her to shore, one of the firefighters took off his jacket and handed it to the cop. He spread it over the girl's thin rib cage and legs. He worked quickly, but gently.

Then the local cop put his baseball cap back on and turned and walked back up the hill. The firefighters filed after him. The sheriff's deputy canceled the ambulance on its way and asked dispatch to send out the coroner. From beneath the jacket, the girl's white hand poked out. I wanted to cover that up, too. The deputy turned his back on me, staring out at the lake, his mouth grim.

I glanced back up the hill. The local cop was standing there alone, watching me closely. The fire department volunteers were climbing back in their truck. As they pulled away, there was still no sign of Windy.

Apprehensively, I walked back up the hill, feeling suddenly like I'd been awake for days without rest.

The local cop wasn't really local because I didn't know him from high school. He was about my age, an Indian man with short black hair. I'd have guessed Joe James had never had any other job than as a cop. He was tall and straight, almost thin but not quite. His face was deeply freckled, making him seem younger than he was. Being a cop suited him. He looked you directly, gravely in the eye.

The first time I had ever seen Joe was at Pitch's trial. I could tell he didn't recognize me. It'd been five years and I was a little thinner, dressed in jeans and a man's shirt. Not the suits I'd worn to the trial.

"Are you the one who called 911?" he asked.

"No," I answered. "She's in the house."

"When did she find the girl?" he asked.

"I don't know," I said. "I came just before you arrived."

"Do you know this girl?" he asked. He tilted his head to look me in the eye when he spoke. I remembered him clearly on the witness stand. He'd been the first cop on the scene then, too. On the stand, he stayed calm, reading to the judge from his notes. My father's blood alcohol had been 0.3 on the night of the car accident. I remembered seeing Joe out in the hallway after his testimony, holding the little girl's mother while she sobbed and sobbed. The noise filled the little hallway like a beating pulse.

"No," I answered truthfully. I had never seen the girl in my life. "Not this one."

I took Joe in to Windy, who had locked herself in her room. He knocked gently on the door. "Windy," he said. "It's Joe James. Do you remember me? I need to talk to you about what you found."

"Go away," she said from behind her door. I could picture her clearly on the other side, her body leaning against the frame. She was crying unsteadily.

"Mom," I said, "the police would like to speak with you. You need to come out and tell them what you know about the girl. When did you find her?"

We heard a shuffling and a fumbling from inside. The noise of a drawer being banged shut. Then Windy appeared at her door, eyeing us through a small crack. When she saw Joe she opened the door all the way. She was still in her nightgown, still streaked with tears, but her face had gone oddly slack. Starkly and noticeably so.

Joe frowned.

"I took some of my pills," she wheezed. "Some of my pain pills for my back."

His frown deepened. She put her hand to her chest, her face crumbling completely. "My chest hurts real bad."

Joe called the ambulance back on his radio.

4

In the end, Windy was all right. The ambulance crew sat her out in the truck and hooked her up to a monitor. She gave Joe her information, which wasn't much, while they worked on her.

She'd been on a walk down along the property line when she found the girl.

She must have been that way a thousand times.

Maybe last week was the last time she'd been out there.

She had never seen the girl before.

She looked young.

She looked dead.

I listened from outside, leaning against the ambulance. I eyed my parked car, its closed door and the bottle inside, still hidden beneath the seat. My throat was so dry it burned and my head throbbed.

I felt the keys in my pocket, calculating how much longer Joe would want to talk. Right then, Joe climbed out of the rig and a new truck with a rusted-out box pulled up. I frowned, seeing Ardell behind the wheel.

Joe waved at him, not seeming surprised at his arrival. He walked over to Ardell's window and leaned in.

"I heard the call," Ardell told him, his eyes sliding to me. I had forgotten he was with the fire department. "I was late on the first one, closing down the bar. Just about turned around when I heard the second ambulance call. I thought I'd stop in."

Joe shook his head. "The coroner's on her way. Not much to do. The lady who lives here had some chest pain, but that's resolved itself."

"Did the rescue squad come out?" Ardell asked.

Joe nodded. "Left maybe ten minutes ago."

Ardell's eyes flicked to me again. "Everyone else okay?"

I stared determinedly at Windy's feet poking out of the ambulance.

Joe reassured him and stepped back from the truck. Ardell backed slowly out of the driveway, pausing at the road to let the coroner's plain white van roll in. The van drove straight down the hill, over the grass. A woman and two men climbed out.

I found myself once again being studied by Joe.

"Any idea who she is?"

I shook my head. "Never seen her in my life."

"Why are you here today?"

"I live here. With my daughter, too. She's with her father now, who doesn't live here," I clarified.

"Did you hear any noise or disturbance last night?"

I shook my head.

"How about this morning?"

"I left when it was still dark and was gone all day."

"Where were you?"

"At the Rush City prison," I said. "Visiting my father."

His eyes flickered slightly, but that was all. He was a good cop. His gaze drifted from me to Windy's naked feet, still poking out of the ambulance, then back again. "I see," he said, and I knew he'd just now remembered me.

He took my full name and date of birth anyways. He asked me for Windy's information as well, though I knew he'd been to the house a million times when Pitch still lived here. He needed our phone number and contact information.

"Here at the house is fine," I said. "I don't work anymore. Not since I moved home."

"Where did you used to work?"

"The Ramsey County Attorney's office as a prosecutor."

He paused in writing, his eyes faintly curious.

"Call Collin Hamstad. Check it out."

"Why would I check it out?" he asked mildly.

"Because you just found a dead teenage girl in my backyard," I said. "Because you're a cop. And you know who my father is."

"I know Collin, too," he said.

"Most everyone does. He was a good boss."

Windy sat up in the ambulance. She pulled off the tape from the monitor, fixing her still-teary eyes on me. "I don't want to stay here tonight," she said.

It didn't happen often, but I agreed with her. The sky was darkening to evening. My daughter, Reine, was going to be home in the next few hours. I didn't want to have to explain this to an eight-year-old. Glancing down the hill, it seemed that the coroner was just starting her work. I assumed it would take a while.

I turned back to Joe James. "Do you know where the Hi-Way Motel is?" I asked. "Put that down for our contact information as well."

He nodded and jotted it down.

"Can we talk while I go inside and pack some clothes for my daughter?"

He waved me away. "We're fine for now. I need to speak with the coroner."

He turned and walked down the hill. I waited a moment for Windy to climb unsteadily out of the ambulance. She trailed behind me like a plump, damp toddler. I noticed a pile of junk by the entryway that hadn't been there this morning, sprawling out a little towards the kitchen. There were boxes of antlers, jumbled together, empty bottles of Pitch's favorite hooch, and some rags.

Ever since Pitch had gone to prison, Windy had been slowly moving him out of the house. Box by box. Inch by inch. All of it to a shed we used to use for boats down by the lake.

"Go pack a bag," I told Windy grimly, eyeing the antlers as if they were thorns. "Just five minutes and we'll go."

The headlights of my ex-husband's silver Mercedes lit up the whole dingy motel parking lot like a bright celluloid meteor. I tucked my bottle into my purse and pulled the zipper quickly closed. Whatever pills Windy had taken had knocked her out in the back seat. She snored softly, still clutching her bulky overnight bag. It rattled whenever she moved it and I suspected she'd packed more pills than underwear.

For a little while Denny and I stared at each other, trying to determine who would move first. I gave up. I wanted to see my daughter, so I climbed out of my car. Still, he made me wait. Slowly, he conferred with Louisa, his wife, and then Reine. He eyed me all the while, staring at the spot where I stood as if I wasn't there. As if he were merely observing a slightly interesting door or light pole.

Louisa locked the door behind him when he finally exited his car. It made me smile grimly at her. She dropped her eyes, fiddling with the radio.

"Jesus," Denny said, looking around the almost vacant parking lot, "what the fuck now? Why the hell would you call and tell me to meet you here?"

I opened my mouth to speak. I closed it again, surprised at the tight feeling in my throat. Rule number one about ex-husbands is to not unravel in front of them. Even on days like today.

I tried again. It was easier to examine his car than Denny when I spoke. It was new since the divorce. The novelty plate read DENNY1. The front hood was smooth and burnished like a pan fish, so sleek it looked wet.

"Windy found a body in the lake," I said, choosing small, tight words. I was worried about my voice. "Unknown girl. About fifteen. A drowning maybe."

Denny tore his eyes away from a couple getting stoned in the other car in the lot. He stared at me—really stared, looking me over from head to toe. I felt the full attention of his blue eyes—maybe for the first time in years. My throat constricted so much, I felt like an actual hand must be throttling it. I looked away.

"Fuck," he swore softly. Then he added in a quiet voice that surprised me, "Is Windy all right?"

I nodded tersely, still not looking at him. I didn't like his kind tone. I didn't need it. It stirred my anger, like a leaf on the wind—impossible to catch. I felt my body go rigid as I worked to smother the urge to chase it. *Reine is watching*, I reminded myself.

Denny wasn't a dumb man. That's why I had married him. He felt the change in the air. He didn't back away, but his voice was harder when he spoke again.

"I've known Windy for almost ten years, so drop the shit, Jane," he said. "She's my daughter's grandmother and I've a right to know if she's okay."

I forced the edges of my mouth into a hard smile. "I'll be sure to tell Windy that you care so deeply. The thought of losing you as a son-in-law has kept her up nights."

"You know, Jane, I called Windy just last week. We're fine. You're the only fucking one who thinks a scorched earth policy is a good thing in a divorce."

"It's my burning ground you're standing on," I hissed. "Go the hell home if you don't like it."

Denny was actually so mad that his face twitched. He took a slow, calming breath that shuddered despite his best efforts at control. "Where are you staying tonight?" he tried to ask more coolly. "Here? With Reine?"

"There's a pool," I offered. "She'll like that."

His eyes bulged slightly. "This place is a shithole. Let me take Reine back to St. Paul."

"She has camp tomorrow. First thing," I said, shaking my head, "I have her clothes ready to go. She's only got a few days left of camp, before you guys go to Florida."

"And you want her to go to camp and be fucking Rebecca of sunny-hick farm. Yeah, I get it, we've covered it before."

We had, so I didn't need to say anything.

"And I told you . . ." he began.

"Can I come out now?" Reine asked, rolling down the window of the car.

We both turned. Denny's eyes cut to Louisa who mouthed "sorry," holding up her hands.

Denny was still obviously skeptical about my assurances that life could continue on as normal with a dead girl in my backyard, us moving to a motel, and Windy passed out in my back seat. But Reine was listening now, and he didn't want to say any more. He pressed his lips into a hard line. Then without another word or glance at me, he turned and climbed back into his car.

Inside, he had a brief conference with Reine. I couldn't hear the words, but I saw their heads bend together, almost touching. All the while, Louisa craned her horse neck around to look at the motel. Reine and Denny talked and nodded, and then suddenly Reine popped out of the car, shrugging her pink backpack onto her shoulders.

"Hi, Momma!" she said, bounding towards me. She smiled and hugged me. I fought the urge to scoop her up into my arms and cling to her fiercely. She was alive and beautiful. She was safe. It was hard to look at one girl, without thinking of another less lucky child now being carried to the morgue.

Reine turned and waved goodbye to her father. With her back turned to me, I took the opportunity to give him the finger. Denny rolled his eyes and started his car.

With Denny and his Mercedes gone, the parking lot dimmed considerably. Reine slid her hand in mine. It was a peaceful summer twilight, slow and blue, even here. Especially now that Reine had arrived. Still, I felt my smile falter slightly when I looked down at her. I felt certain she would ask the reason for this abrupt move.

"Daddy says they have a pool!" she said instead. "Just like in Florida?"

I nodded, grateful. I checked Windy in the back seat. Still sleeping. Swinging our hands together, Reine and I went to the main office. We claimed a key on a worn blue triangle of plastic and the stern warning that the pool closed at 10.

Generally, the Hi-Way Motel lived up to the promise of its name. It was located on the county road and that was its main amenity. Most of the motel was painted a fading baby blue. It was a long, low-slung cement structure, with a row of rooms stretching out from the main office. All of the doors facing the highway were a different battered color. Room 8 was easy to find, in a straight line between 7 and 9. There weren't any pictures on the walls, just a white plastic crucifix near the door.

In back, there was a small pool surrounded by an acre of cement, with old folding lawn chairs scattered here and there. There was no grass at the Hi-Way, just cement and asphalt waiting to be hosed down.

I sent Reine into the bathroom to change into her swimsuit. While she wasn't looking, I practically drug her unconscious grandmother inside and flung her on the bed. Truth be told, I was relieved that Windy had medicated herself so heavily. I wasn't sure I could handle more tears like earlier—at least not in front of Reine.

Reine practically exploded from the bathroom, ready to swim. Windy grunted a little in her sleep. I trailed in Reine's wake across the green outdoor carpet to the pool. Reine dove in. I bought her an orange pop from the vending machine and myself a Diet Coke. I poured half my soda out into the floor drain and refilled it with gin from my purse.

Finally, I sat at the edge of the pool, drinking, dangling my feet, and watching her.

I loved my girl. She flipped and turned and practiced her strokes back and forth across the tiny pool. The water sloshed over the sides everywhere with her enthusiasm. When she saw I was settled, she kicked to me. She chattered about her upcoming annual trip to Florida. When I was still married to her father, we had gone every year.

Despite her fortifying presence, I had to fight off a strong feeling of exhaustion. I let my thoughts simply bump along on her stream of words. When she was done in the pool, we walked down and played both of the games at the little arcade near the vending machine. Then we checked on Windy, who was still sleeping, and watched a movie on cable.

At midnight, Reine was finally calmed down enough to lie down in the bed beside her grandmother. I lay prone in the other bed, listening to her breath grow slow and steady. When she was asleep at last, I sat up again. Restless, tired, I wandered back out to the pool. In the now-complete dark, the pool's underwater lights glowed like the headlights of Denny's Mercedes. I glanced up at the sky above. It was black and I shivered in the evening cool.

I sat in the most sturdy-looking of the old lawn chairs. It wobbled a little rustily beneath me. I eyed my near-empty bottle of gin and considered the shabby door to our motel room. I dug Pitch's five-year medallion out of my pocket, and I drained the rest of the bottle raw.

I closed my eyes as my hand closed around the little coin and my throat burned with unmixed gin. I knew enough about life to not want to have this moment.

Angrily, I felt my eyes tear up. Everything floated in the quiet all around me, Pitch, Denny, my daughter, and the girl. There was of course the girl. All day long I had been moving—in transit—no time to process.

I didn't want to stop moving now and let the day catch up with me. That's always the most painful moment, when the worst is over. That first moment where you have time to think.

I tossed the medal into the pool like a coin and made a wish for all of this to go away. It sank, but instead of drowning, seemed to grow brighter in the watery light. The water clarified it. Magnified it.

I stared at the door of the room where Reine slept and couldn't imagine closing my eyes. Couldn't imagine sleeping. That would feel too much like death. Like the girl. Both of them. I'd seen both of them dead. The tiny white coffin of the one Pitch had killed. The girl in the lake today, her dull, startled eyes.

I rose abruptly. Without much thought, I was back in the car and on the road. I was almost to my final destination before I realized I'd forgotten to turn my headlights on. When I did, the new light startled a pair of deer from the ditch along the narrow dirt road. They clattered across the road and were gone, their white tails bobbing in my blinking, watery eyes. I hardly slowed and almost drove past the turn onto Old Comfort Road. If I hadn't been mainly moving on instinct and memory just then—I would have missed it entirely.

{ 5 }

Until I moved back home again last year, I hadn't thought about Ardell. You might have said his name and I wouldn't have blinked. He'd become one those childhood things that I just didn't visit much anymore. I might have needed a reminder that he was something I should associate with Pitch, growing up, and the bar.

But now that I thought about it, I remembered Ardell. There was one night when I was hidden in Pitch's car, curled in his coat against the fall air and the dark that hung in the trees like the broken deer. And suddenly the light of the bar's door opening broke my concentration on my math homework. I looked up and found myself looking at Ardell. He was in the light near the side door, near his motorcycle and the heaped garbage bins. Maybe he was twenty then. And he wasn't alone.

I forgot my long division entirely, watching transfixed as Ardell reached for his companion and kissed her slowly and deeply. He touched her hair and wound her towards him, like you might coax a bird. She didn't resist. For a long moment, I didn't breathe, and he held her. He pressed his mouth to her forehead, then her eyes and finally again to her lips. They swayed, like the butchered deer suspended all around me.

I had never seen the girl before in Comfort Lake. She was Mexican and beautiful—her long dark hair hung down past the middle of her back. When Ardell lifted her up into his arms, it ruffled lightly and she settled it back from her face. When he murmured softly, though I listened closely, I couldn't hear the words he spoke.

Still carrying the girl, Ardell walked past Pitch's car, past me and the parking lot entirely. I pressed myself down against the seat and pulled Pitch's coat over my head. They never saw me, I'm sure. They disappeared completely into the dark down by the cabins and the lake. I tried hard to concentrate on my math homework, but the numbers slid away from me like slippery, soapy bubbles. I felt more alone than I had before. The dark seemed heavier and all I could hear was the sound of ropes creaking overhead.

I never saw the girl again, or really much of Ardell after that. In a few short months, I moved out of Pitch and Windy's home to foster care. I lived with a minister and his six kids, who my girlfriends and I teased mercilessly at school.

Years later, when I was in high school, the same girlfriends sometimes drove out in packed cars with older sisters to buy bottles from Ardell. The rumor was that he'd trade if you were broke, but only to some girls. The type of girl who was willing to trade, I guess. Not me though. I was too afraid of running into Pitch at the bar.

I always listened to their whispered stories about Ardell, though, while we shared the bottles at parties in cabins whose owners were gone for the winter. Parties that always seemed to get broken up by the police or the minister before I got drunk enough or brave enough to share what I knew.

The bar's parking lot was still packed when I arrived after midnight. Neither Ardell nor his daddy had ever kept a strict closing time. For most, it was a bar of last resort, after everything else was closed. One last chaser, so to speak.

My headlights illuminated a couple at the edge of the lot, smoking cigarettes. They winced in the light, swore, and faded further back into the tall pines that circled the bar. I found a spot and killed the engine.

The blackness of the sky seemed condensed under the trees, as if their boughs were weighing it down, holding it in like a pressure cooker. The night air was warmer than at the Hi-Way, despite the lake. I heard a rustle, and remembering the pair I had disturbed, listened nervously. The rustle came again, but overhead this time. Looking up I saw a pair of broad white wings flicker among the branches of the trees. An owl, I thought, shuddering. Maybe. I went inside.

Ardell had his cousins Rowdy and Primo helping him. Hazy smoke and about three dozen people in jeans and t-shirts crowded up against the bar; the rest huddled in the booths with their caps pulled down. I slid into an empty booth near the wall.

When Ardell appeared, he had a single glass with ice and a bottle of gin. He set it down on my table wordlessly.

I met his eye, then looked away. He opened the bottle, poured for me, then slid into the booth on the other side.

I felt myself blink, my eyes burning. I took a quick sip of gin and hiccupped a little bit. Fuck, I thought, feeling the tears building behind my eyes. I took a deeper sip, letting the ice touch my lips. I focused on that immediate feeling. I closed my eyes and drained the glass.

The minute I set it down on the table, Ardell filled it again.

I eyed it longingly and brushed the hair from my eyes.

"I think this is the first time since you moved back that you've sat down in the bar," Ardell observed.

"I hate this place," I said. "I hate everything about it."

"Me, too," Ardell agreed, looking around with distaste. "So why do you come here then?" he asked.

I shrugged and drained the glass. My face began to feel warm. I eased back into the seat, closing my eyes, resting my head against the wood back. "Must be the booze."

"Must be," he agreed. I could hear him fill my glass again.

I opened my eyes, reaching for it. He was standing now. "You should pay me before you drink that," he observed. "You look like a fucking lightweight to me."

"How about you open me a tab?" I said.

"Sure," he said dryly. "I'll just put it on your dad's."

The second bottle of the day never goes down as easy as the first. And that's a hard truth. The second went down with the grim image of Pitch sitting in his wheelchair, his prison blues buttoned up to his chin.

Usually the bottle I bought on Pitch's visiting day lasted me the whole month. If I followed the rules. Tonight the rules felt like they were written in wavy, colored lines of crayon. I was beginning to feel light-headed. Worse, my eyes were burning again. Without anyone there, with no reason to keep them in check, the tears slid out in a silent stream of misery. I drained glass after glass.

I couldn't outrun this day, but I was sure as hell determined to drown it. I felt the image I didn't want to see, almost as if it were hovering over me. Hovering like a shadowy owl in the dark ceiling. The image of the girl, pale and white, her eyes blank.

I had the sudden, sharp realization—almost painful—that drinking wasn't working. There was this pressure on my chest, like someone was holding me underwater. It hurt to breathe. So I stood and willed myself to walk out of the bar, holding the bottle to my chest.

I collided into the first parked car, then another, sloshing gin down my front and biting my lip. Unsteadily, I stumbled from the parking lot and into the dark. I felt the cool of the lake and walked towards it through the thick trees. My breath seemed to ease at the promise of water. It got easier to think. I found the bank and looked up through the branches. The moon hung wide and bright there, the water reflected white light everywhere.

Abruptly, my knees gave way beneath me. I sat and stared at the lake and poured gin unsteadily into my mouth.

"Are you okay?" Ardell's voice asked from behind me.

I wiped my wet mouth on my sleeve. My stomach had begun to burn, and I knew I probably wouldn't be able to stand up again. My body felt feverish with gin, almost like an allergic reaction. Like a bee sting. I drank some more and stared out at Ardell's old dock. It stretched out into the moonlit lake like a white, roadside cross.

Ardell sat down beside me on the cool grass. He watched me drink, his long legs stretched out in front of him. The rippling cry of a loon echoed across the lake. It was the sound of something being brutally emptied.

"Do you want me to take you home, Jane?" Ardell asked.

I shook my head like a small child.

"You can't sit here all night," he said. "What do you want me to do?"

He reached over and brushed a strand of hair from my hot cheek. His touch lingered for a moment.

I took another long, final drink from my bottle. "You know, Ardell," I said, finding my voice, "if you let me finish my bottle, I won't really care. You can do whatever the hell you want."

For the record, blacking out is against the rules. When I woke to myself again, I was in my car outside the Hi-Way. Just around dawn, grey and cool. My memory of the past night seemed to have the same pale consistency.

My cell phone was ringing fervently, and I was slumped across the front seat. I fumbled for it on the gritty floor of my car and felt a sharp pain in my hand.

As I shook away a small sliver of glass from my index finger, I squinted groggily into the poorly-nourished light. My phone was mixed in with the stones Reine had collected at camp, an old pair of my sandals, and my now—I realized sadly—shattered drinking glass. Its winking girl and her painted red skirt lay in pieces. I didn't remember it breaking.

The early morning air was almost cold, but I was covered in damp sweat. The ringing was too much for my head. I grabbed the phone. "Hello?" I half-slurred.

"Good morning, beautiful!"

I closed my eyes, regretting this conversation already. The unmistakable voice belonged to my old boss. I could see Collin already sitting at his desk in St. Paul, paper files opened all around him. I could picture the river behind him out his broad window and Army Corp ships working the locks.

"Hi, Collin." I sighed. "Can I call you back?"

"You won't," he answered easily. "You and I both know that."

That was true. Collin had been calling me a few times a month since

I moved back home. He only caught me at moments like this when I forgot and answered in distraction.

"I was staring at your empty office across the hall this morning when your local cop called me. About you. Funny, huh?"

"Funny," I repeated, pushing myself up onto one elbow. Smaller words were less painful.

"Are you okay? Is Reine okay?"

"We're fine." He waited for more. "What did you tell him?" I asked instead.

"That I miss you. That you were the best attorney I ever hired. That he should tell you I'm still holding a job for you, because you won't return my calls."

"Thanks, Collin," I said, and I meant it. He'd always been good to me. Even through the tough parts.

"Come have dinner with me," he pressed. "You can tell me what's going on."

"Goodbye, Collin," I hung up. I always did when the conversation went in that direction.

I sat up fully, holding my head. I was wearing my jeans and one of Ardell's shirts. Behind my left eye, there was a pain so intense, it let light in.

When I sat up, I found Windy peering down at me through the open car window, swaying slightly on her feet. I might have jumped in surprise if I wasn't so weak.

"I thought you'd be here," she said, her voice shaking. Windy had a round, chubby face. Her blonde wispy hair made her seem younger than she was—childlike, doll-like. She seemed even more so when she cried, which was often, as I remembered it. She was crying now.

I rested my head carefully against the seat back, pushing my hand against my left eye like I was trying to staunch the blood from a wound. My car smelled overpoweringly of fruit juice and suntan lotion, and my stomach roiled noisily.

"I thought you were asleep. I had to make a phone call," I said, trying to ignore the pain. "I stayed in the car, so I wouldn't bother you."

"I was asleep," she said, "but then I woke up and . . ." She took a quick, gasping breath, a small pathetic sound like a hiccup. "I just kept thinking about that girl."

"Thinking about it won't help," I said. My neck now ached from the effort of keeping my head up. "Just let it go."

"How can you say that?" she demanded. "There was a dead girl in our yard. We . . . we saw her!" She sobbed for real this time and pushed her hand to her mouth as if to smother the noise.

I couldn't think what to say. Our lives together were so littered with bodies. With grief. I felt numb. Maybe I was a little surprised that she could still be so upset.

"If I start falling apart about it . . ." I shook my head. "When you start that, you might not stop. Especially now with Pitch . . ." I hesitated. I hadn't meant to say that. "With everything," I finished quickly.

"What does that mean?" she asked sharply.

I stared out the front window at the blue motel wall. I couldn't think where else you could find that color. It came from a can, weathered, stripped, and painted over again. "It means that Pitch is dying," I said. "He has late-stage colon cancer."

"When did you hear this?" Windy demanded.

"At the prison. About two months ago."

Windy started crying in earnest.

"Please don't," I said, looking away.

She cried more loudly, her face turning an ugly red.

"Don't do this," I yelled, punching the steering wheel. The rest of me hurt so bad I hardly felt it. Windy stopped crying with a strangled gasp. I regretted the outburst instantly. She stared at me, her lips quivering.

"Mom . . ." I started to say.

"You blame me for this, don't you?" she said. "You think all this wouldn't have happened if I stayed."

"No," I answered plainly, "I don't." We'd been over this before.

"Yes you do!" she cried, her voice ragged. "You think this is all my fault. Even that girl—she had to die so I could leave him. So I could be free. All those years he . . ." she couldn't finish.

She turned and ran from me, slamming the motel door behind her.

I heaved myself out of the car after her and managed to strike my head on the doorframe. The pain blinded me. Helpless, I sank back on my seat. I felt something shake in my chest, an out of control feeling, like a bird trying to fight loose. I reached under the seat, groping for the bottle I hoped was there.

It wasn't.

Reine poked her head out of the motel door. Her face was still sleepy and she was wearing her pajamas. "Momma," she said. "Grandma's in the bathroom making weird noises."

I stared at Reine and took a deep breath. It hurt in my chest. Like breathing in smoke and ash. Still, I dashed at my eyes and nodded. I never fell apart in front of Reine. Despite the night before, that seemed to be the one rule that still mattered.

A few hours later, Windy still hadn't emerged from the bathroom. I had to get Reine to camp, but I knew better than to force my way in. I stuck a note on the door, promising to return. Then Reine and I showered down by the pool.

I dug a pair of sunglasses out from the glove compartment while Reine settled into the backseat. My eyes ached now like a stigmata. I shifted the car into reverse and glanced up into my mirror as my foot slid off the pedal and my car rolled into motion. Joe had parked his boxy blue and white immediately behind me. I swore in surprise and stomped back on the brake. The car jerked, and Reine strained around in her seat to see what was the matter.

"There's a cop back there!" Reine announced.

"I know, honey." I sighed. I slid the car back into park.

Joe rapped his knuckles on my window, smiling encouragingly at me to roll the glass down.

I did, but didn't smile back.

"Hello," he said. "Can I talk to you?"

"No."

"Why not?" he asked.

I stared at my hands gripping the steering wheel. *Because I hurt. Bad,* I thought, *and I can't deal with you now.* "Move your fucking car, first," I answered. "Unless you plan on arresting me."

His eyebrows went up and his eyes slid to Reine. I felt the reproach. I clutched the steering wheel more firmly. I prayed silently that he would go away.

"I'll be right back," he said. He went and moved his car, parking a few spots down in front of the main office's peacock blue door. He walked back.

"Can we talk?" he asked again.

I took a long, slow breath. "I have to get Reine to camp. I don't have a lot of time now." I was amazed that my voice stayed level.

"It will only take a minute."

As I climbed from the car, Reine moved to follow. Joe smiled at her and shook his head. "This is grown-up stuff," he said. "You stay there while I talk to your ma for a minute. I promise to only talk about boring things, so you don't miss anything."

Reine looked at me. I nodded. She settled back in the car and took out her notebook and markers from her backpack.

"Maybe you and your mom could swing by my office sometime today?" he suggested mildly.

"I'd prefer not to talk about this in front of . . . anyone . . ." I looked significantly back at Reine.

"I called your old boss," he said.

"What did he say?"

"He said to tell you he's holding a job for you in the civil division. All real estate stuff. No more criminal."

"Does that mean I checked out?"

He nodded, taking out his notebook. "Who was that man that met you here yesterday? The motel manager said he had a funny car."

"My ex-husband in his Mercedes."

"And the woman with him?"

"My ex-neighbor. And before you ask," I said, squinting into the sun back at Reine. "Denny has nothing to do with this. He's a federal prosecutor. The type of man who runs for Attorney General, not the type of man who leaves dead bodies in his ex-wife's backyard."

"Your boss said you quit your job to run his campaign."

I felt that flutter in my chest that had bothered me earlier. That panicky feeling that something winged might actually live in my chest. Something struggling free. I pressed my lips together, not wanting to talk.

What he saw on my face, I don't know. But he must have sensed I wasn't going to offer any more because he put his notebook away. "How is your mother doing?"

I felt my patience give way with an audible snap, as if a twig had broken beneath my foot. "I need to get my daughter to camp," I said, turning away. "I'm trying to keep things as normal as possible for her."

Joe trailed me back to my car. When I opened my door, Reine leaned out the back window. "It's a crime to leave a child unattended in a hot car," she said to Joe. She handed him a small piece of paper scribbled on with marker.

Joe looked at the paper. "What are these numbers for?"

"Those are the state statutes you broke for leaving a kid in a car unattended."

Joe looked at me. "Are these really the right codes?"

I sighed, climbing into the car. "Reine has a photographic memory. She remembers odd things."

"Why are there two sets of numbers?" he asked.

"I charged you with conspiracy, too," she answered, settling back into the car and putting on her seat belt. "Since you both left me here together."

Joe actually smiled. He folded the paper carefully and put it in his breast pocket. "Remind your ma to come see me after camp." He climbed back into his car and was gone.

7

All around our car, children thronged like a tide. Their sharp, excited voices sloshed against us, first one way, then another. I killed the engine and eyed Reine apprehensively.

"Bye, Mom!" she chirped, her eyes already darting everywhere, taking it all in.

I said goodbye back to her alone in my car. Reine hadn't waited. I watched her pink backpack dip along like a determined bobber. Around her, urged by the camp counselors, the younger children formed ragged lines that almost instantly fell apart.

Reine met up with two girls. They seemed to know where to find each other in the chaos. I saw them smile and Reine said something, the words lost to me.

Someone started a song about the house on the rock. Only the smallest campers sang along, clapping their hands and stomping their feet at intervals.

"Why did the police officer want to talk to you?" Reine had asked as we drove over.

"Mom knows a lot of police, honey," I said. "She used to be a lawyer."

"Are we going home tonight? Or will we sleep at the motel?"

"Probably the motel. Just a pre-Florida party. Get you used to the pool."

Reine wrinkled her nose. "The motel doesn't smell like Florida."

All the right things, said the right way.

Reine bent towards the girl on her left. She was taller, a few inches more than Reine, with long, blond braids the color of corn silk. The girl on Reine's other side placed her arm around my daughter's shoulders, possessive and timid at once. Reine had never mentioned these girls to me before.

By some sudden signal—seemingly separate entirely from the pressing counselors—the children turned and headed down the trail, into the woods and out of sight. Reine and her companions were swept along with the crowd. All that was left behind was a drifting flotsam of bewildered parents and a collection of minivans.

I slumped and rested my head against the steering wheel. With Reine gone, the headache I'd been ignoring pressed in on me like a physical weight. On the now-empty seat, I noticed her lunch, comprised of items hastily gathered at the gas station. The chocolate donuts were already melting in their package.

I stared at the crumpled paper bag for a while, wanting to close my eyes and sleep right there. It would be a long day without lunch, I thought. Resigned, I climbed stiffly out of my car. Taking the path I thought I'd seen Reine disappear down, I threaded past three little stations dedicated to Saint Agnes and her miracles. The trail forked here. The saint's right hand was raised aloft. I went that way.

The trail I chose ended up at the lake, with my daughter nowhere in sight. Leaving the trees, I stumbled down the steep bank to the muddy beach and squinted into the sun. To one side, a group of girls crowded into a pair of canoes. A few years older than Reine, they wore shorts and tank tops. They glided out onto the lake, their tanned arms wielding pale oars. I squinted again and saw their destination—a floating dock off shore. They fixed themselves to it and then clambered aboard.

The girls laughed and jostled, peeling off shirts and shorts, stripping down to sleek tanned skin and bathing suits. They pushed and laughed and then leapt into the water, holding hands. They plunged in with a fierce whoop of glee, vanishing instantly, swallowed whole. The brief silence that followed was deep, strange, breaking just as abruptly as glass.

Their laughter surged skyward with them, seeming to start even before they fully broke the surface. They bobbed and giggled until they climbed back on the dock and the process repeated itself.

I realized I was holding my breath. I looked down, startled. The warm green water lapped against my feet and flip flops. I'd stepped into the water without meaning to.

Saint Agnes's camp was on the deeper side of the lake across from the Lost Comfort Bar. When I was a child, the camp had been run by the Revelation Baptist Church. Every Sunday, they had white-robed baptisms here, throbbing with hymns. We washed so many sins away that between the church and Lee Ring's bar on the other side, I was surprised the lake didn't boil.

My phone rang. It startled me almost as much as it had this morning when I was unconscious. I pulled it out of my pocket and stared at the number, not recognizing it.

"Hello?" I answered, still gazing out across the lake. Lost Comfort was shallow and weedy all the way across. The center of the lake had a sandy bed, rising almost to the surface.

"Ms. Darcy?" a voice spoke from the phone. I'd almost forgotten I'd answered it.

"Yes," I answered, pulling my eyes reluctantly away from the far bank. "Who is this?"

"This is the prison health office," she said, and I remembered the voice. We had talked over Pitch's case before visiting time yesterday.

"You're father wanted to me to call you. He's experiencing some bleeding and his blood counts are way off. We're going to move him to the hospital to try to get things under control."

I blinked. The wind rustled the reeds across the lake, a dry sound, barely a whisper.

"Is he going to be okay?" I heard myself ask.

The nurse paused, then said not unkindly, "your father is very fragile, Jane. That's why I'm calling. He could go at any time."

I nodded, even though she couldn't see me. We had discussed all of this yesterday.

"Do you need the hospital information?" she asked.

"No," I said. "I know where to go. Thank you," I added and hung up. I was still holding Reine's lunch in my other hand. I had crumpled the bag.

A shriek from the diving girls pulled my eyes back towards them. I felt as adrift as their dock. I pictured Pitch riding in the ambulance to the hospital. I felt dizzy. My eyes drifted back across the lake. I couldn't see the bar, but I wanted a drink.

I had another memory, as clear as those white-robed baptisms. It had happened across the lake though, almost in a different world. I remembered that once I had taken a canoe from old Lee Ring's dock. I'd tipped it and wasn't able to get it back to shore. Ardell swam out for me. I remembered him carrying me back to the bank, my teeth chattering. I remembered his wet hair plastered against his face and the feeling of my cheek on his bare skin. His chest felt as hard as the knot of fear in my stomach. Nothing Ardell could say would soothe my crying. I was too frightened. Not of almost drowning, but of Pitch waiting for me on the shore.

From behind me in the wood, a crowd of tiny girls shuffled out in a line holding hands. They wore suits and floaties and streaks of still-white suntan lotion. They moved around me as if I were a tree or a rock, fixed and unimportant. They drifted into the water, under the eyes of a watchful trio of counselors.

One of the camp counselors smiled at me. "Aren't you Reine's mom?" I nodded.

"I recognize you from parents' day. Reine is down at the archery range."

I held out the crumpled lunch bag by way of explanation for my presence.

"Oh," she said. "Can you bring that to the main office? That happens all the time, kids huh?" She was maybe fifteen, not much older than the girls in the canoes. She was slim, her skin a bright pink from too much sun and not enough suntan lotion. Her shoulders were peeling under her red hair.

At her feet, one of the little girls tipped into the water. Expertly, she fished her up with one hand. The little one started to cry, coughing out water, and I stepped quickly onto the bank.

I got lost again. I was about to give up when I rounded the trail and found myself at the stations for Saint Agnes once more. I paused, a little surprised to find a small girl sitting beneath the little wooden altar, her curly head turned away from me. For a moment, I almost mistook her, and my heart twinged. She could have been Reine, four years ago.

She had a pair of pink sandals, but had torn these off. She was determinedly itching her ankles with both hands. I knelt down by her. When she looked up to meet my eye, she was very different from Reine. Her eyes brown, and her nose sharper. She pointed at her ankles.

I looked where she directed and gasped. Her ankles were red and blistered. Everywhere. She'd scratched open the larger blisters until she bled.

"That doesn't look good," I told her gently, catching her hands in my own. They were bloody under the nails.

She nodded.

The camp counselor I'd just left came running up the trail. She cried audibly with relief when she saw the girl. "Thank goodness," she said, her chest heaving from her run. "I didn't know what to do. She was there one minute and gone the next." She hugged the girl.

"Did you find Reine yet?" she asked.

I shook my head. "Try the fire circle," she suggested. "They're probably done with archery by now."

"This one has poison ivy," I said, pointing.

The counselor took in the girl's feet for the first time and groaned. "That's the second one this week." She scooped her charge up efficiently and held out her hand to me. "You might as well give me Reine's lunch, then. I need to take her to the office. I can take care of it for you."

She was gone before I could ask her where I should go. Her red hair and redder shoulders bounced around the leafy corner, leaving me with Saint Agnes in her perch. Still kneeling, I stared up at her in consternation, at her bland, ceramic face and painted brown eyes. The little altar pointed up, with a triangular top like a ship's prow. A yellowed ribbon wrapped around the figure read, *The Third Miracle*. Her hand was broken off.

I rose and brushed the dust off my knees. I remembered from catechism class after I married Denny that you have to perform three miracles to be a saint. Despite the sign, with her broken hand and mild face, I couldn't guess what her third miracle had been. There was a ceramic lamb at her feet. It had been touched so many times by little fingers that its painted face was worn off. I touched it for luck, too, randomly picking a trail. I wondered if Pitch had reached the hospital yet.

Whether it was Saint Agnes's blessing that guided me or not, I'll never know, but I found my car without getting lost again. Just in time to join the last stream of retreating minivans. When the narrow camp road T'd up against the main road, I paused. To the left, the road went to town. To the right it wound to Ardell's bar across the lake. I looked one way, then the other. I tried to imagine filling the whole day until I could pick Reine up again. Though I was tired all the way through to my bones, I didn't feel like going back to the motel with Windy. Or worse, back home with its police tape.

I pulled over to the side onto the grass and let the growing line of cars behind me push by. Mainly, the queue was comprised of moms. Many of them drove up from the Twin Cities each day. They'd stop for coffee on the way home and finally wake up in the quiet car alone. I used to do that. They each paused dutifully at the main road, craning their heads to look both ways for traffic. There wasn't any.

I let them all pass. Remembering, I reached over and opened the glove compartment. There was the almost-empty bottle I'd been groping for so desperately this morning. I turned it over in my hand, feeling its warmth. The first swallow went down like medicine. I wiped my lips on my hand. I could feel my headache recede with the lightness I began to feel.

The second swig went down better and emptied the bottle. My lips still burning, I restarted the car and turned left onto the road, heading towards town. I had an appointment with Joe. Unlike the other moms from the cities, I didn't check for traffic, but I kept my eyes open for deer.

The police station was in a pole barn behind the old Red Owl. Joe's desk was one of three behind a simple divider wall, all crammed together. I sat in the plastic chair the police secretary showed me, and glanced over the mess on the desk. It was substantial. On top of the papers and radio wires sat a brown paper lunch sack. The bag was still crisp and folded neatly closed. A female hand had written on the bag, *Five o'clock, Dinner. You promised.*

From my chair, I could just see the back room. A couple sat around a small table there. They both had paper cups, but weren't drinking from them. The woman hugged her purse, looking frail.

Joe stood there with them, talking with the man. The man's head was bowed so much his chin seemed to touch his chest. When Joe noticed me, he paused, as if a little surprised that I'd shown up. He spoke again quietly to the couple, then came out to me, closing the door behind him. The last I saw of the woman was her eyes. They were sunken into her face and red.

Joe tried to smile at me in welcome, but the effort was grim.

"Can you come back later?" he asked, his voice quiet. "They came to identify the body. Drove all night from Milwaukee as soon as they saw my Jane Doe go out."

I examined the closed door. I tried to remember their features, to match their faces with the girl. All I saw was her expression—as if she'd fallen into a deep well. Like a person in shock.

I looked back at Joe's tired face and wondered if he'd slept since the call yesterday.

"Do you think she's theirs?" I asked.

"Don't know. They looked over the photos, but they aren't sure. Their granddaughter's been missing for fifteen days," he said. "Same age. Only way to be certain is to take them up to see the body."

Joe reached over me and grabbed his hat off the desk. When he put it on, I could see his hands shake.

Back at the motel, I parked the car in my same spot right as the phone rang. I looked at the number. It was Collin, strangely enough. He'd called me in this exact place this morning.

I answered the phone. "Hello, Collin."

"Hello, beautiful," his voice echoed and I guessed he was in the court house. "Funny world. I just ran into your ex-husband here at the court house. Twice in one day, I've had to play twenty questions for you."

"Sorry about that."

"Anytime. Just so you know, Denny is pissed as all hell. I don't know what you're doing lately, but you might want to cool it."

I closed my eyes, rubbing my aching temples. I couldn't seem to get the image of that sad couple out of my mind. "I don't care what Denny thinks," I said.

"He said he's taking Reine to Florida in a few days."

"Yes. When she's done with camp."

"Come up and have dinner with me then. Or I'll come there. We can talk about how much we both hate Denny."

"You're the one who introduced me to him."

"Don't I know it," he said ruefully. He hesitated. His voice sounded slightly strained when he spoke again. You might have missed it if you didn't know him as well as I did. "Denny thinks you're drinking again."

I killed the car engine and slid the keys into my purse. "Denny can go fuck himself."

"Are you?" Collin asked.

I eyed the glove compartment, with its empty bottle. "Not at this minute."

"Shit," he swore. "Shit."

"It's no big deal," I insisted.

He actually laughed; it was a harsh, bitter sound. "I'll come get you," he said. "I'll be there in an hour and we'll get you into treatment. Denny can take Reine to Florida a few days early like he wants. He'll never even know."

"I have it under control."

He wasn't having it.

"Look, I'll take myself. Don't go nuts. I just need a week to handle things."

The silence on the phone made me think he'd hung up.

"When is Denny coming for Reine?" he asked at last.

"Tomorrow." I sighed.

"You call me when he comes." He hung up.

I stared at the phone. Angrily, I reached to restart my car. That was when I noticed our motel door hanging open. My stomach sank. I glanced at the clock on my dash, but it had turned off with the car. I wasn't sure how long I'd been gone.

I climbed from the car. Gingerly, I peeked my head inside the door, trying to guess what state Windy would be in by now. The lamp nearest the bed flickered. In the daylight, the room looked bare and dirty. The bed Reine and Windy had shared was still unmade. The television was on, with the sound turned off.

I poked my head into the bathroom. Windy was there, but I cried out when I saw her. She lay on the grimy tiled floor, her dress pushed up over her round knees, her face hidden by long, damp tendrils of sweat-dampened hair. I drug her to the next room and flung her across the rumpled bed. She slipped from me like a fish.

Her breath was slow, almost unnoticeable. I stared at her for several long moments, my own breath filling the quiet in the room like water flooding into a broken hold. I looked out the front door for help and saw only the black asphalt. It took me several tries on the motel phone to hit the right numbers for 911.

The emergency room doctor had a small curtained office. If I looked to the left, I could see Windy's feet in the alcove where she slept peacefully. Reine sat to the right in one of a series of plastic chairs. After Windy was admitted I had run to pick her up from camp. Now she knelt on the floor and used the seat as a hard surface to color on. I watched her with one eye while the doctor leafed his way through Windy's large file. He looked younger than me, but tired. At last he said, "Your mother already has a substantial medical history with us."

I nodded.

He seemed hopeful that I would ask him a question. I didn't. I watched Reine fill in a panel with brilliant green as several groups of patients in white robes shuffled past her, blue slippers on their feet and coffee in their hands. They all looked as exhausted as the young doctor.

Farther down the hallway, I could see a uniformed prison officer standing outside one of the curtained rooms. None of the other rooms were guarded by a man with a gun, so I guessed Pitch was there. No one went in or out of that room. At least not while I watched.

I looked back at the doctor to find he was waiting for me. "Your mother has overdosed before. She actually has a hold on her file for certain pain prescriptions."

I met his eye.

"Did you know this?"

I shook my head. "I only moved back home this year. I wasn't aware that she had any drugs except for a muscle relaxant for her back."

The doctor weighed this carefully, almost as if he were writing out a prescription. "She also has a substantial history of fractures and contusions," he said. "Over the past twenty years, she's been treated here for numerous broken bones. She's broken her left arm five times."

I glanced back over at Reine. Her head was bent so close to the page her nose might have been lost in the fold. To my surprise, Joe appeared in the hallway, still wearing his uniform. He sat in a chair a few feet down from Reine. She didn't notice. He watched her, placing his hat on his knee. He sipped his coffee. Only very slowly did my eyes refocus on the doctor. He was waiting for a response again.

"Has she been to treatment for the drug problem?" I asked.

"Yes."

"Can you send her back?"

"Yes."

I nodded, gathering up my purse, intending to rise.

He wasn't done. "I mentioned her injuries because they are consistent with abuse. Does your mom currently have a spouse or partner? You're the only one listed on her forms as a contact person."

"No."

"Do you have any idea who . . ."

Of their own accord, my eyes fixed on the uniformed man standing down the hall. "Yes."

"We have services to help here at the hospital. We can help your mother."

"Go ahead then, offer them to her when she wakes up," I said and gathered up my purse once more. "But for me it's late and we've been here almost five hours. I need to get my daughter home to bed."

To my surprise the doctor touched my forearm, holding me back. "You need to help your mother," he said. "You're authorized to act for her as her medical authority. I need you to tell me what is going on."

I needed to leave. I pulled myself loose from his hand and his concerned look. "Please let me know when the treatment center comes to pick my mother up," I said. He started to speak again, but I walked away.

"What's wrong with Grandma?" Reine asked when I approached.

"She fell and hit her head in the shower," I said. "At the motel."

I knelt beside her, glancing at Joe, and helped her return her crayons to their box. He watched us silently as we, one after another, arranged them in neat rows. Sky blue. Magenta. Brick red. She leaned into me, watching me work. The magic of order and neat little boxes. I found her slight but steady weight reassuring. I blinked and the threatening tears were gone. "Should we go home?" I asked.

"Home?"

"Back to the motel," I corrected hastily.

"Is there still time to swim in the pool?"

I nodded.

When we stood, Joe rose as well and held open Reine's pink backpack. Reine blinked as if she'd noticed him for the first time. She ducked behind me. Together, Joe and I zipped her things in. I couldn't help but notice that he smiled at Reine while we worked. Behind the nurse's station was a clock. It was well past five. He'd missed his dinner, sitting here with us.

The guard standing down the hall coughed and we both turned. "If you want, I can ask . . ." Joe began.

"I don't," I interrupted. I put my arm around Reine, leading her away from the place. "Not with my daughter here. And I don't like to talk about the past."

"You sure picked the wrong town then," he said. But he smiled and his voice was gentle. Still carrying Reine's little bag, he followed us out the door.

Joe trailed us back to the motel in his squad car. I'd lost my room key, and we were now locked out. He walked to the office for us and talked to the old man at the desk.

Reine slid her hand into mine as we stood outside our room's shabby door and watched him through the office window. I noticed for the first time that someone had written above each of the doors, Revelation 22:12. The old Palmer Method handwriting was painstaking. I wondered if it was the old man at the desk.

"He seems nice," she said. "He reminds me of Daddy." She was talking about Joe, not the old man.

"That's because Daddy used to be a cop."

"Really?"

I was taken aback by her surprise. This wasn't supposed to be a secret. But maybe neither Denny nor I had gotten around to mentioning it.

"He quit when you were a baby. I guess you would be too young to remember that. I used to bring you in to kiss him goodnight when he worked his shifts at the precinct."

"Why did he quit?"

"Because Momma didn't want to be married to a cop," I told her, trying to keep my voice matter-of-fact.

Joe arrived. He held out the key and to my surprise, Reine took it from him before I could. She smiled fully at him. Seeming as perplexed as myself by her sudden warmth, Joe smiled back nonetheless.

She looked at me. "Can we go swim in the pool?"

"Sure," I said. "Why don't you get your swimming suit out of the room."

She let herself into the room and bounded ahead.

Joe watched. "Just so you know, I had one of my officers take away your mother's drugs."

I nodded.

"She had enough in her purse to permanently tranquilize an elephant. Are you sure you want to stay here?" he asked. "This place isn't exactly the greatest. I bust people out here all the time."

I rubbed my temple. I was almost weary of the headache there. "Reine goes to Florida with her father tomorrow. I'll figure out what to do then. But I don't want to move her again."

"You could go back home," he suggested, speaking low so Reine wouldn't hear. "Your mom's house is clear," he said. "All the police tape is gone. You can go back whenever you want."

The idea of taking Reine there didn't feel right.

"How did it go today with the family?" I asked him.

Joe looked bleak. I had to guess that he didn't handle many of this type of case out here. "Wasn't their girl." He shook his head. "Has to be hell for them, you know. They still have no idea where their granddaughter is. Then when I got them off, the Yellow Medicine county sheriff called to say he'll be up tomorrow. He wants to see if it's a missing girl he's looking for."

Joe might have said more, but Reine reappeared. I was grateful for his understanding.

"Are you coming, Mom?" she asked.

I hesitated, glancing at Joe's terse face. For a moment, I remembered him at Pitch's trial, testifying about the accident scene. About the little girl he'd tried to revive. He must have been a pretty new cop then. That hadn't registered with me at the time.

It seemed like I should say something. Instead Joe nodded his goodbye and climbed back into his squad car.

"Mom?" she asked again.

"Sure, honey," I said, taking Reine's hand in my own. It held off the flicker of anxiety I felt when Joe left.

The night above us was dark, clouds hiding the stars. The pool was lit from within, the lights glowing like watery moons or UFOs. Reine glided across the water, then back again. She dove, kicking her legs skillfully underwater. She seemed to glow a little, too.

Some of the fear had drifted away. Not gone. Maybe just submerged like the lights and the moon. I didn't have to think about Windy lying on the floor.

Reine dove again. She came up with a spurt of water, then went under again. I frowned, noticing the glimmering thing on the pool floor she had found. My stomach contracted even as she pulled it up, turned it over in her small hand, reading the inscription on the coin.

God grant me the serenity to accept the things I cannot change.

I didn't need to see the words. Reine paddled over to me with her treasure held over her head. She handed me Pitch's five-year sobriety medal.

"What's that?" she asked. "There's words on it. Like a rosary."

"It's a special prayer," I said, tucking the coin into my hand. "To help people stop drinking."

She smoothed her bangs back from her wet face, looking up at me.

"Will Grandma be okay?" she asked.

"Yes," I answered.

"How did she get hurt?" she asked again.

"She fell in the shower. She'll be okay."

Reine let her legs float up, holding loosely onto the side. "Did you hear about the girl?" she asked.

I shook my head slowly, suddenly not trusting my voice.

"Everyone at camp was talking about it today." Reine's face grew serious, her voice hushed and sad. "A girl drowned in the lake. Lyssa's father is on the police department. She said it was terrible."

"Oh."

"We talked about it at camp," she said. "And the counselors talked to us about swimming. Being safe and stuff."

I studied Reine's face for any trace of suspicion. I was guessing she still hadn't made the connection between our house and the drowning.

"What did they tell you about safety?" I asked.

"We had a drill."

I remembered the drills. All the campers running to the main cabin while the counselors held hands in the lake, moving across the beach. They had practiced the drill when I was a camper, too. Reine rested her head against my knee and I stroked her hair.

"Does it work?" she asked.

"The drill?"

"No, the special prayer. On the coin."

"Of course it does," I answered. "Every blessed time."

I woke to a clicking noise—the sound of plastic hangers in my closet being pushed against one another. It was still dark in my room at Windy's house, but the closet was open and the small, bare bulb inside emanated a halo of yellow light.

I squinted at the figure standing there. She was too tall to be Reine. I frowned, alarmed, getting slowly out of bed. I tried to be silent, but she turned at my slight noise. I froze. Unconcerned, she went back to looking at the clothes in my closet.

My mind seemed to be working slowly, like a clock with missing gears. I recognized her from yesterday, from the yard. The drowned girl. But here she stood, calmly sorting through my clothes.

She wore a simple blue dress. Cotton, with a small ruffle and buttons down the front. Slim and pretty, her long hair fell loosely around her shoulders. My fingertips tingled with fright as if fear alone had made them cold.

Click. Click. Click went the hangers. I took a few cautious steps forward. Hanging in the closet among my suits and shirts was a pair of gutted deer, their tongues lolling out, entrails removed. Their eyes were dead.

The girl took no notice. *Click. Click. Click.* She pulled out one of my trial suits and held it against her, looking in the mirror as if to judge its fit. She put it back.

Click. Click. Click. She pulled out a shirt, brushing against one of the deer carcasses. Where her shoulder grazed the animal, a streak of blood and fur now clung. She didn't seem to notice, turning slightly left then right to watch herself in the mirror. The image was distorted; it rippled occasionally as if it were underwater. It was the same, but also not. Her features were darker, her eyes brighter, almost animal; a bird.

She pulled out the dress I had worn for Reine's baptism. The thought of Reine shook me a little, a nick of panic from a small blade like a scalpel. I didn't want this girl in my house. It wasn't safe. She was already dead. Covered with blood. I eyed the hallway and the door to my daughter's room.

"Who are you?" I demanded, finding my voice as I was waking.

The girl frowned at herself in the mirror. I saw myself over her shoulder, but I seemed farther away. The mirror rippled again, disturbed, unsteady.

She opened her mouth to speak and the motel phone rang, loud and discordant.

I was awake. Awake without crying out. My heart pounded. Dark.

The phone rang again and I dove for it, my movements wild and uncoordinated. I nearly fell out of bed. My eyes strained to make sense of my surroundings—motel room. Reine slept in the bed beside mine. The grubby room was empty. Television. Beds. Chair.

I had almost forgotten the phone in my hand. It was the floor nurse at the hospital. Windy had suffered a mild heart attack, probably brought on by the overdose and the stressful circumstances. Her pastor was with her now, comforting her. She would be fine. Did I want to speak to him?

I pushed the palm of my hand into my right eye. Another migraine starting.

"No," I managed. "My daughter is sleeping. I'll come in the morning. Is that soon enough?" My voice was rough, quiet. I had to repeat myself, so she could hear.

Reine didn't stir.

The nurse hung up the phone and I was alone in the room.

I was still shaking from the nightmare. I was hot and faint. I lay back on the bed, but couldn't stay down. It felt like a weight was being pushed into my chest. I couldn't breathe.

I rose, stumbling over my purse and clothes. I shoved my legs into my jeans and found my keys. I needed to breathe. To leave. I stumbled outside.

The cool evening air rushed into my blood like wine. I staggered and leaned against the hood of my car for support, breathing deeply. I might have fainted, but I gripped my keys, the pain of their edges making my eyes swim.

I opened the car and pulled out the bottle from the glove compartment. It was empty. I felt under the seats and then opened the trunk of the car. I took things out and then put them back in, finding nothing. A semi passed too fast on the highway just outside the motel, filling the whole parking lot with blinding light, rattling and pounding the pavement. It left me shaking and ill, but more awake than ever.

The thought was in me to leave. To go and come back. Sleeping, she would never notice. I looked at my keys in my hand.

I'd spent most of my life waking up alone. In dark cars outside of bars. Alone in my room in an empty house. In worse places and houses I didn't know. I thought of my daughter in the motel room. I thought of her waking up alone, and her voice asking for me.

When she was little she'd been so scared of the dark we'd had a trail of night lights. Little bulbs plugged in the wall sockets that led from her room to the bed I'd shared with her father. When her father left she'd slept with me for months. Pressed close and hard into my back.

I went back into the motel room and closed the door.

This time I lay down in Reine's bed with her and pulled the blanket over us. Her breath was even and calm. It was the only thing in the small room that offered comfort. Not the thin blanket or the parking lot lights shining through the window. Just her.

I was too afraid to close my eyes. I listened to my daughter breathe, until it was the only sound. It drowned out my own heart beating.

The wise man built his house upon the rock.
The wise man built his house upon the rock.
And the rains came tumbling down.

The next day, the music carried us out of camp and down the road to Windy's house. Reine's last day of summer camp left her face glowing with both content and suntan oil. She gripped an art project made from pinecones in her hand.

"Do you remember when Lorraine gave me the coconut?" she asked, thinking already about her trip to Florida, about the resort in Key West where we always stayed.

I nodded, turning off the highway onto the dirt road. We were heading to Windy's house to pack Reine's things for the trip.

"Remember when I found the shell with the dog shape on it?"

I did remember, all the funny shapes and the palm trees and how Reine had cried and cried in our tent the first year we went to Florida. She was three and had loved the ocean, loved the sand and the little turtles. But she hated the tent when we had to sleep in it. It was too strange, too different from her own bed, her pink room and starry nightlight. After two exhausting nights, where she wept halfway to dawn, we scrapped the plan to camp, checked into the Palaces Resort and played cartoons to calm her. Lorraine, the caretaker, had given her coconuts to play with and we'd gone back every year after that—except last year after the divorce.

I pulled into the driveway and Reine jumped from the car. She needed to collect her things and then I'd promised to call Denny.

"Mom?" she called back over her shoulder. "Mom, will you get my suitcase for me?"

She disappeared into the house.

Reine had no reason to hesitate, but I lingered. I found my eyes drawn down the hill. Joe had been true to his word, all the police tape was gone. Only the muddy tire marks, scored into the wet ground down by the lake, gave any clue that something terrible had happened here.

I looked back at the house, almost as if seeing it for the first time. I hadn't noticed before that Windy had it repainted, a pale yellow. She must have done that before I moved back. It didn't surprise me that I hadn't noticed. When it came to things in Comfort Lake, I remembered more than I looked.

I went inside, wondering how much longer I would stay. I'd come home thinking I'd last about a week. It'd been thirteen months now, but this place seemed less like home than it ever had. Ghosts didn't bother me. I didn't really believe in them, but often memory was worse.

"Mom," Reine called again, when she heard the door slam behind me. "Did you get my suitcase?"

"I will," I said, pushing aside another one of Windy's junk boxes filled with antlers and old bottles from the basement door. I knew the suitcase Reine wanted, pale blue from a garage sale. A hard trunk with silver clasps that the airline charged extra to carry. The inside was lined with soft, pink satin pockets. That's why she had wanted it and also why I had given in.

"Are you sure you want the blue one? Maybe you're too old this year?" I asked her, peering down the dark steps to the basement.

"I want the blue one," she called. Her voice was more muffled, as if she was standing in her closet.

The basement stairs were both narrow and steep. They were pitted from Pitch's boots and thousands of trips up and down. As a child I'd chipped my tooth on the third one from the bottom. As I went down, the temperature fell considerably and the air grew damp and stale. It was a smell that always made me think of Pitch, who used to cure deer down there, hanging two or three poached carcasses from the ceiling beams at a time, letting the blood drain into the floor. He stored the meat in a series of antique deep freezes that hummed like airplanes.

There was no rail. I trailed my hand along the cool wall for support. I couldn't remember a time when I had come down here as a child when something wasn't bleeding the floor slick, the pale white translucence of sinew glowing in the half dark like moonlight and chips of broken bone grinding beneath my feet. Pitch butchering. The harsh, mechanical noise of the saw and the freezers.

I flipped on the light and found only an empty space. Windy had been at work here for years now. The floor was clean. The table, hooks, and saws Pitch had used were gone. Even the back room, where he used to sit in a disintegrating chair and watch television for hours, was empty. Now it only held the cedar wardrobe where Windy stored our winter coats and Reine's suitcase. Piece by piece, bit by bit, she had moved him out. Like the changed color of the house, I wasn't so surprised I hadn't noticed.

I pulled Reine's suitcase from the closet and headed back upstairs. In the hallway, passing Windy's room, I paused. I pushed her bedroom door open with my fingertips. These days she had a narrow single bed with a white frame against the wall, a matching, low chest, and a wardrobe. I didn't go in here often. I considered the wardrobe carefully, setting the suitcase down on the floor. The plush, new carpet practically swallowed my feet.

In the top drawer I found her pills. There were two large bottles made out to a woman named Xi Lu. This was in addition to what the police had confiscated from her purse. I pulled the bottles out and set them on her bed. I searched the rest of the room, half-listening for Reine, not wanting to be surprised. I found an almost empty bottle of pills in a shoebox under her bed. The chest, though, held only blankets. Her closet was empty as well.

I swept the pills from her bed to my purse. Then I went to the kitchen, picking up the suitcase once more and lugging it along with me. I pulled open the bottom cupboards and went through her pans. Then I stood on the suitcase to check the top cupboard where Windy stored my grandmother's casserole dishes. There was a small plastic bag of gel capsules tucked into one of the bowls. I kneaded the bag, frowning a little. One of the pills came apart, dusty powder coating the rest of the contents. The suitcase wobbled beneath me.

I climbed off the suitcase, listening across the house for Reine once more, frowning when I didn't hear her anywhere. I tucked the bag of pills into my pocket. Abandoning my first search and starting another, I looked in the bathroom and living room, then her room. No Reine. Reine also wasn't in the back bedroom. I felt a little thrill of worry. That feeling I recognized from my daughter's toddler years when she dashed out of sight at the store. Her voice giggling and excited, my heart pounding.

I paused outside my own closed bedroom door, my mind flickering like a candle to last's night's dream. I pushed the door open a little too quickly. This room was empty, too, the closet open, the mirror reflecting back my own worried face.

The front door slammed loudly, the noise echoing across the house. Like an unspooling anchor, I felt relief. She'd been outside.

"Mom," Reine called. "I forgot my sunglasses at camp! I looked in the car and everything. We need to go get them!"

My phone rang just as Denny arrived. It was the hospital, but I ignored it. There were several other messages that I had missed. I could see that Denny was already angry. It was almost dark and Reine's bags were packed. We hadn't gone back for her sunglasses. I promised to fetch them later, and bought her another pair and some suntan lotion at the dime store.

"What the hell is going on?" Denny demanded. "I thought we were supposed to meet at that shit motel?"

I blinked. I had forgotten this. Reine and I had eaten our goodbye dinner at the diner and come back home, almost out of habit. It was likely he'd been waiting for hours already at the motel, his anger mounting with his blood pressure.

At the tone of his voice, Denny's wife hastily helped Reine into the car and closed the door.

"I forgot," I said, holding out Reine's suitcase for Denny to take. He didn't.

"Of course," he snorted. "You forgot."

I blinked at him, stung. "If I said I forgot, I forgot. Since when have I been the liar in this relationship?" I offered him Reine's suitcase again.

He ignored it.

"Fuck you," I said and dropped the suitcase on his foot.

He swore, wincing in pain.

I turned away. "I'll see you in two weeks when you get home from Florida."

Denny grabbed my arm. His neck was red; he was angry. He clenched the suitcase now, like a weapon.

I relaxed. It was easier when he was mad.

"Do you have any idea what it was like to be married to you, Jane?" he hissed. "With all your goddamn rules that apply to everyone but you? So yeah—that's right, I'm a liar. I'm a cheater. Being married to you for ten years was like being paralyzed from the waist down."

I pressed my lips together. I forced my face into a smile.

"Cheating was a fucking survival mechanism." Denny drew a long ragged breath as if he was being strangled.

I shrugged.

"Jesus," he breathed, "fuck you, wife. Fuck you."

"Reine has her phone on her," I said calmly. "Please have her call me when your plane gets to Florida. I will call her every night to check in. I assume you're staying at the Palaces?"

"Fuck. You."

I shrugged again, showing my teeth when I smiled.

He reached for my arm again.

"Don't touch me again. Ever."

He met my eye and he dropped his arm. He started to speak, but thought better of it. He turned, his back as taunt as the line dividing a highway. I stepped back into the shadow of the porch, feeling the crinkly bag of Windy's pills in my pocket.

The car door slammed like a starter's gun and he started the engine. Reine waved at me out the back window, smiling. He didn't give her a chance to say goodbye, so she mouthed it through the window and gave me a thumbs up.

I waved back at her until she was gone.

His headlights faded down the road, leaving a sudden darkness. I opened my phone and dialed Collin's number. It took a few tries. My hand was shaking; my arm hurt.

"How did it go?" he asked. "Did Denny pick Reine up?"

I could hear his own kids playing in the background. He had three boys and a wife named Jennifer. My lips were too dry. I ran my tongue over them. "Look," I said letting myself back into the house, "I need a little more time. Twenty-four hours."

"I don't think that's a good idea."

"Trust me on this one," I said, once again kicking aside Windy's box of junk and antlers. It always seemed to be in the way. "I'll be fine," I said. "Come get me tomorrow night."

"I'm starting to feel like this is a plea deal we're negotiating. I don't like that feeling."

"One more night. I need to pack."

He didn't believe me, but he agreed anyway. I hung up the phone and sat down at the kitchen table. My legs were shaking, my hands were so unsteady when I opened the baggie that I spilt some of the pills. I thought of my daughter's face disappearing down the driveway and more remotely of little white coffins. I thought of the girl. She was never far from my mind these days.

The foolish man built his house upon the sand.
The foolish man built his house upon the sand.
And the rains came tumbling down.

I sat in the parking lot of Ardell's bar and drank and thought about nothing. He should have been closed hours before. Still there were some cars in the lot, including a massive blue Chrysler that reminded me of my grandfather. Mostly it was dark except for the electric blue glow of the bug lanterns and the small thread of light escaping from beneath the bar's drawn curtains. The trees seemed to hang low over the place, trapping the light with their branches, compressing the air all around me into dense night. When I looked up, it was black and only black.

Ardell was across the room when I stepped inside, but even in the gloom I could feel his eyes find me. He didn't smile or wave me over. He grew still, like a dog that's spotted its mark. He set the bottle he was pouring down on the bar. One of the remaining customers shuffled past him and sensed the change in the air. The man glanced warily at Ardell and quickened his pace a little. He stopped at a table and pulled his girlfriend out of her chair. They left, brushing past me at the door.

That left one old man still at the long wood bar, holding half a glass of warm beer.

"Jess, it's closing time," Ardell said to him, without taking his eyes off of me. "Get the fuck out of my bar."

The old man looked up slowly as if coming out of a deep trance. "The fuck I will," he answered. "Let me finish the beer I paid for."

I walked the length of the bar, feeling his eyes on me the whole while. I sat down on a stool in front of him. He found me a glass and poured it full of gin. Then watched me drink it, his eyes hungry. He filled my glass again. "I'll get you some ice from the back. We're out here."

The old man belched loudly.

Ardell swore and walked around the bar. He grabbed Jess by the back of his shirt.

I drained my glass again and rose in search of ice. There was the noise of a scuffle behind me and both Ardell and the old man yelled.

The little back room had a peephole window. A poster of a deer was taped over the glass with yellowed tape. The door popped open, revealing a bare, dead light bulb and a deep freeze. Over the deep freeze hung a cross. I blinked at the crucifix through the dark.

The front door slammed as Jess was finally ejected out the door. I heard the lock click across the now-silent bar. I opened the top hatch of the freezer. A wave of cool floated up around me like a mist as the light from the cooler flooded the room with a soft glow. I filled my glass and heard Ardell's tread behind me. He kissed the back of my neck and pressed the weight of his body against mine. I stared at Jesus on his cross. My body was melting from the alcohol and Windy's pills. I moaned a little.

He reached around me and closed the freezer door. In the dark now, I turned and slid my arms around Ardell's neck. He picked me up and sat me on top of the freezer and kissed me crushingly. I wrapped my legs around him and reached for his belt. "Not here," he whispered when I touched his skin.

He drug me from the room. I stumbled into the bar and pushed him against a table. "Not here either," he said, his lips on my neck.

"Why not?" I breathed, reaching for him again.

"It's filthy." His voice was very ragged now. "And I hate it here." He picked me up as I started to fall into the well of alcohol. My body started to go numb from the effects of the last two drinks and all the pills and drinks before. My eyes rolled.

"Jesus Christ," Ardell said, "how much did you drink tonight?"

"A lot," I said, letting my head loll back into his arms.

Outside we almost tripped over Jess's passed-out body. He was slumped across the step. Jess must have driven the old Chrysler because it was still there. Ardell swore and ripped open the car door, slinging me across the massive back seat. The old spring seat rocked steadily beneath us as I faded into relief.

I dreamt I was hanging from the basement ceiling with Pitch's deer all around me. My fingertips scraped the floor, my arms stretched out below me, pale and white in the dark like antlers. Blood was draining from my belly.

I woke up already vomiting. Choking, gasping. I heaved myself onto the floor, trying to clear my lungs. I was back in my room at the Hi-Way and alone except for the white, plastic crucifix on the wall.

Something was wrong with my arm. It hurt so badly, I screamed when I hit the floor. I rose, staggered to my purse, found the last remaining pills in the bottle. Swallowed them with a mouthful of vomit and lost consciousness again.

When I woke next, I was in the bed again, sweaty and wet. I rose unsteadily and stumbled into the shower. My body was hot and bruised. I let the water run over me as I leaned into the wall of the shower. I slumped onto the toilet and slowly toweled myself off. My arm didn't hurt now, but it didn't move much either. I didn't remember breaking it. Like so many things lately, my memory wasn't there.

Outside the small bathroom window, I saw the old caretaker in the early morning light. He pulled out his wrinkled member and pissed into the pool where my daughter had been swimming a few days ago. He zipped up and went back to sweeping. I pulled the curtain, stumbled to my bed, and fell asleep once more.

I woke because the drowned girl was standing over me. She wore a white t-shirt and cuffed blue jeans. I blinked at her, certain I wasn't dreaming this time. She didn't seem dead. Her face was calm, and I was struck again with the sudden sad thought that she had been beautiful when she was alive. Her hair fell all around me when she reached over and touched my face. Her touch was gentle, as if she were checking a child for a fever. She smiled. Though her lips never moved or changed, she said, "Don't be upset. I'm here now." She touched my face again, closing my eyes for me, as if I were already dead.

I woke once more because someone was knocking loudly and persistently at the motel door. I was alone in the room again. My body hurt, but only dully now. The knocking came again and I called for them to wait, then called once more because it took me awhile to dress with just one hand. The pills were wearing off, I felt myself wince each time I moved my arm too quickly. I pulled open the door and squinted painfully through the light of full day at the motel's caretaker. I wasn't expecting him.

He was maybe sixty, dressed in shorts, a white t-shirt and sandals. His nose was large and streaked with purple, broken veins. He handed me a piece of paper when I opened the door.

I stared at it, then at him.

"I ran the charges through for your room and your credit card was declined," he explained. "If you wanna stay anymore, you'll have to pay me cash or give me a working card."

Behind him on the highway a pair of white semis rolled by. The building shook.

I tucked the slip in my pocket. "What time do I have to be out?" I asked. My throat hurt to speak. My voice sounded worn and smoky.

"Noon." It was already almost 11:30. "I tried knocking earlier, but you didn't answer."

"Doesn't matter," I mumbled. "I don't have much stuff."

Another semi rolled past, and the caretaker leaned against the jittering door frame. Furtively, he peeked into the room. "Where did your girl go? I noticed she hasn't been here the last few days."

"With her father. To Florida."

He seemed to relax, "Good," he said "I was worried about the little one. I got grandkids of my own. Six of them."

I nodded.

"You get all kinds out here," he said. "Makes me nervous about the kids."

My cell phone rang. "I'll let you get that," he said. "God bless."

I only answered the phone to assure his exit. It was Collin.

"I've been trying to reach you for three days," he said tightly.

I winced internally. *Three days.* I had no memory of how long I'd been floating in and out of consciousness. *Three days.* It had happened before. I pushed the memory away—it carried with it Denny's angry face.

"I was about to give up." I could hear other voices in the background, echoing when he spoke. He was back at court.

"It takes me awhile to pack," I said. He didn't laugh.

"I drove up there," he said.

I felt a tug of something like guilt; it was a long drive. "You shouldn't have done that," I said. "I told you I'd call when I was ready."

"I keep thinking about something you said the last time," he said. "You said it's weird how drinking brings an amnesia. You forget how good you can feel when you're clean. How good it feels to wake up without feeling sick. How good it feels not to have to lie all the time to Reine. Remember we had that conversation?"

"Windy is in the hospital," I said, changing the subject. "She had a heart attack. I've been taking care of her."

I could sense him hesitate.

I felt a sizzle of anger, "It's the truth. I don't need to lie to you."

"Okay, okay," he said, "I believe you. When do you want me to come up? I can leave here in an hour."

I felt a thrill of panic. "Look," I said. "I can't go now. I have to take care of my mom."

"You need to take care of yourself."

"I'm fine. I've just been at the hospital."

He sighed in frustration. "Look, I'll call and check in tomorrow. Give you time to fix things with your mom. And Jane?"

"Yes."

"Take care of yourself. Everything in me is telling me to drive up and get you now. To lock you in the trunk of my car and dump you at rehab. Don't make me regret this." He hung up.

I sat shakily on the creaking bed and pressed the buttons to check my messages. There were over a dozen of them, over the three days I had just missed. I cradled my head in my hands and pressed the phone to my ear. There were Collin's terse missives. Then my daughter had called. "Hi, Momma!" she said almost breathlessly, excited each time. The rest of her message was always garbled, as if she were rushing away to the beach already. She was having a good time.

The prison nurse had called. Pitch's bleeding had stopped enough to move him back to the prison. Windy hadn't called at all.

I listened to the last message. "Jane, this is Denny," he said, his voice crackling with anger like an electric field. "Thanks for the calls at 4 a.m. Don't call me when you're drunk. Don't call me. And by the way—fuck you, too."

I hung up the phone and closed my eyes, trying to put together my thoughts. I was out of pills and I needed to leave. My arm was throbbing now, making it hard to pack. Going through my things, I found Reine's swimsuit. I pressed it to my heart like a stuffed animal, and tried to keep moving. I slung my things into the car one-handed and drove away.

The front door to Windy's house was pushed open. I paused warily. Peering inside, I could see the narrow front hallway. The basement door gaped open as well.

It could have been me that did this any time over the last few days. I wouldn't have remembered. But I didn't want to go inside.

My arm hurt as if someone were slowly pulling it out of its socket and away from me entirely. I needed some of Windy's pills, wherever she'd hid them.

I stood on the porch and stared at the black hole to the basement and felt a sense of foreboding. It was like a physical weight, as if someone were pressing me down, crushing my chest. I didn't remember how I'd hurt my arm, didn't remember the last handful of nights. But against the blank surface of my memory floated something from farther away, something that I had forgotten years ago. Staring at the black, gaping door made me think of it.

I remembered Windy's face, frightened and pale, hanging over me like a nightlight. She shook me awake in my bed. I was small enough for her to carry then, so she scooped me in her arms and ran. I could tell she was already badly hurt; she ran unevenly, panting with pain. Pitch cut us off in the hall and she screamed, screamed like someone being stabbed, and she turned and ran in the other direction. Pitch roared, an animal noise, like a dog and a pig mixed together with beer. But he slipped coming after us, and that was her chance to escape. She made it to the front hall and flung me loose.

"Run!" she sobbed at me, "Run, Jane!"

But I was young and scared. Instead of the front door, I flung myself into the basement and slammed the door behind me. I fled to the bottom of the wooden stairs and hid under Pitch's butchering table. Windy screamed over and over as Pitch laid into her. I lay on the cool floor, trying to be invisible, trying to not exist. My foot tipped the bucket I hadn't seen, and cold blood, clotted and congealed, poured over my ankles, up my legs. The smell overpowered me first and I lost consciousness.

I sat down shakily on the porch. The day got hot. It was August after all. Still I wavered on the porch, trying to decide. The pain I felt made me cry, but even a broken arm couldn't make me go back inside the house now. For the life of me, I didn't know where to go.

I heard a car roll up the driveway. Joe stepped out of his squad car. He took in my pale face and asked urgently, "What the hell happened?" I held out my arm. "I fell down the stairs," I said. "I think it's broken." He touched me, gingerly taking my arm in his two hands. He touched me so gently I felt certain that I must be breaking entirely and I started to cry.

There was coffee down by a curtained alcove at the end of the waiting room. Joe stirred some sugar into his plastic cup and came and sat back down with me. We'd been waiting nearly an hour, the pain in my arm growing more and more urgent.

"You don't own a dog, do you?" he asked, staring distastefully at the coffee.

I shook my head, cradling my arm.

"That's why I was out near you today. About a mile down from your mom's place. Neighbors called, because a car hit a dog."

"What did it look like?"

"Black. Like a lab or something."

"Was it okay?"

"No," he said grimly. "I had to put it down. It was suffering too bad." He gave up on the coffee entirely and set it down by a stack of magazines. "Only the third time I've fired my gun on duty in eight years, I think."

"What were the other times?"

"A deer in the same condition a few years back. Raccoon before that. Rabid." He shrugged. "Life as a small-town cop."

He picked up his coffee cup. "I'm going to try this again." He rose and went back to the alcove. I watched him fiddle with the pots a little, then refill his cup. He added several packets of sugar and little cups of cream. He came back and sipped it carefully. This time was better.

"I've been up all night," he explained. "I hate the hospital coffee."

A nurse walked by, and I looked up hopefully. She kept moving and disappeared down the hallway.

"Have you been to see your mom?" Joe asked.

"Yes," I said. "Why have you been up?" I asked before he could ask any more questions about Windy. "Double shift?"

"Couldn't sleep."

I watched him drain his coffee cup. "How are things going with the girl? Has anyone claimed her yet?"

"No."

"I'm sorry," I said.

He rubbed his face, looking truly tired now. "The medical examiner is going to issue her official report tomorrow. Accidental drowning, lake water in her lungs. No other signs of trauma." He shook his head in disbelief. "I just don't understand why no one is looking for her and no one's claimed her. Young girl like that."

"You'd be surprised how many kids there are out there, who no one gives a shit about."

"No, I wouldn't be surprised," he said bleakly. "I've been doing this job too long."

At the moment, he looked it. I remembered him touching me in the driveway. His hands running down my arm, feeling for the break. I might have reached over and comforted him, but the nurse called my name. He started, rising. He handed me back my car keys. "Here you go. Good luck."

I tried to smile back at him, but I had the feeling I failed.

A doctor wasn't needed to tell me my arm was broken. When the nurse put the x-ray film on the light box, I could see the proof for myself in black and white. The break was there in my forearm, just above the wrist. The bones of my fingers reminded me of antlers, glowing against the dark. I shuddered and looked away.

I thought of Windy and her broken bones, the noise of Pitch beating her that night. It was the worst one I remembered. My arm throbbed. Pitch hadn't ever spent more than a night in jail for any of it. Windy was always too afraid of him to cooperate with the police.

I thought of her on the dirty motel room floor on the day of her overdose, pale and sweaty, almost lifeless. And then the heart attack. Maybe this was where she'd first started taking the pills, at the hospital after a beating. Even in prison, after all these years, it felt like Pitch might kill her yet.

I turned when I felt someone watching me, pulling me away from thoughts I didn't want anyway. She was making no secret of it, staring curiously through the curtain the nurse had left half open. The old woman smiled when I met her eye, a tired kind of smile. She wore a hospital gown and her bare legs and feet stretched out from under it. They were the color of something long submerged, brought to the surface. She looked deeply and gravely ill.

"I hate sitting in these rooms," she said, her voice hushed and worn. "Too cramped. I get claustrophobic." She pressed her hand to her struggling chest, "What are you in for?"

I held my arm up a little, "Broken arm."

She nodded, making a sympathetic face. "I have cancer," she said. "Terminal stage. They like to bring me in here anyways once and awhile. I'd prefer to stay at home."

I wasn't surprised at her diagnosis. She looked as ill as Pitch, who I knew was at death's door.

It took a while for her to catch her breath. "I saw you in the lobby with the policeman," she said, then grinned almost mischievously. "Lucky you. He sat with you the whole time—he's a handsome one. You in any kind of trouble?"

I shook my head. "He was just giving me a ride to the hospital."

She nodded, watching a pair of nurse's aides pass by with a med cart. "I think I know your father, girl," she said. "I recognize you."

"Pitch?"

She frowned, "That doesn't sound familiar. What was his real name?" To tell the truth, I actually had to work to remember. "Leo," I said. "Leo McCullough."

She nodded, satisfied. "I thought so. Most people wouldn't notice the resemblance, but I knew him when he was young. He used to pick cucumbers some summers on my grandfather's farm. Little ones—for the pickle factory. You look like him when he was a teenager."

I knew she didn't mean anything by it, but I felt myself frown. "No one has said that before," I said.

"He was a looker, too, back then. Like your policeman." She chuckled, a dry wheezy sound. "I liked all those farm boys, but my father was the minister for Sunrise Lutheran."

The doctor arrived. "Can I interrupt?" she asked politely.

"Of course," said my neighbor, "I'm just passing the time until it's my turn. Old people like to talk, you know."

The doctor stepped into the room and pulled the curtain. She glanced at the film, then me. "Well," she said, "it looks like you'll need a cast."

Underneath the now-closed curtain, I saw my neighbor's bare feet shuffle away, called back into her room. I was surprised she even had the strength for that. Pitch was just as grey last visiting day.

"Does it hurt?" the doctor asked, touching my arm.

"Yes," I answered emphatically.

Windy was in the opposite wing of the hospital. I stood in the door and watched her for a while. I rubbed the cast on my arm, as if it could feel. The room was small and narrow, and depressing.

Her eyes were closed, and I thought she was sleeping, but when I sat down, she said, "I hate this place. Always have."

I nodded glumly. "Me, too."

She turned her head and looked at me. For a full minute she frowned at my arm in its new sling. "What the hell happened to you?"

"Stairs."

She considered this. "I hate those stairs. I've fallen down them more times than I can count."

"You should move into a condo," I suggested. "One-floor living."

She sat up, slowly, rearranging her wires and tubes. "You must have hit your head, too. Will you get my sweater out of the closet?"

I retrieved it and handed it to her. "Are you cold?"

She shook her head, laboriously sticking one arm in and then another. She shifted her weight to the edge of the bed, and I understood that she was planning to stand.

"Where are you going?" I asked nervously.

She tested her weight on her feet and grunted a little. She pointed at her wheelchair in the corner. "I want to go see the babies up on the fourth floor. The nurses wouldn't take me. But if I have someone to wheel me there and watch my wires, it's okay."

"Oh," I said. "Do you think that's a good idea?"

She shrugged, "The church volunteer wheeled me up there yesterday. There were six new ones and a pair of twins."

I pushed the chair up closer to her and she lumbered into it, almost pulling out one of her wires. She showed me how to unhook her IV bag and hang it from the chair. I banged her around a little, trying to get her in the right direction. It wasn't easy going with only one arm.

"I hate this place," she said again.

"Me, too," I agreed again, pushing her into the hall. None of the nurses protested, so I figured we were okay. I pushed her down the hall to the elevator.

The fourth floor was in the old part of the hospital that had high-vaulted ceilings, hung with bare light bulbs dangling on wire cords. The floor was a green linoleum and the walls tiled with beige squares. I had been born here.

When we arrived, Windy pulled herself out of her wheelchair and leaned heavily against the rail that ran along the window to the baby room. I counted six little infants, in plastic cribs, two with pink and the others with blue hats. They were sleeping, wrapped tightly in white- and blue-striped blankets. I looked from them to Windy's intent face. There were deep rings under her eyes. Her nose and cheek were bruised from her fall and her eye was bloody. The bruises were turning black and yellow. I looked away.

"Your father always wanted a boy," she said. "But I would never let him talk me into another one. I went to the hospital in St. Paul and had them fix that. My cousin drove me out and watched you while I had the surgery. Do you remember that?"

I did remember the trip; one of the few we'd made. Windy's family had been too afraid of Pitch, so visits were rare. The cousin's apartment had been paneled with dark wood and flowered wallpaper. I remembered the apartment owner herself a little less clearly; a tall woman with blonde hair like Windy's. I might have been four or so then. The cousin had spent the day combing my hair and tying it up in ribbons. Before we left, she'd taken a picture of me, standing on the front steps in a new dress she'd bought just for me. No one had ever done that before.

I looked back at the babies. Denny and I had planned on another child. I had quit my job to concentrate on the fertility treatments the doctor recommended. Denny, of course, had announced he was leaving me for the neighbor two weeks after I walked away from the prosecutor's office. I looked away from the babies; like the x-ray of my hand earlier, I didn't want to think about it too much.

Windy pulled me from my thoughts; she sank slowly at first, then with a solid whump of air fell back into her wheelchair.

I glanced down at her. If possible, she looked more tired and drawn than before.

"Are you okay?" I asked.

She shook her head, a little out of breath.

"Should we go back to the room?"

"Not just yet," she wheezed. "Maybe if you wheel me over there, I can still see the babies sitting down."

We tried; the other window around the corner seemed lower. She stared at the babies intently, her fingers gripping the window ledge. A few nurses walked by, then a doctor in a hurry. I waited patiently, eventually sitting down in one of the hard hospital chairs. I contemplated my cast. At last she said, "You know what I was thinking lately? I don't know if I ever told you this, but your great-grandmother—my grandmother— was a midwife. She delivered all the babies around here for years. She delivered both me and your father, too."

I hadn't known this.

"I couldn't sleep last night," she continued. "The medicine they gave me made me sick and every time I closed my eyes I dreamt about that girl. Like she was sitting right there in my room. Next to me." I looked away. "So I was making lists of things in my head," she said. "And I thought about all the things I would still have in common with your father, even if I had never married him or never knew him. My grandmother would still have delivered both of us. Helped us both into the world. Isn't that a strange thing to think?"

"No," I answered. "It sounds about right to me. Are you ready to go back yet?" I asked. "They might be looking for you to give you your medication."

She looked reluctantly back at the babies, but nodded her acquiescence at last. "I've been pretty out of it. I thought you stopped by yesterday?"

"Yes," I lied, slowly turning her in the right direction back to the elevators once more.

"How about your father?" she asked. "Any news on him?"

"No," I lied again.

Behind us, one of the babies woke up and began to cry. I glanced back, watching a nurse enter the room. I stumbled a little over the chair, and winced when I jarred my arm. The prescription they'd given me hadn't started working fully yet. I turned back, concentrating on walking.

Windy leaned forward and pushed the elevator button, grunting painfully as she did so. "I have a favor to ask you," she said as the door slid open. "I have some money in my purse to give you. I want you to buy some flowers from the gift shop, but they're not for me."

15

Ardell was working. He was wearing a white t-shirt torn at the neck over grimy blue jeans. He had all the doors to the bar thrown open to let the cool lake air in. At midday, the inside of the bar was still cave-like, all shadows and blue-grey light. Ardell was taking the chairs off the tables and wiping them down. A mop leaned against the bar. He straightened when I entered and squinted at me in the bright doorway. He wiped his brow on his sleeve and tossed the rag he was using behind the bar.

"Jesus Christ," he observed, "what did you do to your arm?"

I shrugged.

He waved me all the way in. Reaching over the bar, he grabbed a bottle of gin for me. I felt my legs go pleasantly numb when his hand closed around the bottle neck. He sloshed a little in a glass as I sat.

"Where have you been?" he asked. "It's been a few days. I was getting used to you being around."

I shrugged again. "Windy went to the hospital."

"How is she?" he asked.

"Nuts," I answered.

He almost smiled, then pushed the glass of gin across to me. "I'm almost done setting up for tonight," he said. "If you want ice, you'll have to grab it out of the deep freeze." He nodded to the door at the end of the bar.

I rose.

"Can you grab the whole bag? Just dump it in the cooler behind the bar."

"Those bags weigh fifty pounds," I protested. "And my arm is broken."

"You're a big girl," he said. "You can lift it."

I paused at the word big.

"Tall, strong, a fighter," he corrected, "that kinda big. Not fat. No insult intended." He headed back to his mop. "I used to have a great aunt like you—Sister Marie-Regine. When my dad still ran this place, she used to clear the bar on Sundays and haul the drunks to church." He actually smiled at the memory. "Dad hated her. And God she could throw a punch. She and Father Larson both."

The deep freeze must have been as old as my grandmother—it reminded me of the one she'd had in her basement, with a chrome handle and rounded edges. It filled the room with a low hum that was almost comforting. Like everything else in the bar, the white freezer was covered in dust and grime from cigarette smoke. On the lid, two handprints stood out, stark and white against the dirt and grit.

Like headlights hitting a sudden sign in the dark, I remembered the last night Ardell and I had been together; him kissing me, his lips pressed against the back of my neck. I felt myself flush and my knees go weak, a little like when he'd poured the gin. Everything was a blank after that. It was forgotten. It might as well have never happened, except that here I was and here were my handprints.

My eyes slid from my handprints up the wall to the crucifix. I remembered that now, too. In the steadier light, I noticed for the first time a small portrait framed and hung under the cross. Like everything else, it was covered in grey smoke and grit. I leaned forward; making out a black and white picture of a baby, fading into the dirt. She was in a little lace dress, like a baptismal dress. She couldn't have been more than eighteen months old.

I glanced over my shoulder, suddenly feeling like an intruder. Ardell flipped on the radio while he mopped. Randy Travis sang gospel with the conviction of a condemned man. I glanced back at the little picture, then lifted it gently off the wall. I meant to peek without getting caught. My fingertips betrayed me again, leaving marks in the grime.

"That's my sister, Sass," Ardell rumbled from behind me.

I hadn't heard him approach. I didn't jump, but only because I had learned not to long ago. It always irritated Pitch.

"I don't have many pictures of her," he continued. "Just that one really. She was fifteen when she died."

With surprising gentleness, Ardell took the little frame from me. He wiped it clean with the edge of his shirt, and placed it back up on the wall, straightening it until it was in the exact same place as before.

"She drowned," he said, turning away. "I've always considered her to be like my own patron saint. She watches out for me." Ardell touched my shoulder briefly, then returned to his chores. Randy Travis finished his song and the bar fell silent.

"Are you going to grab that ice?" he called back.

Once the chores were done, Ardell poured me another gin and sat across from me at a table. The light filtering in the windows was getting cooler, soft and grey. It was turning out to be a windy day, with white caps running across the lake.

"Do you have any sugar?" I asked.

He rose and found me a jar behind the bar.

"I think I met your sister once," I said. "Dark brown hair? Almost black like yours. Brown eyes."

Ardell didn't meet my eye. He shrugged and opened the sugar, setting it in front of me.

"Tall and thin," I continued. "That's about all I remember. I only saw her the once."

"When do you think that was?" he asked.

I put in a spoonful of sugar, stirred and took a slow sip of gin; my lips burning pleasantly. I closed my eyes and remembered, biting my warm lips thoughtfully. "I was maybe four, so it had to have been a while ago." The second sugary sip was better than the first. I let the feeling burn my throat.

I looked at my memory; it guttered like a candle—too much black and bright at once. The dark edges swirled around me and I felt their pull like smoke floating upward. Light flickered and faded. I remembered only sleeping by fits and turns in Pitch's car, waiting for him to come out of the bar. Even for Pitch, things had been running late. My legs were numb with being cramped into a small ball in the dark, curled altogether, trying to be small and invisible.

I remembered Sass, suddenly shaking me, bending over me, her long hair touching my face. I could hardly see her features. "He's coming," she whispered and the taut fear in her voice woke me completely.

Young children don't often wake easily—but in that moment I was urgently awake. Her voice was like an electric charge. All at once, I was aware of the dark and the trees pressing down on us. I was aware of the smell of pitch and pine and the soft rocking noise of the lake stirring against the shore. And I was already moving, sliding across the seat and out the door with Sass.

My ears were pricked for danger, and the noise of the bar door slamming open, of old Lee Ring swearing and heaving with anger made me jump as if I'd been struck. I froze, as I often did in those situations. I drained the rest of the glass of gin. "He almost had me," I said, not quite meeting Ardell's eye. "He actually managed to grab hold of my arm. I'm sure he was out of his mind. You could see it on his face. But she pulled me loose and we ran like hell into the woods."

The sugar gritted between my teeth. I reached for the bottle in Ardell's hand. He let me have it without protest. I sloshed a lot into my glass, not caring that I soaked the table, too.

"Did he follow you in the woods?" Ardell asked.

I nodded.

"Did he catch you?"

"Not that time," I said grimly. "He was too drunk to go far." This time the drink went down quickly without any burn.

"How old were you?"

"Maybe four, like I said."

I turned the half-full bottle on its side. It spun slowly as I started to feel the gin settle into me like concrete hardening. It felt better.

"I remember you hanging around the bar," he said, his eyes following the slowly spinning bottle. "But I don't remember that." He shook his head. "I spent about two years in juvenile detention in Red Wing. 'Bout when I was fifteen. Couple years later went to prison in Rush. Must have been while I was gone."

"Why did you go to prison?" I asked.

"Fights, mainly," he said. "That time I blinded a guy in his left eye."

The bottle stopped, pointing at Ardell. "Here?"

He shook his head. "No, this was my girlfriend's dad. We didn't see eye-to-eye on a lot of things." Ardell grimaced. "Problem sorted itself out though. By the time I got out, he'd taken her back to Mexico. Never saw them again."

I picked the bottle up to pour another. I paused. "Why did you come back here after that?"

"Where the hell else was there to go?" he said, rising so abruptly it surprised me. "And besides there's Sass." He collected his cleaning supplies from the table, heading back to work. "You should pay me before you drink anymore of that," he said. "It surprises me, given your old man, but when you drink, you're a fucking lightweight."

After Ardell's, I popped some more pills and sat down by the lake for a while at the old turn-out. I watched the water. I tried to return Reine's calls, but she didn't answer. After that, one thing led to another and I woke up early the next morning back in my car, with my head pressed against my steering wheel. My neck hurt and my arm ached. The light was blindingly bright. I swore unhappily; I was parked outside the Hi-Way Motel. From the crick in my neck, I guessed I'd slept there most of the night.

The car smelled sweet and overwhelmingly floral—an almost fermented smell. On the passenger seat was the bouquet of flowers Windy had asked me to buy, already wilted and brown in the heat. Sometime between Ardell's place and the lake, I had forgotten to bring them to the cemetery like Windy asked. I looked around and found my purse. I put my sunglasses on and took some of the pills left in my prescription bottle.

I reached to restart the car, but just then the caretaker emerged from his office. He looked a little surprised to see me.

At this point, there wasn't much use in trying to hide the state I was in. And there was no time to start the car and peel out of there. I rolled the window down and tried to smile at him. He'd never been unpleasant to me. I owed him an apology at least for getting confused and driving back here.

He didn't ask me any questions though. He leaned on the open window.

"I was wondering if you'd come back. I have your things in the office. You left some stuff behind."

The old man gestured me into a chair by the motel's front desk while he drew out his keys. "I put the stuff back in the safe," he explained. "Otherwise my cleaning person sometimes throws things away."

I sank obediently into the chair while he disappeared. For a while I looked down at my feet and the green shag carpeting. I listened to the window air conditioner hum mechanically and burble. It reminded me of the deep freeze at Ardell's. I found myself thinking about white handprints and stared at the crucifix on the old man's wall. It was behind the desk, large and white, plastic like the ones in the room. This one was big enough to take up the whole back wall. It made me wonder if crappy old motels by the highway had a particular patron saint. If Ardell's bar did, why not here as well?

The old man returned, holding a folded manila envelope. He saw my eyes on the crucifix and shrugged ruefully. "My late wife was a little bit of a holy roller, you know? Used to drive me insane. She'd have the Gideon Bible people out for the rooms and everything."

"I would take the crosses down and she would put them back up," he added. "We would argue and I would say, 'no one checks into a motel to hang out with Jesus.' But she didn't care. She'd get those church people over to lecture me."

He sighed and sat next to me.

"But you know the day of her funeral, I came home and looked at that cross on the wall. And I told myself it wouldn't ever be me who takes him down again."

His worn face looked sad, like an old wound.

"What did she die of?" I asked.

"Cancer," he said, shaking his head, "Ate her all up. Went fast though." He handed me the envelope.

I turned it over in my hand, frowning. I couldn't think what I had left here. I glanced at him again, then opened the envelope. Inside were a handful of Reine's barrettes, arranged on the ribbon she liked, and Pitch's sobriety medal.

My heart sank.

"Found them by the bed. Slipped down along the wall," he said. "Normally I would have just thrown the barrettes out, but those medals are important."

I nodded, hastily closing the envelope. My throat had a sudden lump in it, like I swallowed something whole. Something dry and painful, like purple thistle.

The old man rose, "Tell you the truth, girl, you look like you could use it. I've got one myself you know." He held open the office door for me.

I rose creakily.

"Do you have a sponsor you can call?" I shook my head.

"'Bout a year after my wife died, my two girls came over and told me I wouldn't be seeing my grandkids anymore if I didn't sober up. I love those kids, so I figured 'well that's it for me.' I went to treatment the next day."

He followed me out into the parking lot to my car. "You know," he said, not unkindly, "if I find you sleeping here again, I'll charge you for a room. And I don't like having to call the police."

I flushed with embarrassment.

"I tell the same thing to all the teenagers who think this parking lot is a good place to hang out and get stoned. I don't need that kind of trouble."

I nodded sheepishly.

"You should go home, anyway," he continued. "You said your daughter was with her father. When is she coming back?"

I had lost track. "Soon," I mumbled. "I tried to call her yesterday." He turned to leave, then paused, remembering. "You know, I didn't realize it when you checked in at the time, but I think I used to know your mom. We might have worked together at the restaurant when we were teenagers. She sure has changed." The old man patted my shoulder and left this time. He went back into his office and flipped on the motel's "open" sign.

I climbed into my car and tossed the envelope onto the passenger seat. I looped the sobriety medal around the car's mirror, then I rested my head against the steering wheel for comfort. *God grant me . . .* I thought, but really, I already knew better.

16

I parked in the turnaround at the cemetery at the end of the rows of graves along the lake shore. The gravel crunched under my feet when I climbed out of the car. Before I closed the door, I rolled the windows down so the car stayed cool. The lake was still and green, crowded near the shoreline with a thick bank of weeds and cattails. A tall white egret picked its way delicately through the tangled growth.

I thought of my daughter and pulled my cell phone from my purse. She hadn't called.

I swayed a little in the soft lake breeze. The pills were wearing off again and I felt the beginnings of a headache. I reached through the window and grabbed the flowers. I was too rough; battered and wilted, they started to fall apart in my hand. I sighed, glancing up the hill at the row of stones. It was easy to make out the little stone with its perched lamb that I had come to visit. I considered the flowers again. I didn't have anything else to bring at that moment.

Just then, I hated Windy for asking me to do this. She came every month like penance; every twenty-first day faithfully. I climbed the hill and put the flowers in front of the stone. Pitch had killed this little girl and shattered her mother's face and ribs. She would have been the same age as Reine now. They might have even been in camp together, leaning into one another, telling secrets in the parking lot.

The noise of tires on the gravel drive made me look up quickly. The girl's parents had moved to Kansas City, leaving this sad little grave behind. Must have been a few years ago now. Still, I felt nervous—criminal perhaps—standing here. I relaxed a little when I saw an unmarked squad car slowly roll down the drive. Joe parked next to my car and walked back up the hill. He wasn't wearing his uniform now, but somehow still looked like he was.

If he was surprised by my presence here, he didn't show it.

The breeze off the lake had grown cool; I shivered and hugged myself. I touched on my earliest memory of him, as a face across the courtroom, before I knew him. He'd aged since the trial, I realized. He'd been there for every day of it, often holding the mother's hand, standing with her in the hallway.

"Are you okay?" he asked. I knew he wasn't just asking about the cast on my arm this time.

I shook my head slowly. "Doesn't really matter," I said.

He reached out and gently touched the little stone lamb on the grave. "I heard her folks moved down south. Almost two years ago."

"I know that," I answered. "Windy keeps track of those things."

He seemed about to ask a question I didn't want to answer, so I spoke instead. "What are you doing here, Joe?" I asked.

"Lew Hanson just died," he said, letting his hand fall. "Did you know Lew?"

"My father did," I said. "They might have fished for steelhead together."

"He died of a heart attack in jail two days ago," Joe continued. "In the drunk tank. His family won't claim him and the jail won't pay for the burial. So it's up to the city. I'm looking at two lots here."

"The county won't bury him?"

Joe grimaced. "I was still at the jail filling out the paperwork when he had the heart attack, so technically he was still in my custody. So he's my problem. The county offered a plot out along Old Poor Farm Road. They got a facility out there, mainly for prisoners and the unclaimed. I'm going to check that out after this." He paused and studied me for a moment. "You don't look so good."

The pain I had felt earlier in my temple was growing into a full-bore migraine. Still, I pushed back at him and the concern written so plainly on his face. "How do I look?" I asked.

He wasn't rattled. Cops are used to blunt questions. "Pale," he answered, "and a little tired, too. You could use something to eat."

It was a simple observation, but it made me blink as if I'd been struck. I looked down at the grave. That too was a mistake. There was a hot needle of misery inside me. I felt it loosen and collide with my stomach, tearing at my insides. I couldn't hold it close anymore. "Sometimes it doesn't help to talk about a problem." I spoke softly, but he felt the warning in my voice nonetheless.

"You think I'm trying to help you?" he asked gently.

I met his eye, taking full stock of this man. There was something about him that was as grey and comforting as the wool jacket he wore over his plain clothes cop jeans and his neat black boots. "Yes," I said. "Yes, I think you are."

He shrugged easily. "Maybe I'm just being nosy. Cops do that," he suggested.

I looked away.

"Where's your girl?" he asked. "Is she up at the summer camp? I didn't see her when I took you to the hospital this morning."

"No," I said and my voice actually wavered. I hated myself. "She went to Florida with her dad. We—they," I corrected, "take the trip every year."

"Probably a good idea to get her away from this," he added shrewdly.

I nodded, not trusting my voice again.

Joe sighed and put his hands in his jacket. "Well," he said, "since we've agreed that I'm definitely not helping you out, why don't you come with me for a while? Take the drive down to Old Poor Farm Road with me. It would help me, to have some company looking for a place to bury Lew. I'm even getting a little sentimental for him. Feels like I spent more time with him than my girlfriend. I must have picked him up for the drunk tank at least once a week. When he got enough in him, he'd cry in my back seat for his daughter."

"Did she die?" I asked.

He shook his head. "Nope, near as I could tell she lives in Los Angeles and just wouldn't send him money anymore."

"Sounds about right."

"Did you know him?" he asked.

"I already said I did."

"I remember that," he acknowledged.

"But you asked again anyway?"

"I did," he answered.

"Why is that?"

"Because sometimes," he explained patiently, "it's not the answer I'm after, but the way people say the answer. Helps me read the situation."

"You learn that in cop school?"

"Yes," he nodded. "So what do you think, will you take a drive with me?"

I should have said no outright. Instead I said, "Why would I do that? You can't really miss Lew that much."

He looked out at the lake. "I was thinking about the girl," he acknowledged. There was no need to ask which girl. "If no one claims her, I'll be looking for a place to bury her, too. And I don't like that idea. That's not at all like burying Lew Hanson."

"Someone will claim her," I said. "It might just take a while."

Joe bit his lip and shook his head. "I've put it out everywhere . . . that we have a Jane Doe here. But I've got a bad feeling about this one. A bad feeling like it's going to be me putting her in the ground."

"Why?" I asked.

"Dunno, but that's how I feel." Our eyes met. "So why don't you ride with me today? Truth is you can help me out. I'm just a small-town cop who writes a lot of speeding tickets. I didn't sign on for this."

Joe turned onto the highway. "So," he said, starting the conversation, "when I called him, Collin, your old boss, said you handled his worst cases. Does that mean you handled those gang murder trials two years ago? The ones in the paper."

"I don't talk about my cases," I said, crossing my arms. "Sorry, I never have."

Joe's car was dusty but otherwise clean. The dirt from the back roads he patrolled lay in a soft sheen on the blue dash. "Was your dad a cop?" I asked, changing the subject. "Is that how you got started?"

He shook his head. "He worked for the highway department his whole life. Hard worker. He died about fifteen years back."

"I'm sorry to hear that."

He smiled, "He was a good dad. An Arapaho man. Met Mom out here and swept her off her feet. Promised to take her out to Montana where he was raised. They made it about as far as St. Paul. I've got three brothers and a younger sister. None of them are cops either."

"Why did you move way up here?"

"Sister Marie-Regine—my mom's great aunt," he answered. "She always helped my mom out after Dad died. She liked me. So she left me her house when she passed on—right about the time this job opened up. Been here ever since."

Outside the window, the lake slid by us, a long slice of blue on the horizon. Then Joe turned off the highway and pines rose up on either side.

"Why did you move back?" he asked.

It seemed a fair enough question. I fiddled with the lock on the door.

"My divorce," I said. That was the easiest answer anyway. "Home seemed like the place to end up."

"Starting over?"

"People don't wind up here to start over, Joe," I said.

He almost smiled, thinking I was joking. I wasn't, and the smile slid off his face. That was the most we talked for a while. We were getting close to the old cemetery. The sign for Old Poor Farm Road leaned at an odd angle, almost falling into the ditch. There weren't many houses on this stretch of road. A few old farms and a new house with an unfinished porch. We passed stretches of electric fence along damp fields. Joe slowed and turned off the road onto a narrow trail that was mainly two tire tracks heading into a tired-looking field. The car jolted when we slopped into the ditch a little.

The cemetery wasn't much. There wasn't a gate or a fence to separate the yard from the field, just a mowed line against the long prairie grass. The center of the graveyard still held the crumbling foundation of a barn with the oldest stone graves pressed up against it. The newer graves were closer to where Joe parked, marked by metal crosses. Apparently the county didn't pay for first names on the crosses, just the last. "How can you tell who's buried where?" I asked.

"The county's got a list." He shrugged. "But they don't bury many anymore. Most people will come for family. Even the ones in prison. Sometimes the hospital has an unclaimed stillborn and they end up here, too."

I counted about forty metal crosses and two dozen old and crumbling stones; most of the oldest looked like children's graves. No names on these, just a few dates hardly days apart. I turned my back on them. They were too hard to look at.

"Poor farm used to mean orphanage, but they kept some old folks here, too," Joe explained, frowning off across the field. "But it's mainly kids here and prisoners."

A flutter of ribbon caught my vision at the edge and I turned. I walked over to a grave that stood at the end of all the little grim white markers. This one had an iron cross, but someone had tied a ribbon over the name. My foot touched stone and I looked down. Grass mostly covered a modern, flat marker of black stone. It looked newer than anything else here.

"That would be Sass Ring," Joe said. "Ardell's sister."

"You know Ardell?" I asked, surprised enough to pull back the hand that was reaching to soothe grass away from the stone.

Joe nodded.

"How?" I asked, thinking of the little smiling baby on Ardell's wall.

"Ardell and I are cousins on my mother's side. You shouldn't be so surprised really, everyone up here is related. Besides I like to think there's a certain logic to my relationship with Ardell. He gets them good and drunk, and I arrest them. Almost like a family business," he joked. I didn't smile. I was looking at the stone again. I squinted more closely at the dates, adding up the simple arithmetic in my head; she was fifteen when she died.

"She was killed," Joe said. "They never found out who or why. Probably one of the drunks at the bar or some drifter passing through. Lee Ring always had a rough crowd out there."

I touched the ribbon hung on the cross and its paper picture of the Virgin Mary. The blue of her dress had faded in the sun to a soft baby blue. Her face was almost completely worn away. I was certain Ardell had hung it here recently. I let the little paper flutter from my hand. The prayer on the back began, "Hail Mary, full of grace . . ."

"She was drowned," Joe said, though I didn't ask. "Sister Marie-Regine never got over it. I don't think Ardell did either, though he never talks about it."

"Did you know her?" I asked.

Joe shook his head. "I was too young. But I remember my mom talking about it."

I rose, brushing grass from my knees. "Why is she buried out here?"

"Because her father was a sonofabitch," Joe observed calmly. "She was an unclaimed up at the county morgue."

"The stone looks new though," I frowned.

Joe nodded again. "Ardell put that in just a few years ago—right about when he sobered up. He asked me to come out, because we're family. Just the two of us and the crows while the stonemason set the stone. Listening to the wind." He hesitated and touched the old iron cross. "It's sad when you think of it. Neither one of them could have had much of a life, growing up in that bar. Lee Ring was about the meanest drunk I ever met, too, except for your dad."

I looked away. There was a movement near the fringe of pines beyond the mowed yard. A threesome of crows rose from the trees, circled briefly and alighted on the foundation. They shook their wings at us. I didn't like thinking about Ardell or either of our fathers when I was sober. Things started to crowd in on me. I looked around at the iron crosses again. They were blackened from the weather. Most of them crooked. It was a shabby, dirty place and suddenly, I'd had enough of it. Joe was looking around, too, his face grim.

"Do me a favor, Joe," I said. "If you have to bury that girl, don't do it out here. This is fine for Lew. But not her, don't leave her out here."

Joe met my eye and nodded seriously. He was about to speak when my phone suddenly rang, its little trill startling even the crows. They cawed angrily and flew away, settling in the pines over Joe's car.

"Hi, Mom," Reine's voice burbled on the other end and I smiled, even as my eye fell once again on the row of battered gravestones. The line wasn't clear, but I thought I could hear the wind in the background. I pictured her outside and closed my eyes. It helped me listen, but more than anything it closed out the image of babies' graves.

"Did you make it in safe and sound?" I asked, going back days. We hadn't talked yet. Just messages. "Sorry I missed your calls before."

"That's okay." I could feel her smile on the other end and that warmed me. "Yep, the plane landed fine."

"Are you at the Palaces? Is the cabin close to the pool like you like?"

"No, Daddy changed his mind." She giggled. "Guess what! We're not at the Palaces this year. Daddy rented a whole house on the beach and it's on stilts and it's pink. And there's a kitchen."

"But we always go to the Palaces," I blurted out and hated myself for doing it.

"Louisa knew this place," Reine said. "Hold on a minute, Dad's talking."

"Yes,"Reine said, not talking into the phone. I heard Denny's voice in the background. "Okay," she said to him, then started speaking to me again. "Dad said we're going to head out to the beach. I forgot my flip flops and my bathing suit, but Daddy bought me some at the airport."

"You left them at the motel," I said.

"And at camp," she said. "Remember, you promised to get my sunglasses? They're my favorite ones."

I had forgotten. "I'll go get them," I promised, "and I'll call you tomorrow." I could practically feel her straining toward the water. "Love you, Reine."

"Love you, too." She hung up the phone first, leaving me staring at the grim row of iron crosses alone again. They swept away the beach and my daughter like a hard wind. I looked down at the ground and frowned at the scratchy grass that climbed to my knees.

"Everything okay?" Joe asked. I had almost forgotten he was waiting for me. I slowly tucked my phone back in my purse and zipped the bag closed, taking my time, trying to piece myself back together.

"That was just my daughter," I said. "Just checking in with me."

I straightened my shoulders and turned around. I was glad I had taken my time because Joe was watching me closely. I smiled falsely, which he returned automatically. Neither of us was fooled.

"How about you let me take you out to eat?" he asked.

I shook my head. I had already let this day get too far away from me. I didn't want to be with Joe anymore. I couldn't take the concern that was so clearly written on his face. It made me uncomfortable, leaving me feeling out of place, the way I always had with Denny.

"Joe," I said, "you better get smarter if you want to stay living in a small town."

He smiled. "Who cares if people talk?"

I eyed him, thinking of his girlfriend, trying to remember the last time I had seen her. We went to high school together; I think she worked at the bank.

"When was the last time you ate anything?" he asked more seriously.

I thought about it, slowly piecing together the days since Reine had left. There were a lot of holes in my memory. If Reine were here, I wouldn't have forgotten to cook for her. I suddenly felt frayed and ragged. I had forgotten to eat; maybe for days now. I knew enough to remember that wasn't a good sign for me.

"Get in the car," he urged, still gently, "I have to drive you back to your car anyway. We'll stop somewhere." Behind him another crow landed on the pines and shook her wings. She eyed me with her black and beady eyes.

Suddenly I felt too tired to argue.

In the end we drove out to the highway past two towns and found a fast food restaurant with a lighted plastic sign. I took the last of my pills in the bathroom while Joe ordered our food to go. Then Joe drove down to the public dock on Big Comfort Lake where the police department had their boat tied up.

We climbed in and Joe let us float out, not bothering to start the motor. We drifted not that far from the shore. The pills I took were taking off a bit of the anxiety I felt from the graveyard. We floated toward the thick reeds, Joe sitting next to me on the metal bench. He tapped my leg and pointed silently at a dozen enormous white birds—egrets picking their way through the reeds on their tall, rickety legs. I watched them poke here and there, dipping their beaks into the weedy water, pulling fish out and swallowing them whole.

The boat rocked gently one way then swayed another. We drifted within a few feet of the reeds. Joe didn't seem to mind. He let us drift back out again while he ate his burger. He rubbed my back. "Eat your food," he said encouragingly, his voice quiet so that he didn't frighten the birds. "It's getting cold."

I slowly unwrapped a burger. "How long have you been with Tessa?" I asked.

He grimaced and ate a fistful of fries. "'Bout five years, I think."

I raised my eyebrows. "Five years is a long time to just date in this neck of the woods," I observed.

He shrugged. "We're engaged and all that."

"Congratulations."

Two of the white birds wandered close to one another. They seemed to face off against each other warily. I waited for a warning or a call. They eyed each other some more, then silently one bird shook its whole body, a little like a dog, and then awkwardly launched itself into the air. Its great gangly wings were as wide as the boat. It rose and we watched as it slowly glided back down to the water, just a few yards away from where it was before.

"Do you have a date picked out?" I asked.

"We did," he said, grimacing again and finishing his fries. "We had to cancel it." He crumbled the box in his hand and put it back in the sack.

"What happened?" I asked.

Joe opened up a metal tool box at our feet and rummaged in there, finally pulling out the boat's light. He yanked out the cord. "I started to have anxiety attacks," he said. "It felt like this weight on my chest. I couldn't breathe. I called 911. The only time I ever had to do that in my life. I thought it was a heart attack, but it's just the anxiety. So we put things on hold for a while."

He finished fiddling with the light and we were bathed suddenly in its soft, white glow. The glow and the cool evening pulled me more steadily into the lethargy that was growing around my edges from the pills. I started eating my food, trying to move away from the sluggishness I felt.

Joe smiled to see me eat.

He dug my fries out of the enormous paper sack of food and handed them to me. He ate another burger and let the boat drift farther along, only now and then steering things with the battered wood oars when we got too close to the shore.

The sky faded out and the little light seemed to grow brighter. As the sky darkened, the lake became completely black, without depth. To my surprise I actually finished all the food Joe gave me and started to drink my now-warm pop. I finished that too, and then asked him. "Why do you think you started to have anxiety attacks? Do you know?"

He shrugged, "They say it's really common with cops. Just a part of the job I guess."

"But you've been a cop for years. They just started up a little while ago?"

He nodded.

A great white bird along the shore emerged again from the curtain of reeds. In the twilight, its plumage stood out like a ghostly, mysterious light. It swayed there for a moment, then disappeared into the curtain again. I looked around for its companions and couldn't find them. All six had disappeared, silent and unnoticed. I felt a twinge of sadness, soft and slurry along with my consciousness.

"I think it started—the attacks," Joe said, "when Tessa started talking about kids. Being a cop has never bothered me. But all of a sudden . . ." he shook his head, "I felt like the back of my mind—the part you just don't pay attention to—had been keeping track of all this stuff for years. All of a sudden it tallied up the bill and handed it to me. All at once. Everything that ever scared me or kept me up at night."

"So you put the wedding on hold?"

"Yep. We put it on hold. Canceled everything—the hall, minister, dress. Until I get this figured out."

"How long?"

"About two years now."

I couldn't imagine that going over well. "She must be getting impatient."

"Yes. Yes, she is." His face was grim. "We were supposed to have this big dinner a few days ago to talk about it. I kinda skipped it. That was the same day we found the girl."

The evening's peaceful quiet was suddenly broken by Joe's cell phone ringing. We had drifted once more against the reeds. The noise startled the flock of white birds hiding in the green curtain. They rose as one with an eerie cry that made me shiver. Their white wings—like seraphim—were suddenly threatening and large. We both shrank back and the boat rocked violently. The bag of food and the loosely attached light fell into the lake. Joe grabbed both sides of the small boat, trying to calm its rocking as he grabbed his cell phone.

Then suddenly the birds were gone. Joe answered his phone.

I couldn't hear the voice on the other end of the line, but the change on Joe was dramatic. His cop face appeared like the birds surging out of the reeds. "I'll be there," he said and hung up.

Joe climbed onto the back bench and pulled on the motor. He had us to the shore in two minutes. I followed him to the car, feeling as if my legs were rubber—I couldn't tell if it was from the water or the pills. I felt chill and wished for the sweater I had back in my car at the cemetery. Joe handed me his jacket.

"I'll drop you off at your car," he said. "I hope you don't mind."

"What's wrong?" I asked.

"The girl," he said tensely. "There's another family come to see the body."

I wrapped his still-warm jacket around me, feeling with a painful certainty that life was costing us both more than it should.

{17}

We didn't talk during the brief drive. I wondered if he could; his face was so taut he seemed to have been muzzled. He forgot to say goodbye and left me standing alone in the dark cemetery by the lake and my car. I fumbled for my keys in my large purse. I was shaking so much I could barely drive home.

Reaching Windy's house, I was suddenly over my earlier skittishness. I walked through the black, gaping door without thought. Hell, I'd have walked through anything at that moment. I'd taken all my pills in the bottle I had earlier and I needed more.

I'd been here before. Been this sick, been this shaky, and knew things weren't going so well for me. I found some pink pills tucked in one of my mother's shoes and stuffed them into my mouth like berries. I slumped back into her closet and closed my eyes. I knew it was time to call Collin. Like the last time. There wasn't much more that I could get away with in my current state.

It was then that I heard the noise from the basement, an odd and unexpected sound. The sound of water rushing unfettered. I pulled myself up by Windy's dresses, then teetered unsteadily to the stairs and peered down. The bottom of the stair was black as always, shadowed and hidden. But then it rippled. The noise of water rushing past grew stronger. I clung to the wall and let myself down.

The basement was flooded. Flooded all the way to my waist with water that reeked of the lake. I peered around in the dark, too afraid to turn on the light. I could make out the strange forms of floating chairs as my eyes adjusted. Something hard bumped against my leg, and I pressed my hand to my mouth—I knew better than to scream. Pitch hated the noise.

It was the little station for Saint Agnes that I'd seen at the camp, torn loose. Shaped like a prow, it floated past me. It was mostly submerged, but still afloat. I tried to catch it in my hands, but felt suddenly the pull of the water it was caught in. Strong, startling and unnatural, I stepped back quickly.

I watched the little boat's path, watched the drowning saint float away, her face serene as she slowly sank. The water rushed away from me, across the long basement to Pitch's old drinking room. It was almost as if there was a storm drain beyond that door, just beyond my vision, pulling everything in.

I could see more in the dark now. Wedged against the door to Pitch's room was his old butchering table—too big to fit through the narrow opening. It was acting like a dam, everything caught against it—antlers, pieces of broken bows and furniture, canning jars, knives, and yard tools. The little saint station popped to the surface again and caught there as well.

And then I saw it, half-submerged in dark and water: the girl's body, pale and lost, sad and dead. It was caught up against the table, mixed with all the other things.

I couldn't scream now. I didn't have any breath. My chest, my whole body was empty. I fell backward into the water, fell under the current. For the second time in my life, I lost consciousness from fear.

I revived still slumped over in my mother's closet. Dry and unhurt, clutching my phone in one white hand, and the now-empty plastic baggie in the other. Beneath my ear was one of my mother's practical, brown leather shoes. The house was quiet. I was alone. My phone rang, and I answered it more because of that than anything.

"I changed my mind," Collin said abruptly. "I can't shake this bad feeling in my stomach about you. It's like someone keeps punching me there. I'm coming to get you."

"That might be a good idea," I admitted, shakily.

"Good," he said, with an exhale of relief. "I'll be there in two hours. The room is bought and paid for. Everything is arranged. You just need to man up and show up."

A little prickle of a thought touched me. "What do you mean paid for?" I asked.

I could feel Collin wince on the other end. He had misspoken.

"Who paid for it?" I asked. "You? They charge like five hundred bucks a night."

Collin didn't answer.

"Collin?" I asked, except it wasn't a question.

"Where are you at?" he asked.

"The hospital like I said. Taking care of my mother. Who paid for the room?"

Collin swore under his breath.

I waited.

"Denny," he admitted at last. "Denny called me last month and said he'd pay for everything if I could just get you in."

In an instant, I was so angry I felt bloodless, weightless. I could have levitated from the closet. "Goodbye, Collin," I said.

"Wait!" he yelled. "Wait a goddamn minute, Jane. I don't give a fuck who pays for this, but you have got to go in."

"You know I don't want a dime from him. I didn't even ask for alimony," I hissed. "He can take all his money and shove it up his ass. He isn't going to buy me off."

"This isn't about him. This is about taking care of you. It's time to kiss your pride goodbye and come clean."

"Come clean?" I breathed. "Come clean? How about you, Collin? Have you told Jennifer about us yet?"

"You know I haven't," he said quickly, more quietly. Wherever he was—home I suspected—I heard the noise of a door closing. "Amazingly, I haven't mentioned to my wife what happened. I went back to treatment."

"So because you're back on the goddamn wagon, that makes you so much better than me?" I yelled.

"I never said that."

"Fuck you."

He drew a long ragged breath, "Stop this. You know I would never say that to you."

"Fuck you," I repeated. "Fuck you for plotting this with Denny. Fuck you and never call me again."

He might have answered. I never knew, because I hung up.

I slumped onto the floor. I felt as if I'd been beaten, physically shaken until my teeth and my bones hurt. One thing was certain: I needed to get out of my mother's closet. It was too hot there, as if the air itself were smothering me. The heat was a second skin, reptilian, grating—I needed to shed it.

I looked above me, at her skirts hanging over me. Her church clothes, heavy and woolen, almost with their own shape. Her years of restaurant uniforms, worn almost to nothing. I grabbed ahold and tried to pull myself up. The hangers gave way and the whole mass came falling down on me, burying me.

I lay there for a moment, chest heaving, smelling my mother's scent all around me, mixed with soap. It made me feel like a very small child. I closed my eyes for a moment.

When I woke, it was near midnight, cool and dark.

An odd noise reached my ear, the phone ringing. Not my cell phone, but the one in the house. An odd sound indeed, one I didn't often hear anymore. Like Windy's clothes, it reminded me of my childhood. I bumped through the darkness and caught the phone just barely.

It was the hospital. Pitch was there now. It didn't look good. Did I want to visit? The nurse would make arrangements with the guard.

"Yes," I said. "I'll be there."

They had him propped up in his bed, with a bolster of white pillows. Nonetheless, he slumped uncomfortably to the side. Pitch's skin reminded me of a salamander, grey and sickening, hairless and loose against the bone. When I entered the room, he didn't move—he was too weak—but his eyes turned toward me. Blue and pale, they were the only thing left that reminded me of him.

"They called you?" he asked softly.

I nodded, sitting in the chair beside his bed.

"Do you want to lie down?" I asked.

"No," he said, his voice too dry. I handed him a little cup from his bedside table. He drank it shakily. "I asked them to prop me up like this. Hard to get comfortable."

His arms were covered in tubes. I traced the lines with my eyes all the way up to the IV bags hanging over him. It seemed like there were too many.

I dug in my purse and pulled out his little sobriety medal; the one he had given me just days earlier. "I brought this back to you," I explained. "I thought you might want it." I had to press it into his hand and close his fingers around it.

"The priest was already here," he said, pointing his chin at a little wheeled table across the room. "The one from the prison. I was glad he came."

I rose and went to look at the table. There were two little prayer cards—the kind priests leave; one of Mary, with her kind face, and the other of Jesus, wrapped in a red cloth. His sacred heart glowed just as brightly red, with its flame and crown.

I picked up the blue Mary card and turned it over, reading the little prayer. It reminded me of the one I'd seen today, tied with faded ribbon to an iron cross. I thought of Ardell's hands tying it there. For the first time it occurred to me that Pitch would soon be buried at the Poor Farm Cemetery as well, just an iron cross among the other prisoners and unclaimed, with Sass and maybe the drowned girl.

I turned back to Pitch, still holding the little card. I never meant to ask him the question that came next. It was almost as if it were written there for me on the little card. As if I were just reading it aloud, after *Hail Mary, full of grace . . .*

"Dad," I said. "Can I ask you what happened to Sass Ring?"

He looked away. That was all I needed. Just in the way he turned from me. I didn't need him to speak. I didn't want him to speak anymore. "I made a mistake," he said, still not looking at me. "I was drunk. Out of my mind and I thought she was you."

He took a sip of water. It dribbled down his lip. Whatever I had expected him to say, it wasn't that. I sank back into my chair, the little card of Mary pressed to my chest for comfort.

"You thought she was me?" I repeated. The room filled with quiet like a flooding basement. Only the mechanical noises from his machines pulsed or kept the time.

He set his cup down shakily one last time. "I always wondered," he said at last, "how much you remembered. *If* you remembered anything. You were there, but I always thought you were sleeping in the car."

I shook my head fiercely, pressing my hand to my mouth. I had already started to cry.

"Your mother took off," he said. "Took you, too, down to St. Paul with that cousin of hers. And she comes home and tells me she had herself sterilized like some animal. So I decided," he shrugged, "that if she didn't want my kids no more, I'd show her.

"I was coming out of the bar," he continued, "and I was drunk and I thought that girl was you. Saw her down by the lake—you were always down there messing around. It only took a moment. I just held her under. She was such a little thing."

I was crying in earnest now, my hand pressed so hard against my face that I felt my mouth bruise.

He didn't say anything. He didn't offer any comfort. I didn't want him to. Pitch didn't like tears. I'd learned that young. It always made it worse.

Finally, Pitch pressed his call button for the nurse. "Can you help my daughter?" he asked the nurse, still not looking at me.

The nurse took stock of me and nodded. She helped me from the room when I couldn't stand on my own and put me in an empty waiting area down the hall. I cried so hard that at last I did vomit. She pressed an emesis basin to my mouth and pulled my hair back from my face while I heaved sickly green and yellow bile that burned my throat.

"We have a grief counselor I can call," she offered.

I shook my head, hugging myself.

"It might help," she pressed gently. "This is hard to deal with, I know. But if you help yourself, you can help your father better."

I laughed, a hard painful sound, like one of Pitch's hunting arrows being pulled out of me. It surprised us both.

"I'm sorry," I told her, relenting. "Pitch and I have a complicated relationship."

"Lots of people do with their parents," she said. "That's why it sometimes helps to talk to the counselor, too."

I shook my head. "Can you get my purse from his room?" I asked. "I don't want to go back tonight. I might fall apart again if I do."

She considered me for a while, then relented. By the time she returned, I'd dried my eyes on my sleeve. I stood and gave her the rumpled prayer card I still held in my hand. It was creased and damp now. "Will you give this back to him?" I asked her. "He might need it."

"Are you sure you don't want to go say goodbye?" she asked. I could tell she didn't expect him to live until morning.

I shook my head, pulling my purse on to my shoulder. "Don't worry," I said because she'd been kind, "we already did."

I got lost in the old part of the hospital again. I felt too unsteady to stop and ask anyone for directions. When I finally found the lobby, with its tall glass windows, in the newer part of the hospital, I drew up short. Near the door was Windy, sleeping in a waiting room chair, her extra clothes and shoes in a bag at her feet. Behind her the tall windows seemed flat, one-dimensional like a solid wall of black. She seemed small. She was breathing softly and evenly.

I stood over her for a while, trying to collect myself. I couldn't imagine why she was waiting here, but I didn't want to wake her. There was a woman behind a tall reception desk, carefully studying her computer screen. She looked maybe fifty, her hair neatly cut and styled. At midnight, her pale rose suit jacket still looked fresh and she wore some type of brooch.

I looked back at Windy. She looked like a fat, squashy baby. Her stomach was a soft lump. Her shirt wasn't buttoned all the way, revealing the soft white skin of her belly. It rose and fell with her breathing. I thought about her age for a moment and realized with surprise that she must be nearing sixty-five.

When I turned back to the receptionist, she was watching me, her face neutral, her hand poised above the phone. I realized I must look a little wild.

"This is my mother," I explained. "Can you tell me what's going on?

Has she been discharged? I didn't get a call."

She nodded and picked up the phone, speaking into it with low tones that I couldn't quite hear. A doctor I didn't recognize emerged a little while later.

Yes, he explained. They'd left several messages; my mother had indeed been discharged. There wasn't a bed in a rehabilitation center open for at least another week. She'd have to make do on her own until then because there wasn't a medical reason to keep her.

I checked my phone. There weren't any messages. They must have called the motel or the house.

An overhead page came for the doctor and he left. I watched my mother sleep, unsure what to do. No one materialized to help me, so I finally found a wheelchair near the door and put Windy's things in the little basket. I woke her gently, and was surprised that she let me place her into the chair. She tucked her feet up and watched me mutely, and I pushed her out with me into the black curtain of night that waited beyond the gleaming glass windows.

{18}

I woke to the noise of shuffling in my room. Windy was there, quietly going through my dresser, looking under things. I kept my eyes closed, listening to her move here and there. She had noticed that her pills were missing. I let her look and drifted back to sleep. When I woke for good, hours later, she was gone, and so was her car. Since the house was empty, I left, too.

I didn't like going to the liquor store in town. It was down from the old Red Owl and on the same block as the Methodist church. But I couldn't face Ardell anymore. Not after what Pitch had told me. I parked my car outside the store; it was a brick building, the city municipal. For a while, I read the neon signs and posters and didn't decide. I watched some people go in and then come back out. I felt tired and thought about my bed back home.

I took out my phone and called my daughter.

"Hi, Momma!" she chirped. "We just got up!"

I leaned back in the seat, letting her voice fall over me like the tide.

"Momma?" she asked.

"I'm here, honey," I said. "I'm just happy to hear your voice. What are you doing today?" I was already crying, so it was safer to ask a question and let her talk.

They were going to the beach and diving today. They were going to see dolphins at the dolphin center. She asked me a question. Only the pause made me register it.

"I'm sorry, honey," I said. "The line is bad, can you say that again?"

"Did you get my sunglasses yet? The ones from camp, like I asked?"

I had forgotten. "I called and had them set them aside," I said. "Why are they so important?"

I could feel her shrug, "Dunno. You bought them for me and I like them. They have blue stems, so they look different from everyone else's. It's easy to tell mine apart."

"Okay," I promised, "I'll go get them today."

I could hear Louisa's voice in the background calling. "I have to go now," she said.

"Okay, I love you. See you soon."

"Love you, too."

I hung up the phone, and sank back in my seat once more. The phone rang. She was calling again. She must have forgotten something.

"Hello?"

Instead of Reine's voice on the line, it was Denny's. "I wanted to make sure you'd answer," he said, his voice hard. "I'm sick of leaving fucking messages."

"What do you want?"

"I want you to stop," he said. "Stop calling me when you're drunk. Stop leaving me profanity-laced messages that my wife is afraid to hear."

"I'm your wife," I said and hated myself.

"No," he bit out. "No, you're not. We're done with that. And if you don't get your shit together, I'll have you back at court. I'll ask them for Reine."

"Fuck you."

"Fuck you, too." He hung up.

I sat there, stung, staring at the signs and the lights, but not really reading them. The clerk peeked nervously out the window. I'd been there too long and was attracting attention. I went into the liquor store.

It was still the same place I remembered from years ago, same bottles and crowded shelves. Just no Pitch. The thought made me pick up my pace. I chose two bottles of gin with girls in red dancing skirts on the bottle. I put them on the counter with my card and went back to a sunglasses display they had near the door. They also sold cigarettes, and candy flavored like rum. I whirled the display until I found a pair of sunglasses with blue stems.

I brought these with me to the counter. The clerk shook his head. "Your card was just declined," he said. "Do you have another one or cash?" My eyes flicked to the bottles. "Can you try it again?" I asked. "Maybe try to run just one bottle through."

He was a young man with a nest of untidy, long hair. I could tell he didn't believe me. I felt myself redden. Still, I stood there and watched him run everything through again, my heart sinking.

The card was declined again.

"What about the sunglasses?" I asked.

He shook his head, looking bored.

The motel clerk had told me my card was bad, but I'd forgotten. I looked through my purse, but I knew there was nothing there.

My head started to hurt—just behind my left eye. A nest of undulating snakes, the beginning of a migraine. "I'm sorry," I said. "I'll have to come back later."

Ardell's front door was busted in when I arrived. It looked like there had been a fight. Someone had kicked in the side of the already-broken jukebox and there was glass everywhere. Ardell was on his knees picking up pieces of it when I walked through the door. A few tables were turned over. A chair was on the bar.

The police radio chattered. There were loose cattle on Olinda Trail. A suspicious person outside the Methodist church.

We stared at each other a little. Some part of me felt like he must know, must know about Pitch. I waited for him to yell, steeling myself.

He seemed to shrug, coming to the decision he needed to make. "Are you going to help me or what?" he asked.

I nodded, walking into the bar and setting my purse on a table.

"Do you have a broom?" I asked.

We worked in silence, and it took us a while to get everything back together. Eventually I got tired of cleaning up someone else's mess and sat down at the bar. I started drinking. Spilled sugar and gin were starting to cover the bar's countertop and most of the fuzz in my brain when Ardell sat a little beaded hair tie on the bar next to me. Its orange plastic bead smiled at me, like an eye.

"Don't know where the hell that come from," he said. "Must've fallen out of someone's purse. I don't allow kids in the bar."

"Why not?" I asked. "Your old man did."

"I used to, too," he said. "You remember Drew Engel? He used to play ball at the high school. One day he left here and I heard this screaming from the parking lot. I go out there and he's trying to rape his little girl, right there in my parking lot on a Sunday afternoon. He had her pinned against his truck, the other little ones standing there. I beat the shit out of him and called the cops."

He shook his head. "You know how I told you I sobered up a few years ago. Well, when I walk into those meetings, you can guess who wanted to be my sponsor. I said fuck that. I may be a drunk, but at least I'm not that."

I picked up the little bit of stretchy elastic and pulled on it absently. It reminded me of Reine.

Ardell was thinking something similar. "Reminds me of you. Pigtails and everything. God, you were a pain in the ass when you were little." He smiled when he said it.

I shrugged and set the hair tie down to refill my glass. "It gets a little boring sitting around a bar all day, waiting for your dad to finish drinking himself shitface."

"Your dad had a hell of a leg on him, too," Ardell acknowledged. "He and my old man could sure put it down."

"I don't want to talk about them," I said. My tone was a little sharper than I thought it should be, and I frowned. Ardell frowned, too. I drank some more.

Finally Ardell said, "I wasn't talking about them. I was talking about you. You were a pain in the ass." He sat next to me and rubbed my back. "Remember that floating dock we had down by the lake? I sank that motherfucker six years ago and all I could think of was how many goddamn times I had to wade out in the hip-deep water to pull you off that thing. Never made any sense to me how you could swim out there and then be too terrified to swim back."

"Maybe I just wanted you to carry me," I suggested, stirring sugar into another glass. My hands felt heavy and I spilled more than I should have.

Ardell paused as if he were almost surprised by the admission. The look on his face made me blush. I pretended it was because of the sugar. I brushed it off the counter. My words were coming out a little too fast for my thoughts.

Ardell watched me and I felt more self-conscious. I put my drink down. It struck the counter a little too hard.

He touched my arm for a moment, then thought better of it.

"Some folks around the bar last night said they saw you out with JJ in his plainclothes," he said. "Last night, having dinner, they said."

"JJ?" I asked, genuinely confused.

Ardell shrugged. "Joe James. He's my cousin. JJ or fucking JJ is usually what I call him when he's busting up the bar."

I poured the rest of my drink down my throat and shook my head. Ardell didn't try to touch me this time when I turned away. "Jesus, this is a small town. We went for burgers at a fast food joint on the highway and that's news?"

"JJ isn't my only cousin in this town. Word gets around."

"Why do you even care?" I demanded.

"I don't," he said quickly. "Don't get mad. I'm not like that. I'm not a jealous man, never have been. You can see who you want. It's just . . ." he hesitated. "It's just I thought maybe I could take you out to dinner sometime, too."

Ardell was a part of me that I only found in the dark. But he wasn't the wild boy I remembered anymore. I rested my head on the bar, feeling the grit of sugar on my cheek and needing the cool of the wood. He was a sober man now—almost at the end of forty, and wondering what the hell was left of the rest of his life. I closed my eyes. I missed that boy in my memory and his wild kisses, covering my skin like a blackout. I almost felt myself sob, a ragged flutter in my chest, but I pressed my lips closed and was lost for a moment in my own drunken dizziness. It was like I was standing on that old floating dock, waiting for his eighteen-year-old self to come get me.

"You okay, Jane?" he asked, touching my cheek. His skin felt warm on mine. I didn't want him to stop touching me. But then there was Sass. And Pitch in his hospital room. And too many things between us. I opened my eyes.

"Ardell," I said, "you know there isn't anything about us that can last past my next drunk."

He took his hand away.

"Why not?" he asked, and I knew he was hurt.

"Because my daughter is coming home next week," I answered.

"Hell, that doesn't bother me," he said. "If you want, we can all go out to dinner together. We can find something fun to do for your kid."

That wasn't what I had meant. I shook my head. "But then what?"

He frowned. "What do you mean, 'then what'?"

"After dinner, then what?" I asked. "Then we bring her back here and she can hide under the tables while we fuck and grow up in a bar just like you and me. That didn't turn out so well for us, you know."

"It doesn't have to be that way," he said quickly.

"How else would it be?" I asked. "You going to fix that old jukebox up to play lullabies? Did that work for Sass?"

Ardell flinched as if I struck him. I shouldn't have said her name. It was too painful for both of us. It made me feel more miserable, more ashamed. I couldn't stay anymore. I stood, unsteadily at first, bumping against the bar for support.

"I'm sorry, Ardell," I said as I turned to leave, and I meant it.

"Do you need a ride home?" he asked, not looking at me.

"No, I can make it," I said, fixing my purse on my shoulder.

"Fine," he said when I reached the broken screen door. He reached up and turned his police radio back on. "Just make sure you take the back roads home. If Joe James catches you, that will be the end of your dinners down by the lake. JJ doesn't fuck around much on the straight and narrow."

It had started to rain, and Windy was sitting at the kitchen table when I got home. She made a face when she saw me. "You smell like a sewer every time you come home from that bar. Just like your father."

When she spoke, she sounded like her hands, shaking on her coffee cup. She had opened all of the cupboards and emptied everything onto the floor. She wasn't trying to hide it anymore. I stepped over the mess and opened the refrigerator. The last time I had eaten was with Joe. The refrigerator was empty.

"Do you want me to go get some food?" I asked. "Do you have any money?"

She shook her head. "You'll just go back to Ardell. Why should I let you do that?"

"I'm not going back to Ardell," I said, "but I'll go get you something to eat if you think it will help. They said they'd get you a treatment bed next week."

She set her coffee cup down, more forcefully than she intended and it shattered.

She and I stared at the mess for a while, not really sure what to do.

"My back hurts," she suddenly quavered. "I don't know what to do. Every time I lie down, it's like someone is digging a stick into my back. I need my pills."

I held my hands up, "I don't have them, Mom. The cops took them."

"When?"

"When they took you." I started to put the dishes and cups back into the cupboards. "Do you want me to make you some more coffee?"

"They say Lee Ring used to pass Ardell's mom around the bar like the beer." She laughed harshly. "She was like—what do you call it—a cowbird, a brood parasite. She came to the bar pregnant with Sass and left her behind. That's why old Lee never liked Sass. Rumor is the dentist in Chisago City raised Lee's twin boys, 'cause she didn't stay there long either."

When I didn't respond, she asked, "Why do you go there? Don't you know what they say about Ardell?"

"Yes," I said grimly, stacking one plate on another. "Yes, I certainly do."

Windy wandered off down by the lake despite the gentle rain that started. I went to get groceries with money I found in her purse. I made it as far as the gas station on the state highway. It overlooked both Big Comfort Lake and the police station down below. I didn't see Joe's car in the lot. At the gas station, I bought a loaf of bread, eggs, and a case of beer, which I hid in the trunk of my car. I bought Windy some cereal and milk and a few bananas from beside the counter. I went back for ice for the beer, and then I drove to the lake. The beer tasted like frog piss, but it helped. I played the radio for a while, then got sick of it.

Windy wasn't any better when I got home. She'd taken all the dishes out of the cupboard again, as if she'd forgotten she'd already searched there. Everything was everywhere. I paused at the door and Windy looked up at me. She was shaking and her puffy face was red.

She had a little kitchen knife in her hand, which she pointed at me. "If you don't give me my pills," she sobbed, "I swear I'll cut my own goddamn head off."

I set the groceries down and tried to grab the knife out of her hand. "Calm down," I said.

She jerked back out of my reach, her face panicked, then struck down. The knife struck me on my collarbone, sliced through the skin and stuck into the bone with a strange, wet noise. Almost like a kiss.

I stared at her. Though I didn't, Windy screamed and her legs gave way beneath her. She fell on her bottom, still screaming, and covered her face.

I looked down. The knife wobbled in me when I moved. "Sonofabitch," I murmured. I staggered a little and sat down at the kitchen table. Windy scrambled to her feet and ran, disappearing down the hallway. I heard her door slam, then lock.

I looked down again. I was bleeding now. Looking down seemed to be a mistake. I realized I still had my purse on my shoulder. The groceries still sat on the floor. The whole thing would have seemed ridiculous if it wasn't starting to hurt.

With my good arm, I reached into my purse and found my phone. My vision started to swim a little when I dialed 911. I could hear Windy howling, sobbing in her room. Despite my dizziness, I went to wait for the ambulance on my mother's front porch.

The fire department arrived before the cops and the ambulance, but Ardell got there first in his truck.

"Jesus Christ," he swore. "Did you do this?"

I shook my head. I was sitting now on a rocking chair on the porch. That felt easier.

He stared at me, his eyes sliding grimly to the door behind me.

"She didn't mean to do it," I said quickly.

Ardell shook his head. "Joe won't take that," he said flatly. "You know that."

Talking was starting to grow difficult. My arm hurt, and I pressed my lips tight against the pain. The fire department crew surged up the driveway. "Maybe he's not on duty today. Can you go in and take care of Windy?" I asked him. "I don't want her to hurt herself."

"Jane . . ." he started.

"Please Ardell, I'm asking you . . ." I struggled on the right word, "as a friend. Go make sure she doesn't do anything I'll regret. She's not armed." I glanced down at the knife and almost laughed. "Not anymore, at least."

Ardell didn't find it humorous, but he went inside. I closed my eyes and waited, feeling the uproar of sound around me like I was sinking into deep water. When I opened my eyes, Joe was there, standing over me. The county sheriff had Windy in his car. I couldn't see Ardell. Joe's face was as pale as I'd ever seen a man.

"Hey, Joe." I tried to smile. "I'm okay. Nothing serious. Sorry to bother you."

He seemed unable to speak. He stared at the knife in my shoulder and worked on several words for a while, then he managed, "Who did this to you, Jane?"

I didn't answer.

He pointed at the car, where Windy sobbed. "What the hell is she doing home? She was supposed to go to treatment."

I shook my head, which was a mistake. It made my shoulder sting and the world start to fade. Joe grabbed me and held me up in the chair.

I winced. His touch wasn't exactly gentle. "The hospital sent her home last night. They couldn't find a bed . . . you know the routine."

He shook me a little. "They sent her home strung out like this. And you took her?" He was angry.

I might have been angry back, but I was too distracted by pain. "She didn't seem so bad last night."

"Are you going to press charges?" Joe demanded.

"Against the hospital?" I suggested, being stupid on purpose. "The insurance companies do this all the time."

"You know what I mean!" he barked and shook me again, and hard, jostling my shoulder until I cried out. Startled, he released me.

My blood was on his hand.

"I'm sorry," I said, and we both knew it wasn't about the blood. I could read his face as clearly as the rainy sky just then. I knew that Pitch and that little girl would haunt Joe forever.

"Please don't press charges," I said. "She didn't mean to do this. She's sixty-five years old, Joe. What's going to change now? What he used to do to her when I was a kid . . ." I broke off. "That's why she started on the pills."

I met Joe's eye and I thought he'd regained some of his composure. "What do you want me to do?" he ground out.

"Take her back to the hospital. Find a way to keep her there until there's a treatment bed open for her next week."

"You want to ride in the same car and hold her hand while I take you to get stitched up?" he asked bitingly. "Because in case you haven't noticed, you've got a goddamn kitchen knife still stuck in your shoulder and you want me to just take her to the hospital, like I don't goddamn see that?"

He was getting beyond reason.

"Joe . . ." I began.

"Don't . . ." he took a deep breath and turned away. "Jesus Christ, Jane," he said. "That little girl died while I was holding her in my arms right on the damn road. Five years old. There isn't a day that goes by—a morning that I don't wake up thinking about her. I made sure he was put away for good after that. But here I am, still driving out here, wondering whose body I'm going to have to clean up next."

I wanted to answer him, but something more urgent was happening with my shoulder. I couldn't push the pain away anymore. And just then, I couldn't talk. I felt myself slipping into a stupor, something like shock. Ardell's familiar voice suddenly rumbled calmly, "Mind if we cut in, JJ? The ambulance guys would like to take a look at Jane. Maybe you can investigate later."

Joe glared at Ardell. Ardell didn't flinch away from his hot stare. He crossed his arms, the two ambulance crew guys on either side. I recognized one—Jerry—from high school. The other small, dark man I didn't know.

Joe looked from Ardell to me and then back again. His face was red with anger. He looked like he might speak, and then thought better of it. "I'll have the sheriff take your ma to the hospital," he said, and left the porch.

I slid slowly off the rocking chair to the ground. Ardell and the ambulance crew leapt forward, interrupting my fall. Just two weeks ago, I sat with Reine on this same chair, talking about the start of summer camp. She was perched on my knee, so excited that her whole body tensed with anticipation when we talked—like a cord pulled tight between two hands.

My head rolled back suddenly, heavy as a bowling ball. At the same time it felt like my body went weightless.

"I was wondering when that was going to happen," the EMT said calmly. "She looked pale enough to faint." I could still hear him, though everything else was getting foggy. He tugged on my arm, examining it. "Nasty cut there. I'll get the stretcher."

"Don't bother," Ardell rumbled from close by as I struggled to remain conscious. "She's my girl, I'll carry her."

As he lifted me up, my thoughts drifted completely, cut loose into memory. In my mind, I was six again—and the movement was like the old dock pitching beneath my feet. I stumbled and practically jumped into his arms, wrapping my arms around his neck in my panic. The lake water was up to his waist. I let my feet drag in the water, though I was shivering from cold. He shook his head, trying to get my hair out of his mouth.

"One more time," he growled, holding me tightly as we reached the shore. "One more time, Janey, and I swear I'll leave you out on that damn dock."

The cold was making me drowsy. I was soaked to the skin. I rested my head on his shoulder, not the least bit scared. After all, we both knew an empty promise when we heard one.

Technically I was conscious, but I didn't feel fully awake. I felt like I was swimming in hot, cloudy water. I wasn't disoriented. It was more like I knew where I was, I just wasn't fully there myself yet.

The doctor had pulled the curtain closed around me in the emergency room. He was finished. Then he was gone. My broken and now-cut arm was bandaged from wrist to shoulder. My pain had left with the doctor and his syringe. The discharge nurse had already handed me more pills, small green beads in an orange-brown bottle. She was speaking to me. I blinked at her.

"Go where?" I asked.

"Pardon?"

"Where do I go?"

The nurse herself seemed confused for a moment. "Home?" she suggested.

For a moment the word home conjured up my former living room in St. Paul—boxy and open. Light streamed in all the windows, filtering through the curtain, creating lacy shadows on the floor. Reine was sitting beside Denny on the blue couch I had just bought.

I was surprised at the tricks memory played. They seemed cruel. I turned away from the nurse. My hands trembled while I zipped the pills into my purse. My mouth tasted like vomit and my throat was so dry it ached.

The nurse offered me the rest of my possessions in a plastic bag. I peeked inside at my jacket, keys, and blood-spattered shoes. "There is someone here to drive you," she said.

I frowned, but followed her to the lobby in blue hospital booties. I wasn't ready to put my shoes back on.

Rowdy, Ardell's cousin, was waiting for me in the lobby, looking out of place. I didn't know who I expected—Joe or Ardell or someone else. Rowdy wouldn't have been my first choice, but I felt relieved that it wasn't either of my first two guesses.

Rowdy rocked a little nervously in his work boots as we sized each other up. He was a thin man in tight, dirty jeans and a baggy t-shirt. The shirt was frayed around the collar. He wore a red ball cap over his long, stringy blond hair.

"Ardell had to go open the bar," he explained. "So he called me to drive you home. Are you ready to go? Been waiting like an hour."

I nodded.

"Do you want me to carry those things?"

I didn't. I hugged the bag and bloody shoes as I followed him to his boxy van and climbed in. The van was filled with crap and smelled of hamburgers and fast food. I sighed as I sank into the seat, and watched him jog around the front to the driver's side. I realized that I was nauseated and pressed my face into the cool of the plastic bag. Rowdy said nothing. Maybe I wasn't the first woman he'd driven home like this.

A little while later, Rowdy waited while I sat and eyed the front door of my house. Rowdy wasn't exactly company, but still I didn't want to let him go. I couldn't think of the last time we'd said ten words—if ever. But I asked anyway, "Didn't Ardell need you at the bar?" It was getting dark, seven or eight already.

Rowdy shook his head. "He's got Maggie there tonight, too. I'll head out there when we're done. You want me to walk you in?"

I shook my head, but still didn't move from his van.

Rowdy looked around. "I remember this place. Used to drive your daddy home some nights. Is this where you found that girl's body?"

I nodded.

"Cops still haven't found out what happened to her, have they?

Everybody is talking about it down at the bar." He spat out his window. "Fucking JJ. Couldn't find his own fucking dick if he needed to."

I felt too nauseated to respond. I nodded tightly.

"Where'd you find her?"

I pointed down off the hill with my good arm and Rowdy stared.

I opened the van door; the cooler fresh air helped the sick feeling in my head and stomach. I decided the little green narcotics in my purse weren't settling well with my system. They were different from what I'd had before.

"Yep," Rowdy said, still looking down at the pines and not seeming to notice my distress. "I used to bring your dad back here all the time." He shook his head, "Your old man had a fucking temper on him. One time he fell asleep in my backseat." Rowdy gestured over his shoulder. "When I went to wake him—boom! Fucker kicked me right in the stomach. Knocked me flat on my ass." Rowdy grinned.

I felt pale. Rowdy misinterpreted my expression. "Sorry," he said quickly. "But your old man was just mean when he drank. That's the truth of it. Meanest damn drunk I ever saw."

I nodded.

"Wasn't always like that," Rowdy continued. "When he was sober, he was different. I remember once, after my ma died, he came into the bar and just sat next to me and cried, like we were old friends. He told me all these things about my ma from when they were kids. Stuff they did in school and shit." He shook his head. "I never would have known any of that. When I think back on being a kid, all I ever remember her telling me was to shut up, eat my dinner, and go outside." He laughed. "But your old man had some stories. Crap you never think about your folks."

As Rowdy talked, I watched the front door. It was getting dark and the sickness I felt inside made me dizzy. I rose, using the van for support. I winced—even through the drugs my arm hurt when I pulled on it. "Thanks, Rowdy," I said and slammed the door.

Rowdy started up the engine, but he leaned out the window. "Are you sure you don't want me to walk you in? Ardell said to make sure you got settled right."

I shook my head and kept walking. My hospital slippers made an odd shuffling noise on the dirt when I walked. The plastic bag with my shoes bumped against my knees with each step. I dug out my keys, then let the bag of bloody shoes fall to the ground by the porch. I left it there. I went in and called my daughter. I left a message, then I took another pain pill.

I woke feeling like my arm was on fire. I rolled to my side and was noisily and uncontrollably sick. The smell made me retch more and I stumbled from Reine's room, where I was sleeping in her little bed. I threw up again in the toilet and then curled up on the cool tile floor. I drifted into unconsciousness, but only for a moment. My eyes opened as if they were on an old hinge and I slowly rolled onto my back.

I let my head tilt to one side—I was still holding the bottle of pain pills clenched in my hand. The nausea rolled over me, making me feel like I was lying at the bottom of a rough sea—the pressure crushing me, while my stomach seemed to roll like the tide. The house was hot and I felt dangerously faint.

Windy's phone rang and I frowned. It rang again, with an urgency I couldn't match. My arm throbbed in unison with the sound. I stared at the ceiling and let it call out in vain while I fell back asleep on the bathroom floor.

The second time I woke, I was able to sit up slowly. Cradling my arm, I bumped from the bathroom to the hallway. I leaned against the wall. In the kitchen, I put my whole head in the sink and drank. Then I threw up. The new pain pills definitely weren't working with my stomach. I looked around at the kitchen. Everything from the cupboards was still on the counters, the drawers all ransacked. Windy had left one hell of a mess behind her.

I sat slowly down in my mother's kitchen chair. On the kitchen table, there was an overturned bottle of scotch. She must have unearthed one more bottle in her search. I righted it—there was maybe a finger of drink left. The bottle was Pitch's brand.

My eyes found the perennial box of junk she kept at the door. It was empty. She must have visited the shed. I drank the scotch and then rose, feeling more steady. I needed more. The pain in my arm, along with everything else, was just killing me.

The shed was usually locked, so I carried a hammer down with my good arm. The shed was an old chicken house, a long, low wood structure where Pitch would sometimes keep a fishing boat. In the bright sunlight I squinted at the metal deadbolt. It looked solid, but when I jiggled it, it fell open. Windy hadn't bothered to really lock it. I set the hammer down and slid the door aside.

From the bright to the dark, it took my eyes a little while to adjust. Boxes and loose junk were heaped nearest me and the door. There was a basket of bowling trophies, some tools, and a few black plastic bags. The shed smelled of mildew. As my eyes adjusted, the back of the shed came slowly into focus.

She'd moved Pitch's whole basement room out here—chair and all. The chair faced the TV along the back wall—a huge cabinet affair from the '60s that only ever ran in black and white. What caught the eye, though, were the antlers she had piled from floor to ceiling all around the television. In the half dark of the shed, they gleamed like bleached bones. I stared at the odd, macabre splendor and walked slowly forward. Hanging from the tips of the antlers here and there were old Christmas ornaments. I shook my head as my eyes drifted upwards and I noticed the ceiling.

Dangling there were hundreds of bottles—mostly Pitch's beer bottles, but also bottles of brandy and scotch. They hung from wires, with a little wire noose wrapped around each glass neck. Pitch's favorite brand had featured a silver buck's head on the label. Hundreds of beady black eyes floated above me, keeping watch. Like chimes they played a soft music, still swaying from when I had jostled the shed open.

I shivered. Sometimes, I thought, you had to admire the full power of Windy's craziness.

I climbed on Pitch's chair and tugged gently at a bottle of still-full scotch, sniffed it, and then went back up to the house. Pitch didn't drink gin. I was always grateful for the fact that gin didn't smell like him. Not the way beer and scotch did. But this would have to do.

I was still on the porch later that day, slowly melting into the warm afternoon when Ardell arrived. Ardell's face was black and blue. The damage around his right eye was pretty heavy. The tissue was swollen and the white of his eye was red and bloody.

"What happened?" I asked him.

He grimaced. "There was a fight at the bar last night. I had to break it up." He looked a little sheepish. "I'm getting slow and old, I guess. I don't think anyone's landed a punch on me since I was seventeen." He shook his head. "And I ain't seventeen anymore."

Ardell seemed to creak a little as he eased down on the porch beside me. I had a feeling that more punches had landed than what showed on his face. "Dad and me always prided ourselves on never having to hire a bouncer to stand at the door."

"Did you drop him at least?" I asked.

"Of course I did. It just took me longer than it used to. I got a lot on my mind lately." He picked up the bottle I was drinking and read the label. He frowned a little. "Did you get that from the bar?"

I shook my head. "This is what's left of Pitch's old stash. Windy has it all down in the boat shed."

"Must be," he said. "I don't carry shit like that. Not since Dad died. Only fucking bums come around if you sell shit like that." He looked me over. "How much of that have you drank? It will hit you harder than the gin you usually take."

I shrugged. "Want some?"

"You know I don't drink."

"Not anymore."

"Not anymore," he amended. "I used to tie it on pretty regular."

"Why did you quit?" I asked.

He looked out at the lake. "About a year after the old man died, I had a dream about my sister."

"That was it?"

"That was it," he repeated.

I took my bottle back from him and took a long drink. "Must have been one hell of a dream."

"I dreamt I was sitting across the table from my old man in that filthy old kitchen at the lodge," he explained. "And there was a bottle of my favorite whiskey in between us and I was shooting shots of it. But for some reason, he wasn't drinking. He was just sitting there watching me drink. And he kept laughing like he knew something I didn't, every time I poured a shot in.

"So the more I drink, the more he laughs and the angrier I get. And I can't see what this crazy old fuck thinks is so damn funny. So I keep drinking. But then while he's laughing, he starts to play this game where he peeks under the table. Real obvious, like he wants me to look, too.

"But I won't. I just keep pouring it down. And it's hot and I'm miserable. It's like I can hardly breathe, but I keep drinking. And nothing works. I can't get drunk.

"And he wears me down. And finally, I say 'fuck this' and look under the table and there's my sister, Sass, lying there dead with her throat cut.

"And the old man is laughing at us both. I want to kill him, but I'm too weak, too drunk to get up out of my chair. And suddenly I look down at myself and I realize I'm covered in blood and just soaking wet. And I get that the old man cut my throat, too. I've just been pouring the booze into my own lap while he laughs." Ardell looked nauseated. "Shot after shot and I never noticed."

"Was that like a recurring dream?" I asked.

"No," he answered, taking a slow breath. "Just the once was enough." He looked me over again. "Why don't we go inside and get you some coffee?"

I shook my head. "Don't feel like coffee."

"How about you?" he asked. "Ever been to recovery?"

I nodded, watching the lake. It was so peaceful out here, with Ardell and the wind moving through the reeds. "Twice before," I said. I held up my glass, like a toast. "I guess they say the third time's the charm."

"When was the last time you went?"

"Before Reine was born. When I got pregnant."

"And you started up when your husband left?"

I shook my head, "Before that."

We watched the lake some more.

"We were going to have another baby, you know," I said, surprised to find myself talking. Especially about the baby. "I wonder if Denny suspected that maybe I was drinking and thought it would help. It was easy for me to stop when I was pregnant with Reine."

"What about the first time you quit?'

"I was nineteen then, and stayed sober until a little after I married Denny." I held up the bottle, "I started young—drinking Pitch's stash. Just like this." I shrugged. "It was a good way to get to sleep and not wake up. Not hear them going at it. When I got away from home, I could quit. My last foster parent was a judge. I knew his daughter at school. He took me in and helped me find a program."

"Ever think of going back?" he asked. "To treatment?"

"No."

He nodded sadly, but sat there with me while I drank myself a little closer to unconsciousness.

"Tell me about Sass," I said after a while. "Not just the dream. Something real."

"Like what?" he asked.

"Well, you call her a saint; why is that? Don't saints have to perform three miracles?'

"She has. She sobered me up. That was the second miracle."

"What was the first?"

"I don't like to talk about that," he said, his face grim.

"Why not?"

"A little bit before I gave up drinking, I tried to kill myself. After Dad died. JJ found me hanging in the bar."

I blinked and took another drink. It helped.

"I always thought Sass must have been watching out for me," he said, looking away. "There wasn't no real reason for JJ to be out there that day."

I didn't mean to, but I touched his arm. He looked at my hand, surprised, and covered it with his own.

"Did you ever find out how she died?" I asked. "Do you know?"

He didn't look away. He didn't take his hand from mine. Instead, he met my eye. I didn't hide anything. I didn't even know where to hide the painful things anymore. A tear slid down my face and he brushed it away for me. He knew.

"Your old man wrote me about three months ago," he said at last. "He must have known he was terminal then. He told me what happened."

It was hard to breathe. It felt like the scotch I had drunk was an ember of fire in my chest. "Does anyone else know?" I asked.

"Joe. I showed him the letter."

That surprised me. "Why didn't you have him arrested or anything? Why no charges or trial?"

"He's dying, Jane," Ardell said gently. "What good would that have done? JJ and I talked about it, and we decided not to unearth everything right now. Would hurt more than it would help."

"Who would it hurt?" I asked, confused.

"You, Jane," he said, and my heart contracted. "I didn't want to hurt you."

I shook my head, "Ardell, I don't want that . . ."

"By the time the letter arrived," he said, "you had already started coming into the bar, and I just thought if it were in the paper and all that . . ." He shook his head. "You didn't look like someone who needed any more trouble."

The ember of pain in my chest grew hotter, harder. It was like someone was thrusting a poker into my heart. I was crying freely now. "How do you live with this?" I asked him. "Knowing these things."

He shrugged. "We don't have much of a choice, do we? You're gonna wake up tomorrow, even if you don't want to. Life," he said gently, "is more than the terrible things we do to each other."

"You know I haven't seen any proof of that," I said.

He put his arm around me and drew me close to him. I leaned my head on Ardell's shoulder. "Do you love me, Ardell?" I asked, taking another drink.

He took a ragged breath. "I do, Jane. God help me."

We sat until dark while he sadly watched me drink myself unconscious. Then he carried me to my bed.

I woke slowly, coming back to the surface from deep underwater currents of dreaming—from water that never saw the light, but moved in unseen streams in the depths of the ocean, layer upon layer of liquid black. It was late now. Almost midnight. His warmth infused the blankets, surprisingly hot where his hand rested on the bare skin of my shoulder. I listened to his breathing and woke up a little more. We were both still dressed. I still wore my robe and nightgown.

I rolled over and pressed my face into his side, into the white t-shirt that he was wearing. His shirt smelled like soap, and his skin beneath smoky and human. He woke when I stirred and pressed his body to mine. He kissed me and then pulled me on top of him and began to work my nightgown up my thighs, kissing me all the while. We wrestled off my robe around my injured arm, and he flipped me back onto the bed, pressing his weight into me. He moaned softly with the pressure.

I broke away from his mouth, "You should . . . you should put something on if you're going to do that," I said as he tried to kiss me.

He ignored me, pressing against me once more.

"Ardell," I squirmed, trying to push him away a little more while still kissing him.

"I hate those things," he said, unbuttoning the top of my nightgown. "You never made me wear one before." I let him kiss my bare skin for a while, falling back into the pillow—it was a little like falling back into sleep, into the current. And then he was inside me, holding me, and I couldn't float away anymore.

I opened my eyes and pushed on him firmly. He made a noise and rolled off me, back onto the bed on his back. He eyed me, slightly wary, slightly angry.

My head hurt. I stood and pulled my robe back on. I was hung-over and the thought of making love slid off me when I moved. Ardell watched me tie my robe shut, but I didn't meet his eye. I mumbled something and wandered out into the hall, then the kitchen. Behind me, I heard him swear softly, then climb out of bed, put his belt on, and tuck his shirt back in. He rejoined me fully dressed and looking grim.

I rummaged in the kitchen cupboard, pressing my hand to my temple where a migraine had opened up like a small ball of light. I felt nauseated. I couldn't find my bottle in the cupboard. I remembered the porch.

Outside it was dark, the moon was slight. In my bare feet, I inched across Windy's acorn-strewn porch, wincing when the hard little nuggets hit my feet. I stooped down to collect the bottle and my glass. That wasn't such a good idea. All the blood rushed to my head—suddenly dizzy, I needed to steady myself, holding onto the nearest rocking chair. I felt like my nose was going to start bleeding.

When I went back to the kitchen, Ardell was still there. He leaned against the kitchen sink, watching me carefully. I felt a wave of anger start to slosh around messily inside me. I set the glass down on the counter too forcefully; the noise made me wince. I started pouring.

"Why do I get the feeling that if I made a run to the store for condoms, you wouldn't let me back in anyways when I came back?" he asked.

I ignored him. The second glass went down better than the first.

"Jane," Ardell said softly. It almost startled me. I didn't want him to be there. I stared at my glass to make him disappear. It didn't work; he touched my elbow. "What's going on?" he asked. "I thought we made up."

I closed my eyes so I could pretend he wasn't there. My head hurt so bad that a soft sob escaped me. Ardell wrapped me in his arms, and I pressed my face into his chest. It was like the warmth in our bed. It was like my memory. Like I was watching him kiss that beautiful woman, with her fringe of black hair. He pressed his lips to hers. I hid in the car, a small child, the gutted deer hanging in the trees all around me. The image came to me so strongly then that I wanted to reach over with my closed eyes and check the lock on the car door. I wanted to be safe and away from him.

He kissed me; he kissed her in my memory. In my memory I was that other woman. He picked her up and carried us safely away. I was there, and I was also hiding, wanting to run after him in the dark. I had loved him since I was a child. I kissed him and that opened the floodgate. He kissed me tenderly again and again. He unbuttoned my robe and slid his arms around my body and held me up when my legs gave out. He picked me up and carried me back to our still-warm bed. In my memory I was the woman he was kissing. Not the girl in the car.

He put me on the bed and I pulled him down on top of me. I imagined how he had kissed her, how dark and cool the night had been. I saw him slowly kiss her again and again.

"Jane," Ardell murmured as his lips kissed my chest. "God, Janey, I love you."

When he said my name, my eyes flew open. It felt like I fell into my body with a solid smack and, no matter what, he couldn't catch me. I found myself staring at the ceiling, my whole body hurting. My arm suddenly ached with all the pain I felt yesterday. I stiffened. Ardell felt it, he faltered. For the second time, I pushed him away.

This time there wasn't any anger in his face. But he knew it. He already looked like I'd kicked him.

"What's wrong?" he asked, touching my cheek.

I shook my head, shook his hand off me.

I didn't want to tell him to leave. I looked at my hands. I was starting to feel the effects of the alcohol. But for the first time, it couldn't wash this away. It was too painful.

He tried to smile. "Why not?" he said, "I promise you'll like it. Trust me. You always did before."

I looked away, feeling a burn of embarrassment. "Don't talk about it like that. I don't . . . I don't like what it says about me . . . that I can't remember things."

"That's not what you mean to me," he said gently, reaching for my hand.

I shook my head, pulling away from him.

He made a noise of frustration and rose from the bed. He paced the room angrily.

I felt myself shrink and I hugged myself.

He paused and stared at me cringing on the bed. When he spoke, he couldn't hide his anger. "Are you really telling me that you can't make love to me sober? You really think I'm that bad? You gotta wash me down like that?"

My throat constricted painfully. I felt a sob rising and I pressed my hand to my mouth.

It seemed like Ardell might speak again. He loomed over me, staring at me for several moments. I felt dissected, like something small and filthy. He shook his head, swore and tried to speak again. His frustration and anger were getting the better of him. It filled the room. I wanted to shrink even further into my hands.

"Fuck this," he said at last and walked out of the room. I heard the front door slam. I strained to hear it open again. But he didn't come back. I started to cry in earnest now, and this time he wasn't there to comfort me.

Half an hour later, the Rush City prison warden called me to offer his condolences. I had never talked to him before, just the nurse. He wasn't nearly so kind, just direct. Pitch had died at the hospital. Prison policy required me to come collect his things within forty-eight hours. The county coroner already had the body. The undertaker of my choice could collect him after the pathologist's exam, which was standard with a prison death. If I didn't claim him, the prison would see to a burial.

After the warden hung up, I stared at the phone for a long while. The house was silent around me. It smothered me with its stuffy heat. I laid my head on the kitchen table; it felt cool to my feverish skin. It was almost 1 a.m., and I couldn't call my daughter this late, but I longed for her. Not to grieve. Not to have her comfort me—she was too young for that. But I missed her with an intense, painful longing that seemed ready to claw itself out of my chest. I sobbed. And suddenly it was all too much. The house was too hot and I was suffocating.

The deer antlers gleamed like teeth in the dark. Stark and white, they seemed to have their own foreboding presence at the back of the old shed. I paused, uncertain, and contemplated the swaying bottles playing their soft music in the wind. They danced in and out of my flashlight's beam. The myriad of antlers on the labels caught the light, then spun into darkness; a little bit of a strobe effect. It felt like a thousand black eyes watched me, not quite real, but there nonetheless.

A car pulled into the driveway. I squinted up into the light of the house and recognized the boxy shape of Joe's squad car. He got out, his eyes finding my light, and walked down the hill.

His presence broke the spell I felt, the inertia, and I hunted around in the black shed for something to knock down a bottle. In the dark I was having trouble telling which ones were full or empty.

"Maybe we should talk," Joe said from the shed door behind me.

"You realize it's 1 a.m.?" I asked.

"I'm working the night shift." He shrugged. "Besides, you're up."

I poked at a bottle, trying to unhook it with a rake. "That I am," I agreed. "Why is that?"

"Because my arm hurts. Because I can't leave well enough alone."

Slowly he looked around, first at the shadowy forms behind me, then at the bottles hanging like so much strange fruit from the ceiling.

He shook his head. "What is this place?"

"Windy put it together from Pitch's old things." I poked my chin at the wall. "All the deer he poached, his stuff from his room. Dunno." I shrugged. "Maybe she meant it to be like art or something."

"Feels more like a crime scene," he observed bleakly.

"I don't think Windy wanted it in the house anymore," I explained. "Anything to do with him had to go. Hard to blame her." I was still looking for a full bottle. Something with a different shape from his beer bottles. "Feels to me like something from my memory though, you know? Like from when I was too young to really remember. Or like a dream." I took in the strangeness of the place again, almost as if with Joe's eyes. "Don't know how Windy does it. But she gets inside my head like this."

"Why are you inside your head at 1 a.m.?" he asked, coming close. He shone his flashlight into the shed, taking in all the corners. "Maybe you should get some sleep. You look a little ragged to me. Time to call it a night."

I was getting frustrated with trying to fetch down another bottle. And I could see Joe wasn't in the mood to help, even if he was taller than me. I looked around for the little chair I'd used earlier. I tried to stand on it, but with one injured arm, my balance was off. I staggered a little and fell.

Joe caught my arm, steadying me. He was so warm to the touch. "Are you even listening?" he asked. He was angry, or rather, I understood then, he was still angry and running out of his ability to hide it. His voice betrayed it. "Your whole arm is wrapped in a sling. Your shoulder is stitched up. You probably haven't eaten since I fed you and it's time to goddamn go to bed." His voice rose sharply with each statement.

I didn't push away from him. "Can I tell you something about Tessa?" I asked.

He blinked. I was struck again by how much he reminded me of Denny. Handsome and sincere. I'd never felt comfortable in my marriage. Not once in ten years. I'd never taken the thing head on. It was easier to drink the hard conversations away.

"Someone who waits five years for you isn't just biding time," I told him. "You're a fucking fool if you don't see that she loves you."

"Why are we talking about this?" he asked, and his face might have gotten red. It was too dark to see.

"You're just going through a rough patch—and I know something about rough patches," I said. "Don't burn your bridges."

"What about you?" he asked. "You've got enough proof in you to burn every bridge in this county, and you're out here looking for more at 1 a.m."

"Me?" I looked up once more at the bottles swinging above me. They turned slowly in the gentle night wind. "You know all those little things that only you know about yourself. All the things you've seen and done. They seem like they don't amount to much, but all those little things are who you are. If you could see that about me, you'd see this." I gestured at the shed, the bottles and the antlers. "Like a crime scene."

"You are better than that," he said. "You're like me. You're just going through a rough patch, too."

I shook my head. "I used to think that. I used to think if one more goddamn thing happened, I'd explode. Denny. Pitch. My job. All the pressure from it. I couldn't handle it anymore. But I'm not going to explode. The more I drink, the more it feels like I'm just going to fall apart little by little where I stand."

I was tired of this game with the bottles. Of everything feeling out of reach. Even Joe. I staggered back a little, losing my balance. I almost fell, but Joe caught me one more time, steadying me. This time, I pulled away, turned, and started walking back up the hill, back toward the house.

"Where are you going?" Joe asked.

"I changed my mind about Pitch's old piss-water," I called, looking back. "I'll go get my own."

He shook his head angrily. "It's goddamn 1 a.m., Jane, where are you going to go?"

"Don't worry," I said, reaching my car. "I know a place that's still open."

He followed me, of course. I could see his headlights behind me. When I hit the gravel of Old Comfort Road, he turned his squad lights on. I swore and drove a little ways farther. He didn't stop, just pulled closer to my bumper so that the lights played like a strobe in my rearview mirror. I was almost to the bar, so I pulled over to the side. It wasn't a good idea to arrive at Ardell's with the police in tow.

I fumed in my car. Joe fumed in his. Finally, I got out and walked back to the squad car. He moved to get out, but I stood in front of his door and kneed it closed again.

"Turn your lights off," I said angrily. "Everyone will see."

"I know where you're going," he said.

"I wasn't making a secret of it."

He gripped his steering wheel angrily. "Go back home," he ordered. "I don't need to be back here at 5 a.m. cleaning up another mess for Ardell."

"I'm an adult. You can't tell me what to do."

"Go. Home," he repeated.

"Don't you have better things to do than follow me around? Have you found that girl's family yet?"

I'd gone too far. His expression went flat. His cop face emerged.

"I've cut you all the slack I can manage, Jane. You're not supposed to be driving with your arm in a sling. You're on medication and shouldn't be drinking. If I find you driving these back country roads drunk, I'll arrest you," he said with quiet anger. "Just like your old man."

"I used to *pray* the cops would arrest my old man." I shook my head angrily. "You think what he did to Windy was bad? I could tell you things about what he used to do to me. Even when Windy called the cops, they wouldn't arrest him."

"That was back then," he said. "We don't operate that way anymore."

"Forgive me if that seems like too little too late. Pitch is dead, and that's the only thing that ever stopped him."

Joe blinked, surprised. "When?"

"They called about an hour ago. " To my surprise, my voice actually broke when I said it.

Joe turned off his lights, his face grim. "What do you want me to do, Jane?" he asked, and he seemed less angry. "You know I can't leave you out here like this."

Suddenly I felt too tired to fight with Joe anymore. And too tired to drink anyways. "I'll go home," I said. "Just don't follow me. I hate that." I turned and walked back to my car and opened the driver's door. I glanced back at Joe. He was tense, watching me. I think he was afraid I might run or do something stupid, but his face was more worn now than angry.

I turned back to the car and I paused, startled, frozen. There in the front seat, as real as if she were my own daughter, was a young girl wearing a pale blue dress and flip flops. In her arms she cradled the chipped statue of Saint Agnes with its little banner enumerating miracles, the worn lamb. She met my eye, watching me, and I recognized her, even in the dark. Not the drowned girl. Alive as she'd been in my dreams, in my memory. There was no mistaking her now.

"Sass," I breathed.

For a second, everything slowed down around us. A bright light on the road suddenly flooded where we stood—a car coming too fast on the narrow road from the bar.

"He's coming," she said urgently, and her whisper cut across the darkness. She beckoned me into the car and I obeyed.

The light filled the car. Filled and illuminated us. In the background, I heard Joe yell. I didn't pay attention. The light was so bright now, so close now that it shattered, exploded all around me.

From the dark, it seemed from a great distance, I heard Joe scream. It was the noise of someone dying.

There was no confusion about where I was. I wasn't entirely sure, though, whether I was conscious or not. The hospital room was filled with hushed noises that seemed louder than they should have been. A heavy vinyl curtain separated me from the old man next door and his whispering family. The whispers themselves crowded around my bed, moving like cottonwood fuzz on the wind, gathering in the nooks and crannies. Curtains were softly wheeled back on their tracks. Nurses padded by on thick-soled shoes.

So I knew where I was, but the ceiling confused me. The ceiling rippled oddly. Like the surface of a deep green lake, it moved on the wind above me. When I peered into the water, I could see the face of the old man in the next bed looking down at me, submerged, floating away, sinking deeper into the depths.

I couldn't move. The weight of all that water held me down. The old man's face was calm, though. Had I been awake, I might have panicked—but the lake was soothing and I couldn't look away. I couldn't feel anything. It seemed that beyond the water was the sky, but it was strange, inverted. The tops of the trees along the horizon met the lake. The surface shifted, and the old man's face disappeared. It seemed as if there was a shape in the ripples. I squinted to make it out, but couldn't.

Reflected through the lake, green light rippled across my room as if a stone had been thrown in the water. The ripples crossed my hands and I felt their cool with relief as on a hot summer day.

It was easy to sleep in the quiet, lapped by the light.

The rippling light carried me in and out of dreams. I dreamt I was driving my car in the deep, green lake. With the windows tightly closed, we floated like a submarine. My steering wheel turned us first one way, then easily glided us another. It felt safe. The little dome light on my car was comforting, as all around us streams of bubbles raced to the surface through the dark.

Reine and Sass sat in the back seat together, giggling and talking. They spoke the language of girls, breathless, staccato laughs, then whispers. I couldn't make out what they were saying. I turned down the knob on the radio, but it seemed like it was broken. Each time I touched it, Patsy Cline's song just grew louder.

> *I go out walkin'*
> *After midnight*
> *Out in the moonlight*
> *Just like we used to do . . .*

I could steer the car both up and down through the water, explore the bottom of the lake, at times sandy, then filled with vast fields of green weeds. I had to pay attention because around us floated pieces of debris, things from the basement: antlers, the statue of Saint Agnes, bottles, and pieces of broken furniture. There were more ominous things, too, gutted deer suspended and floating, tethered to the bottom on the lake. Similar shapes wrapped in white sheets that looked like human bodies, ghostly in the deep green.

I glanced at the back seat for comfort and adjusted my rearview mirror so I could see the girls more clearly. They whispered, touching hands, smiling mysteriously into each other's eyes. I felt a familiar stab of motherly panic. I wondered if I should warn Reine not to play with the dead girl, as if she might have germs or a contagious condition.

> *And as the skies turn gloomy*
> *Night winds whisper to me*
> *I'm lonesome as I can be . . .*

The music played on and on. My hands on the steering wheel gripped the bit of plastic and steel so tightly that my skin turned white. The bones of my knuckles stood out in stark relief against the dark gloom beyond my windshield. I realized vaguely that I was terrified. I glanced at the girls again and adjusted the car just a little bit to the right.

Sass sat beside my hospital bed in the visitor's chair. I opened my eyes slowly; it was as if she had been there a long time, her hands folded across her lap. I knew her with certainty now. With every fiber of my being. Her dark hair framed her face like a soft cloud. She had the same eyes as Ardell. Almost the same broad, clear sweep of forehead. I wondered if they'd both gotten that from their mother.

It was a normal hospital room this time. No water, no submerged submarine cars. My body hurt with a dull intense pain whose source couldn't be located. It hurt everywhere the same, but distantly, almost like a forgotten memory.

Sass took my hand in her own cool fingers. With her other hand, she drew aside the top of the simple blue dress she wore. I cried out at what I saw. She had been opened up, gutted like an animal—cut from neck to stomach. Inside the terrible wound, I could see her sacred heart. It glowed like an ember at the center of a campfire, shifting with strange blacks and blues.

She pressed my unwilling hand into her chest, touching her heart. It was the same as sticking my hand in a stove, and I screamed. The fire spread through me and my eyes flew open, startling the nurse standing over me. She had been taking my pulse. She jumped a little, her eyes refocusing on me.

"I'll get the doctor," she said, hustling from the room. "We're glad you're awake."

Four days later, one of Joe's officers came to see me while I sipped apple juice from a carton. He was a tall, bulky man with blond hair cut military-style. I knew him from teen parties by the lake long ago. He'd been friends with the sister of someone I went to school with.

The officer was Cullen Rogers. And I knew when I saw him that Joe was done with me. It was hard to blame him. There's only so much one man can take, after all.

Officer Rogers filled the chair next to my bed and it creaked. He had some paperwork to finish and he was glad I was awake.

The nurse peeked in, then disappeared when she saw my visitor.

"Do you remember what happened?" he asked.

"I do," I said. "But it all happened so fast, I'm not sure I'll be able to describe anything. I was talking to Joe and we said goodbye. And then I tried to get back in my car . . . it happened fast."

I remembered Joe screaming when the car hit—a raw, ragged noise torn out of him. I remembered the lights, so bright they seemed to light us from within. I didn't say any of this to Officer Cullen. I didn't mention Sass's appearance in the car. I knew better than to sign my own mad confession. She'd seemed so real then. She still seemed real.

"What about the driver?" I asked. "In the other car?'

"The other driver died."

"Oh," I said, and took a sip of apple juice.

"You're lucky to be alive," he told me. "You got back into your car just in time."

"Who?" I asked.

He frowned. "Who was the driver?"

I nodded.

He read me a name that I didn't know from his notebook.

"Old or young?" I asked.

"Fifty-eight. Male. He was coming out of Ardell Ring's bar. When he hit you, he was ejected. Broke his neck and a lot of other things. No seat belt. Blood alcohol was pretty high."

I nodded again.

He closed his notebook. "I just wanted to let you know that the bar owner has been out here a few times."

"Ardell?" I said. When I spoke his name, it was as if I remembered everything that had happened in the last few weeks all at once.

I closed my eyes.

"He and Joe had it out. I had to separate them the night of the accident.

Joe told the hospital staff not to let him in anymore. Not to bother you. We know Ardell from way back. He's probably got some angle going on. He might be afraid we're going to charge him for the sale and wanting to talk to you about that." He rose. "Do you want me to call your nurse back?" he asked. "I think she had your lunch."

I shook my head.

"Feel better," he said. "Do you know when you'll be out?"

I didn't. My ribs were broken in two places. I'd reinjured my arm. But I was lucky it wasn't worse.

The cop paused at the door. "Joe wanted me to tell you that it was best for me to handle this," he said. "You should call me with any questions. Joe being a witness and all, it's best not to complicate things."

I nodded, surprised at how tight my throat felt. My eyes started to sting ominously, and tears welled up behind my still-closed lids.

"Is there someone I can call for you?" he asked. "Joe said your mother is in treatment, and he wasn't sure how to get ahold of your ex-husband. Do you want to give me the number so I can call him?"

I opened my eyes, shaking my head emphatically. I didn't want Reine to end her vacation. To see me like this. "There is someone you can call for me, though," I said. I gave him Collin's phone number. "Tell him I'm ready for him to come get me."

The noise of tires screeching woke me. Sitting up in bed, I listened for Reine across the small house. I heard her steady breathing, just across the hallway. Rising slowly with the weight of the baby I carried, I padded into her room. She slept in her bed, all the blankets pushed to the floor.

It was January already, and though we hadn't had much snow yet, it was cold. I covered her again and looked out her window, down to the road.

There were two cars there. It looked like someone had hit a deer.

I glanced at her clock; it was near midnight, and I wondered if they needed me to call someone. I touched my stomach and rubbed it meditatively. The baby seemed to be sleeping, too.

I went out to the hall and pulled a coat from the closet. I buttoned it around my stomach and slipped on my boots. I reached for the door with my left hand, forgetting. I missed the knob. There was still some numbness there from the accident. I opened it with my other hand and went outside.

The new house was on a little hill, with more yard in front than back. I trod carefully down the driveway, between the trees, feeling the frosty ground crunch beneath my feet.

I arrived at the two cars, illuminated by their headlights and the winter moon. There was an old man in a ball cap, who seemed to be driving one car. The other man was maybe twenty. Between them was the deer; unfortunately it was still alive.

It still breathed raggedly, sharply. It couldn't rise, but the panic in its eyes raced as fast as its broken legs still trying to run on the pavement. Calmly the old man stepped on its throat, crushing it and putting an end to its misery. I looked away. The young man vomited violently, crying now.

"Do you need any help?" I asked.

"No," the old man said. "As soon as dipshit here stops crying, we'll be on our way."

From the damage to his car, I guessed the young man had hit the deer.

"Do you need me to call the police?" I asked.

The old man nodded. "Sure, we'll need a tag for the deer. Do you want it?"

I shook my head. We both looked at the young man again.

"What are you doing here, son?" I asked. "Where are you headed?"

"I was looking for a diner. Someplace to stop, so I turned off the highway. Got a little turned around on the roads and then . . ." His eyes strayed back to the deer. I thought he might start crying again.

"Where are you going?"

"Back to school in Duluth."

"There's no diner out here," I told him. "You need to get back out on the state highway. That will take you to the interstate about twenty miles down. Do you think your car will still drive?"

He nodded slowly. "Do I have to stay for the police?"

"Of course you do," the old man spat. "Dumb shit."

"I'll call them," I said, turning back up to the house.

I didn't go back outside after the call, just watched from the window. Eventually the police arrived. The young man left, and the police officer came to my door. I didn't recognize him. He took my name and information and asked me if I wanted the deer.

"No," I said. "I've never had much of a taste for venison."

When he left, I settled back into my bed. The sheets had cooled, and it was nice to lie in the still and the quiet, listening to my daughter breathe steadily.

Joe arrived the next morning when I was making Reine breakfast.

I opened the door for him and blinked, though I wasn't really surprised.

He had his uniform on and a baseball cap. He had a small box in his hands. His face looked hesitant. We hadn't seen each other since the night of the accident, over five months ago.

I smiled. "Come in."

"I saw your name on the log book this morning," he said, following me the few short steps back into my kitchen. "Everything okay?"

"Just a deer got hit on the road," I said. "Eat with us. How do you like your eggs?'

"Runny," he said, and sat at the small table with its two chairs. He settled his box on the floor then peered at Reine in the living room, only her feet were sticking out of the end of the couch. She was watching cartoons. His eyes took in the rest of the snug place. It was more of a cabin than a house, with a view of Big Comfort Lake.

"My ex-husband helped me find it," I said, "after the hospital. Windy and I needed a little space from each other. Denny had it painted and fixed the windows. Recarpeted."

His eyes settled fully on me. The cast was off my arm; I had healed and gained weight. I was starting to show. "You look good," he said.

I finished his eggs and set them on the table across from him. I buttered the toast and settled down for breakfast.

We ate in companionable silence. Pushing his finished plate away, he said at last, "I had a little trouble finding you after the hospital." He held out the box. "The prison told me you never came from your father's things. So I went up and got them, just in case. After the accident, I'm sure you had a lot on your mind."

Hesitantly, I took the box. Looking inside, I saw a manila envelope, a pair of shoes, and the clothes Pitch had been wearing the day he left court after his sentencing.

I set the box on the table and took out the manila envelope. It was mainly papers, a few photos of Windy and me from when I was young. A picture of me petting a deer was on top. I remembered the deer park. I was wearing a little plaid dress. Along with the pictures Pitch's sobriety medal slid out. It landed on the table with a small *thunk.*

God grant me the serenity to accept the things I cannot change. I picked the little thing up and put the chain around my neck, then tucked it into the top of my shirt.

Joe was watching me carefully.

"Thank you," I said simply.

He nodded and rose to go. I trailed him to the door. "How about you?" I asked. "How are things going for you since the accident?"

He paused, and it was difficult to judge the expression on his face. It was a mix of many things. "Tessa is pregnant," he said. "She's due in the spring."

"Me too," I said.

He smiled then, and I was relieved to see it. "Things are better," he said. "I'm not having the panic attacks anymore. I was so worried about having kids, about everything. But now that it's really happening . . ." He shook his head. "I guess you just move on. No time to worry about it too much. She keeps me busy, too. Tonight I have to paint the baby's room. And the rest of the house to match."

I touched his arm. Just for a moment. He looked at it, then covered my hand with his. "It will be okay, Joe," I said. "Life is about more than the terrible things we do to each other. There's good stuff too."

He patted my hand, and then let me open the door for him.

"How about you?" he asked. "Is your husband excited about the baby? Did you get back together after the hospital?"

"Oh," I said, shaking my head, quickly glancing at Reine, "this isn't his baby."

"I'm sorry," Joe said, and he actually blushed. "I thought because of the house . . ." He trailed off. "Since he fixed it up for you. Sorry for being stupid."

I smiled reassuringly. "Denny just helped me get back on my feet. For Reine. And besides, maybe he owed me. The doctor says the baby is going to be just fine, even after the accident and . . . everything else."

"A miracle, then," Joe said, and I could see from his face that he was still thinking of the accident. From the look in his eyes, I was glad I remembered so little of that night.

Joe turned to go once more, then hesitated. He looked like he was speaking against his better judgment, but he spoke anyway. "I just thought you might want to know," he said. "Ardell closed down the bar after the wreck."

"I didn't know that," I said quietly. I hadn't seen Ardell since the accident either.

Joe nodded, "Not sure what his plans are. Next week the fire department is going to burn the whole place down. The old house and the bar, too."

I glanced over at Reine again. She was still just a pair of bare feet, poking out from her blanket. Her hand emerged and she turned up the cartoons. I smiled, turning back to Joe.

"Thanks for telling me," I said. "Maybe I'll see you around town."

The pink brush fell smoothly through Reine's hair. I stood behind her and brushed it straight until it was almost down to her shoulders. She watched me seriously in the bathroom mirror, still sleepy. Still in her pajamas.

"What do you think of the name Lionel?" she asked.

I paused, a little surprised. "Are we picking out boy names now?" I asked. The subject had been forbidden for the last week.

"Well," she answered, playing with a beaded hair tie, "are you sure it's a boy? For sure, sure?"

"Pretty sure," I said, beginning to separate her hair into the three plaits needed for her braid. "You can look at the ultrasound pictures again if you want."

She frowned at me through the mirror. "Well, if we can't use our girl name anymore, it might as well be Lionel."

I tried to suppress my smile since she was watching me closely, but it was hard. I picked up the brush again. "There are lots of boys' names, too," I said. "And we have a lot of time to think about it still. A few more months."

At last she asked, "When will Daddy come?"

"Soon. He said Louisa will pick you up at noon."

I worked in silence for awhile on the few knots in her hair, but Reine tired of my brushing before I did. She squirmed loose. "I should get dressed," she said. "If Louisa is coming."

I nodded, following her though the house, missing already the soothing motion of the brush pulling through her hair, like water running through my fingers. I missed the earthy smell of her skin that each brush stroke brought up like a plough.

I sat carefully on her bed, trying not to jar the baby, and watched her dress, then pack, for her weekend. She smiled at me. "What will you do all day, while I'm gone?" she asked.

"Probably work," I told her, trying to assemble a truthful statement. I wasn't really sure what I would do without her today, when I was alone with my thoughts and the news Joe had brought. "I brought some of my files home for the weekend. I'll probably just sit at the window, look at the lake, and read."

She folded a pair of jeans into her duffle bag, then found a pair of socks and a few shirts. The sound of the door-knocking interrupted our quiet ritual.

Reine glanced at the clock, which read almost noon, and then back at me. "Do you want me to get it?" she asked, not quite hiding the concern behind the question. Ever since the accident, especially since I'd told her about the baby, she'd been convinced I was fragile somehow.

I shook my head and rose slowly. She watched me and smiled encouragingly.

Louisa was at the door, her arms wrapped tightly around her, holding closed the red coat she'd forgotten to button. The now-empty Mercedes was still running behind her, leaving clouds of exhaust in my tiny, frozen yard. I hadn't noticed much about the day until then—it was sunny and bright, the white snow making everything brighter somehow.

Reine was within earshot, so I smiled a welcome at Louisa and invited her in. She met my eye only briefly and stepped inside, her eyes darting around for Reine, who hadn't appeared from her room yet. She smiled at my elbow, not sure of herself. "How are you doing?" she asked.

"Just fine," I answered calmly as Reine appeared, her bag zipped and ready. From the closet by the door I retrieved her coat and handed it to her. Louisa and I watched her put it on in silence. When she was done, Reine reached up and kissed me. I couldn't help but stroke her hair again.

"Let's go," she said, turning to Louisa and squaring her shoulders. I handed her the duffle bag. "I'll be back Sunday night," she told me. "But

I'll call tonight to check on Lionel."

Louisa's mouth seemed to twitch a little in surprise at the name, but she kept her face in order. With a nod to me, she herded Reine out the door and into the waiting car.

Through the open door, I watched the car disappear into the trees and down the driveway. Ridiculously, I realized I was still holding Reine's hair brush. I set it down and took a deep, almost-steady breath.

"Lionel?" I tried the name in the quiet, touching my stomach. I shook my head and closed the door on the empty yard. Then I went and made myself a cup of tea.

At my desk, my half-empty teacup at my elbow, I flipped through my assistant's messages from yesterday. They were written in her neat Palmer Method handwriting. She'd handed them to me outside the courthouse as I headed out to pick up Reine from school.

There wasn't anything there that couldn't wait until Monday. I stared at my files and considered working. I was still new at the county prosecutor's office, so my caseload was light. "I promised Collin not to work you too hard," my new boss had said with a grin as he showed me my desk.

I realized I wasn't going to open the files as my eyes wandered out the window. I'd only brought the files home to distract me, because I knew Reine would be away. But I was already too distracted. I took in the lake. It had snowed again last night, a light dusting, leaving everything new and slightly rounded.

On the very top of the papers was a warrant I needed the judge to sign on Monday. I'd have the sheriff's office serve it for me. Mostly I worked with the county officers on my files. I'd managed to avoid Joe entirely until now, respecting his request for distance.

But he had been the one to visit. I thought about his fiancée and pictured the notes she'd soon be writing on his lunch bags—*buy diapers, dinner at 5, you promised.* I used to write notes like that for Denny. I turned that memory over in my hands, the way you might test a cup of hot tea just out of the microwave, feeling the heat, wanting to see if it was bearable.

I smiled and thought about Joe being a father. It wasn't a hard image either—warm, like the tea. I sipped my drink and studied the lake outside my window again. If I squinted hard, I could make out my mother's place on the other side in the distance. I had a small yard—for here anyway—only half an acre. The snow had covered our tracks to the lake, the path Reine and I had made to go ice-skating. Well, Reine ice-skated and I watched, trying not to fall and damage Lionel. The poor baby had already been through enough in his brief months inside me.

I felt more sure of myself now. More sure that it wouldn't be overwhelming. So I let myself think through my whole conversation with Joe, letting myself replay his words in my head. Like our tracks in the snow—only obscured, not gone—I knew where my thoughts would lead.

I remembered my assurance to Joe—that life was more than the painful things we did to one another. I touched my stomach; there were good things too. Ardell, of course, had told me those same words first. I remembered hearing them, sitting on my mother's porch, slowly losing consciousness to Pitch's scavenged scotch.

I let myself think of Ardell, really think about him for the first time since the accident. Staring out at the sheets of white on the lake, I imagined them burning the bar—the flames consuming the old lodge. I pictured all the snow and ice melting, hissing billows of steam into the cold air, like spirits. And then I pictured it over, the fire extinguished, leaving behind the gaping black hole of the foundation, and the firefighters taking apart what remained with axes and picks. I wondered if Ardell would join in, or if it would be too much.

I realized with a sudden little jolt of pain that I had hold of Pitch's sobriety metal. I'd twisted it a little too tight, the chain cutting into my neck. I dropped it instantly and reached for my tea. I didn't dare drink it. My hands were shaking too much. I just held onto its gentle heat instead, feeling that fade as well.

I had been putting off thinking about Ardell for a long time. I hadn't even mentioned him to my counselor at the recovery center. Joe's arrival and this new information made everything more immediate. Uneasily, I rubbed my stomach. What would Ardell do after the bar burned? Would he leave? Where would he go? For months since I'd finished rehab, I'd done my best to only think about the soothing present—the immediate minute—easy things like brushing Reine's hair, picking out paint colors for the new house, doctor's appointments, arranging the files on my new desk at work, and making cup after cup of tea. I'd walled everything else off.

But the boundaries I'd imagined between the livable present and the darker past and the scarier future weren't as hard or fast as I'd imagined. They weren't even walls at all. It was more like I'd wrapped myself in a gray and wooly blanket, like a child playing a game, choosing not to peek out. But it was all waiting for me the moment I did—the memories fell around me as softly as snow touching the ground.

I could no longer think of Ardell—and it was amazing to me how clear his face, his expression, his smell even, came to me then after months of absence—without tracing in his features, the traits he shared with Sass. They had the same high forehead, the same brown-almost-black hair, the same long mouth that defined their faces.

I remembered Ardell holding me on my mother's porch, his arms tight around me. What had he called his sister that day? My memory was sloshy like gin. He'd called Sass his own patron saint. He'd said she'd saved his life. Her first miracle. She'd convinced him to stop drinking. Her second miracle. I suddenly wanted to know what he thought the third miracle had been.

Maybe I knew it already. Sass had saved me, though I had been too young to remember. It was too hard to think some thoughts. I could only do it if I pretended that Ardell's arms were still around me. I thought back to the day Windy had found the drowned girl. Joe had buried her months ago. I'd read in the paper that the Lutheran church had paid for her stone in the city cemetery. Had Sass looked like that girl when they'd found her? Her eyes shining like flat, dead stars beneath the water, her black hair floating out like a net around her. Her mouth open. Her skin naked, white like snow.

I could remember it all now, things only hinted at in terrifying dreams and hospital rooms. I remembered myself huddled in Pitch's car. The bar door flew open. At the terrible sound of the drunk growling, every nerve in my body suddenly exploding in panic. The drunk's face—Pitch's face, that I saw clearly now—contorted with rage that was beyond reason. Contorted until it was animal and deadly.

Sass tried to shake me fully awake and out of my panic, her eyes as frightened as mine. How had she known to be there? "Run," she urged, a command no one could ignore—not even me, frozen in fear of Pitch. She practically pulled me from the car, willing me to run with her for the safety of the woods.

She didn't make it. I remembered the sudden feeling of her absence. He caught her, his hands around her mouth before she could even scream. Her pale white arms reached for me through the dark. One last look—the panic in her eyes—dead, bright like stars—and then she was gone. They were gone and I ran on and on.

I remembered the night I had wound up in the hospital. The accident. The same eyes. The same face. Everything becoming clear in my broken mind. Everything lit as if by the oncoming headlights—too bright to ignore the truth. I had thought then, as I heard the tires screech towards me, that her name would be the last thing I ever spoke: "Sass."

Part of me wondered if I'd lost my mind. I knew the tricks the mind could play. Memory was the most unreliable of strangers.

A sudden snap shook me loose from the hold of my thoughts, back to the present. I looked at my hand. I'd pulled Pitch's sobriety medal loose from my neck. The broken chain dangled from my hand. I stared at it in surprise, becoming more aware of myself. My breathing was ragged, labored; darkness flicked before my eyes, like a shadow passing through the trees.

I was hyperventilating. Simply knowing that was useless. It did nothing to slow my breath. I struggled, closing my eyes. I thought of Ardell. I thought of his arms around me. It almost worked. My breath calmed slightly. I struggled to regain control, realizing then, that just the memory of his arms wasn't going to be enough.

I realized now that this stretch of road—that Lost Comfort Lake itself—would always bring to mind Ardell. But he was more than that; he was like the water itself in the rock beneath, connecting us all. The baby stirred inside me when I took the right turn at the fork, driving slowly into the pines along the poorly-plowed road.

The lot was empty when I arrived. If possible, the old lodge house looked even more grim than I remembered it. Like it knew the fate that had been meted out for it. It was hard to believe anyone had ever lived there. That Sass and Ardell had grown up—almost grown up in Sass's case—beneath that saggy, moldering roof. The front entry and broken windows had been unboarded, and the door itself removed and discarded. The bar was in a similar condition, door stripped, standing wide open. I looked away.

All around the bar and house, the trees had been clear-cut to the ground and butchered into piles of logs. Everywhere great rivulets of sap bled slowly into the snow. The smell of the pine was sharp and clear on the cold air; almost antiseptic. Most disorienting was the intensity of the sky above, a bright ring of blue circling the spot. It was almost as if we'd been located on a map. I felt small and nervous, exposed in the great wide space. The house brooded and sagged on its beams. It wasn't much comfort.

Climbing out of the car, I looked around and didn't see Ardell. My breath made little puffs and I hugged myself. Peering down at the cabins closest to the lake, I saw wisps of smoke from Ardell's wood stove. I hesitated and then reached into the car and retrieved the box of Pitch's things. I needed to walk carefully down the slick ground.

Behind his cabin, Ardell was cutting kindling. The sound of splitting wood, the axe hitting home, was unmistakable, and I followed it. Despite the winter day, he'd taken off his jacket, working in his t-shirt with only a cap pulled over his ears to protect him from the cold.

He didn't see me at first, and I watched him work. His arms came down and the wood split. His axe stuck, and he heaved the whole thing into the air, bringing it down again. He picked up the bits, threw them on his pile and turned for another log.

He froze when he saw me, then straightened slowly.

I hugged Pitch's box a little tighter, until it crumpled some. I tried to smile, but my face didn't seem to be working at the moment.

Ardell swung his axe, sticking it in the stump he'd been using, his expression neutral.

"I didn't come to drink," I said quickly. "That's not why I'm here."

His eyes dropped to my stomach. Behind him the lake was a sheet of ice, over two feet thick. It had the color of pale milky jade. I felt the cold again and shivered.

"The bar's closed anyway," he said at last, studying my face. "You heard that?"

I nodded. "When is the burn?"

"Tomorrow," he answered, shrugging on his jacket. I watched him strip his gloves off his hands and stuff them into his pocket. Our eyes met, and I realized he was waiting for me to speak.

I held up the now-battered box again. "I was wondering if you could burn these for me. Just set it in the bar."

He came close, peering inside the box. It wasn't much to look at—some folded clothes, the broken medal, and a few envelopes of papers and pictures.

"It's Pitch's things, from prison," I explained. "There's not much. But I don't want it. And I can't see bringing it out to Windy. That wouldn't do any good."

"How is your mother?" he asked as he gently took the box.

I shrugged, looking down at the lake once more. A little wind had risen and it was making swirls in the snow. "Same as always, I guess."

He nodded, then frowned fiercely, but not at me. He was looking over my shoulder. I turned, following his gaze. An old truck had pulled into the lot up at the bar.

"God damn drunks," he said. "I've been closed for five months and they still show up."

"Go inside," he said pointing at his cabin, as he headed up the hill. "It's too cold for you to be out here with the baby." He added grimly, "I'll be right back."

I opened the cabin door. There was a little wood-burning stove in there and it was warm, as he'd promised. Still I lingered at the door, watching his back, hesitant. I ducked inside when the shoving started.

Ardell's little cabin wasn't more than two rooms, a bathroom, and a closet. It was clean and neat, and mostly empty now. I supposed I had been here before, but I didn't remember it. The narrow closet contained a small sink and a refrigerator. His clothes hung on hooks all along the bedroom wall. His bed took up most of the space. It was neatly made and covered with a quilt. The window over the bed let in more sunlight than I'd expected under the pines. It filled the whole room.

There was no chair, so I sat on the bed. It was hot now from the fire. I took off my coat and hat and laid them beside me.

Everywhere in the tiny cabin there were signs of the move. There was a suitcase and a duffle bag open beside the bed. Stacked against the wall were several cardboard boxes of books—books on birds, hawks mostly, like *Bedwith's Guide to North American Birds*. I felt a stab of worry over where Ardell was going.

My eyes fell on an open box pushed under the bed. I pulled it out and saw an old camera and a dozen cloth-bound notebooks. They were frayed and the spines had been taped to hold them together. There was a stack of mail, bills rubber-banded together, and the picture.

I knew this one. Of course, he'd brought it down from the bar—Sass's baptismal picture. She looked tiny and peaceful in her white dress.

I touched her baby cheek with fingers that were suddenly cold again. If I hadn't been in such a safe place—with Ardell so near—I knew I would have started hyperventilating again.

I wasn't sure how long Ardell had been standing there, but I jumped when I finally noticed him. He stood in the doorway and watched me sitting on the bed. For the first time I felt how alone we were together. The careful way he examined me, his eyes lingering on my stomach again, made me blush. I hugged Sass's picture to my chest and wiped my eyes, realizing they were wet.

"Are you okay, Jane?" he asked gently.

I shook my head, not trusting my voice.

Concerned, he came and sat beside me on the bed. He took my hand. For a long while we sat like that, me holding Sass's picture like a warm compress to my heart, his eyes dark and sad.

At last it seemed like I had to say something, but the things I wanted to say were too much for words.

"What do you think of the name Lionel?" I asked instead, grasping at a topic that, while it wasn't exactly safe, wasn't balanced over burning ground like all the others.

"No."

"It's not a bad name." I almost smiled at the immediate certainty in his answer.

He shrugged. "That doesn't make it a good name, either."

Talking about the name brought to mind my daughter, and that made me feel stronger, more present in the room at least. "Where are you moving?" I asked, brave enough to try a more difficult question.

He considered this for a while. "Not far," he answered. "I'll move in with Rowdy for the time being. Until I figure things out. I didn't want to leave if you still . . ." He broke off awkwardly. "Well, until things worked out."

"Does he have room?"

"I'm not keeping much. Most everything is going in the fire tomorrow." He looked around the room. "Bed, furniture. Everything."

"What are you going to do with this?" I asked, holding up the picture.

Ardell looked away, folding his arms across his chest. "I was going to get rid of that, too," he said. "It feels like the right time to let some things go."

"No," I protested. "You can't do that. This is the only one you have. You told me that."

It was still hard for him to meet my eye. "It costs me to keep it, Jane," he said carefully. "To keep this place. I don't think you understand that. Besides, Sass wouldn't mind. She hated this place. When we were kids, she used to pray every night that we could leave here."

He was wrong. I did know—I could see—how much this was costing him. It was written so clearly in the lines of his face.

"Let me keep it for you," I said. "Then if you change your mind, you can have her back." I gripped the little picture tighter, anxious for him to say yes.

At last he nodded.

Nervous that he would change his mind, I rose and shrugged into my coat again. He watched me intently. I tucked the picture into the pocket, where it just fit. The light through the window was changing, cutting a straight shadow between me and Ardell now. Ardell rose reluctantly. I put my hand protectively in my pocket, knowing as I did that I was overreacting a little. Ardell stepped aside to let me out of the bedroom and we stood in his kitchen, by the little closet and sink. The wood in the stove popped and shifted, the heat turning it efficiently to ash.

"I'm not drinking anymore," I told him. That seemed important to say. "I'm taking care of the baby. I wanted you to know that."

"You're out at the old Rendon summer place?"

I nodded. "How did you know that?"

"Small town." He smiled. "I have a lot of family. Some of them are cops."

"Did you and Joe patch things up then?" I asked.

"He stopped by this morning. He's pretty happy about the bar closing for good. I told him this bar's been keeping cops employed for three generations."

He reached over and fixed the collar of my coat for me. "Let me walk you to your car," he said. "Joe seemed worried about Tessa and the baby."

"He did look a little pale when I saw him," I said. "Babies will do that to you. It will all work out all right."

"That's what I told him," he said, opening the door.

Outside, the cold seemed even worse after the warmth of Ardell's cabin. The wind had picked up and the sun started its path down towards the horizon. I leaned into Ardell a little bit, and he put his arm around me, steadying me as we walked.

"Maybe I could come visit you," he said as we reached my car. "After all this stuff with the bar is done. Visit my picture of Sass," he added, smiling. "I'd bring some groceries by for you and Reine and the little one. Make sure you're eating right."

"I'd like that," I said. Looking over his shoulder, I realized I was seeing the bar for the last time. My eyes drifted to the wrecked lodge again. I wondered how much of Ardell would still be left in the house when it burned tomorrow.

Turning back to him, I met Ardell's eye. "Tell me why you're doing this," I asked him.

He didn't answer.

"Are you doing this for me?" I pressed. "Because if it's for me, you don't have to. This is your whole life."

He shook his head. "I know what it's like to have a past you can't live with, Jane," he said. "What it's like to wake up every day and still be living when you don't want to be." He took a shuddering breath and looked beyond me to the ruined old house, his face almost burning with pain. "When you accept that there are things you can't change . . . when that sinks in, that life is like that . . ." he shook his head again, "your path forward gets pretty clear after that."

"Burning down your whole livelihood? That doesn't seem like much of a path forward."

"I threw that drunk out that night, Jane," he said. "I put him in his car and told him to go." The pain in his face seemed to surge, like the fire was reaching new oxygen. "You shouldn't be alive, Jane. The crash shook the bar. Like an explosion. I was sure you were dead. Blood everywhere. Drunks everywhere and Joe screaming that I'd killed you.

"Would I have been any better than your old man if you'd died that night?" he asked. "If our child in your belly had died? Or was hurt. Could still be hurt . . ." He lost his ability to meet my eye—to speak.

"It's not like that," I said quickly. "The baby is fine. Every doctor says he's fine. They did ultrasounds, everything."

A little wind stirred, blowing a new chill across us, tugging at my hair.

The cold was getting to be too much. Ardell reached over and smoothed the loose strands from my face. "That's what Joe said this morning," he acknowledged, but I could see on his face that he wasn't convinced.

What had Joe said to me about the baby? He was a miracle. I felt that word with new strength. I slid my hand into my pocket, touching the hard-pointed corner of Sass's picture. It brought back everything I hadn't been able to ask in the cabin.

As if he could sense the turn of my thoughts, Ardell asked, "Jane, do you remember what I said on the porch that day about Sass being my patron saint?"

I nodded. "You never told me about Sass's third miracle."

"That's because I was waiting on it." He looked back to the crumbling house again, but he seemed more sad now than angry. "I can always feel her around. Like she's still near me." He looked unsurely down at me. "Does that sound crazy?"

There was so much I wanted to say to him—things that might have surprised him, things that might have made him question my sanity. Instead I said, "No." The sound was husky. I cleared my throat, looking for my voice. "No, it doesn't."

"Lately when you're near me . . ." he said and touched my hair again, "ever since you came back—that first day in the bar—whenever you're near me, that's when I feel her strongest. Almost like she's standing right there. I think that she's trying to tell me that you're it."

"I'm what?" I asked confused.

"Her third miracle," he said. "I keep thinking she's telling me it's you."

"How can you believe that?" I asked. "I'm a mess. Barely sober. Barely anything. I already lost one husband because I couldn't . . . couldn't ever . . ."

Ardell leaned down and kissed me, cutting off my protest. "Right," he said. "Exactly. And after all that we've both been through, we're still standing here. Sass or not, it seems like a miracle to me."

He covered my hand jammed halfway into my pocket over the little picture with his own, then haltingly touched my stomach. "I should have trusted that feeling a little more," he said. "I should have come over sooner. To see you. I thought you were staying away, because you were angry with me. I thought . . ." He took an almost-shaky breath. "I thought you were done with me. After our argument. After the accident."

I rested my head against his shoulder, speaking to his shirt. "I needed to get some things straightened out first." I wasn't certain he heard, but it didn't matter. For a moment, I closed my eyes and let him hold me, leaning my weight into him, letting him carry me for just a little while.

Going home, I took the long slow curve around Lost Comfort Lake as carefully as I could, thinking through everything, not so much with my mind, but my heart. For that quiet ride, thought, memory, feeling, all seemed connected—like the lakes—by waters deep beneath the surface, deep in the ground where we'll all—one day—be buried.

ABOUT THE AUTHOR

Rachel Coyne is a novelist and poet who lives in Lindstrom, Minnesota. A graduate of the Perpich Center for Arts in Minnesota and Macalester College, she is a devotee of Pablo Neruda, Don Williams songs, and vintage editions of *Jane Eyre*. Her previously published works include the novel, *Whiskey Heart*, and a children's book, *Daughter, Have I Told You?*

ABOUT NEW RIVERS PRESS

New Rivers Press emerged from a drafty Massachusetts barn in winter 1968. Intent on publishing work by new and emerging poets, founder C. W. "Bill" Truesdale labored for weeks over an old Chandler & Price letterpress to publish three hundred fifty copies of Margaret Randall's collection, *So Many Rooms Has a House But One Roof*.

Nearly four hundred titles later, New Rivers, a non-profit and now teaching press based since 2001 at Minnesota State University Moorhead, has remained true to Bill's goal of publishing the best new literature—poetry and prose—from new, emerging, and established writers.

New Rivers Press authors range in age from twenty to eighty-nine. They include a silversmith, a carpenter, a geneticist, a monk, a tree-trimmer, and a rock musician. They hail from cities such as Christchurch, Honolulu, New Orleans, New York City, Northfield (Minnesota), and Prague.

Charles Baxter, one of the first authors with New Rivers, calls the press "the hidden backbone of the American literary tradition." Continuing this tradition, in 1981 New Rivers began to sponsor the Minnesota Voices Project (now called Many Voices Project) competition. It is one of the oldest literary competitions in the United States, bringing recognition and attention to emerging writers. Other New Rivers publications include the American Fiction Series, the American Poetry Series, New Rivers Abroad, and the Electronic Book Series.

More information can be found at newriverspress.com.

EARLY PRAISE FOR G

"The Amazon is burning. Our oceans are dying. And our fellow humans and animals are still suffering in the billions. But there is a radiant hope on the horizon. In **Gene-trepreneur**, Brett shares the stories of those who have chosen to fight for change with science. I highly recommend that you read this book and then get ready to join the mission-driven cause. You can help build a better and more sustainable future. Onwards and upwards we go together!"

—Ryan Bethencourt, Biohacker, Biotech Entrepreneur and Investor, *Shark Tank* alum

"Science and technology helped humanity become the rulers of our planet, transforming it in ways that often benefit us but to the great detriment of many other species. Can those same disciplines that placed us on the throne now be used to lighten our footprint and make Earth a more habitable place for us all? Brett Cotten argues persuasively that's the case, and gives several compelling examples of biotech entrepreneurs trying to do just that."

—Paul Shapiro, Author of *Clean Meat: How Growing Meat Without Animals Will Revolutionize Dinner and the World*

"**Gene-trepreneur** is a world atlas of biotech: a navigable guide to the intertwined fields of industry, sustainability, and science. Brett Cotten takes you through all the steps to impactful biotech success. Aspiring entrepreneurs listen wisely."

—Simon Jude Levien, Harvard Student & Science Writer published in the New York Times, NJ Herald, & Boston Globe

We have lost a lot of Earth's biodiversity, but there is ALWAYS hope. Cotten produces a lively gaze into how global sustainability in food, materials, and wildlife conservation are vastly intertwined while capturing how one can be a part of the exciting and innovative changes to come.

—Forrest Galante, Conservationist and Host of Animal Planet's *Extinct or Alive*

*"Cotten manages to root a sometimes intimidatingly technical topic into history and pop-culture that EVERYONE can relate to. **Gene-trepreneur** is an absolute must-read for anyone even adjacent to the field—it brings scientific depth into focus and builds bridges we'll need to progress into our best future. Bravo!"*

—Shannon Theobald, Author of *Printing Your Dinner: Personalization in the Future of Food*

*"**Gene-trepreneur** leans into the power of the biotechnology revolution to solve the world's greatest global challenges like biodiversity loss and climate change. Brett Cotten's enthusiasm and passion shines through as he takes you on a journey of how to become an impactful Gene-trepreneur."*

—Shen Ming Lee, Author of *Hungry for Disruption: How Tech Innovations Will Nourish 10 Billion by 2050*

*"Brett cleverly delivers on the new and fast-growing biotechnology industry and explains how we can bring the most value out of our finite resources in this world. **Gene-trepreneur** is a must read for those who are interested in the future and how we can grow our wealth and prospect for the next generation."*

—Chong Hwan Kim, Author of *IoT 2030*

"It's incredible to see the way Cotten broke down the innovations in biotech and the future of the industry into a fun and educational book we can all learn from. In **Gene-trepreneur**, he includes his own interviews of some amazing, insightful founders and CEOs. This is a book you definitely don't want to miss."

–Jason Kraus, Author of *Venture Forward: Lessons from Leaders*

"Maybe becoming a bio-entrepreneur is not hard as it looks. Ditto for saving the world from climate change, species loss, deforestation, pollution, animal and human maladies. The time is ripe for these bold messages–enabling competence and hope. Each chapter is brimming with lively discussions, allusions to relevant sci-fi becoming real, sage advice and copious reference resources."

–Dr. George Church, Harvard Medical School Professor and Co-Author of *Regenesis: How Synthetic Biology Will Reinvent Nature and Ourselves.*

GENE–TREPRENEUR

Cultivating an Entrepreneurial
Mindset in STEM to Impact
Sustainability

_____

BRETT COTTEN

NEW DEGREE PRESS

GENE−TREPRENEUR
Cultivating an Entrepreneurial Mindset in STEM to Impact Sustainability

ISBN   978-1-64137-480-4   *Paperback*
       978-1-64137-268-8   *Ebook*

To Mom, Dad, Bri, and Kiele

Also, to people who are nice to animals.

CONTENTS

Acknowledgements

When setting out on a long journey you've never embarked on before, you never know how much work it will take to reach your final destination. I've discovered along my journey writing *Gene-trepreneur* that publishing a book takes a village, and I am so grateful for all of the support. Fulfilling this dream would not have been possible without you.

Thank you first and foremost to my family for supporting me through every step of the way, always.

Kim Cotten Gerry Cotten Briana Cotten Kiele Cotten

Thank you to the publisher, New Degree Press, especially Brian Bies and those on my publishing team who helped turn my words on a page into an actual book I am proud to have written.

Brian Bies (Head of Publishing) Ty Mall (Developmental Editor)

Linda Berardelli (Marketing Editor) Amanda Brown (Copyeditor)

Srdjan Filipovic (Cover Designer) Grzegorz Laszczyk (Formatting Editor)

Thank you Eric Koester, of the Creator Institute, for inspiring me to write a book now—not to put it off until I'm an old goon. You have changed my path forward in the best of ways.

And thank you to everyone who: gave me their time for a personal interview, pre-ordered the eBook, paperback, and multiple copies to make publishing possible, helped spread the word about *Gene-trepreneur* to gather amazing momentum, provided their insight in content editing, design, and publishing strategy, and to those whom I've played Settlers of Catan with—I'll get you next time. I am sincerely grateful for all of your help.

Abra Sitler	Christian Gibson	Ian Clark
Adam Zorin	Christian Tillegreen	Ian Wolfe
Adrielle Espinosa	Dana Bistritz	Isaac Shoemaker
Alexis Vanderhye	Dana (Robin) O'Brien	Jack Durbin
Alex Patin	Daniel Burchard	Jade Warn
Allison Fletcher	Daniel Uribe	James Huang
Allison Mielke	Dan Smith	Jean Donahue
~Andra Necula	David Benzaquen	Jeanmarie Lynch
Andrew Bickeron	David Gress	Jennifer Vermet
Andrew Blower	David Rabuka	John Mulligan
Angela Trzcinski	Debra Dearien	Jonathan Muth
Angelique Donati	Denver Greenawalt	Juliana DeMarici
Anja Dietrich	Dylan Gambardella	Kang Chi Lin
~Austin Che	Ed Goodall	Katie Casselton
Austin Heimark	Elli Tatsumi	Katie Forte
Ayna Arora	*Emily Johnson	*Kenneth Klacik
Ayush thomas	Erick Young	Kenny Joyner
~Barry Canton	Erik Vos	Kimberly Pfeiffer
Ben Bradbury	Francisco Jaubert	Kim Ulaky
Brad Vanstone	Geena Matuson	Kishore Nannapaneni
Brendan Doherty	*George Chiang	Kotaro Sasaki
Brent Gerbec	Gianna Olivo	Krzysztof Zembrzuski
Brian Spears	Godwin Chan	Larry Norder
Brooke Iveta Fecko	Guadalupe Alvarez	Lauren Scott
*Cal Cacciaguida	Haley Hoffman Smith	Leslie Olivos
Carly Newfield	Haley Janowitz	Letitia Tajuba
Cassi Leigh	Hilde Coumou	Ling Ka Yi
*Chloe Cacciaguida	Hunter Tiedemann	Lisa Lloyd

Luciano Bueno

Madeleine Cuan

Marcos Vega-Hazas

Margaux Woellner

Mark Donahue

~Matthew Markus

*Matt Meltzer

Meredith Lloyd-Evans

*Michael Graf

Michael Hsun

Michael Meisel

~Michael Selden

~Molly Morse

Next Gen Community

Nicole Tarlton

Norman Rogers

Pam Marrone

Paul Bevan

Paul Shapiro

Peter Prestipino

Philip Chwistek

Philipp Ziegler

Rachel Leigh Gross

Rich Keller

Rick Weyer

River Goh

Robert Beaury

Rohan Iyer

~Ryan Bethencourt

~Ryan Phelan

Sally Lee

Sandhya Sriram

Sarah Rudd

Sara Huser

Shannon Theobald

Shen Ming Lee

Shu Li

Simon Levien

Socrates Leotsakos

Stephan Salinardo

Stephen Botelho

*Steve Dearien

Stuart Powell

Tanvi Prabhakar

Thomas O'Neill

Thor Sigfusson

Timothy Librizzi

*Todd Erdley

Tom Speedy

*Tyler Berry

Wayne Puglia

Key: *multiple copies/campaign contributions, ~featured interviewee

SEVEN LESSONS FOR GENE-TREPRENEURS

There are *hopefully* many valuable takeaways for you throughout this book, but here are seven big-picture lessons for a look at what is to come. They are expanded upon individually much more in the conclusion as well.

1. Ideas alone don't mean anything. Execution on those ideas means everything.
2. Opportunity recognition isn't about creating something entirely new. It's about bringing together things that have never been combined in that way before.
3. Only work on something if you'd still do it for little to no money. Money is a by-product of mission-driven endeavors.
4. Operate with 100 percent transparency. People support causes (and people) they care about.
5. Fast fish eat slow fish, so build the most agile, adaptable teams.
6. Think BIGGER. Don't limit yourself to what others think is possible.
7. And give yourself permission. Sometimes nobody else will, but you absolutely must.

Preface

"We shall escape the absurdity of growing a whole chicken in order to eat a breast or a wing, by growing these parts separately under a suitable medium."[1]

−WINSTON CHURCHILL, "FIFTY YEARS HENCE," 1932

Almost one hundred years ago, one of the world's foremost leaders dreamed of making chickens an obsolete technology. In the decades since, this aspiration has been added to by countless writers, filmmakers, entrepreneurs, activists, scientists, politicians, and everyone in between. The concept has been widely shared amongst our favorite books, shows, movies, projects, and nerdiest sci-fi dreams.

But how close are we almost a century later to making this collective ambition a reality? Are we even scratching the surface of Churchill's "suitable medium"?

We are now closer than ever before to telling chickens good-bye and good "cluck" in favor of new research and medical-grade technologies. These progressions are giving us unprecedented abilities to grow real meat without factory-farming animals. It's appropriate timing too because forthcoming generations increasingly want to live longer, healthier lives that are less disruptive to the world around them. It's difficult to understate the potential impacts such a change could bring. But how can we make it possible?

The key to making this dream a present-day reality lies in STEM entrepreneurship. The people leading and supporting impactful

---

1   "Fifty Years Hence (Popular Mechanics, 1932)." New Harvest. January 15, 2016.

STEM initiatives through an entrepreneurial mindset, we'll call them Gene-trepreneurs, will lead us into the sustainable, bio-based future. While ending animal agriculture is an extremely important component of this dream, there are still untold pieces left to connect into the overall puzzle. The good news? Perhaps now is the best and most hopeful time in human history to keep adding those pieces in at a faster rate than ever before.

Even though we are now immeasurably close to living in a world that Churchill and so many others have long coveted, it's been a lengthy road to get here, and truthfully, there hasn't always been so much hope.

∞

As Ryan Bethencourt, one of the fantastic Gene-trepreneurs in this book, will tell you later on, at age ten he witnessed a pig being slaughtered. The animal was evidently terrified, and Bethencourt could do nothing but helplessly watch the shocking scene play out before him. In this moment, ten-year-old Ryan felt what so many others eventually go numb to: that what he saw and knew to be happening to billions of animals from then on didn't feel right, and he was convinced it didn't have to be this way forever.

Like Ryan, as children we all eventually learn where meat comes from. So why didn't Ryan Bethencourt grow up to become numb to the meat industry like so many others? Why did the feeling stick? (And I'll tell you a secret. It wasn't due to the wonders of Duck Tape.)

Perhaps it was because witnessing the incident first-hand left an everlasting impression—a reminder never to go numb. We all have these reminders for various things in our lives, and I suppose like fight or flight, we choose to either suppress or embrace them.

Bethencourt chose to embrace his pain point with the state of food production. Today, this biotech entrepreneur's path has led him to become the co-founder and CEO of a food innovation startup, Wild Earth. Ryan and his company were eventually featured on *Shark Tank* season 10 where he successfully struck a deal with Mark Cuban for $550,000 in investment. We'll get a chance to talk much more about Ryan Bethencourt and Wild Earth in chapter 3, but in this full-circle moment, the child who once watched helplessly as a scared pig was slaughtered was able to show the world how he is building a tremendous company—one that will mitigate our reliance on doing the same to billions of animals in the future.

∞

In writing this book, I realized the world needs more people growing up with a desire to be like Ryan Bethencourt and others later featured such as Pat Brown, Andra Necula, Eben Bayer, Molly Morse, Michael Selden, and so many more. They have all embraced the injustices and inefficiencies they have seen in the world by dedicating themselves to improving those circumstances through STEM entrepreneurship. You are most likely unfamiliar with this list of Gene-trepreneurs right now, but you will soon know who they are, what they stand for, and hopefully how we can all get some of that magic dust they've been rolling around in to rub off on us by the end of this book.

These Gene-trepreneurs make their pain points their purpose and wield the intersection of biology, technology, and business as their tool to increase sustainability in the world around them; that's what makes them Gene-trepreneurs in the first place—and such powerful ones at that.

The truth is that most people don't recognize how many amazing opportunities are now at our fingertips. With the help of biotech, we have the potential to solve some of our greatest and most highly interconnected global challenges such as deforestation, ocean pollution, animal agriculture, human health, microplastics, species loss, climate change, and more.

But there's an inherent problem in the system. Opportunities to transfer STEM and other valuable skillsets into novel areas that significantly impact sustainability simply aren't taught about much, if touched upon at all, in most educational programs (high school, undergraduate, and graduate-level). So how can we prepare the rising generations of today, *tomorrow's Gene-trepreneurs*, for their greatest inherited and globally shared challenges? How can they be educated to recognize and capitalize on new STEM opportunities to impact sustainability and essentially save the world?

The answer isn't to try and cover as much material as possible and hope something sticks. Rather, it is to teach what is commonly referred to as the "entrepreneurial mindset", or perhaps in this case we should call it the "Gene-trepreneurial mindset"? Through teaching the next generation of problem-solvers to operate effectively in environments of uncertainty, recognize opportunities, and take action upon them, we will cultivate tomorrow's Gene-trepreneurs.

∞

But why does this matter to you?

Well, now is truly the time for today's best and brightest to hop on the bandwagon and go after the world's biggest, most pressing sustainability problems. The funding tap is on for biotechnology startups. And many companies are finding they can be more successful following the "doing well while doing good" philosophy. This is in large part due to consumers' increasing demands for companies to step up their sustainability game in order to win customer dollars.

This optimistic change in customer behavior brings with it huge market potentials for individuals and companies who can share their stories of purpose—how they're not just selling products and services, but how they're inducing positive impacts as a direct result. Plus, all this new biotech at our fingertips is transforming entire industries to create cheaper, more sustainable, and healthier products. Suddenly, consumers with differing priorities (costs, ethics, personal well-being, etc.) have their barriers lowered, and it becomes easier and more appealing for everyone to make changes in the right direction regardless of diverging motivations.

Companies and consumers can make the world a better place while simultaneously getting what they want. It's truly a case, and a very profitable one at that, of "have your cake and eat it too."

∞

Fascinatingly, this wave of bio-based innovation mirrors the rise of the internet in the 1980s and 90s, but we're programming a different type of code this time not with the purpose of connecting the world, but rather saving it.

Bill Gates has said that if he were a young student today, he'd study artificial intelligence, energy, or biosciences, as they are all "promising fields where you can make a huge impact."[2] He went on to say, in reference to young students and professionals, that "you know more than I did when I was your age … You can start fighting inequity, whether down the street or around the world, sooner." Winston Churchill might have had the vision, but he and others of his time lacked the tools to bring these big ideas to life. However, today, we have the tools to enact significant change on a genetic level. I like to call it microbe-managing our future.

The goal will now be about teaching others not only how to wield these tools, but in service of what higher purpose. My hope is that through reading this book, you will discover the common threads in sustainability that weave our world together and how you have the power to enact direct change by utilizing the skills and resources at your disposal to achieve *your* greatest impact (this is called effective altruism).

As another Gene-trepreneur, Dan Widmaier of Bolt Threads (a company brewing spider silk amongst other amazing projects), will iterate later on, sometimes the right person for the job doesn't exist yet, so we have to build them. And wouldn't it be great if you could use this book as a toolkit with takeaways for how you can begin building yourself into your own version of Ryan Bethencourt, of Dan Widmaier, of Andra Necula, of … you?

---

2   Weller, Chris. "Bill Gates Reveals What He'd Study If He Were a College Freshman Today." *Business Insider.* May 15, 2017.

The Anthropocene and Riding the EAC to Sydney

Before we jump into it with our first Gene-trepreneur, Dr. Molly Morse of Mango Materials, and her founder story, I think it's important for us to get some quick perspective to better understand exactly when you and I are living across the vast timescales of human history.

∞

Earth's geological timeline is split into several main parts called eras. Each era is split into periods, and each period is divided into a number of epochs.

Right now, we are living in an epoch known as the Anthropocene, which basically translates to a time when the Earth's environment is *significantly* impacted by the presence and will of the human race. I don't know how you feel about this, but I find it both extremely exciting and absolutely terrifying. I guess it depends on how much faith you have in collective humanity.

Paul Crutzen, the Nobel prize-winning scientist who actually coined the human-dominated term for this epoch, stated that "this name change [from the previous twelve-thousand-year Holocene epoch during which human civilization originally sprouted] stresses the enormity of humanity's responsibility as stewards of the Earth."[1]

Even though we know we are currently living in it, we have difficulty pinpointing exactly when the Anthropocene began. Nearly every scientist agrees about humanity's impact on the environment,

---

1   Carrington, Damian. "The Anthropocene Epoch: Scientists Declare Dawn of Human-Influenced Age." *The Guardian*, Guardian News and Media. August 29, 2016.

but the nature of various scientific fields has led to some differing opinions about where to place the official Anthropogenic stamp on Earth's timeline.

From a biological perspective, some hypothesize that the ball began rolling some fifty thousand years ago when humans burned down forests and hunted animals to extinction—so long, giant kangaroos.[2] But most suggested starting dates are far more recent: the 1600s, 1800s, and even the 1900s. Let's quickly look at each.

The 1600s: Colonialism leading up to the seventeenth century left a dark shadow in human history with mass deaths from disease and slavery. But these dark times were like a rejuvenating face mask for the environment! Human catastrophe allowed regrowth of vegetation on lands previously used for farming, leading to a measurable decrease in atmospheric CO_2 levels around 1610.[3] This direct correlation between decreasing human presence and decreasing CO_2 levels presents solid evidence of humans' impact on the world.

The 1800s: The early nineteenth century is also claimed to be a good candidate due to the rapid industrialization that negatively affected the environment and increased those CO_2 levels right back up again thanks to fossil fuels.[4] During Britain's Industrial Revolution, landscapes close to cities were so soot-covered that they caused British peppered moths to change from their normal white color to a black pigmentation in order to blend in. This is a great example of humans completely altering natural selection pressures, which in this case favored mutations for dark coloration in moths to avoid predation.[5]

Lastly, the 1900s: Perhaps the most agreed upon time to mark the beginning of the Anthropocene is the mid-twentieth century. This is when various scientific disciplines can agreeably converge based upon their own qualifying criteria. You see, for geologists, concrete signals

---

2   Biello, David. "Did the Anthropocene Begin in 1950 or 50,000 Years Ago?" *Scientific American*, April 2, 2015.

3   Lewis, Simon L, and Maslin, Mark A. "A Transparent Framework for Defining the Anthropocene Epoch." *The Anthropocene Review*, vol. 2, no. 2, 2015, pp. 128–146.

4   Steffen, Will, et al. "The Anthropocene:" *Environment and Society.* December, 2007, pp. 12–31.

5   Webb, Jonathan. "Famous Peppered Moth's Dark Secret Revealed." *BBC News*, BBC. June 1, 2016.

need to show up in the global geological record in order to make a distinction between epochs.[6] The best signal to check off that box corresponds to nuclear bomb tests (and their resulting radioactive particles being spread out across the planet) in the mid-1900s.[7] This "Great Acceleration," as Crutzen calls it, brought about by nuclear waste and rapid technological advancement post-World War II, is the most widely accepted time to mark the transition from the Holocene into the Anthropocene.

No matter where the specific starting point goes down in the textbooks, though, we have more signals now than ever before that tell of the alarming power humans wield over the fate of the planet. Atmospheric changes, deforestation, mass extinctions, rising sea levels, incredible amounts of damaging marine plastic, and more all show us how we're having more impact on Earth than any other animal in known history. And as the adage goes: "With great power comes great responsibility."

Encouragingly today, with new advancements in biotechnology, we are not only able to recognize the wrongs of our historical past, but we are also able to right a few of them as well, thereby redefining our relationship with the Earth to shape a better present and inspired future.

∞

For example, humans have driven many species to critical endangerment and even extinction. It is now within our grasp to genetically rescue or even resurrect species in some cases that humans have negatively impacted. We can do this with cutting-edge genetic engineering tools, which we will discuss forward from chapter 7. We will also talk about renowned Harvard professor George Church and non-profit Revive & Restore, some of the world leaders in the spaces of genetic rescue and de-extinction, later in chapters 9 and 10.

6   Stromberg, Joseph. "What Is the Anthropocene and Are We in It?" *Smithsonian.com*, Smithsonian Institution. January 1, 2013.

7   Carrington, Damian. "The Anthropocene Epoch: Scientists Declare Dawn of Human-Influenced Age." *The Guardian*, Guardian News and Media. August 29, 2016.

Biotech is also enabling us to move away from one of the most environmentally detrimental practices in our society—relying on an animal-based economy for foods and materials. We can apply medical-grade tissue engineering and food-grade microbial production (just like brewing beer) to create protein-rich foods and goods without the methane-producing machines commonly known as cows. There is a multi-trillion-dollar market to improve the food and materials space around the world in this way, and it is currently taking off not only in Silicon Valley, but also globally as we see more support from forward-thinking governments like Israel, Japan, USA, UK, Singapore, and more.

Additionally, microbes are being used to help solve the impending food crises predicted to occur from the rising population by increasing crop yields. Simultaneously, bacteria can help protect crops from pests and diseases naturally, thereby vastly reducing our reliance on harmful agricultural chemicals and leading to countless beneficial outcomes in a sort of domino effect down the line. This is just the tip of the iceberg too. There is so much more to be optimistic about—bioremediation, solving infertility, tackling invasive species, etc.—and we will delve into all of it as deeply as we can within the scope of this book.

As amazing as these prospects are, what really excites me now, and will hopefully invigorate you as well, is that the biotechnology and entrepreneurial culture we have today is allowing small groups of individuals to take on established industries and affect more positive global change at a faster rate than was previously thought possible.

Through the efforts of those who think BIG and have the mindset to improve the world around them out of curiosity and their intrinsic sense of duty, we are seeing a major shift toward the power of the few to help solve the problems of the many. Synthetic biology (a.k.a. synbio: applying engineering principles to biological systems) and sustainability founders are truly saving the world, and you will hear the stories, impacts, and visions for the bio-based future from the amazing Gene-trepreneurs profiled and interviewed in this book. Some of them have even made it onto the *Inc.* and *Forbes* "30 under 30" lists!

For this reason, I think we really do have cause for hope. There are a rising number of synbio and sustainability superheroes like our first featured Gene-trepreneur and her inspiring tale, but of course, more are always needed. It's time to bring all hands on deck to change our current circumstances for the better. "Avengers assemble…"[8]

Main Takeaway:
It's an exciting time to be alive, and it's truly do or die.
— Humanity has come to a crossroads in our relationship with the world around us, and it's going to be mutual success or mutual destruction.

Mango Materials and Finding Nemo

"And I was floored … completely horrified," Molly Morse told NPR. "It changed my life and I was like that is freaking ridiculous, and I'm going to change it."

What was so horrific?

"There was this huge, gigantic-like fish-tank-type structure full of clamshells, like [plastic foam] clamshells from McDonald's," she recalls.[9]

That simple scene horrified an elementary-school-aged girl so much that she'd go on to found an incredibly promising company dedicated to ridding the world of the massive problem she witnessed that day. Dr. Molly Morse of Mango Materials is a biopolymer Gene-trepreneur.

Morse and her startup Mango Materials produce biopolymers to create plastic replacements that are cost competitive with traditional, polluting, and generally petroleum-based varieties. She founded the company in 2010 out of Stanford University and has grown it into a multi-million-dollar operation since. Their technology has the potential to revolutionize the plastic replacement industry with a product that is carbon-neutral and can help tip the scales in Mother Nature's favor. And to give you some context into the great problem

---

8   *Avengers: Age of Ultron.* Directed by Josh Whedon. Performed by Robert Downey Jr., Chris Evans, Scarlett Johanssen. Marvel Studios. May 1, 2015.

9   Joyce, Christopher. "Replacing Plastic: Can Bacteria Help Us Break The Habit?" NPR. NPR, June 17, 2019.

that Mango Materials is posed to help solve, let's take a quick dive into the world's oceans.

∞

Our oceans are absolutely littered with plastics. Go to the world's most desolate islands or into the deepest ocean ravines and you will certainly find plastic and man-made trash scattered about. If you venture to any beach in the Pacific especially, you will likely see garbage washed up along the shore in vast quantities due to the countries that surround this body of water and the ocean's natural currents.

But this is nothing compared to the huge conglomeration of trash you'll find offshore in an area called the Great Pacific Garbage Patch (GPGP). Sitting at three times the size of France in the middle of the Pacific Ocean, the GPGP is filled with plastic waste, fishing equipment, and tsunami debris that is a gauntlet of death for wildlife to mistakenly consume and become entrapped within. It's also still growing.

By 2025, it is estimated that the output of plastic into the world's oceans will be around 155 million metric tons.[10] To contextualize this, the average weight of an adult person is 137 pounds, which means that the mass of plastic going into the oceans will be equivalent to almost 2.5 billion people (about one-third of the world's current population) every year.[11] Isn't that crazy?

However, all hope is not lost as progress is being made.

Many solutions today include government policies taxing plastic bags or banning single-use plastics like the United Kingdom is planning to do.[12] Enterprising individuals have also turned to making products like the 4ocean bracelets that advertise themselves as taking one pound of plastic out of the ocean for each bracelet made.[13]

---

10   Liu, Marian. "Great Pacific Garbage Patch Now Three Times the Size of France." *CNN*, Cable News Network, March 23, 2018.

11   Quilty-Harper, Conrad. "The World's Fattest Countries: How Do You Compare?" *The Telegraph*, June 2012.

12   Chiorando, Maria. "UK Government Announces Plans To Ban Single-Use Plastics." *RSS*, 26 Oct. 2018.

13   4ocean. "4ocean Is Actively Cleaning Our Oceans and Coastlines."

Furthermore, the Seabin Project is essentially a floating waste bin that sucks up trash in harbors before it gets swept out to sea.

Additionally, a large-scale operation by The Ocean Cleanup is getting underway. The operation involves dragging what looks like an extremely large pool noodle with a ten-foot hanging skirt below it across the water in a U-shape to capture and tow all debris to an area where it can be collected and removed. The Ocean Cleanup states that when fully deployed, their operation can expect to remove about 50 percent of the GPGP every five years, which is brilliant![14]

We certainly need to support a variety of ways to clean up this marine crisis and to help prevent more sea creatures from dying. We also need to keep what is currently out in the oceans from breaking down into dangerous microplastics.

Synthetic biology actually offers a promising solution to this called bioremediation wherein microbes can be selected for, or even engineered, to more efficiently consume plastics. Bacteria have long been breaking down leaking hydrocarbons (what plastic is chemically made of) from the seafloor as food, so it's nothing new. But humans can take advantage of them to employ this bioremediation process where we have congregated high quantities of plastic, such as in land-fills, or when we want to clean water, like in water treatment plants, for oil spills, etc.

Microbes can be immensely helpful machines, like little Roombas for the sea, to help remove dangerous toxins from the environment. But it cannot all be about cleaning up the mess we've made. We have to fix problems at their sources too, and that's where companies like Mango Materials can really shine.

Mango Materials is using methanotrophs, a type of methane-consuming bacteria, to convert methane gas (heavily responsible for global warming) into polyhydroxyalkanoate (PHA) polymers. These biopolymers can be crafted into biodegradable replacements for a wide variety of commercial uses including packaging, cosmetics, apparel, and more. It is not an easy feat though!

14   Ocean Cleanup. "The World's First Ocean Cleanup System Launched from San Francisco." *The Ocean Cleanup*, September 8, 2018.

Dr. Morse is accomplishing this via gas fermentation, meaning that bacteria are taking the methane right off your local wastewater treatment plant and formulating it into these carbon-based polymers beneath their cell walls—kind of like chipmunks stuffing their cheeks. Typically, fermentation requires sugars in solution, like in the beer-brewing process, so you have to be clever about fermenting from gas.

Furthermore, these methanotrophs are not readily industrialized, so they basically must be trained for the job. You might think this training would include genetic engineering to buff up the microbes' carbon-fixation capabilities, but at Mango Materials not much genetic engineering is actually required because Dr. Morse has been doing controlled selection of these bacteria since the company's founding to improve their efficiency. It's like choosing between steroids to build muscle rapidly or consistently working out. And these bacteria have been hitting the gym for a long time getting buff. (In fact, you may see them come out with their own annual calendar sometime soon just like those annual firefighter calendars—which methanotrophs will be Mr. / Mrs. January through December?)

Interestingly, the biopolymers at Mango are also specially formulated depending on the intended end use—whether the PHA polymer will be used with injection molds to create packaging or will be fiber extruded to create filaments for apparel.

Dr. Morse says that about 90 percent of their time and energy is now focused on creating PHA fibers for apparel because Mango's primary concern is with plastic in the marine environment. According to the company's site, 60 percent of clothing contains polyester (which is plastic-based) and only 17 percent of our clothes are recycled. The other thirty billion pounds of textiles are discarded into landfills where the plastic breaks into small pieces that leach into our water supply.[15]

Additionally, many small polyester fibers come out of our clothes during normal, everyday wash cycles. These fibers then find their way into the oceans where they are consumed by small organisms and make their way up the food chain into humans, not to mention the

---

15   "Applications." *Mango Materials.*

damage they impose on sea life in their own right. The great thing about Mango's process is that the biopolymers they create are biodegradable (meaning prone to enzymatic attack), therefore minimizing the microplastic threat to wildlife and us.

If an animal, like a sea turtle for example, consumes any (as they are often known to mistake pieces of plastic for jellyfish—a very delectable food item if you are a sea turtle), in the long run they won't be harmed. Crush, Squirt, and the rest of the *Finding Nemo* turtle gang riding the East Australian Current (EAC) will definitely owe Mango a fin tap and noggin bump of gratitude.[16]

Obviously, it's better if these materials have a chance to be recycled so the methane can be recaptured and turned into biopolymer-based products once more. But again, if any of Mango's polymers happen to end up in the oceans, there are plenty of microorganisms to break them down safely.

Business-wise, Mango Materials is very competitive with traditional PHA plastics, but the problem, as with most biotech companies, comes with scaling up. (Biotech is generally pretty expensive compared to building a software as a service—a.k.a. SaaS—business as they require lab equipment, lab space, reagents, scientific software, etc.)[17] Dr. Morse says the greatest challenge the company faces is acquiring funding to scale.

Mango Materials generates plenty of interest from investors, but the issue is angels and venture capitalists (a.k.a. VCs) want quick returns, and the cost of equipment to expand Mango's operation is not cheap. Additionally, investors want to see the concept proven over a long period of time. The company currently has years of data as they have been employing their technology in the field since 2015 in an anaerobic digester (no oxygen) at a Redwood City, California, waste treatment plant. Dr. Morse says they will likely be there for another year or two but will then build a larger unit if everything works out with their funding model.

---

16   *Finding Nemo*. Directed by Andrew Stanton. Performed by Ellen Degeneres and Alexander Gould. Pixar Animation Studios. May 30, 2003.

17   Hyde, Embriette. "Building Synthetic Biology Companies at Scale: Practical Advice from Seasoned Investors and Entrepreneurs." *SynBioBeta*, September 19, 2018.

Very promisingly, though, Dr. Morse stated that even within the past six months, she has seen a massive change in the demand for plastic replacement. It stems from growing consumer awareness brought about by National Geographic and other organizations drawing attention to the huge issue of plastic pollution.[18] As demand grows, financial backing of biopolymer companies like Mango Materials will likely see a substantial boost. It's really about playing the long game for the good of the world and not about making a quick buck.

I really believe that Mango Materials with Dr. Morse at the helm can have an extraordinary impact on sustainability and is employing exactly the right strategy by focusing their efforts in apparel. Since their biopolymer can be extruded into filaments and incorporated into clothing like traditional polyester, there are countless opportunities in the truly colossal fashion and textile industries. And I have a brief personal story related to this next.

But first, I also want to pass this question off to you. Given the choice between purchasing a normal cotton/polyester blend shirt or one with Mango's biopolymer in it (and assuming similar price points), which one would you choose?

Grad Gown Gifts and Black Hole Closets

Coming out of my senior year of college, I dedicated a couple of months to working on a "side-hustle" if you will to reduce some of the plastic-based fabric waste I witnessed coming from the graduation industry.

Every year in the US, more than 3.6 million students graduate from high schools and 3.7 million students graduate from various college programs, plus all of the children who have middle school, elementary, and kindergarten / pre-k ceremonies utilizing gowns as well.[19] Most of the graduation apparels (caps and gowns) are made out of single-use, plastic-based polyester and are simply worn to take pictures in and walk across a stage.

---

18   Treat, Jason, et al. "We Depend On Plastic. Now, We're Drowning in It." *We Depend on Plastic. Now We're Drowning in It.*, May 16, 2018.

19   "The NCES Fast Facts Tool Provides Quick Answers to Many Education Questions (National Center for Education Statistics)." *National Center for Education Statistics (NCES) Home Page, a Part of the U.S. Department of Education.*

Ask yourself, if your school did not offer rentable, re-usable graduation apparel, what did you do with your overpriced, single-use cap and gown? After that momentary usage, most are typically thrown into the garbage or tossed into that black hole of a closet or drawer you've got never to be seen again (at least until you move and decide to finally throw them away because they don't "spark joy" for you anymore).[20]

I thought of this startup idea about one hundred days before graduation and called it Grad Gown Gifts. The mission was to recycle caps and gowns into personalized keepsakes post-graduation (throw pillows, decorative caps, signing frames, etc.) so they wouldn't end up in landfills like the millions that already call those places home. It was like the 4ocean bracelets removing plastic from the ocean but for grad apparel.

∞

My vision for the company was to become a hybrid between Shutterfly (a company where you send them pictures and receive a scrapbook) and online artist-based marketplaces like Design By Humans, Society6, Threadless, or in some cases Etsy (where artists and artisans sell their craft from personal online storefronts).

And since you should always have an exit plan, even when you first begin a startup endeavor, my proposed exit strategy, if successful, was to sell it to Jostens—a behemoth supplier of graduation apparel, or a similar enterprise down the line. I thought it would be perfect for a company like Jostens because they could sell their apparel products on the front end and then recycle them into personalized keepsakes as an environmentally beneficial, back-end business too. It would make them more of a company with a cause.

But when you look deeper into it, what would have stopped Jostens from just replacing me? What barriers to entry were in place preventing them from doing their own version of Grad Gown Gifts?

My advantage was weak: being ingrained in the university infrastructure as a student/recent graduate while Jostens was already a

---

20   *Tidying Up with Marie Kondo.* Netflix, 2019.

widely distributed grad apparel brand with relationships established around the country. I could have also possibly applied for a patent on a frame design to house graduation caps in place of the felt backing, but they could have come up with their own version just as easily. And I thought perhaps my company would be so small that Jostens wouldn't want to invest their time and money into setting up their own operation when it would be cheaper to acquire me or let me keep taking a small cut of the pie. But if it was small forever, it wouldn't really be creating the desired BIG impact, would it?

Additionally, I ran into many problems with the supply chain (contract manufacturing, the insane cost of personalized framing, licensing art, building an artist base, finding quality content from the public domain, etc.). For example, I went to a local framing shop to inquire about pricing for a ten-by-ten-inch custom frame. From this small local business, I was quoted approximately $45 each. I also ventured to a well-known craft store—that may or may not have been the name of the regional manager of Dunder Mifflin's Scranton branch—and they quoted me around $90, which included a substantial discount from a custom framing sale they were running at the time! Ridiculous, right?

Looking at the insight from potential customers I had obtained (mainly freshman college students straight out of high school), most said they would pay something like $25 for a framed decorative cap. The custom framing cost alone, not to mention the price of shipping, the labor costs for artists/artisans, licensing, etc., made this absolutely impractical on a small-scale to run. And if I somehow managed to figure the supply chain and financials out, again, what would stop a big graduation apparel company like Jostens from copying the process over to their infrastructure?

There were many other considerations, and I learned many valuable things from the process. But in the end, Grad Gown Gifts was not meant to be.

However, even though Grad Gown Gifts did not fully come to fruition and was not an endeavor in synthetic biology (simply satisfying my passion to aid in sustainability), I am so grateful I pursued the idea because it taught me that some problems do not have viable business fixes on the back end; usually the best way to solve a problem is at its roots.

In this case, the option far better than Grad Gown Gifts would be to use a more eco-friendly, biodegradable material to tackle the problem at its source in the cap and gown manufacturing process— something like gas fermentation with microbes perhaps? And this is exactly what Dr. Morse is so well-positioned to accomplish with Mango Materials. If anyone from Jostens reads this, please reach out to her.

The best outcome of this project was that it led me to attend an entrepreneurship conference in NYC called Next Gen Summit. There, I encountered entrepreneur Eric Koester, who inspired me to write this book, which has driven me to connect with so many amazing synbio and sustainability startup founders and experts you will read about in the upcoming chapters. This personal experience also goes to show that entrepreneurial failures, even small ones, can lead you to your next big thing in unexpected ways. Onward and upward!

Main Takeaways:

If you desire long-term returns, make sure your endeavor is in a space with barriers-to-entry or you'll get eaten up alive.

- For example, nothing was really stopping people from selling fidget spinners in their heyday, was there? Heck, I even sold 3D-printed fidget spinners for a course project, and my team raked in $1,500+ over a couple of weeks.

One company's profitable, back-end fix to a sustainability problem is not 100% transferable to your back-end fix to a sustainability problem—in my case, 4ocean bracelets versus my endeavor with Grad Gown Gifts.

- However, note that if you believe you have something worthwhile, you *must* put in all the ground work—including the very important step of asking your potential customers questions to find out if you're actually solving a meaningful pain point.
- You will learn a lot more by taking action and asking questions rather than simply stewing on a stagnant idea.

Failing at one thing can lead to your next BIG one; you truly never know what lies around the corner for you so always keep pushing forward
- But at the same time, be reflective and smart about choosing your next steps so you can be efficient with your time and energy—as famed author Neil Gaiman would say, "Does it bring you closer to your mountain?"[21]

A Note to the Reader

Through consuming all of the plant and cell-based meaty content in the upcoming chapters, my hope is that you will learn and become truly inspired to get involved in this magical space in whatever way you choose.

Whether simply by talking more about biotech and sustainability with friends and family, writing a paper, article, or book, joining a lab or club, helping out on the financial side of these endeavors, or pursuing one of your own inspired ideas, please know that no matter your background, no matter your age, you can join the cause and help drive the development of our bio-based future.

We're all in this together, and your part can be as little or big as you want to make it.

The rest of the chapters are structured similarly to this introduction in that we'll mostly deep-dive into the sustainability challenges followed by a discussion of the amazing Gene-trepreneurs and start-ups rising to meet them.

And now that your feet are wet, let's do one giant cannonball into the pool of STEM and sustainability; off to chapter 1!

---

21   Gaiman, Neil. "Neil Gaiman: Keynote Address 2012." University of the Arts. May 17, 2012.

CHAPTER 1

CLEAN SEAFOOD PART I: A SEA OF SUSTAINABILITY CHALLENGES AND FISH DEATH STARS

You know how in *Back to the Future Part II*, Marty McFly and Doc Brown travel to 2015 where hoverboards and flying cars are the norm?[1] Well, looking back now that was a bit ambitious, right? But hey, we're getting there!

Shockingly, all the way back in 1932 (as we touched upon in the preface), Winston Churchill had a similarly ambitious prediction about the future of food in an article titled "Fifty Years Hence": "We shall escape the absurdity of growing a whole chicken in order to eat a breast or a wing, by growing these parts separately under a suitable medium."[2] Churchill went on to affirm that "... the new foods will be practically indistinguishable from the natural products from the outset, and any changes will be so gradual as to escape observation."

Today, this is exactly the world we are immeasurably close to living in with what is being called clean, cell-based, or cell-cultured meat.

Obviously, it's a little later than the fifty years Churchill predicted when he mentioned this in 1932, but better late than never! I wholeheartedly wish that Winston Churchill's forecast had come to fruition in a timelier manner, though. For the first ten years of my life, my parents managed to convince me I had been eating "vegetarian meat"—real meat that didn't require animals to be killed. Cell-based

---

1   *Back to the Future Part II*. Directed by Robert Zemeckis. Performed by Michael J. Fox and Christopher Lloyd. Universal Pictures. November 22, 1989.

2   "Fifty Years Hence (Popular Mechanics, 1932)." New Harvest. January 15, 2016.

meat wasn't even on the cusp of commercialization at this point. And to say the least, I was very surprised when I found out the truth.

Maybe you can relate to this brief childhood story before we get to the "meat" of this chapter.

∞

Growing up watching Animal Planet shows such as *The Jeff Corwin Experience* and *The Crocodile Hunter*, I *really* grew to love animals; I treasured the pictures I'd get in my monthly *Ranger Rick* wildlife magazines. I also grew up in the woods of New Jersey watching deer, bears, turkeys, and the like with a beloved yellow lab named Lexi. Being surrounded by animals, I felt no desire to eat them. In fact, even as a child it seemed odd to me why I or anyone else would want to consume another living thing. I've since changed a bit becoming a slight form of pescatarian, meaning okay with seafood, which admittedly is a step in the less sustainable direction, but this chapter is about breaking all this down.

My parents wanted me to have a protein-rich diet to be a healthy, growing boy so they fed me beef and chicken and called it "vegetarian meat." I believed this until fourth grade when my teacher, Ms. Henderson, told me vegetarian meat didn't exist. Even though I always had classmates tell me they'd never heard of it before either, no adult had previously given me reason to question this animal-free meat. It's kind of like the legend of Santa Claus *spoiler alert*. Lots of kids say they found out he wasn't real in elementary school, but you don't really believe those naysayer kids until you're told the truth from a credible adult or discover your "presents from Santa" hidden in the trunk of your mom's car two weeks before Christmas. Ms. Henderson's skepticism in my ten-year-old assertions made me inquire to my parents, who then spilled the beans (which I should have promptly made into a black bean burger).

Fortunately for children today who share in the same mindset I had growing up, the alternative protein revolution now emerging will allow them to consume plant-based and clean, cell-cultured meats like never before.

Unlike bean and other conventional veggie burgers, some really phenomenal companies like Impossible Foods and Beyond Meat are coming up with novel, plant-based burgers that "bleed" (which we'll talk about in detail in chapter 3).

At the same time, other startups are cultivating *real* animal tissue with cutting-edge, medical-grade technology (the same used to grow human tissue and organs for life-saving procedures). The result of this tech is meat molecularly identical to animal-derived versions, except it is made to taste better, be more nutritious, and have no toxins or agricultural chemicals (not to mention already being better ethically and for the environment). Plus, it won't require billions of animals to be farmed and harmed. It's a brilliant win-win-win all around—truly a "have your cake and eat it too" option for agricultural and wild animals, the environment, and for us hungry but still health-conscious humans.

Another really cool aspect with synbio upgrading the meat industry is that alternative protein startups are making sustainable foods so much more inclusive by catering to everyone's unique tastes and preferred diets: passionate meat-lovers, vegans, vegetarians, the Jewish community, and so many others will all have options on par with and eventually exceeding traditionally harvested proteins.[3] It's extremely thrilling because this new era of food production will monumentally improve our global sustainability, which as we know, is urgently needed.

Even Bill and Melinda Gates, two of the most important, knowledgeable, and charitable people of our time, are also throwing their support behind cell-based meats. They're doing this alongside other movers and shakers such as Richard Branson.

Bill Gates, when writing in regard to feeding the growing population set to reach 9.6 billion by 2050, stated, "Put simply, there's no way to produce enough meat for nine billion people. Yet we can't ask everyone to become vegetarians. That's why we need more options for producing meat without depleting our resources."[4]

3   Friedrich, Bruce. "Why Clean Meat Is Kosher." *The Good Food Institute.* June 22, 2017.

4   Morgan, Rick. "Bill Gates and Richard Branson Are Betting Lab-Grown Meat May Be the Food of the Future." *CNBC.* March 23, 2018.

Right on, Mr. Gates, right on.

∞

But how does this food innovation apply to the world's oceans? Can we really produce higher quality seafood products? And what exactly are the big dangers for us and wildlife in the seafood industry as it stands anyway?

For one, mercury levels pose a very real threat to those who rely on seafood—human or otherwise. Oceanic mercury levels have more than tripled since the Industrial Revolution, primarily due to human activity. The greatest mercury disaster to date came to Minamata, Japan, in the 1960s after chemical plants dumped the dangerous element into the ocean.[5] Over the following years, thousands of villagers became ill, died, and even had children with birth defects all due to consuming mercury-laden seafood. Fortunately, in the past several years more than one hundred countries have come together to sign the Minamata Convention on Mercury to curb the addition of even more into the oceans by humans.

Although the worst mercury disaster was over half a century ago, the downstream effects are still present today. This is especially prevalent when people consume a lot of king mackerel, swordfish, marlin, shark, tuna, and other predatory varieties as these fish feed on many smaller mercury-containing species. The element congregates into larger and larger amounts as you move up the food chain. So when you eat a lot of these top-tier fish, you become the next congregation point for all that dangerous mercury to get passed along to you.[6] Yikes!

Another huge concern in the seafood industry, as we briefly touched upon in the introduction, is microplastics. All of the plastic that ends up in our lakes, rivers, and oceans degrades into microscopic bits, with many microplastics coming directly from clothing fabrics going through everyday wash cycles.

---

5   You, Jia. "Mercury Levels in Surface Ocean Have Tripled." *Science*. December 10, 2017.

6   Brown, Mary Jane. "Should You Avoid Fish Because of Mercury?" *Healthline*. September 14, 2016.

Small creatures ingest these microplastics, and just as with mercury, the amount builds up as you ascend the food chain.[7] No human wants to consume plastic along with their food unless they're one of those unusual people on *My Strange Addiction* snacking on TV remotes and newspaper bags. Plastic also hurts the wildlife that it ends up in (shellfish, sea birds, fish, etc.) by compromising their immune systems, affecting growth rates, diminishing their ability to successfully reproduce, and clogging their digestive systems, which can absolutely lead to death.[8]

The problem for us and wildlife will only go away if we attack the issue at its origin, much like our first Gene-trepreneur, Dr. Molly Morse at Mango Materials, working to provide better options to companies in materials sourcing and manufacturing. Of course, it's also important to support large-scale endeavors like The Ocean Cleanup with their high-tech pool noodles too because the spout that plastic pollution is spewing out of won't just be abruptly shut off; it'll be a slow trickle that we will be wiping up with our metaphorical Sham-Wows for generations to come.

The total amount of plastic waste currently within and being added to our oceans is rapidly growing, and until we stop or at least greatly minimize the outflow, we must realize that when the water our seafood comes from is polluted with plastic, we ingest some of that plastic too. And you're no remote eater, are you?

Overfishing and Cod Bless You
Aside from mercury and microplastics, perhaps the largest problem in the wild-caught seafood industry is overfishing. Trawling for certain fish and shellfish often kills many other animals in the process. Dolphins, seals, sea turtles, sharks, whales, and many more species become caught in the nets and drown. Nobody really knows the actual number of animals that die by-catch either because the

---

7   Parker, Laura. "Ocean Life Eats Tons of Plastic-Here's Why That Matters." *National Geographic.* August 18, 2017.

8   Thompson, Andrea. "From Fish to Humans, A Microplastic Invasion May Be Taking a Toll." *Scientific American.* September 4, 2018.

majority of it happens off-shore and is undocumented. But research-ers estimate that by-catch in the US alone could be up to two billion pounds.[9]

Beyond the tragedy of by-catch in and of itself, fishing gear is also commonly lost beneath the waves. When these huge fishing nets, sometimes miles long, are lost in the ocean, they don't stop doing their jobs. These "ghost nets" keep snaring fish and other creatures in them for as long as they are below the surface, and it can take many years, decades, or even longer before they degrade and stop the cycle of killing.[10]

Apart from the unintentional casualties in the fishing industry, the overfishing of high-demand target species—like bluefin tuna, for example—has driven many seafood varieties to the brink. Too many are harvested to maintain healthy populations. The good thing is that agencies create fishing limits so that depending on location, vessel, and permit type, anglers can only catch a certain number of bluefin tuna per day or overall trip to help protect wild numbers.[11]

Fascinatingly, in the past many fishermen were restricted to keeping fish of a minimum length depending on the species, which allowed juveniles to grow. However, this ultimately backfired because it removed the fertile, big fish out of the gene pool. Many fish varieties today have become smaller on average, as well as more shy and not producing as many offspring as a result.[12] Policies have now changed to prevent anglers and commercial operations from taking the largest members of specific species to ensure their conservation. Unfortu-nately, these measures don't always work. One example that hits quite close to home for the Brits is their iconic fish 'n' chips.

∞

9   Keledjian, Amanda, Gib Brogan, Beth Lowell, Jon Warrenchuk, et al. "Wasted Catch: Unsolved Problem in US Fisheries." *Oceana*, March 2014.

10 "Ghost Nets, among the Greatest Killers in Our Oceans..." *Mission Blue*, May 23, 2013.

11 NOAA. "Bluefin Tuna Angling Category Daily Retention Limit Adjustment." *NOAA Fisheries*, April 23, 2018.

12 Uusi-Heikkila, Silva, et al. "The Evolutionary Legacy of Size Selective Harvesting Extends from Genes to Populations." *Evolutionary Applications*, John Wiley & Sons, Ltd (10.1111), 27 May 2015.

Cod numbers dropped 90 percent between 1971 and 2004 (oh my Cod!), and overfishing has made it hard for their numbers to bounce back quickly.[13] This is further compounded by warming ocean temperatures due to anthropogenic (human-derived) climate change, as British waters are now becoming more suitable for some Mediterranean species while cod move northward to find colder climes.

Since catching cod will become more difficult as marine temperatures continue to climb, Dr. John Pinnegar, who led a study at the UK's Centre for Environment, Fisheries and Aquaculture Science, said he "would anticipate that currently small-scale fisheries targeting warm-water species such as squid, sardine and anchovy will continue to expand" and that "they will probably represent a greater share of the UK fisheries catches in ten years' time."[14]

So you know what that means? Get ready for squid 'n' chips everybody! (Which actually doesn't sound that bad, does it—calamari and french fries might even be something Rachael Ray would call "delish" or would make it into Binging with Babish's "Clean Plate Club.")[15]

Some people may also try to create aquaculture farms to rear cod, but this has been attempted before with minimal large-scale success. Today, salmon and tilapia are the most popular fish in aquafarming environments, but it took a while for humans to transition from fishing the oceans and rivers to raising them in fisheries.

Interestingly, as stated by aquaculture expert Paul Greenberg, World War II actually had an *enormous* impact on the seafood industry. During the war, fish populations were able to significantly increase because fishing vessels were under threat of being blown up by underwater mines or Nazi U-boats on the prowl. But after the war, new military technologies such as sonar, which was previously employed to detect enemy submarines, became embraced by fishermen to find schools of fish, thereby dooming many fish populations forever more.[16] So yeah, Nazi Germany was good for fish the same

---

13 Kentish, Benjamin. "Fish and Chips Are Being Replaced by Something Much More Disgusting." *The Independent*, Independent Digital News and Media, December 12, 2016.

14 Ibid.

15 *Binging with Babish*. YouTube.

16 "The Future Of 'Wild Fish,' The Last Wild Food." *NPR*, NPR, July 1, 2011.

way the DMZ, that highly militarized border between North and South Korea, is pretty much a wildlife sanctuary.[17]

To provide you with some context, in the 1950s, what Greenberg refers to as the total "fishing effort" exploded. Twenty million metric tons of fish were caught every year. A couple of decades later, however, we began transitioning more into aquaculture because wild stocks were plummeting. These farmed fish could be cultivated in high numbers in small, defined areas, which was a big plus for fishery owners because they didn't have to spend long durations out at sea away from their bonnie lasses or be limited by catch quotas. Over time, improving aquaculture tech began allowing for more pounds of fish to be obtained per unit of water outflow, and certain species could suddenly be raised with much more success using inland tanks than in the past.

Fast-forward to today, and currently around half of the marine fish consumed in the US are farmed. The other half comprising wild-caught is equivalent to around eighty million metric tons annually, which is at the absolute carrying capacity the oceans can withstand.[18] Demand for fish has more than doubled since the 1960s (because more people plus a rise in pescatarian or similar diets), and by 2030, society's consumption is set to double once again. Even though we cannot take more from the oceans, we do not necessarily need to double-down on traditional fish-farming. It has its own host of problems, and that'd be like trading in your car with 250,000 miles on it for one that has 225,000 miles—really just exchanging one set of clunker problems for another, right?

But just like with plastics, the tap will not be turned off all at once in favor of plant and cell-based seafoods. A transition must be made, which is why there are efforts to improve traditional fish-farming by Gene-trepreneurs to make it more sustainable during this transformational period.

17   Harbage, Claire. "In Korean DMZ, Wildlife Thrives. Some Conservationists Worry Peace Could Disrupt It." NPR. NPR, April 20, 2019.

18   Greenberg, Paul. "The Four Fish We're Overeating — and What to Eat Instead | Paul Greenberg." *YouTube*, YouTube, January 13, 2016.

MicroSynbiotiX and Medical Lettuce

You've heard about the threat antibiotic resistance poses to us humans, right? The thought of getting an untreatable infection is pretty frightening. Well, fish are vulnerable to attacks from bacteria too.

Farm-raised fish are loaded up with antibiotics and growth hormones. Farmers treat their fish with antibiotics to prevent diseases and parasites in their often-overcrowded pens, but it can contribute to the ever-growing and very scary problem of antibiotic resistance.

With aquaculture for sustainable food production being the fastest growing food sector worth over two hundred billion dollars, this equates to a lot of antibiotics being introduced into the environment every year from the industry. Yet, ten billion dollars' worth of product is still lost due to disease outbreak annually.[19] Although this is only 5 percent of the total market, any improvement in disease prevention would be *massively* valuable to fish farmers. This is where a really cool company called MicroSynbiotiX comes into play.

Instead of using antibiotics, MicroSynbiotiX is creating vaccines that utilize the fish's own immune defenses to protect against illness. It's a lot better for us too because we don't ingest the antibiotics left in the fish tissue when we consume them. Traditional vaccines that you and I get at the doctor are mostly either attenuated versions of the virus that aren't strong enough to do any damage or inactivated virus particles that are just plain dead. Also, similar to us when we get our shots, fish and other aquaculture foods species on the farms are often vaccinated manually, which entails labor costs and requires the fish to be of a certain size and maturity before doing so.[20] However, new vaccine technology is on the rise that offers another method.

You may have heard about research at the University of Pennsylvania around 2014 that revolved around using lettuce to grow vaccines.[21] Led by UPenn biochemistry professor Dr. Henry Daniell, the premise was not to use the pathogens themselves at all, but instead to

---

19 "MicroSynbiotiX." *Microsynbiotix*.

20 Komar, Cedric, et al. "Understanding Fish Vaccination." *The Fish Site*, March, 21 2019.

21 Pennsylvania, University of. "Delivering Medicine Through Lettuce, World Altering Medical Advancements." *YouTube*, YouTube, April 10, 2014.

produce vaccines by injecting therapeutic proteins into lettuce cells. Once the plants produced these proteins, the leaves could then be ground up into a powder, placed into oral capsules, and stored without refrigeration for years! Normally vaccines require refrigeration to remain viable, which can become a huge problem when transporting to rural areas around the world.

Dr. Daniell and his research team have since been able to produce over thirty vaccines in this unique way with lettuce cells, which is going to revolutionize the way we vaccinate the globe.

MicroSynbiotiX took this same premise and applied it to aquaculture vaccines. Instead of lettuce, though, they have engineered transgenic microalgae to produce the necessary proteins (basically using the algae as 3D printing machines and programmed them to print out these specific, useful proteins).[22] The ideal outcome of their tech is to vastly lessen aquaculture's dependence on antibiotics.

Interestingly, they got their start by entering and winning the 2017 Nutreco Feed Tech Challenge. After their triumph, they received sponsorship from Nutreco that enabled them to run their first animal trials for their initial vaccine candidate. The team was also able to close a one-million-euro seed round.

Main Takeaways:

Putting yourself and your idea out there can be so rewarding because you never know who you'll meet and what will come out of it.

- Even if you don't win a pitch contest, you might spark the interest of an investor in the audience or find someone who can make a key connection with a financial backer, mentor, or others who may become valuable assets to your team.

Also, don't be afraid to shoot your idea out into the universe because you're fearful someone may steal it. Only be worried if someone *will actually* do something about it, and even then, if somebody does take action, there's likely plenty of room for you both in the arena.

- The more people working to open up a novel space → the more value can be carved out of it → the more valuable the piece you take home can be worth.

---

22   "MicroSynbiotiX." *Microsynbiotix.*

You don't have to create some brilliant, entirely new idea.
- If you can take a concept like creating vaccines from lettuce for humans and transfer it over to creating vaccines with algae for fish, you can develop a successful endeavor too.
- So take ideas from different sources and roll them over into a field where you can create value and make an impact. That's a winning formula!

InnovaSea Systems and Kampachi Farms

Aquaculture as we've discussed it is usually inland or utilizing nearby coastal waters, but what if we could venture out into the great expanse of the open ocean where there are no bays to be fouled by highly concentrated groups of fish? It'd be like taking fish to space. "Ground control to Major Tom..."[23]

Steve Page of Ocean Farm Technologies (which merged with another company to create InnovaSea Systems), while not on the biotech side of being a Gene-trepreneur, certainly checks off the box in the sustainability aspect. He has been a very important figure in the effort to move near-shore fish farms out to sea, essentially sending fish out onto their space odyssey.

Page's background as an Environmental Compliance Officer at Atlantic Salmon of Maine, a traditional fish-farming operation, allowed him see a huge pain point and inefficiency in traditional aquaculture. So many fisheries are all right on top of one another near the shore, and there is so much disease spread between pens. These pens are also anchored to the bottom where fish waste amasses because there's too much for the surrounding environment to absorb. It's really not good for the fish or the surrounding area, and after observing all the harm these fish farms are causing, Page knew that moving further offshore was really the only way to continue farming fish sustainably.

He began developing something that could bring aquaculture out into deep water. He co-designed a unique geodesic dome called the Aquapod, which can venture far out into the deep ocean. The result of doing so is much more eco and fish-friendly than traditional close-to-shore and inland fish-farming operations. One unit, if built

---

23   Bowie, David. *David Bowie: Space Oddity.* 1969.

large enough, can also house hundreds of thousands of fish in ample space. After seeing a video about the Aquapods, one witty YouTube commenter referred to them as "Death Stars for fish," which is a hilarious analogy![24] Although, hopefully the pods don't have thermal exhaust ports, which the Rebel Alliance can exploit to destroy them.

These fish Death Stars are actually made from recycled polyethylene plastic with fiberglass reinforcement, and one Aquapod contains the equivalent of 350,000 plastic milk bottles. Page and his team have proven their viability through tests and have been continually taking data points to study the fish domes in the open ocean environment. Now, the Aquapods are becoming more widely adopted amongst companies contributing to the push for more sustainable aquaculture.

One of those companies working really hard to employ Aquapods and grow their role in sustainable aquaculture is Kampachi Farms. Kampachi's team work off of the west coast of Hawaii's island of Oahu where they let the swirling currents carry their initial pod tethered to a boat anywhere from three to seventy-five miles off the coast.[25]

The Aquapods are more beneficial than traditional, stationary fish-farming operations because out deep there are no lines that drop down twelve thousand feet to anchor the enclosures in place, as well as little to no gas burned to maintain their location. And because the Aquapods are miles offshore, this not only lets the fish grow up in a cleaner, more natural habitat, but it also allows for their waste to be absorbed by the vast ocean.

Kampachi Farms, after conducting a long and comprehensive study, found that no measurable detrimental effects have resulted from the Aquapods in Hawaiian waters. This promising conclusion suggests that the calamitous algae blooms and coral garden devastation on the seafloor, as well as the rampant disease usually associated with stationary fish farms, could possibly be avoided with widespread adoption of Aquapod technology—fleets of fish Death Stars.

---

24   "Deep Sea Fish Farming in Geodesic Domes: Upgrade." *YouTube*, Motherboard, December 18, 2014.

25   EarthSky. "The Aquapod: A Free-Floating Fish Farm." *Fast Company*, Fast Company, July 24, 2012.

Addressing the previously mentioned concern of invasive species, the pods are outfitted with brass mesh that allow little chance of escapees (unless they've got Netflix showing re-runs of *Prison Break* in there). In Kampachi's case, they raise native Hawaiian fish in their pods, which is good because in the unlikely case that any escape they are native to those waters so no harm, no foul.

The sturdy mesh is also just as necessary for keeping the fish in as it is essential for keeping other animals out. The fish must have robust protection because millions of dollars' worth of farmed fish are lost every year due to predators finding their way into enclosures: sea lions, sharks, predatory fish, that weird fish man from *The Shape of Water*, etc.[26] It also helps to keep the pods together so they can withstand storms, the accompanying rough seas, and any collisions with floating debris (no Titanic situations). Additionally, the pods become a kind of floating reef that many other species congregate around, which makes them quite a happy place full of life out in the great expanse of the open ocean.

The ultimate goal with such tech is to eventually use trackable water currents to deliver the pods with automated feeding and guidance systems across entire oceans![27] This is much like Alphabet's (Google's parent company) moonshot project Loon, where they are working on balloons that travel in air currents to deliver internet to rural areas.[28] But much in the same way Loon is operating with natural air streams, the Aquapods could be outfitted with a small propeller and GPS system and navigated into the world's powerful ocean currents. They could travel thousands of miles with little fuel consumption and their buoyancy adjusted to avoid harsh waves along the way—kind of sinking it like the lost city of Atlantis and bringing it back up as necessary.

Ideally, by the time the fish reached their final destinations they could be ready or near-ready for harvest. This could become a great global success, saving a lot of money on resources, being much more

---

26   "Deep Sea Fish Farming in Geodesic Domes: Upgrade." *YouTube*, Motherboard, December 18, 2014.

27   Ibid.

28   Wells, Sarah. "Project Loon and Project Wing Graduate from X." *TechCrunch*, TechCrunch, July 12, 2018.

eco-friendly than traditional farming operations, and being healthier for the fish as well. Additionally, it could certainly help wild populations to recover their numbers too. But as exciting as floating fish Death Stars are, they alone are not the sustainable silver bullet for society's increasing demand for fish. While Aquapods are certainly an improvement, synthetic biology can offer an emerging and impressive solution that could help mitigate the negative aspects of consuming both wild and farm-raised fish altogether.

Main Takeaways:

Just like Steve Page, ask yourself what problems, pain points, and inefficiencies you're seeing in your work or daily life.

- There was an opportunity right in front of him that he was able not only to recognize but also to take action upon.
- Actions are greater than ideas.

Again, it's not about creating anything jaw-droppingly new; incremental improvements can be *powerful* too.

- Aquapods fill the void between traditional fish-farming inland / near-shore and the next step of not having many fish farms at all.
- Sometimes, if you can find your spot between what exists now and what will become—not being where the ball is and not able to get to where the ball will be yet—you can make that intermediary, mezzanine step in the right direction a sustainable, impactful, and profitable business.
- Like with Aquapods, the spigot for fish-farming won't be turned off all at once and most likely will never be completely; Aquapods are riding the trickle, and there is some decent long-term opportunity in doing so. Are there any opportunities for you to do the same?

CHAPTER 2

CLEAN SEAFOOD PART II: TUNA AND THE GENE ... WILDER

"If I can't SCUBA, then what's this all been about? What am I working toward?"[1]

—CREED, *THE OFFICE*

If traditional aquaculture is the majority baseline now, and if offshore aquaculture using technology like Aquapods is the mid-tier step, you might be starting to feel how Creed in *The Office* feels about SCUBA. What's this all been about and what are we working toward? What's the big vision?

Remember Churchill's prediction about the absurdity of growing a whole chicken for a wing or a breast and the mention of medical-grade technology to grow real tissue?

Today, Gene-trepreneurs are bringing that foresight to life by transferring cutting-edge med tech to the food sector. They are creating real, genetically identical meat to traditional, animal-derived varieties, but they will be able to do so much more with it once it begins hitting restaurant menus and supermarket shelves over the next few years. This clean, cell-based, or cell-cultured meat as it's called, can be more nutritious (more vitamins, better amino acid profiles, less cholesterol and salt, etc.) as well as better tasting because it's expertly crafted, just like beer, by the best food scientists in the biz.

---

[1] "The Office: Gossip." *The Office*, September 17, 2009.

To me, the whole space emerging around clean meat is almost like the scene in *Willy Wonka & the Chocolate Factory* (the original Gene Wilder version) when he's singing "Pure Imagination." Wherever you look around that room, it's filled with so many extraordinary possibilities, and this food innovation space is no different. Well, there's no questionably sourced workforce, and we're not losing Augustus Gloop in a chocolate river.[2] But aside from those things, pretty similar!

On top of that too, instead of just one man responsible for it all, the Wonka man himself, this field is made up of many Wonkas—growing numbers of men and women joining a community of people from all backgrounds (finance, branding, marketing, journalism, art, and of course STEM) dedicated to building the more sustainable and healthier bio-based future together.

This community in seafood specifically is working on so many exciting endeavors they could have their own chocolate factory eventually. Shiok Meats for example, led by Dr. Sandhya Sriram in Singapore, is cultivating clean, cell-based crustacean proteins (shrimp, crab, lobster). And on the more finned side of things, or rather "finless," I should say, is Michael Selden at the helm of Finless Foods—a startup out of San Francisco focusing mainly on clean bluefin tuna for all your tuna-loving needs.

Finless Foods and *Silicon Valley*

Michael Selden and Finless Foods are creating a lot of chum in the water around cell-cultured fish, and the sharks are coming ... to invest. While we know clean fish products won't suddenly take over the global markets (which is why Aquapods and other aquaculture tech are vital to lean on and employ in tandem with clean fish proteins for the time being), this Gene-trepreneur is helping cell-based fish swim off to a very healthy start.

With the advent of clean fish meat specifically, cell-cultured fish fillets and sushi will be able to deliver mercury-free, microplastic-free, and sustainable food to people all around the world.

---

2   Willy Wonka & the Chocolate Factory, Directed by Mel Stuart. Performed by Gene Wilder. 1971.

I was actually able to speak with Finless Foods' CEO and co-founder Mike Selden to learn about his startup story and what the company is working toward in the clean meat space. But before I delve into Selden's story, here is some important background info about the market and the venture.

So, we know Mike Selden and the Finless Foods team are essentially taking the existing medical technology of culturing living tissue and transferring it into the seafood space, but how exactly? They obtain tissue samples from fish and subsequently proliferate and differentiate the fast-growing cells into the muscle, fat, and connective tissue that we are accustomed to eating. Selden has stated that "instead of using a fish as a piece of machinery that makes fish meat for people to eat, we're going one step beyond that, or one step lower than that, and building ... directly from the cells themselves."[3]

This is all happening in what are called bioreactors, which you can think of being very similar to the fermentation tanks used in the beer-brewing industry. The difference is instead of feeding sugar yeast to generate alcohol, growth factors and nutrients are fed to muscle and fat cells to generate real, healthy, sustainable, and delicious meat. If you are interested in learning more about the science behind cell-based seafood, I highly recommend reading the paper titled "An Ocean of Opportunity" from The Good Food Institute (a.k.a. GFI).[4] Whether it's growth media, scaffolds, or scalability, there are many areas where technical Gene-trepreneurs can apply their skillsets and add valuable pieces to the puzzle if they're up for the challenge and want to make a substantial impact.

As you know now, the main project Finless is currently working on is bluefin tuna. Currently, they can create a sort of combination of protein-rich muscle and healthy fats but are working hard to structure the clean fish meat into fillets and sashimi with 3D tissue printing technology.

In general, across the whole cell-based protein space, scaffolding for the cells to grow on in order to create structured fillets, steaks, etc. is one of the greatest obstacles to overcome (much more about

---

3   Fletcher, Rob. "The (Finless) Future of Fish Production." *The Fish Site*, March 21, 2019.

4   Specht, Liz, et al. "An Ocean of Opportunity Action Paper." *The Good Food Institute*, 2018.

this can be read in GFI's many helpful articles and papers at gfi.org/essentials).[5] Finless has decided to focus on bluefin as their main species because the smartest business decision for them is to make a high-end product and tie their name to it. Many people don't realize that when they eat bluefin, they are actually eating an endangered species that has lost 96 percent of its pre-industrial population.[6] Yet every year we continue to harvest them. Isn't that nuts? Why are we doing that if this is the case?

Well, I guess people just LOVE tuna.

In Japan, the biggest consumers of this species, they hold fish auctions where one 612-pound bluefin sold for $3.1 million this year (an especially high price even for a bluefin, but the first auction of the new year can usually bring in some record-breaking prices).

As a whole, tuna has a forty-two-billion-dollar worldwide market of which bluefin alone makes up two billion worth.[7] The bluefin market also has great price points, making it a fantastic initial product for Finless to work with to gain investment and rapidly grow via funneling profits back into the business. Their overall goal is to take the cultured fish meat, created with medical-grade technology, and bring it down to competitive food prices so when consumers go to the store they can choose between poorer quality fish or the clean, sustainable Finless Foods option. Which would you choose at similar price-points? I think it's a no-brainer.

∞

Now that you know a little more background, the story of Finless Foods begins with its two co-founders—Mike Selden and Brian Wyrwas, who were also named in *Inc. Magazine's* 2018 "30 under 30" list.[8]

---

5   "Explore Our Library of up-to-Date Resources." *The Good Food Institute*, January 6, 2016.

6   Press, Associated. "Bluefin Goes for $3 Million at 1st 2019 Sale at Tokyo Market." *NBCNews.com*, NBCUniversal News Group, 5 Jan. 2019.

7   Selden, Michael. "Making Sustainable, Lab-Grown Fish Meat a Reality | Finless Foods | HT Summit 2017." *YouTube*, Hello Tomorrow, March 8, 2018.

8   Khan, Ahmed. "Finless Foods Raises $3.5 Million in Seed Funding To Grow Cultured Fish." Medium, CellAgri, June 21, 2018.

The two were peers at the University of Massachusetts Amherst, both studying biochemistry and molecular biology for their undergrad.

After graduating, they moved to New York City where Selden researched colorectal and thyroid cancer using a fruit fly model at Mount Sinai medical school, and Wyrwas worked testing cancer treatments on human tumor samples at Weill Cornell Medical College. The two frequently met up for lunch between the two hospitals, and one day over a couple beers and some plant-based Impossible Burgers (which we'll talk about next chapter), the two decided they could actually go out and pursue an idea they had been tossing around for a while—cell-cultured fish meat.

Selden and Wyrwas worked toward building a pitch although neither had utilized any entrepreneurship resources at school or taken business courses before. Selden said knowing some people who had started businesses of their own—such as one of the founders, Seung Shin, of Ephemeral Tattoos (tattoos without the lifelong commitment)—really helped them in those beginning stages and gave the pair models to learn from. The duo then applied in late 2016 to IndieBio, the world-renowned life sciences accelerator headquartered in San Francisco. They ended up withdrawing their application due to not feeling their ideas were ready yet. Instead, they re-applied with a revamped tech workflow and were accepted at the end of February 2017 into the next batch of IndieBio accelerator companies.

Snapshot Lesson:
If you need to take a step back and work things out, do it (but don't get too comfortable there). By revamping time effectively, Selden and Wyrwas were able to capitalize and get more out of the opportunity IndieBio presented. You may initially think it's a step back, but what if that momentary step back saved you time and allowed you to get not one, but two steps further than you would have gotten had you went in full tilt feeling things weren't quite ready yet?

∞

After being accepted, Selden and Wyrwas left their jobs, packed their bags, and moved to San Francisco to begin pursuing Finless Foods full time—a dream, but a scary one, for any entrepreneur! It wasn't easy at first. Mike comically shared that his early founder experiences often mirrored many portrayed in the popular show *Silicon Valley*, especially in the first season.

For example, just like Richard Hendricks (Thomas Middleditch's character), Selden went to the bank to deposit funds and abruptly learned that he needed a separate business account for the company. A lot of things seem obvious looking from the outside in, but as a young and first-time founder there really is so much thrown at you all at once, and it can be overwhelming! Selden and his co-founder blame this particular mishap on not getting into the series until after the first season aired. Nowadays, Selden says he watches the show as homework so he knows what entrepreneurial pitfalls to avoid. (Hmmm, a very good excuse to catch up on a favorite show, huh?)

Getting down into the business of Finless Foods, Selden has previously stated that they run on the Impossible Foods model, which is a successful startup producing plant-based meat that we'll get to in chapter 3. The general outline is to start out in a luxury market, prove the viability of the product, and then lower the final price as the product becomes more widely adopted as a commodity.

Even if Finless Foods was not able to shift from their position solely in the luxury market and just stayed within the top end, the company would still have a tremendous impact on the environment. Selden, while speaking on a Climate One panel, mentioned how the top 10 percent of people in the world are creating 50 percent of the greenhouse gas emissions due to their lifestyles.[9] Those people are also eating endangered species like bluefin tuna in massive quantities. If just this group decided to eat Finless Foods' fish rather than wild-caught or farmed varieties, it would certainly have a positive and measurable impact moving forward.

I asked Selden how they decided upon that "Impossible Foods" strategy, and he said that Finless Foods' entire business model drastically changed after getting into IndieBio. It got a major overhaul

---

9   "Climate One." *Climate One - The New Surf and Turf,* 2018.

by listening to mentor and investor feedback as well as watching how other new companies were operating. It helped that cell-based meat powerhouse Memphis Meats had been in the previous cohort at IndieBio several months before them too. It's nice to have a group of companies forging the clean and plant-based meat spaces together because founders can learn from each other's successes and mistakes.

Selden remarked that he really likes the "Impossible Foods" strategy of releasing in top restaurants served by master chefs for several reasons:

1. Professional preparation at top-notch establishments ties Finless Foods' bluefin tuna to a luxury idea.
2. The consumer, likely trying clean bluefin tuna for the first time, is seeing and tasting the cell-based fish meat as a high-quality product from the start, not some sort of "Frankenfood." First impressions are really important, and people eat with their eyes first!
3. Educating people about the product can be a hurdle, but the waitstaff help sell it. As Selden points out, it "builds in a set of evangelists" who encourage people to try the product.

These reasons make this "Impossible" strategy a perfect way to launch into the market with a clean meat product like Finless Foods is gearing up to deliver. And when you think about the high costs of educating consumers in any industry, the waitstaff at high-end restaurants are truly a fantastic and cost-effective method of direct customer education and can act as a kind of inherent salesforce if they like it.

Obviously, funding is also a big deal for startups. It can be especially important for those in biotech because they can burn through cash quickly from purchasing necessary equipment, lab materials, hiring various scientific experts, and running tests to hone their products. You might wonder how Finless was able to get their beginnings. When it came to funding the startup, IndieBio actually provided them with pre-seed money; each company in the four-month accelerator program receives $250K for 8 percent equity.[10] It's a really

---

10   Kopelyan, Alex. "FAQ." IndieBio. IndieBio, January 24, 2017.

healthy start, but Finless eventually needed more backing, which is when they began looking to venture capital (VC) for seed funding.

I inquired to Selden how they approached acquiring VC backing since there are some very important considerations—such as if the VC has experience investing in life sciences and whether they will be likely to invest again in future rounds.[11] Selden responded that the company approaches VC funding, as well as hiring in general, from the perspective that they are always trying to fill gaps in their skill-sets. You can use this in your life too by finding partners who have complementary skills to your own.

Selden and Wyrwas considered their company to be strong in cellular biology and brand-building and wanted help with marketing, operations, finance, etc. So they brought on successful venture capitalist Tim Draper (early and growth-stage investor in Tesla, SpaceX, Twitter, Solar City, Coinbase, Patreon and many more significant companies), which gave a lot of credibility to the venture started by two entrepreneurs in their mid-twenties.[12] The pair also brought on experts in aquaculture, tissue engineering, and many more facets of synthetic biology and STEM to build up their impressive team.

Additionally of interest, Finless Foods did not behave like the typical company when seeking their VC funding. Usually companies will approach the firms to deliver their pitches for investment. However, Selden having many reporters and writers in his network, utilized these connections to drum up as much press as possible. This made the VCs who really believed in the company and cared about their mission approach Finless Foods first. It evidently worked because the company has already secured over $3.5 million in seed funding from some great firms that really try to invest in world-benefiting ideas and ventures.

With fundraising, you have to be really careful who you accept money from because there are some entrepreneurial horror stories. (I had a professor who always called venture capitalists "vulture capitalists.")

---

11 Kasireddy, Preethi. "What I Wish I Knew about Fundraising as a First-Time Founder." *Medium*, Medium, May 31, 2018.

12 *Portfolio | DFJ Venture Capital.*

Snapshot Lesson:
Fill gaps in your skillset in hiring and partnering with VCs. Also, having multiple-time backers, especially ones with notable names, displays faith in the founders and company. It's like if you tell someone how cool or smart you are, nobody will believe you. But when a seemingly reliable person or group of people say, "Hey, Esmerelda over there is so super fly and a very stable genius," others will be more likely to take that to heart.

∞

Curiously, knowing that many traditional meat operations are investing into their own disruptors in cell and plant-based beef, I asked Selden if he found this to be true for his company and the clean seafood space as a whole. His answer was yes. There is a lot of interest because these aquaculture companies can't produce the species that Finless Foods currently works with. Only one operation in the world can farm bluefin tuna successfully, which is Tuna Princess in Japan.

Selden also mentioned during his appearance on the 2018 Climate One panel how bluefin tuna aquaculture really struggled for about ten years as people tried to figure out how to actually raise these fish.[13] During this time, the bluefin seemed to be healthy and eating fine into adolescence, but then they just stopped eating. For a while nobody knew why. Only later it was discovered that there was not enough DHA (docosahexaenoic acid) in their diets, which is a critical fatty acid that affects brain development and photoreceptor function. Basically, the reason these fish stopped eating was because they became blind. So for a decade, the aquaculturers trying to raise bluefin tuna blinded and starved their fish to death.

The fact that there is only one company farm-raising the fish now is also a contributing factor to why bluefin commands such a high price today. But if you think about the Tuna Princess operation and wild-caught fish, the tuna themselves haven't really changed in a very long time and take quite a while to go from swimming to being

---

13   "Climate One." Climate One - The New Surf and Turf, 2018.

served on a plate. Bluefin sexually mature at around five years and can live to about twenty-five years of age.

A real advantage for Finless Foods is that they can modify their product on a dime and will be able to produce the same amounts of clean fish meat in a matter of weeks that the traditional tuna industry would take years to grow. And as culturing tech continues to develop, so much can be enhanced with cultured tissue to make the fish meat more nutritious and better tasting (aside from already being microplastic, mercury, and antibiotic-free). This makes everyone, whether in the wild-caught or aquaculture space, interested in getting in on the clean bluefin tuna venture that Finless Foods is cultivating.

∞

Finless isn't the only clean seafood venture operating though. Companies like Wild Type, BlueNalu, and as mentioned above, Shiok Meats are also developing cell-based seafood products. Nevertheless, Selden says he doesn't see these companies as competition because Finless Foods is the only one producing bluefin tuna for now. If anyone comes into the tuna space, it still won't be a problem because as we now know, bluefin is a two-billion-dollar industry. Finless Foods is playing on a worldwide scale, and there is room for multiple players—multiple majestic and powerful tuna in the sea.

Even if Finless is only able to get a piece of the cell-based bluefin tuna market in the future, they'll be doing just fine. Plus, Selden and Wyrwas run the company very transparently. Selden stated that they "are in it for the right reasons" and people are reacting well to their message. This is a very common theme across all of synthetic biology; transparency and honesty are paramount.

I also brought up whether he thinks that technologies like Aquapods are here just for the interim or whether they will have a place amongst clean meat in the full-fledged future of the seafood industry. Very astutely, he believes in a diversity of tactics because we need all hands on deck to get people consuming more sustainable fish meat and not dwindling wild-caught products. If the ocean ecosystem collapses, so do we. Aquapods and better aquaculture methods are definitely part of the solution right now, and Selden just sees clean fish products as the next step for those looking further down the road. He and his team have so much respect for all of the people working toward this common mission, and it is exactly why Selden and Wyrwas started Finless Foods in the first place.

Unfortunately, not everyone has the same commitment to sustainability, which is why I inquired what foot they are leading with in their marketing strategy—the sustainability approach or the fact that their product is healthier by having no microplastics, mercury, or antibiotics? He was clear that Finless Foods will be selling mostly on the health aspect because, sadly, studies show that people make their decisions concerned more with their health than our collective sustainability and animal welfare. Selden sees the best way to get others to eat more sustainably is by offering Finless Foods as a second, healthier option to traditional fish. And most plant-based and cell-based protein companies are moving in this direction.

It's the best and fastest-acting tactic to achieve a desperately needed change in food sustainability. There's simply no time to waste in lessening our reliance on animal agriculture and mitigating anthropogenic climate change.

∞

Looking beyond their bluefin tuna product, Selden stated they are also looking to branch out into other fish species eventually. It won't be hard to expand their line to tilapia, skipjack, swordfish, mahi-mahi, and other fish varieties because the process of culturing any of these is relatively the same as with bluefin. They are already working with many different cell lines from different species. With tens of thousands of fish varieties in the world and more being discovered every year, the possibilities are plentiful! It's a *Willy Wonka & the Chocolate Factory* situation for sure.

I also asked Selden whether they would ever venture outside of fish and into animals of other categories like shrimp, lobster, octopus, or even whale meat to stop the useless killing of whales in certain

Scandinavian countries and Japan.[14] He said that while he would love to work with those species, most of the company's branching out is into fish because their systems have been studied much more. A lot of academic work has dealt with goldfish and zebrafish, which makes the transition into other fish species much easier because they are closely related evolutionarily to those well-studied organisms. When it comes to creatures like lobsters, they are more like insects and spiders than fish. There simply isn't much previous research to build from there, and it would be like starting from the beginning again for Finless, or at least close to it. Sounds like they'll leave that market to Shiok Meats and stick with fish.

Interestingly, I also know many synbio companies will be able to take genetic material and turn it into completely novel or hybrid products in the future (such as new scents, flavors, better protections for crops, etc. that we will talk about in coming chapters). I curiously asked Selden whether he and the team were looking to combine fish species into hybrid clean meats or even make clean meat from extinct fish varieties down the line? He responded that it would be really cool to create something totally new, and that he had recently tried mastodon gummies produced by a company called Geltor.

Let me say that again ... literal mastodon gummies derived from genetic material that was used to create mastodon gelatin![15]

While it would be cool to create something totally new, that's going to be years into the future for Finless Foods because they are currently focused on bluefin tuna. The next set of species they will commoditize in the clean meat market will probably be pretty closely related to bluefin evolutionarily, so maybe swordfish or some other similar top-of-the-food-chain fish. Whatever they choose, I am (and hope you are now too) very excited to see Mike Selden, his co-founder Brian Wyrwas, and the Finless Foods team achieve their goals. They are certainly a flagship amongst some of the cultured seafood fleet, and I sincerely look forward to seeing where they help lead the clean fish space moving forward.

14   Kirby, David. "One More Reason the World Should Stop Eating Whale Meat: It's Filled With Pesticides." *TakePart*, Mar 13, 2015.

15   Shapiro, Paul. "Making Mastodon Gummies, Geltor Is Recreating a Truly Paleo Diet." *TechCrunch*, TechCrunch, March 12, 2018.

Main Takeaways:

It's not a bad idea to choose a product that has a high price point and billion-plus market.

– You can launch in a luxury space, be profitable, and ride the value curve as you commoditize to bring to larger markets.

If you've already done most of the footwork for one thing (like bluefin tuna), your next product should be something you can use all of that footwork on (evolutionarily similar species to bluefin).

– Double-dip into the resources (time and money) you've spent getting the first product off the ground. It's a wise move when you're a resource-strapped startup.

Don't get distracted by all the possibilities. Be aware of them but focused on building your best option.

– Consider impact and return on resource investment.

It's okay to take a moment to pause and revamp / re-calculate your current course. The right timing can increase your yield from an opportunity.

– But don't get too comfortable. Continue progressing forward.

Build a team of co-founders, employees, investments partners, etc. that have complementary skillsets but also believe in you and your shared vision.

CHAPTER 3

TERRESTRIAL MEATS AND NOBLE GOATS

Let's set the scene of the crime.

There was an incident at a local livestock auction house in Hackettstown, New Jersey, where dozens of goats and sheep were brought to be sold. Late one night, about sixty escaped from their pens.[1]

But who could've done it? A disgruntled ex-employee? An animal rights activist?

What about a former pen inhabitant?

The town has a well-known goat, nicknamed Fred, who roams around the area and who also ran to freedom from this very same auction house a year prior. Could he have come back and freed his friends?

Hackettstown police were hot on the case.

The police stated that Fred was spotted in the area a couple of hours before the escape, and the auction house manager believes Fred let them out by headbutting the pen door. He said Fred "must have put a lot of force into that."

And later the next day, Fred showed up again and began headbutting the gate to jailbreak a new group of animals brought in. Unfortunately, Fred was shooed away before his valiant mission could be completed, but we'll remember his boldness and altruistic efforts.

Honestly, jokes about over-the-top crime shows aside, it's pretty sad because goats have been found to be of similar intelligence to breeds of dogs.[2] This might sound crazy to some, but there was an emotional drive to Fred's actions. And it's not just goats. Pigs, cows, and other animals used in agriculture are capable of forming

---

1 Bain, Jennifer, and Amanda Woods. "Rogue Goat May Have Helped Dozens of Farm Animals Escape." *New York Post*, New York Post, August 10, 2018.

2 MacDonald, Fiona. "Goats Are as Smart And Loving as Dogs, According to Science." *ScienceAlert*, June 30, 2018.

emotional relationships with humans and other animals. Evolutionarily speaking, they are all really similar to us humans in their ability to feel happiness, sadness, fear, pain, etc. because they have the same neurotransmitters and nervous systems that we have in our bodies; it's basic science (comparative anatomy, genomics, and evolutionary biology) and common sense.[3]

Unfortunately, this common-sense "animals have feelings and form relationships" fact is too often out of sight and out of mind. Many people have to be reminded of that mammals have a lot in common, and others haven't even considered it. To say that animals aren't conscious or don't feel emotion and pain is akin to the ridiculous, self-aggrandizing notion that the sun and all the known universe revolves around the Earth. In fact, this is exactly what the Catholic Church believed when they convicted famed astronomer Galileo Galilei of heresy in 1633 and sentenced him to house arrest for the rest of his life.[4] The point is, be nice to animals, and Fred is a very noble goat.

Some Meaty Numbers and Vegan *Fight Club*

Cell-based and plant-based seafoods as we've discussed in the past couple of chapters aren't the only sustainable protein spaces gaining momentum. Scientists all around the globe are taking medical-grade tissue-culturing and microbial technology and applying it to terrestrial meats such as beef, pork, foie gras (duck liver), and chicken.

In 2013, Dr. Mark Post of the Netherlands, who has gone on to found the very successful clean meat company Mosa Meats, created the world's first cultured hamburger at a cost of roughly $325,000. Seems expensive, right? But Mosa Meats is projecting that they will soon be able to offer clean beef patties at $10 each and come to market in 2021.[5] If they are successful, that will be 0.003 percent of the original prototype's cost, which is remarkable. It shows just how fast clean and plant-based meat startups are bending the cost curve in their favor.

---

3   Dvm, Nigel Caulkett. "Do Cattle Feel Pain the Same Way We Do?" *Canadian Cattlemen*, April 3, 2017.

4   "Galileo Is Convicted of Heresy." *History.com*, A&E Television Networks, November 13, 2009.

5   Peters, Adele. "This Lab-Grown Beef Will Be in Restaurants in 3 Years." *Fast Company*, Fast Company, July 27, 2018.

People have been raising livestock for millennia, and factory farming has been going on for many, many decades—throughout the 20th century.[6] If factory farm operations have been squeezing out every penny and making this horrendous process like a well-oiled machine for that long (doing things like selective breeding, using growth hormones, sourcing cheap feed from corn and soy, etc.), yet cultured beef burgers are able to become competitively priced in the marketplace within just a couple of decades, who do you think is going to win this race? Who would you bet your money on in the foreseeable future?

I can't even begin to imagine what the protein industry may look like in ten, twenty, or even fifty years if this is the rate of progress. Even more mind-boggling is that it's a constantly accelerating rate. Innovation is coming in hot and will be an extremely heavy hitter in the ring against factory farms. I mean, we're fighting for the future of the planet here, right?

Dr. Post says, "We know where to improve the technology to get the price down."[7] And for Mosa Meat, the biggest driver of their cost reduction will be the implementation of a huge twenty-five-thousand-liter bioreactor. (Again, think of the big fermentation tanks used in the beer-brewing industry.) This is where the cells can grow and multiply in a clean, nutrient-rich environment. Developing large bioreactors while finding a way to lessen the cost of media (the nutrients and growth factors the cells thrive on) are two of the most significant steps in scaling up and successfully commercializing the first widely distributed cell-based meats in the coming two to ten years.

Eventually, these cell-cultured and plant-based proteins will not only be indistinguishable and more affordable than meat from animals, but they will also be much more desirable for their increased nutrition and tastier benefits compared to traditional meat. Less saturated fat is better for your cholesterol levels. You'll be able to obtain more vitamins, more minerals, and more amino and healthy

---

6   "Intensive Animal Farming." Wikipedia. Wikimedia Foundation, September 4, 2019.

7   Peters, Adele. "This Lab-Grown Beef Will Be in Restaurants in 3 Years." *Fast Company*, Fast Company, July 27, 2018.

fatty acids, not to forget being toxin, antibiotic, agricultural chemical, and disease-free.

Along with the classic meat staples of beef, pork, and chicken, the market will also likely expand to what are considered exotic meats such as alligator, bison, kangaroo, wild boar, elk, ostrich, and maybe even species that don't roam the Earth anymore (or just for now) such as mammoths and dodo birds. Remember from the last chapter that Geltor has already created mastodon gelatin and used it to create mastodon gummies![8] As long as companies have the genomes of animals to study, the possibilities are endless as to what they can achieve in food innovation and production.

∞

The reason it is so important for us to transition into clean, cell-cultured meats and plant-based proteins is for sustainability. Animal agriculture contributes very heavily to climate change—more so than you might think.

Cattle farming specifically requires enormous amounts of deforested land and water. Cows are also methane-producing machines! Just ask Dr. Patrick Brown, the founder and CEO of Impossible Foods. While water consumption and methane creation are certainly big issues, he affirmatively states that by far the most destructive aspect of farming animals for food comes from their land requirements. About 50 percent of Earth's land area is used for animal agriculture one way or another, whether it's fields for them to graze or land to grow feed crops.[9]

Animal farming is one of the main reasons (along with mining, drilling, urbanization, and plantations for products like palm oil) why millions of acres of biodiverse rainforests are cut or burned down every year in places like South America and southern Asia. The loss of all of these trees is causing more annual carbon emissions than eighty-five million cars would over their whole lifetimes, and

---

8   Shapiro, Paul. "Making Mastodon Gummies, Geltor Is Recreating a Truly Paleo Diet." *Tech-Crunch*, TechCrunch, March 12, 2018.

9   "Climate One." *Climate One - The New Surf and Turf*. 2018.

if tropical tree loss were counted as a country, it would be the third largest producer of CO_2 emissions in the world behind China and the United States. [10]

So in large part, the lungs of the Earth are being set ablaze so that humans can dine on steaks and burgers—long-term sacrifices for short-term gains. Maybe not a wise investment choice when we're talking about the shared future of the entire planet, right?

Humans require so much meat in fact, that the biomass of cows is now ten times greater than the biomass of all the living vertebrates left in the wild.[11] And according to the World Wildlife Fund's 2018 Living Planet Report, "On average, we've seen an astonishing 60 percent decline in the size of populations of mammals, birds, fish, reptiles, and amphibians in just over forty years."[12] To be precise, this is an average, so it means some species have declined by 10 percent, 50 percent, 90 percent, or have gone completely extinct while a number of others are actually growing stronger. The average between all of them is a loss of 60 percent, so when you realize this includes the ones who haven't lost that much or are on the rise, you know that the ones who are suffering losses are suffering *severe* losses.[13]

Professor Ken Norris, who is also the director of the Zoological Society of London, stated that "if half the animals died in London zoo next week, it would be front-page news, but that is happening in the great outdoors. This damage is not inevitable but a consequence of the way we choose to live."[14]

I mean, it's almost as if Thanos from *Avengers: Infinity War* and *Endgame* sneakily got rid of enormous percentages of wildlife populations over the course of decades instead of in one immediate snap. Many of us are blind to this shocking change since we either didn't

10   Gibbs, David, et al. "By the Numbers: The Value of Tropical Forests in the Climate Change Equation." *By the Numbers: The Value of Tropical Forests in the Climate Change Equation | World Resources Institute*, October 4, 2018.

11   "Climate One." *Climate One - The New Surf and Turf.* 2018.

12   Grooten, M., and R.E.A. Almond. "Living Planet Report 2018." WWF. World Wildlife Fund, 2018.

13   Yong, Ed. "Wait, Have We Really Wiped Out 60 Percent of Animals?" The Atlantic. Atlantic Media Company, November 1, 2018.

14   Carrington, Damian. "Earth Has Lost Half of Its Wildlife in the Past 40 Years, Says WWF." *The Guardian*, Guardian News and Media, September 30, 2014.

exist forty years ago or weren't galavanting around the woods counting animals like the Count on *Sesame Street* ... one bat ah ah ha ... two bats ah ah ha ... three bats ah ah ha ...

But this is where we rely on the work of our predecessors, the data they gathered, and carry the torches they passed along to us in order to recognize that things are taking a very wrong turn here. Forty years is significant in a human's lifetime but only a blip on the geological time scale; a blip shouldn't have such a drastic rate of change where the average wild animal populations shrink by 60 percent.

"Shame" *Bell Rings* and a More Human Approach

To raise awareness of this animal agriculture issue and try to bring about change, many people have shamed meat eaters in the past, which has not only proven to be ineffective but has also led to a lot of backlash and jokes about vegetarians and vegans always letting you know they are vegetarians or vegans. For example:

"What's the first rule of Vegan Club?"

"Tell everyone about Vegan Club!"

"Ahaha, that's so funny, Chad! You're hilarious!"

It shows up a lot in movies too, like in *Scott Pilgrim vs. the World* when Todd commits Veganity Violation Code Number 827 by ingesting half-and-half milk and is subsequently stripped of all his superpowers by the Vegan Police.[15] Although the jokes can be hit or miss, there is certainly a lot of tension and division among people based on their diets. It's become almost like a political rift of tribalism.

Personally, I don't believe anyone should be looked down upon for their choice to not eat or eat very little meat, or for respectfully encouraging others to become more knowledgeable about the food industry as well. (Most people don't like willful ignorance or a lack of respect for life.)

Quantitatively speaking, vegans and vegetarians require far less animal lives to continue their own, which I think is something that should be commended for both the ethical and environmental impacts:

---

15   Wright, Edgar, director. *Scott Pilgrim vs. the World.* Universal, 2010.

- The average American consumes 222 pounds of meat per year.[16]
- This equates to around 7,000 animals over a lifetime.
  - 11 cows
  - 27 pigs
  - 2,400 chickens
  - 80 turkeys
  - 30 sheep
  - 4,500 fish

And all this isn't even counting the number of animals used to feed our food, as is the case with fish meal for example.[17]

Of course these numbers vary from person to person and across different countries and cultures, but if you consider the increasing number of vegans, vegetarians, and people reducing their intake of meat around the world (especially driven by younger generations like Millennials and Gen Z), we're talking billions of lives saved from the supply-and-demand meat industry.[18]

Nevertheless, asking people if they believe their life is worth over seven thousand still isn't very likely to cause anyone to make dietary changes. Instead, it generally makes you come off as a jerk on a high horse. And as mentioned last chapter, people care more about eating what they want rather than what their diets are doing to animals and the planet.

It's also common sense that most people don't like feeling as if they are being told what to do by holier-than-thou individuals. This is why it's impossible to talk everyone into scrapping meat from their diets, despite the facts.

This became really apparent to Dr. Brown, founder of Impossible Foods, when he attended the COP21 climate talks in Paris. There, he saw some super dedicated environmentalists, who were there to discuss and obtain international agreements and policies to fight

---

16 Purdy, Chase. "The Average American Will Eat the Equivalent of 800 Hamburgers in 2018." *Quartz*, Quartz, January 4, 2018.

17 Solomon, Ari. "USA Today: Meat-Eaters Consume 7,000 Animals in a Lifetime." *Mercy For Animals*, March 13, 2015.

18 Loria, Joe. "Forbes: Millennials Driving Force Behind Global Vegan Movement." *Mercy For Animals*, March 27, 2018.

climate change, eat steaks after the sessions.[19] It doesn't imply they're bad people—I mean, they were fighting for measures to protect the environment—but it just shows how hard it is for many to shake the steak. After all, meat has been ingrained in many of our daily meals from an early age. And it can be especially difficult to cut meat out when there is such convenience in obtaining it along with an easy dissociation that the meat in nice packages at your grocery store was once part of an animal.

∞

Whereas shaming has been proven to be an ineffective method of swaying meat from the masses, there is a genuinely good-hearted movement on the rise to simply make others more aware about factory farming without the finger-wagging.

Natalie Portman, who is an incredibly intelligent, accomplished woman and has earned a degree in psychology from Harvard University, produced a documentary called *Eating Animals* that served to educate others on what goes on behind the scenes at factory farms.[20] The industry is so secretive because if people really knew what was happening, they would be appalled. The nightmarish stories of animal cruelty at factory farms are true: the cramped conditions, force-feeding, disease, mass murder, etc. And the meat industry masks itself behind a curtain so no one can see what is really going on. Certain states even go as far as to have laws that prohibit people from disclosing the details of these operations.[21]

This is why when it comes to putting meat on the table, I and many others respect ethical hunting and family farming much more than the abhorrent factory farming industry. Hunters and small farmers are more connected to the land and animals, know the value of life, and what it means to take it.

---

19 "Climate One." *Climate One - The New Surf and Turf.* 2018.

20 Portman, Natalie, producer. Quinn, Christopher, director. *Eating Animals. Eating Animals,* June 2018.

21 CBS This Morning. "Natalie Portman on 'Eating Animals,'" Rise of Factory Farming, and Harvey Weinstein." *YouTube,* YouTube, June 15, 2018.

With the almost 100 percent of meat that comes from these horrible, large operations on the other hand, it becomes all too easy for people to forget or become willingly blind to how that nice cut of beef ended up at the store and eventually onto their plate. The majority of animals are moved on big trucks (you've probably unknowingly passed them on the highway) to industrial slaughterhouses. However sometimes, we happily hear stories about animals falling off those trucks or escaping the slaughterhouses and then getting to live their lives in animal sanctuaries. I'm always rooting for them, and I think most people feel that way too. That's why at the end of *City Slickers* *spoiler alert even though it came out in 1991* Billy Crystal's character Mitch buys Norman, the baby cow, after learning that the cattle owner intends to turn the herd into burgers.

Anyway, I highly recommend watching Natalie Portman's project. It really approaches this topic from a place of sharing information about the factory farming industry and what it does to the environment and these animals instead of being like the nun lady, Septa Unella, in *Game of Thrones* ringing her bell and saying, "Shame."[22]

Impossible Foods, Meat Chefs, and Bovine Technology

Dr. Patrick Brown might be familiar to appreciative researchers and college students for his open access scientific journal called the *Public Library of Science* (a.k.a. *PLOS*), which launched in 2003. However, his founder story with Impossible Foods began eight years later while he was on sabbatical from his medical professorship at Stanford University.

Dr. Brown asked himself what he could do that would have the most positive impact on the world given his skillset and knowledge of cellular biology and genomics. (This is the philosophy of "effective altruism" that he and so many others in the synbio/sustainability spaces practice. This scientific approach analyzes how we can make the greatest positive impact in others' lives and on the world at large with a set amount of skills and resources.)

He quickly concluded that he must tackle the use of animals as a technology for food production because it is by far the most

---

22   "Game of Thrones: Mother's Mercy," June 14, 2015.

detrimental practice on a global scale that we face today. Dr. Brown began by putting together what he describes as the best research and development team to ever work on food and studying meat as if it were a disease given his medical background. Just as he would study cancer in his old lab, he and his team studied the mechanisms by which meat is given its flavor, texture, etc. Once they understood the mechanisms, the goal became to find plant-derived proteins that mimicked those characteristics and were more sustainable to produce.[23]

A key finding was that heme plays a vital role for us in recognizing a food as meat. Heme is an important iron-containing biomolecule in our blood that allows oxygen to be bound and carried throughout our bodies by hemoglobin, myoglobin, and other hemeproteins. Many different varieties of heme exist within the same organism, and you probably consume upwards of one thousand molecularly distinct hemeproteins every single day. Both plants and animals have heme in their systems, but as Dr. Brown mentions, the concentration of heme in our food makes us recognize meat for what it is.[24] A beef patty contains far more heme than spinach, for example. Since Impossible Foods is all plant-based, the team looked to hemeprotein varieties that could replace those found in traditional meat.

Leghemoglobin, a hemeprotein located in the roots of leguminous plants like soybeans, was found to be a terrific substitute for animal hemeproteins. One whole acre of soybeans can only produce about one kilogram of leghemoglobin, however, so the Impossible Foods research team designed a strain of yeast to produce leghemoglobin via fermentation much in the same way yeast produce beer.[25]

The scientific premise behind this idea is very simple. Everything has DNA, and certain sequences of DNA make up genes. Genes encode specific proteins and molecules to be produced. The scientists took the genes for leghemoglobin and added them into a strain of yeast. Then, much like one brews beer by having yeast ferment barley

23 "Climate One." *Climate One - The New Surf and Turf.* 2018.

24 Ibid.

25 Simon, Matt. "Inside the Strange Science of the Fake Meat That 'Bleeds'." *Wired*, Conde Nast, September 21, 2017.

sugars into alcohol and carbon dioxide, the yeast ferments sugarcane and corn into leghemoglobin. In theory this seems easy, but in practice this process is not as rudimentary as it sounds. There's a lot more scientifically to consider, but for the sake of being concise, we'll save this jargon for another time.

The Impossible Foods team also carefully crafted the Impossible Burgers to include essential amino acids akin to those found in traditional meat. Just in case you aren't familiar with amino acids, there are twenty of them, nine of which are called essential amino acids because our bodies cannot produce them and thus must be obtained via the foods we consume.[26] Vegans and vegetarians usually supplement their diets by eating legumes and nuts to get their daily dose of amino acids. Positively, the company conducted an amino acid study that found the availability of essential amino acids in a group of people fed a week-long diet of Impossible Burgers matched the availability of a group fed beef burgers.[27]

Impossible Foods is currently working to take that a step further by developing a version that will have an even better balance of amino acids than cow-sourced burgers. Dr. Brown comically stated, "That's doable, and the cow is not working on this problem." Plant-based meats as well as cell-cultured clean meats have the ability to be so much better than traditional varieties from slaughtered animals.

∞

Dr. Brown made the interesting parallel that the transportation industry didn't call it quits when automotive technology could keep up with the horse, and Impossible Foods doesn't have to hit a stopping point on progress either.[28]

---

26   Kubala, Jillian. "Essential Amino Acids: Definition, Benefits and Food Sources." *Healthline*, June 12, 2018.

27   "Climate One." *Climate One - The New Surf and Turf.* 2018.

28   Ibid.

Sidebar

Speaking of the automotive industry, quick story I heard from Seth Goldman, the co-founder of Honest Tea and executive chairman of Beyond Meat (Impossible's competitor). On a Next Gen Summit panel, Goldman recounted a comparison of two Henrys:

- Henry Ford: founder of the Ford Motor Company who revolutionized the automobile industry by making cars more accessible to the masses
- Henry Bergh: founder of the American Society for the Prevention of Cruelty to Animals (ASPCA) who have the commercials with Sarah McLachlan singing "In the aaarrrrms of the angel..."

Let's say you love, I mean LOVE, horses. While I am fully supportive of the ASPCA, as they do incredible work for many different animal species, who do you think did more for horses specifically?

Henry Ford's auto empire pretty quickly got out ahead of the horse and buggy and relieved many equines from their labor. If it weren't for Ford commoditizing cars when he did with his assembly line, perhaps millions of additional horses would have been forced to pull carriages for who knows how many more years.

Snapshot Lesson:

You don't have to work full time in the field where you want to make a difference. Through a domino effect, side-chains can lead to you having a more meaningful impact than you might realize. Just something to consider in your current studies and career. The answer might not be in front of your face, but with a little searching, you may find a unique way to make your impact in a cause you deeply care about.

Dr. Brown and his team also looked at the life cycle of their product to examine the environmental effects from start to finish, and they asserted that compared to traditional cattle farming, the Impossible Burger:

- Needs only 5 percent of the land
- Needs only 25 percent of the water

- Produces only 12 percent of the greenhouse gas emissions[29]

That's fantastic, especially considering that currently we have ten times the biomass of cattle than the biomass of wild vertebrates left on the planet!

Imagine how much the environment would benefit if even just half, a quarter, or a tenth of the total cattle biomass was replaced with the Impossible Burger growing method. It would have a notable impact on the planet. I don't think this is far off either because a cow is simply a cow, and that's what you're getting when you eat traditional beef. However, wouldn't you rather have the healthier Impossible Burger—that has been optimized for flavor and nutrition—on your plate? Dr. Brown states, "The way we win is we think about the meat eater and what they care about: deliciousness above all, nutrition, convenience, affordability."[30]

In fact, the company pinpointed that most of their consumers are meat eaters—about 75 percent actually. They also concluded that most devout meat eaters don't cherish the fact that their meat comes from slaughtered animals. The plant-based and clean burgers can cater more to what meat eaters care about and are simply more versatile in every way (flavor, health benefits like lower saturated fats, texture, and more energy, water, labor, time, etc. efficient) than meat sourced from animals.

This illustrates how important it is to correctly identify your customers and do your research to know what consumers want and value in a product. Impossible Foods is 100 percent hitting the nail on the head in this regard, which is why they are one of the most exciting startups out there today in plant-based protein with the potential to make a really significant and positive impact on the world.

---

29   Simon, Matt. "Inside the Strange Science of the Fake Meat That 'Bleeds'." *Wired*, Conde Nast, September 21, 2017.

30   "Climate One." *Climate One - The New Surf and Turf*. 2018.

To turn this potential into reality doesn't just come down to creating a fantastic product. Excellent products don't sell without a great business strategy behind them. Dr. Brown states that Impossible Foods strategically adopted the Tesla model, wherein they started their prices on the higher side in the luxury market. As they scaled up, their prices began to come down, thereby becoming more affordable for a larger customer base. Impossible Foods actually implemented an extremely clever launch strategy wherein they targeted the restaurants of elite chefs known for not cutting anyone any breaks on quality of ingredients, especially alternatives to traditional meat.

Their first chef was David Chang, who at one point banned all vegetarian dishes from his menu. Dr. Brown knew that if he could convince top chefs like Chang to serve the Impossible Burger in their restaurants, it would be a game-changer. And that's exactly what he did. People took notice too because these well-respected chefs were not going to serve anything subpar as meat. Brown states that it was "an implicit endorsement that was invaluable to us."[31] It gave Impossible Foods immense credibility.

Additionally, because Chang's and other top chefs' reputations are attached to their food and restaurants, Dr. Brown knew he was securing a positive first interaction for consumers with his product. This is very important considering that for most people eating the Impossible Burger at these restaurants, it would be their very first exposure to it. What better way to ensure a positive experience than having the burger professionally prepared and served to customers?

It's an efficient and skillful strategy for bringing a new food product to the market, especially one as groundbreaking as Impossible Foods' elevated take on plant-based meat. Dr. Brown said that the

---

31   Ibid.

delivery strategy combined with "... the incongruity of these famous meat chefs serving a plant-based product, plant-based meat, amplified the buzz and attention for us."[32]

Impossible Foods has progressed quite a lot since their launch, now having a new, tweaked version of their Impossible Burger optimized for any and all meat dishes. It is available at over 5,000 locations including 377 White Castles, all 570 Red Robin locations in the US,[33] and recently rolled out at Burger Kings as the Impossible Whopper.[34] It's a success!

Dr. Brown is very confident that within the next few years, Impossible Foods will make their product at less cost than any beef from a cow. It's *possible* because Impossible Burgers use less land, water, fertilizer, etc. in manufacturing than the animal-based system we have used up until this point. All of the costs of an operation are factored into the final product price you, as a consumer, pay. So, if Impossible Foods can beat the traditional animal system on manufacturing cost (even with the cattle-farming industry receiving government subsidies, by the way), Impossible Foods can beat them on price for consumers too while simultaneously serving up an all-around better burger.

Dr. Brown stated, "We'll change the world more dramatically than any company possibly in history has ever done it because when you look at the impact of the system we're replacing, almost half of the land area of Earth is being occupied by the animal farming industry, grazing, or feed crop production." (Simon)

It might sound ambitious, but all of the greatest entrepreneurial minds always think BIGGER! Never limit yourself to what others think you can achieve. With the track Dr. Brown and Impossible Foods are on, they are already creating an impact that will only multiply from here.

---

32   (n 91)

33   Watson, Elaine. "Impossible Foods Replaces Wheat with Soy Protein Concentrate in Its Plant-Based Burger; Says Color Additive Petition Won't Delay Retail Launch." *Foodnavigator*, January, 2018.

34   "Burger King—Impossible Foods." Impossible Foods.

Main Takeaways:
The domino effect: consider how what you're doing now or plan to do will impact causes you care about and how distant that impact may be.
- You might be able to make a direct impact, but you may also be a couple or many steps removed from the end result of your actions.

Figure out everyone's selfish motivations and top priorities and align them to a common end goal.
- If your product satiates all personal desires and concerns, you've made something that all, or at least many, roads can lead to, and that's a rocket you want to be on.

Think bigger.
- It might sound kitschy, but if you shoot for the stars and hit the moon, are you going to be upset or absolutely elated?

New Age Meats and Jessie the Pig

The world loves bacon of all kinds, right? There's American actor Kevin Bacon, whose namesake the "Six Degrees of Kevin Bacon" game was derived from.[35] There's English philosopher and statesman Sir Francis Bacon, who is credited with formally developing the scientific method.[36] And of course, there's bacon the food, which so many people and animals around the world love to consume with eggs, on sandwiches, in salads, and even as bacon-flavored chips.[37]

But what if bacon, and hopefully all forms of pork protein as well, received a sustainable and health-conscious overhaul just like Impossible Foods is doing with the beef burger?

Another company in the food innovation space, although doing cell-cultured protein and not plant-based, is New Age Meats. This startup was founded in June, 2018 by chemical engineer Brian Spears and molecular biologist Andra Necula. The two applied into IndieBio, worked within the accelerator for the latter half of 2018, and are currently making huge strides in clean, cell-cultured pork. I interviewed

---

35   "Six Degrees of Kevin Bacon." Wikipedia. Wikimedia Foundation, August 30, 2019.

36   "Francis Bacon." Wikipedia. Wikimedia Foundation, September 4, 2019.

37   Andrew Grantham, and Talking Animals. "Ultimate Dog Tease." YouTube. YouTube, May 1, 2011.

Necula and read a lot of material from Spears, and although they are only in the seed stage, I am extremely optimistic about their endeavors at New Age Meats!

Interestingly, Necula was in an accelerator program called Entrepreneur First in London after finishing her PhD at Oxford. She knew she wanted to make a big impact with her biology background, really embracing the effective altruism philosophy mentioned previously, and she was there seeking a co-founder to work on a startup in the clean meat space.

Entrepreneur First (EF) is unique in comparison to most other accelerators because generally entrepreneurs already come in with a team and a business, whereas at EF they arrive to find the right co-founders first within their selective cohort before building out a business. After interviewing many candidates, though, she joined The Good Food Institute's entrepreneurial community, GFIdeas, to look outside EF for the right, highly specialized partner. Through this group she found her co-founder, Brian Spears.

The first problem they encountered was that to work together at EF, Spears needed to apply into Entrepreneur First as well and immediately move to London. Not messing around, he did exactly that! The pair worked there for months honing their initial concept—to become a company that assisted others in clean protein to automate and scale up. But after speaking with many clean protein founders and iterating their concept, the pair realized the industry was still in such early stages that there were simply not enough companies interested in their vision yet.

So what to do now?

Pivot!

Necula and Spears figured out they really needed to become a fully integrated vertical operation that could pull together the top players and developments in bioreactors, growing media, and scaffolding to put clean protein products on the market—the ultimate end goal any cell-based protein entrepreneur wants.[38] Circling back to a main takeaway from our last section, they thought bigger! And

---

38   Spears, Brian, and Alex Shirazi. "Brian Spears of New Age Meats - Clean Meat Founders Series - Live Recording." *Cultured Meat Future Food*, YouTube, August 5, 2018.

when it came time to pick their poison, so to speak, the two landed on pork as their primary objective.

This was for several reasons:

1. Most other companies are focused on beef, poultry, and fish. However, pork holds a huge "hock" of the meat market—over twenty billion dollars in the US alone.[39]

2. Many pork products are processed and don't require much structure (sausages, dumplings, pepperoni, etc.).

    a. In order to build pork chops, an edible structure needs to be designed for the cells to grow and differentiate on to become muscle, fat, and connective tissue.

    b. Although scaffolding technology is still in its infancy, developments are being made with decellularized apples and spinach leaves (similar to renovating a building—taking out the plant cells but leaving the overall structure and then re-inhabiting that structure with muscle and fat cells to multiply).

    c. Many clean meat companies are working hard to create suitable scaffolding for their products, such as Finless Foods' quest to produce sturdy tuna fillets. But to be ahead of the curve, pork offers many unstructured options to start making an impact sooner.

3. They aren't starting from scratch.

    a. An overwhelming amount of literature from the medical and pharmaceutical industries discusses how best to culture and differentiate pig cells. (They are extremely similar to humans.)

    b. It's basically like having a recipe book that tells you what temperatures, pHs, growing mediums, etc. will culture the cells best.

Necula and Spears visited a farm and collected some tissue samples from a pig named Jessie. Over the course of a couple of months, and after some recipe-testing as it were, those sampled cells were able to

---

39 "Pork Facts." *National Pork Producers Council.*

differentiate and multiply to the point where they could be turned into sausages.[40]

Obviously, as the company expands and uses bigger bioreactors, more cell-based sausages can be served up. But this impressive rate of production is at least three times faster than the time it takes to grow a 280-pound, market-ready pig for food in factory farming, which is generally around six months.[41]

Necula also says they can customize what type of cut the cells would equate to at the company. Cuts of meat are designated as the ham, loin, hock, spare ribs, blade, belly, etc. New Age Meats can culture cells from each of these areas to create these desired cuts of pork for consumers.

Imagine culturing cells from only the highest quality parts of the pig much quicker than factory farming can put out the same cut of meat, not to mention this top-quality pork protein is designed to taste better and be more nutritious than any traditional pork on the market. Wouldn't that be game-changing? That's what New Age Meats will be capable of serving up to you and any fellow pork-lovers if everybody's cards get played right—regulators/policy-makers, customers, financiers, the co-founding pair, etc.

∞

In September, 2018, the company employed the assistance of Matt Murphy, a chef and butcher in the meat industry for the past twenty years. Murphy, being well-versed in meat, states that factory farming animals isn't sustainable at all the way it's currently done.[42] He helped Spears and Necula cook up some of New Age Meats' cultured sausage samples as a taste test for the press and investors, and it went really well. Everyone was taken aback by the product saying how much it tasted exactly like pork sausage (because technically, it is real pork sausage since there were actual pig cells making up the meat)!

---

40   Spears, Brian, and Alex Shirazi. "Brian Spears of New Age Meats - Clean Meat Founders Series - Live Recording." *Cultured Meat Future Food*, YouTube, August 5, 2018.

41   "Life Cycle of a Market Pig." *Pork Checkoff.*

42   New Age Meats. "New Age Meats Pork Sausage Tasting Event." *YouTube*, YouTube, October 19, 2018.

The go-to-market strategy for New Age Meats is also tremendously well-thought-out and a bit different than the luxury restaurant strategy Finless Foods has planned and Impossible Foods has executed on. They envision launching in craft breweries. It is so clever because it will highlight their cell-cultured meat alongside established products that also require an in-depth preparation process.

Spears said, "Beer and bread are things that aren't exactly natural. We don't dig up beer from the ground. We don't pick bread from a tree."[43] And thus by having their product in craft breweries, they can showcase the bioreactors for culturing their pork right next to the fermentation tanks for producing the brewery's beer on-site—an incredibly brilliant and transparent way to introduce their clean pork sausage into the market. And transparency is key for establishing public education and trust.

Spears and Necula say New Age Meats is a food company first and foremost and are acutely aware that transparency is and will always be paramount. If they are to succeed against the factory farming industry—for themselves, their future consumers, pigs like Jessie, and the planet—there's simply no other way it can be or should be.

If New Age Meats can inject themselves into craft breweries across the country and abroad (I mean, think about Oktoberfest alone), do you think they will stand a good chance at achieving impactful success and accomplishing their mission to help mitigate climate change, stop the breeding of animals into lives not worth living, and greatly improve human health?

Main Takeaways:
After talking with your target customers, if your initial concept isn't what they want or need at the time, ask yourself:
 — What do they need that I can offer value on?
 — Am I potentially going after the wrong audience?
 — Am I thinking BIG enough in the first place?

---

43   Spears, Brian, and Alex Shirazi. "Brian Spears of New Age Meats - Clean Meat Founders Series - Live Recording." *Cultured Meat Future Food* , YouTube, August 5, 2018.

Have your ear to the ground and listen to what pain points are out there and ready to solve.
- If an issue out there already has some groundwork and research completed that you can use, great; you just put yourself a few steps forward and hopefully saved a lot of time and money by doing so!

It's great to have peers and models to learn from in business, especially for go-to-market plans, but hopefully your product has a unique value proposition and occupies a space that can set you apart.
- For example, what a match made in heaven breweries and clean pork sausages can be; New Age Meats is wise to have their sights set on that pairing strategy.

Wild Earth, Man's Best Friend, and Visiting the *Shark Tank*

One of the most important avenues of sustainable food that is often overlooked by many feeds some of our closest companions—our pets. You may have grown up with a furry family member, or I hope you at least had some friends with them so you could get your dog or cat fix.

One of the pups I've grown up with is Kiele ("Kee-Lee"). She's a half German shepherd/ half yellow lab who we rescued after she survived parvo (a canine virus that can kill dogs, especially puppies because they are most susceptible). She's still back in New Jersey with my parents playing with her stuffed animals and chasing squirrels. She's also a big fan of this section's Gene-trepreneur and company, but more on this shortly.

The most popular furry companions are dogs and cats (over 163 million in the US alone, which is about half the number of human residents in the country).[44] And while dogs are omnivores, cats are obligate carnivores, meaning that they don't have a choice but to eat meat.[45]

The pet food industry has been notoriously sketchy over the years with its animal-derived food products resulting in multiple poisonings and mass recalls due to contaminations with bacteria like *E. coli* and salmonella, as well as discovering traces of the euthanasia drug pentobarbital in some pet foods.

Additionally, the protein ingredients themselves can come from a slew of questionable sources like the entrails of animals, remnants from dead and diseased ones, animals with tumors, etc.—basically not only the parts of meat that humans choose not to consume, but also many components unfit for animal consumption as a whole.[46] Wild Earth calls these "4D animals—dead, dying, diseased or disabled—so there could really be anything in there."[47]

Even if you were to put aside all of the contaminations and questionable qualities of meat, pet food still leaves a nasty "bark" on the environment. The United States pet food industry contributes to 25–30 percent of the overall greenhouse gas emissions given off as a result of the US's animal agriculture industry.[48] But this is where serial entrepreneur Ryan Bethencourt is coming in to save the day both for animals and for the planet.

---

44 Fox, Katrina. "Why Wild Earth Cofounder Ryan Bethencourt Is Applying The Science Of 'Vegan Biohacking' To Pet Food." Forbes. March 16, 2018.

45 "Why Are Cats Called "Obligate Carnivores?"" CANIDAE®.

46 Martin, Glen. "Should Our Pets Be Vegans, Too?" Cal Alumni Association. July 11, 2018.

47 Webber, Jemima. "Can Dogs Be Vegan? 5 Meat-Free Foods to Try." LIVEKINDLY. Publisher Name LIVEKINDLY Publisher Logo, June 8, 2019.

48 Fox, Katrina. "Why Wild Earth Cofounder Ryan Bethencourt Is Applying The Science Of 'Vegan Biohacking' To Pet Food." Forbes. March 16, 2018.

Ryan Bethencourt is one of the utmost leaders in the realm of biotech startups, having invested in and helped build more than seventy companies as part of IndieBio's co-founding team (the world's leading life science startup accelerator).[49] Now, he is the CEO and co-founder of Wild Earth, a startup founded in 2017 that is positioned to drastically improve the pet food industry under his leadership and palpable passion for helping animals. I had the pleasure to connect with him and learn more about his story founding Wild Earth.

Ryan shared with me that he grew up in Miami with lots of animals in the house—everything from birds to snakes—and a love of science fiction. At around ten years old, he had the unpleasant experience of witnessing a pig being slaughtered, and it didn't really sit right with him. He expressed how he could see the animal was terrified, and he knew there had to be another way for us to source meat down the line.

When Bethencourt co-founded IndieBio in 2014, he was able to directly impact startups working on this other way: plant and cell-based meats like we've been talking so much about. He helped many fellow Gene-trepreneurs at companies like Finless Foods and Memphis Meats, both working to vastly lessen our reliance on animal agriculture, through mission-driven investment and his expert mentorship. At this time, while everyone was looking at creating plant and cell-based proteins for human consumption, Bethencourt began turning his sights toward the food supply of our four-legged friends. Pets had been an underserved market in the food innovation space still left untapped, and this opportunity was ripe for bringing sustainability to a very unsustainable industry.

Today, with the pet food market worth over thirty billion dollars in the US alone, Wild Earth has the potential to make an incredible impact in the health of pets around the globe if it can successfully go tail-to-tail with the field's top players.[50] But just like Big Dairy and the meat industry for humans, in this battlefield, ground

49   Canal, Emily. "This 'Shark Tank' Founder Valued His Company at $11 Million With No Sales. Here's Why Mark Cuban Invested $550,000." Inc.com. March 18, 2019.

50   Martin, Glen. "Should Our Pets Be Vegans, Too?" Cal Alumni Association. July 11, 2018.

won't be won easily without a fight. If anyone can do it, though, it's Ryan Bethencourt.

$$\infty$$

To start, Bethencourt and his team have created plant-based dog treats made from human-grade koji, a relative of food fungi like mushrooms often used in delicious soy sauces and miso. They have also formulated a koji-based dog food that provides high-quality protein for your canine companions without killing tons of animals to provide that protein. I was able to get Kiele some of their peanut butter treats and Wild Earth's first commercialized run of koji pet food, and let me tell you, she's one happy pup!

Comically, Bethencourt shared that he was the first test animal for the products since he didn't want to give his pets an upset stomach if the first batches were a bust. But fortunately, and as I would have expected from him, it all went remarkably well. He has since gotten the paw of approval from many dogs, including picky-eater Kiele, as well as cats who steal their dog siblings' food. And as a high point in this R&D process for Wild Earth as well is that after testing on themselves, they let pups voluntarily taste-test from the comfort of their own homes. Traditional pet food companies test their products on caged animals, and you certainly won't find the CEOs of those big businesses eating any of their company's products themselves.[51]

Bethencourt has actually regularly challenged big pet food company executives to taste-test their own pet food on social media and has yet to find a soul brave enough to do so. Shouldn't that tell you something? These incumbent execs know exactly what is in their products and don't want to put it *anywhere* near their mouths, yet they will happily feed it to *your* four-legged best friends.

That's the difference between them and Wild Earth; Ryan Bethencourt is leading by example and stands by the products Wild Earth makes. The quality is so high he'll happily take a bite. And don't tell anybody, but I may have tried the peanut butter treats. Kiele likes

---

51 Grefski, Lorie. "Is Your Pet's Food Tested on Animals?" One Green Planet. February 10, 2015.

them more than I do obviously, but hey, if you run out of protein bars they'll do in a pinch.

Another awesome aspect about Wild Earth, which will certainly give them an advantage as they expand their product offerings, is that they will be able to create and readily change the texture, flavor, and ingredient profiles of their animal food products to cater to the specific dietary needs of different breeds. Furthermore, they are beginning to explore development of cell-based proteins as well, such as clean mouse meat for cat food.[52] As Wild Earth branches out, they are also looking to partner with clean meat companies like New Age Meats for pork and Finless Foods for fish protein so they can accelerate the adoption of sustainable pet food as quickly as possible.

There really isn't any time to waste, and the founders in this field are more than willing to support each other's mission to lessen reliance on animal agriculture, whether that's for human food or our other animal counterparts.

Wild Earth isn't going to be an expert in every cell-based protein, but you now know some of the ones who are in their specific niches. If Wild Earth and New Age Meats come to a deal with cultured pork, for example, it could be very mutually beneficial as New Age Meats would have another customer channel in pets. At the same time, Wild Earth could not only expand their product line sooner to beat out the big pet food brands, but more importantly that would mean they'd be able to create bigger and more meaningful impacts in animal welfare and environmental sustainability sooner. This is all assuming both can successfully scale up, which is tough for any startup, let alone ones in food innovation. But the point is, with no time to waste, you have to be smart and figure out the most time-efficient, most promising, and most impactful path forward.

Snapshot Lesson:
The right partnership strategy can potentially accelerate your growth and overall impact vastly. You can't be an expert at everything, so if you want to go far (and fast in this case too), it can be best to work together.

---

52   Brodwin, Erin. "'Cat Parents Think It's Cool': A Peter Thiel-backed Startup Pursuing Mouse Meat for Dogs Has Begun Selling Its First Products." Business Insider. October 1, 2018.

Moving as a lean startup also allows Wild Earth to get a leg up on the much larger (for now) competition: the Purinas and Pedigrees of the world. And whether it's you with your own startup or Ryan with Wild Earth, going up against the incumbents can feel like David vs. Goliath.

Bethencourt shared a quote relating to this: "Speed is safety." Being able to quickly maneuver and sneak up on competitors allows a growing startup to avoid getting squished by the big guys. And these large corporations are also starting to take notice of Wild Earth in a variety of ways.

Some are directing fire at Wild Earth in the same barrage the other clean protein companies are facing. It's the whole untenable spiel saying what they're making can't be labeled as a product made with real meat. It's quite the contrary, though, because it *will be* real animal protein in every way, just without the bad ethics, antibiotics, parasites, agricultural chemicals, toxins, diseased animal carcasses, etc. included.

The smart companies are actually beginning to develop their own plant and cell-based products or are investing in their own disruptors. Mars Petcare is one of the largest players in the pet business, and they have invested in Wild Earth to help their sustainable mission. It's like the Starks of Winterfell say: "The lone wolf dies while the pack of ethical and growing sustainable pet food companies survives." That's the quote, right?

∞

Peter Thiel, co-founder of PayPal, is also in the corner of Wild Earth as an investor. And on a season 10 episode of *Shark Tank*, we got the chance to watch Ryan take a plunge into the shark-infested waters of Daymond John, Lori Greiner, Kevin O'Leary, Mark Cuban, and guest judge Matt Higgins. He was tested early on by John who thought the evaluation Ryan was asking for of $550,000 for 5 percent ($11 million evaluation) was outrageous for a company that did not have sales numbers to show proof-of-concept yet. And Ryan also took some flack from O'Leary (a.k.a. Mr. Wonderful) poking fun at the thought of making dogs vegan. The shark who had faith and vision in Wild Earth was Mark Cuban.

Cuban said he'd do the deal at $550,000 for 10 percent, double what Ryan originally offered. And then Cuban resisted any attempts by Bethencourt to negotiate him down. Presented with this once-in-a-lifetime moment that we've all seen so many hopeful entrepreneurs flop at in the tank, Bethencourt made the wise move of accepting the deal, even if it had to come from his own ownership of the company he co-founded.[53]

As Bethencourt reflected on his experience and shared some lessons he learned from the tank, his mindset was that "... one yes from any of the Sharks can transform you and your company into one of America's leading brands, but all too often entrepreneurs hesitate, get distracted or get greedy. Don't!"[54]

Another great lesson he shared was to be yourself:

"The Sharks invest first and foremost in people. We've all seen people on the show whose business idea wasn't exactly going to save the world, but the passion and integrity that entrepreneur showed made us root for them.

If the Sharks bite, what they're really trying to do is understand you. They want to see your excitement and dedication. They want to see if you've got what it takes to take the full pressure and survive. If you do, you might just have what it takes to be a Shark Tank entrepreneur and of course, make them a lot of money!"[55]

∞

Moving even further out into the distant future, Bethencourt stated to me that they could even consider venturing beyond plant and cell-based domestic dog and cat food. This could mean extending into realms like meat for captive lions, tigers, leopards, and more

53   Berger, Sarah. "Mark Cuban Just Invested $550,000 in a Vegan Dog Treats Company on 'Shark Tank'." CNBC. CNBC, March 18, 2019.

54   Bethencourt, Ryan. "5 Lessons I Learned from Going on ABC's Shark Tank." Wild Earth. Wild Earth, March 22, 2019.

55   Ibid.

carnivorous creatures around the world. The same could be said for snakes, bears, foxes, ferrets, and many more meat-eating species in homes, zoos, rehabilitation centers, and animal sanctuaries. The timelines for this are unknown and certainly a significant number of years away, but wouldn't that be amazing? What if Wild Earth and its partners could help every zoo set up bioreactors in-house to provide their omnivores and carnivores with all their protein needs?

I want to end this segment on my favorite part of interviewing Ryan Bethencourt. I asked him what advice he would give entrepreneurs trying to enter the sustainable spaces of plant and cell-based proteins. His response: "Give yourself permission."

People will ask who gave you the right to do something, which in Bethencourt's case are things such as being the co-founder of the incredible accelerator IndieBio and being a disruptor of the thirty-billion-dollar pet food industry. And you know what? Bethencourt gave himself that permission to pursue those ambitions. You obviously need a community of friends, family, and entrepreneurial individuals to help motivate and support you while building any startup, but the most important person you need permission from to chase your dreams is you. And that is, perhaps, my most favorite piece of advice in this entire book.

Main Takeaways:

Use partnerships to your advantage when planning your growth strategy.

Don't be greedy.

- Know what you're willing to give up before you walk into any investor meeting.
- Recognize the size of the opportunity before you. A small piece of a big pie can be worth a lot more than a big piece of a small one.
- If you are like Bethencourt and have a social impact component, consider which is more important to you—your financial reward or making an impact sooner, even if it means less money going to you.

Think big, and when you do, give yourself permission to follow through.

CHAPTER 4

CLEAN DAIRY, BETTER EGGS, AND GAYLORD FOCKER

If you look in the Merriam-Webster Dictionary, one of the definitions for milk reads: "a food product produced from seeds or fruit that resembles and is used similarly to cow's milk."[1] It even goes on to provide the examples of coconut milk and soy milk for further clarification.

Why is this important?

Just as clean and plant-based proteins are disrupting the harmful meat industry, advancing food tech is also knocking on the door of Big Dairy. And as you might guess, sustainably minded Gene-trepreneurs are not receiving a warm welcome. Dairy groups like The National Milk Producers Federation have long pressured government bodies like the US Food and Drug Administration (FDA) via political lobbying to target popular plant-based milk alternatives like soy and almond milk.

Their goal is to prevent these types or any non-animal-based products from calling themselves milk.[2] They view it as a threat to their industry, and rightfully so. Non-dairy milk sales, like those of soy and almond milk, rose 61 percent from 2012 to 2017. In that same time frame, traditional milk from cows saw a 15 percent decline in sales.[3]

In 2018, then acting FDA Commissioner Scott Gottlieb stirred up quite the cause for concern when he proposed moving forward with

---

1   "Milk." Merriam-Webster. Merriam-Webster, n.d.

2   Choi, Candice. "FDA May Force Soy and Almond 'milk' Companies to Change Labeling." USA Today. July 19, 2018.

3   Sibilla, Nick. "FDA Crackdown On Calling Almond Milk 'Milk' Could Violate The First Amendment." Forbes. Forbes Magazine, February 1, 2019.

labeling laws against alternative milks using the word "milk" in their product name. Luckily, since then, cases brought against alternative milk producers by dairy groups over mislabeling have been dismissed on the federal court level, establishing more of a precedent in favor of sustainable innovation that can give us some forward-looking hope in the judicial system as it relates to biotech. Plus, if Big Dairy is really trying to argue that consumers are supposedly getting confused about almond milk's origin not being from a cow, maybe we should take a look into our education system, right?

I do like to imagine a comical scenario in the courtroom where maybe the FDA and Big Dairy try to use Gaylord Focker's (a.k.a. Greg, played by Ben Stiller) line from *Meet the Parents* to argue against alternative milks. I can envision it now:

Dairy Industry and FDA Lawyers: "As Greg Focker stated in the 2000 box office hit *Meet the Parents*, Your Honor—with an 84 percent on Rotten Tomatoes, I might add—'You can milk anything WITH nipples.'[4] But soy beans and almonds Don't. Have. Nipples, Your Honor! It's that simple. Call it nut juice instead! We rest our case."

Judge: "Well, you got me there, Hank." *gavel bangs* "Case closed!"

Just as with milk, the same untenable arguments are being applied in the clean and plant-based meat sector to bar labeling anything as meat unless it comes fully from an animal.[5] In the end, however, I think we can safely predict these ridiculous efforts will be in vain because technology will eventually overtake traditional methods of protein production in the meat and dairy industries on economical, ethical, and nutritional levels. I guess you could say the incumbent industries are really trying to "milk it" (*drum and cymbal hit*) and hold out for as long as possible.

---

4   *Meet the Parents.* Directed by Joe Roach. Performed by Robert De Niro and Ben Stiller. October 6, 2000.

5   Popper, Nathaniel. "You Call That Meat? Not So Fast, Cattle Ranchers Say." The New York Times. February 09, 2019.

Chief the Cow and Counting Your Chickens Before They Hatch

Trends show that milk consumption in the US is actually down 36 percent since the 1970s. However, in that time the dairy industry has been able to more than double the milk output of individual dairy cows while the total number of them has dropped by a quarter.[6]

Interestingly, part of this bump in productivity per cow is due to just one male back in the 1960s, whose full name was Pawnee Farm Arlinda Chief. Chief was a bull whose sperm was the stuff of dairy farmers' dreams because his daughters, of which he had 16,000, were amazing milk-producers. His genes led to really high milk production, and so his genetic material was highly sought after by farmers to increase their revenue. But in Chief's genes lurked a killer. He had a mutation in one copy of his *Apaf1* gene.

Mutations are common. We all have them, but sometimes they can be problematic such as in the development of cancer, or in this instance, reproduction. Chief passed along the mutated version of the gene (called an allele) to some offspring (which became carriers), whereas other offspring received a normal copy of the allele (because that's how reproduction works—half from mom, half from dad, but there are infinite possibilities for which alleles across the whole genome combine to create the offspring).

Chief was such a popular bull that he had half a million grand-daughters and over two million great-granddaughters, which meant there were a lot of carriers of the mutant *Apaf1* gene. His sons were also frequently used to sire more strong milk producers.

Inevitably, descendants of Chief who were both carriers of the deadly allele ended up producing babies (probably most often using artificial insemination). If the resulting offspring received zero or just one copy of the altered allele, they were fine, but to draw the short stick and receive copies from both parents was a literal killer. It led to spontaneous abortions of all calves who inherited the mutant allele from mom and dad. To date, the mutant *Apaf1* gene has cost the dairy industry over five hundred thousand pregnancies, but the use of Chief's DNA has also made them an estimated thirty billion

---

6 Cardello, Hank. "How the Milk Industry Went Sour, and What Every Business Can Learn From It." Forbes. January 04, 2013.

dollars in additional profits. Currently, Chief's descendants make up 14 percent of all Holstein cows—the most popular breed in the dairy industry.[7]

∞

Nowadays, genome sequencing is so cheap that dairy farmers regularly use it to avoid mutant genes like the killer *Apaf1*, as well as to determine the profitable genes that will lead to more milk ... always more milk. Despite utilizing tech to avoid health defects, it is important to realize that the industry is still very unethical (and in my perception, using the tech is more about making money rather than concern for the cows).

I don't think many people are aware that dairy cows do not produce milk all of their lives. Cows and humans are both mammals. Like our species, cows only produce milk after giving birth. And only the females do, of course. This means that the milk being used for human consumption comes at the cost of the baby.[8] If that baby happens to be a male, it really has little value to a dairy farmer, right? That male calf can't birth more milk-producing cows and is just consuming resources, which is why it will either be killed right after birth to be incinerated or turned into pet food, raised to about eight months to then be sold to veal producers, or raised to about twelve to fourteen months when it will be slaughtered and sold as beef.[9]

The selectivity of sexes seen with cows is also commonplace with other species: sheep, chickens, and additional animals across the entirety of the agriculture industry. People will become emotionally numb and tell you that "it's just business" like they're the evil Lord Beckett in the third *Pirates of the Caribbean* movie, but it doesn't change the fact that we're literally killing billions of baby animals

7   Howard, Lisa. "How a Genetic Mutation From 1 Bull Caused the Loss of Half a Million Calves Worldwide." UC Davis. October 13, 2016.

8   Stauffer, Krista. "Average Age of a Dairy Cow." The Farmer's Wifee. June 21, 2014.

9   Levitt, Tom. "Dairy's 'dirty Secret': It's Still Cheaper to Kill Male Calves than to Rear Them." The Guardian. March 26, 2018.

here.[10] It would be a great improvement if we could obtain 99 percent females on these farms using biotech and only breed the males we need to continue reproducing (that is until plant and cell-based inevitably overtake the traditional animal ag industry).

Science has already offered some solutions that can bring us close, one being sex-sorted sperm. Sex of the baby is determined by the male's genetic contribution because typically speaking, females always pass one of their X chromosomes (females are XX) while males have the possibility of either providing another X or their Y sex chromosome (which would result in a male calf, XY).

Since 2004, sex-sorted sperm has been commercially available, and having improved over the years, it can now create 85 percent to 95 percent of the desired sex (being female) when employed. However, it doesn't make sense for a lot of farmers to use semen selection on a mass scale because it is more expensive and can lead to less reproductive success.[11] You can think about it as the process of sex selection takes time (sperm can't swim forever), not all swimmers survive the process, you're halving the number of bullets in the chamber, and this all contributes to less success hitting the target in the end.

I actually learned quite a bit about the subject of cattle reproduction when I co-authored a "How to Artificially Inseminate a Cow" guide with two pre-vet students for an English project several years ago. I will never use it though because I don't want to find myself elbow-deep in a cow's anus manipulating the reproductive tract so I can guide in a semen-straw successfully.

If you liken direct artificial insemination into the cow to shooting an arrow at a target and hoping you're as good of a shot as Robin Hood, one method that can help improve artificial fertilization effectiveness is basically the equivalent of Robin Hood walking up to the target and placing his arrow in the bullseye; it's called in vitro fertilization (a.k.a. IVF).

You've probably heard of IVF being used for humans, but you may not know about it being used for cows. IVF is a treatment where eggs

10   *Pirates of the Caribbean: At World's End.* Directed by Gore Verbinski. Performed by Johnny Depp, Keira Knightley, and Orlando Bloom. May 25, 2007.

11   Rhinehart, Justin. "How It Works: Sex Sorted Semen." AgWeb. January 21, 2016.

are collected from the ovaries, fertilized outside the body, allowed to develop for about a week, and then transferred into the female's uterus to continue growth.[12] Many people use IVF to have children today, but when it first came out with the successful birth of a baby girl in 1978, much of the public was uncomfortable with it, and many headlines referred to children of IVF as "test-tube babies."[13] We don't really hear that term anymore because it's now so commonplace and publicly accepted.

Snapshot Observation:
Educating the public about new biotech can be frustrating and met with a lot of pushback, which is why teaching scientific literacy is so vital today. (Just think about anti-vaxxers and flat-Earthers.) Bio-innovation is only increasing in its rate of progress along with our circumstances around climate change and sustainability becoming more dire. As we've seen with IVF, people eventually come around to technology. It's just a matter of when. So scientific literacy is now more important than ever to accelerate the rate of not only passive public acceptance but also active public support.

IVF can be an alternative to artificially inseminating directly, but the upfront cost can be expensive ($20–$25K per attempt in humans, for example)![14] There is a novel genetic engineering tool called CRISPR (which we'll delve deeper into later in chapters 7 and 8) and as it develops to become more accepted by the public, more regulated by government organizations, and of course cheaper, we may see emerging startups use it to take on the task of genetically engineering male animals out of the factory farming industry almost altogether. This would be done by essentially gaming the biological system such that males would only pass on their X chromosomes, resulting in XX female offspring. This genetic engineering method of sex selection would be done with what are called "gene drives" and will be especially important in other areas like tackling invasive species (but

---

12   "IVF Process | IVF Information." Monash IVF.

13   Sanders, Laura. "40 Years after the First IVF Baby, a Look Back at the Birth of a New Era." Science News, July 25, 2018.

14   Flora, Carlin. "IVF and Gender Selection: What You Need to Know." Parents.

again, much more about all of this exciting innovation later in the species conservation chapters).

When you think about it, gene drives for sex selection in traditional farming might just be the equivalent of what Aquapods are to the aquaculture industry—an intermediary step with decent but most likely declining long-term value. We forecast that plant and cell-based proteins will eventually take the lead, right? However, every opportunity to step in the right direction needs to be taken. Even minuscule improvements can lead to large impacts when we're talking about the animal agriculture industry that affects billions of lives every year.

∞

Aside from cows, agtech Gene-trepreneurs are finding ways to accomplish sex-selection in chicks for the poultry industry, mainly chickens. Male chicks (seven billion every year) are either suffocated in bags or ground alive because roosters don't lay eggs or make enough meat to warrant their survival.[15] But recently, Gene-trepreneurs at an Israeli startup called eggXYt, founded in 2016, are working on a method to screen eggs so that males never have to be born just to be killed almost immediately after hatching.

The way eggXYt is counting chickens before they hatch is via CRISPR where simple biomarkers will show up in eggs that would eventually go on to produce male chicks. The male eggs, when put under eggXYt's screening tech called seXYt, fluoresce a yellow color. This same practice of utilizing biomarkers is extremely common in academic research as it allows scientists to easily observe where certain proteins are expressed in cells or in different parts of the body—highly useful.

The male chicken eggs, once identified by eggXYt's seXYt tech, can then be sold to cosmetics companies or other industries while the female eggs (with no biomarker, thus do not give off a signal) will be allowed to incubate into chicks and hatch. Obviously, this sorting method is very beneficial for the chicken industry on the egg and

---

15   "Count Your Chickens Before They Hatch." EggXYt.

poultry sides to prevent half of all resources put into egg incubation being useless. That's why they use it. But if I had to guess, the founders of eggXYt probably founded their startup to help stop the killing of billions of day-old male chicks every year.[16] It's another example of different primary concerns leading to the same sustainable result.

> **Snapshot Lesson:**
> Again, it's all about how you position your company—solve others' pain points so that in doing so, they are contributing to solving yours.

Overall, around the world over seventy billion terrestrial animals are killed every year to produce meat, dairy, and eggs—ten times the entire human population on Earth. That's not even including the number of aquatic animals raised or caught annually, which goes into the trillions.[17] You can see how animal agriculture is a truly abhorrent industry, both in terms of ethics and inefficiency. However, the good news for everybody who loves dairy is that there are some really exciting startups developing plant and cell-based milk products and scaling up to replace the incumbent industry in commercial markets.

Perfect Day Foods and Plant-Based Cheese

One of the synthetic bio companies building strong bones and shooting cruelty-free milk in the eyes of traditional dairy is Perfect Day Foods, a startup producing milk proteins without a single cow in sight. Founded in 2014 by Perumal Gandhi and Ryan Pandya, the name Perfect Day comes from the song of the same name by Lou Reed because two scientists discovered that calm, happy cows produce more milk. The researchers played the cows music, and that particular song was one of the most efficacious for increased milk production. What a thoughtful story behind the name.[18]

Perfect Day Foods brews casein and whey proteins (the protein foundations of milk) with yeast in a fermentation process and then adds in plant-based sugars, minerals, and fatty acids to create a

---

16   Ibid.

17   "Factory Farms." A Well-Fed World.

18

product that tastes just like the real thing. The immense benefit of this method is passed on directly to customers as people can consume a wide variety of dairy products without the hormones, lactose, antibiotics, and agricultural chemicals that are typically found in dairy-containing beverages and foods.

And in regard to the environment, Perfect Day Foods' process uses a lot less resources:

- 98 percent less water
- 65 percent less energy
- 91 percent less land
- as well as emits 84 percent less greenhouse gases![19]

These benefits have attracted a lot of investor attention. The company raised a Series B round of $34.8 million in February 2019, thereby bringing their total investment up to $61.5 million (see Crunchbase for ongoing updates).[20]

Perfect Day actually became the first cellular agriculture company ever to launch a product to market! In July of 2019, they released a limited run of animal-free dairy ice cream selling one thousand three-pint packs of Milky Chocolate, Vanilla Salted Fudge, and Vanilla Blackberry Toffee. They sold out in hours.[21]

This limited run was to drum up excitement and simply test the waters to gauge market appetite for any future products offering their animal-free dairy. This is important because the team at Perfect Day Foods is currently partnering with existing food and dairy companies to bring their novel dairy to a wide array of products on the market, and they're looking to partner with more. They aren't looking to be confined to a tiny spot in the supermarket with one brand of milk, but rather are smartly focused on integrating into many products through strategic partnerships.

To build one brand, let alone many (imagine Perfect Day ice cream, other frozen desserts, milk, cheese, yogurt, etc.) would be

19   Murray-Ragg, Nadia. "'Vegan' Milk Brand Perfect Day Secures $24.7 Million to 'Disrupt the Dairy Industry'." LIVEKINDLY. February 28, 2018.

20   Perfect Day. Crunchbase.

21   Scipioni, Jade. "This $20 Ice Cream Is Made with Dairy Grown in Lab-and It Sold out Immediately." CNBC. CNBC, July 16, 2019.

excruciatingly difficult, resource-devouring, and risky! But positioning Perfect Day as a supplier of animal-free dairy to companies with established ice cream, milk, etc. brands while utilizing their manufacturing and delivery infrastructures, purchase order forms, and more can save Perfect Day a lot of time and money.

Additionally, partnerships allow Perfect Day to be much quicker to the punch with their company's growth strategy and ability to make significant impacts in environmental sustainability and animal agriculture. It's like with Wild Earth planning to cultivate partnerships to keep being the "fast fish" in the pet food industry.

Snapshot Lesson:

The better you can do as a business in "X" amount of time, the more you can accomplish in your sustainable mission that is likely at the heart of your business to begin with. The right partnerships can accelerate and expand your impact, but it's a matter of scaling successfully (not getting ahead of yourself as a company) and figuring out which partnerships may lead to a 2x, 5x, 10x, or even a 100x impact.

With the successful test run of ice cream now under their belt, Perfect Day Foods now has a very promising proof-of-concept to approach potential partners with and to help seek another round of funding if they deem necessary for keeping up with their growth.

If all goes well, which udders crossed it will, then get ready to see a significant rise in animal-free dairy options from your favorite products courtesy of Perfect Day Foods and other alternative dairy suppliers. It's actually predicted that the alternative dairy market will rise to become a thirty-four-billion-dollar industry by 2024. It already had a 9 percent growth in 2018 from the previous year while traditional dairy lost $1.1 billion in 2018—8 percent down from 2017.[22] Vegans and those with lactose intolerance, rejoice!

∞

22   Ettinger, Jill. "Experts Predict Dairy Industry Could Disappear in 10 Years." LIVEKINDLY. April 07, 2019.

Many more startups and Gene-trepreneurs are right behind them, opening up the alternative dairy markets in all sorts of areas like cheeses, spreads, desserts, etc. with ingredient bases like coconuts, avocados, hemp, almonds, soy, hazelnuts, oats, cashews, and many more.

Some are plant-based, such as Plant Based Cheese out of Amsterdam in the Netherlands. I spoke with founder Brad Vanstone and was absolutely intrigued by the process of turning nuts into cheese. It uses a lot of fermentation, again, much like beer. He's even able to create a plant-based cheese fondue. And this reminded me a lot of another Brad, Brad Leone, of *Bon Appétit* (a popular food and entertainment magazine). Leone actually has a fermentation series with Bon Appétit online called *It's Alive*.[23] It's one of my favorite video series online, and it will certainly instill a love of fermentation in you too.

Other startups similar to Perfect Day are using more of a cellular agriculture approach. Either way, both plant and cell-based dairy can really shake things up for the better in an industry that has long been on the outs. And if you'd like to explore more into dairy innovation, you should check out Olivia Fox Cabane's Alternative Food Industry Landscapes.[24] She puts together amazing visual databases of all the rising food tech startups in dairy and meat along with startups using fungi and algae for cosmetics, materials, and more. Additionally, you can look into the corporate partners, accelerators, NGOs, VCs, etc. involved in these spaces on these landscapes. It's incredibly helpful for seeing the scope of innovation now upon us and finding companies and other organizations in each sector of interest.

Main Takeaway:
Nothing is built alone; you'll go a lot further and create more impacts if you build something together.
- Have a successful proof-of-concept to approach and attract partners with.
- Be smart and strategic about who you collaborate with and when as you do not want to outpace the speed you can realistically grow.

---

23   Leone, Brad. "It's Alive with Brad." Bon Appétit Videos, n.d.
24   Cabane, Olivia Fox. "The Landscapes." *The Alternative Protein Show.*

CHAPTER 5

CROP TECH AND COFFEE

Attention all housewives, college students, fans of *The Bachelor* franchise, and people who uncomfortably try to show off their knowledge of wine during their annual visit to the local Olive Garden, I have some terribly worrisome news. Climate change is coming for your glasses of whites and reds. Prepare to shell out more for your "grape juice for adults."

But as always, there's hope. So how can synthetic biology potentially save the world's food supply of crops and your reasonably priced bottles of wine?

∞

The wine industry is taking a huge hit at the hands of climate change because grapes require cold winters and dry, arid summers. Prime areas for vineyards are moving further away from the equator as climate conditions change; regions like France, Italy, and the Napa Valley are going to be losing grape yields while places like England, Michigan, and Tasmania will become new hot spots for wine-making.[1] And while we can selectively breed and hybridize grape varieties for increased durability, it may not be fast enough to adapt to the quickly changing climate.

This is happening to many more crops all around the world, too. For every increase of two degrees Fahrenheit, crop loss is estimated to be 3.2 percent in rice, 6 percent in wheat, and 7.4 percent in corn.[2] This is attributable to pests making their way into previously

1   Rathi, Akshat. "The Improbable New Wine Countries That Climate Change Is Creating." Quartzy. November 10, 2017.

2   "Climate Change Will Cut Crop Yields: Study." Phys.org. August 15, 2017.

uninhabitable areas that are getting warmer and also due to changing growing conditions—plants like grapes have very specific environmental ranges for optimum growth.

It's such a big concern because, according to the United Nations Department of Economic and Social Affairs, the global population will be approaching ten billion by 2050.[3] Climate-controlled vertical farming (which is using urban warehouses for example with artificial light, temperature control, etc.) might be able to help optimize growing conditions as well as help maximize the crop output per square foot of space, but not all crops can be grown in this manner, especially larger ones like corn for instance.[4]

So the question becomes can we engineer corn, wheat, grapes and other crops to speed up their adaptation process? Can we facilitate their success in our rapidly changing climate conditions in this way?

The answer is yes, and in the cases with many crops we already have. But genetically modified organisms (GMOs) have gotten a really bad rap because of companies like Monsanto, so a lot of public mistrust and misunderstanding must be repaired.

Although recently acquired by Bayer, Monsanto had long been abusing their overwhelming choke hold on GMO seeds and harmful herbicides like Roundup in order to shut out small farmers and amass corporate wealth. This has given GMOs a lot of bad press and negatively impacted the public's perception.[5] However, genetically engineered foods are actually great for the most part! They can allow for less agricultural chemical usage because the plants are engineered to have built-in protection, not to mention having drought resistance and increased hot and cold tolerance.[6] So when most people go picketing against GMOs, they are really just against the abuse of GMOs by companies like Monsanto (or rather, Bayer now).

3 "World Population Projected to Reach 9.8 Billion in 2050, and 11.2 Billion in 2100 | UN DESA Department of Economic and Social Affairs." United Nations. June 21, 2017.

4 Oshima, Marc. "How Vertical Can Farms Get? | Marc Oshima | HT Summit 2017." Hello Tomorrow. December 01, 2017.

5 Caldwell, Tommy. "GMOs Aren't That Bad, But Monsanto Is the Worst." Vice. June 06, 2013.

6 Heikkinen, Niina. "Genetically Engineered Crops Are Safe and Possibly Good for Climate Change." Scientific American. May 18, 2016.

While it would be much more beneficial for public awareness to target a specific company for wrongdoing rather than condemn GMOs as a whole, I think the strategy will improve as scientific literacy increases in further generations.

∞

On a side note about pesticides, France recently became the first country to ban all five of the pesticides that scientists believe are responsible for killing bees.[7] Synthetic neonicotinoids were first used in the 1990s, and they attack the central nervous system of insects. The chemicals alter the bees' sperm counts and disrupt their very important homing abilities. In fact, evidence suggests that this family of pesticides contributes to colony collapse disorder, the mysterious condition that has decimated up to 90 percent of bee populations in some areas. Good on France for taking a step to protect bees because without these pollinators, we would only be able to produce a fraction of our dietary staples.

For France especially now, genetic engineering can help make up for the lack of chemical protection their crops will have. And aside from some outliers, engineering crops is a really necessary aspect to improving agricultural technology moving forward. Not only can it help save the bees via less pesticide use, but it will also help feed—and quench the thirst for wine—of the rapidly growing world population into the future.

∞

In addition to genetically engineering or selectively breeding to affect the plant genome, another method is rising in the ranks to improve the crop industry. Scientists are turning their attention toward the bacteria that live in, on, and around plants to boost plant protection and productivity more naturally.

---

7   Samuel, Henry. "France Becomes First Country in Europe to Ban All Five Pesticides Killing Bees ." The Telegraph. August 31, 2018.

Microbes have evolved alongside plants for millions of years to help defend them from pests and diseases and to provide them with nutrients. But today, many places suffer from soil infertility and depleted plant microbiomes from decades of agricultural chemicals being sprayed everywhere.[8] These chemicals prevent healthy populations of microbes and thus suppress potential high-yield plant growth.

A number of companies are working to help bring back what has been lost, one being Trace Genomics. They analyze soil samples and interpret the data so farmers can know what microbes are living in their fields, assess risks of disease, track nutrient profiles, and more. The farmers can then use this information to take action by choosing what crop varieties to plant in which fields for example.[9]

Taking that a step further, though, companies like Joyn Bio, Pivot Bio, Indigo Agriculture, and AgBiome are not just analyzing but actively utilizing these microbes in the field to farmers' and consumers' advantages.

Joyn Bio and Pivot Bio

Joyn Bio is a company formed in 2017 out of the partnership between synthetic biology powerhouse Ginkgo Bioworks (featured in the next chapter) and life science giant Bayer.[10] Yes, I know Bayer bought the great, evil Monsanto, but this effort is a really positive one that could have a beneficial impact on energy and food sustainability.[11]

Together, the two companies are pooling Ginkgo's synthetic biology expertise and Bayer's agricultural knowledge (and collection of more than one hundred thousand proprietary bacterial strains) to tackle the problem of synthetic fertilizer.[12] Joyn Bio has, to date,

---

8   TechCrunch. "Indigo Bets on Microbes to Boost Plants." July 21, 2016.

9   Diane Wu. "Unlocking the Power of Our Soil I Diane Wu, CEO of Trace Genomics." Hello Tomorrow. April 16, 2019.

10   Bayer. "Bayer and Ginkgo Bioworks Unveil Joint Venture, Joyn Bio, and Establish Operations in Boston and West Sacramento." PR Newswire: Press Release Distribution, Targeting, Monitoring and Marketing. June 27, 2018.

11   "10 Reasons Why Monsanto Is Corrupt from Its Core." Seattle Organic Restaurants.

12   Bayer. "Bayer and Ginkgo Bioworks Unveil Joint Venture, Joyn Bio, and Establish Operations in Boston and West Sacramento." PR Newswire: Press Release Distribution, Targeting, Monitoring and Marketing. June 27, 2018.

completed a Series A round of $100 million, and they have set their eyes on creating nitrogen-fixing bacteria to lessen dependence on crop fertilizers.[13] This is driven by three major sustainability points.[14]

- Three percent of natural gas goes toward creating nitrogen fertilizers for agriculture.
- Three percent of worldwide greenhouse gas emissions stem from fertilizer production.
- Fertilizer in water runoff has caused a dead-zone the size of New Jersey in the Gulf of Mexico, as well as many other environmental and human health problems.

These are three very good reasons to focus on bacteria to convert atmospheric nitrogen into fixed nitrogen to grow plants instead of backing traditional fertilizer usage.

Interestingly, legumes, peanuts, and soybeans already have long-established symbiotic relationships with nitrogen-fixing bacteria and can therefore gain nutrients from them quite easily. Plants like corn, wheat, and rice, however, do not have those same long-lived relationships. The bacteria that colonize them and many other crops do not provide enough nitrogen to meet their nutritional needs.[15] This is why fertilizer is so often used to cultivate them.

Joyn Bio is working on identifying and engineering some of those bacteria to become better nitrogen-fixers to these crop varieties so in the future, they will no longer need to be supplemented to the same degree with fertilizer. Joyn Bio could simply focus on increasing the amounts of natural microbes that would benefit plants, but optimizing the bacteria by editing, deleting, or adding genes will make them much more efficient than the natural microbes ever could be. The company is trying to create strains that grow quickly, inexpensively, are pesticide-tolerant, shelf-stable, and colonize the plant efficiently.[16]

It's a tall order, but with the partnership between the extremely successful microbe-engineering company and the agriculture

13   Joyn Bio. Crunchbase.

14   "Joyn Bio." Joyn Bio.

15   Splitter, Jenny. "These Super-Microbes Could Fix Agriculture's Nitrogen Problem." Forbes. September 21, 2018.

16   Ibid.

behemoth, they certainly stand a good chance of accomplishing their goals. And if this leads to Joyn Bio cutting the 3 percent of greenhouse gas emissions caused by fertilizer down by even just a quarter of a percent, it will make a remarkable difference in the battle to fight climate change on the global scale.

∞

While Joyn Bio is still in the development phase, another company called Pivot Bio is years ahead and already launching their first beta product, PROVEN, "eared" to corn. Founded by Karsten Temme and Alvin Tamsir in 2010, Pivot Bio is "awakening" microbes' innate ability to fix nitrogen, which has been turned off due to one hundred years of inundating the fields with nitrogen fertilizers.[17]

One way that Pivot Bio differs from Joyn Bio is that the Pivot team is not genetically engineering their bacteria. Yes, it will take more time to naturally select and optimize the bacteria for efficiency, but it also means that Pivot has to deal with less regulation regarding transgenic organisms. The company will also be better aligned with current market trends.[18] Plus, they have a head start on Joyn Bio, so we will see which method wins out in the long run.

Pivot's microbes are applied during planting and colonize the roots of the corn crop as it grows. The bacteria supply the plant with nitrogen daily, thereby yielding a partially self-fertilizing corn crop that relies much less on supplemental nitrogen fertilizers for growth. According to recent data, Pivot's bacteria create about twenty-five pounds of nitrogen per acre, which could be up to 25 percent of the nitrogen a farmer would normally apply to their crops.[19] As Pivot creates more improved generations of their microbes, that percentage will likely increase. The goal is to create a fully self-fertilizing crop

17   Pivot Bio. "Pivot Bio Advances Toward Commercial Launch of First Sustainable Nitrogen Product." PR Newswire: Press Release Distribution, Targeting, Monitoring and Marketing. August 06, 2018.

18   Splitter, Jenny. "Pivot Bio Secures $70M Investment For Nitrogen-Producing Microbes." Forbes. October 03, 2018.

19   Ibid.

system in the future to completely drop our reliance on synthetic fertilizers for commercial farming.

In a recent interview, CEO Karsten Temme stated, "The industry has been working to develop self-fertilizing cereal crops … for nearly fifty years. For the first time, Pivot Bio is making this possible. Our rivers and lakes cannot wait another fifty years for a clean alternative to today's fertilizer."[20]

Much of fertilizers' components degrade into a greenhouse gas three hundred times worse than CO_2. It's called nitrous oxide (chemical formula: N_2O), and this contributes substantially to global warming.[21] But if Pivot's microbiome tech is applied to all US corn fields, that would be equivalent to removing one million cars from the road![22] Around the globe, forty-one billion bushels of corn are produced annually, so the opportunities for expansion with corn, and even into other crops such as wheat and rice, are sizable.[23]

Pivot Bio has been gaining a lot of momentum too as they have raised $86.7 million as of late-2019,[24] and have struck a partnership with Bayer to work on enhanced nitrogen production with a bacterial strain for soybeans.[25]

It was also announced that Pivot's product for corn actually outperformed chemical nitrogen fertilizer during the 2018 growing season on eleven thousand tested farms and research facilities. Fields with Pivot's PROVEN product, which is composed of a nitrogen-producing bacteria for the corn microbiome, had an average of 7.7 more bushels per acre compared to fields only treated with chemical

20   Pivot Bio. "Pivot Bio Advances Toward Commercial Launch of First Sustainable Nitrogen Product." PR Newswire: Press Release Distribution, Targeting, Monitoring and Marketing. August 06, 2018.

21   Temme, Karsten. "Pivot Bio: The Crop Microbiome Is the Future of Fertilizer." World Agri-Tech USA. March 13, 2018.

22   Temme, Karsten. "Pivot Bio Nearing Launch of First Sustainable Nitrogen Product." Pivot Bio Nearing Launch of First Sustainable Nitrogen Product. August 6, 2018.

23   Ibid.

24   Pivot Bio. Crunchbase.

25   Pivot Bio. "Pivot Bio, Bayer Announce Research Collaboration." Pivot Bio, Bayer Announce Research Collaboration. November 8, 2018.

fertilizer.[26] We can expect that this number will only improve as the company progresses forward.

Overall, Pivot Bio is certainly a big player to keep an eye out for in agtech and the sustainable food space. They are capable of helping a lot of farmers improve their crop yields and profits, contributing to the growth of top-notch foods that will end up on your plate, and benefiting the environment through preventing significant amounts of fertilizer runoff and greenhouse gas emissions.

Indigo Ag and AgBiome

Another player in crop tech is Indigo Ag, a company founded in 2014 that has raised a sizable $609 million in funding as of late-2019.[27] They have collected plant samples from every continent except Antarctica and every latitude they possibly can in order to find thousands of microbe varieties that can benefit plants.[28] The genetic sequences of these microbes help identify which among them would be most beneficial to certain crop growth.

Traditionally in the industry, most commercial seeds are coated in fungicide and insecticide to prevent the seed from being eaten before it germinates. Indigo is sustainably evolving that by coating seeds in their special elixir of microbes. The bacteria are taken in by the germinating, young plant and rapidly multiply as it grows.

Right now, Indigo is increasing crop yield anywhere from 6 percent with corn to 14 percent with cotton.[29] They also have soybeans, rice, and wheat seed products that fall in between those numbers, but they will assuredly improve those increased yield percentages as development continues.

Farmers are fans of Indigo because the microbes in Indigo plants typically lead to thicker, more robust stems and a larger root mass (which is especially important for soaking up water in

26   Pivot Bio. "Pivot Bio PROVEN Outperforms Chemical Fertilizer." Pivot Bio PROVEN Outperforms Chemical Fertilizer. February 6, 2019.

27   Indigo Ag. Crunchbase.

28   Perry, David, and Signe Brewster. "Indigo Bets on Microbes to Boost Plants." YouTube. July 21, 2016.

29   Indigo Ag. "For Growers." Indigo Ag.

drought situations).[30] While the company focuses a lot on supporting plants under water-stressed conditions, they are also experimenting with bacteria to counter insects, fungi, and disease. David Perry, co-founder, CEO, and president of Indigo Ag, believes that at some point in the near future we will all look back and question why we sprayed so many agricultural chemicals when we could have just looked to microbes as a more natural defense all along.

∞

AgBiome is another company also taking aim at fungi. The startup, founded in 2012, has completely sequenced over sixty thousand bacterial strains so far and found one that they have now crafted into a fungicide product called Howler.[31] Coincidentally, the strain was originally collected in agricultural soil.

The microbe ingredient in Howler colonizes plant roots and produces a natural antibiotic, which combats more than five diseases commonly affecting plants like tomatoes, onions, lettuce, grapes, etc. It also creates an enzyme that breaks down cell walls of fungi, thereby preventing spore attachment to plant leaves and taking away their sweet fungal buffet.[32]

AgBiome has many other microbe-based products in their pipeline, and they are certainly another positive force exhibiting the shift from agricultural chemicals to a more natural, microbe-managing approach in the crop-farming industry.

Coffee Beans and Beetle Kryptonite

Whereas a lot of crop tech is focused on the microbes in soil and plants, it can also encompass targeting the bacteria within insects. Unwanted pests, as well as climate change, are coming for one of the largest staples in the beverage industry—coffee.

---

30 Perry, David, and Signe Brewster. "Indigo Bets on Microbes to Boost Plants." YouTube. July 21, 2016.

31 "Platform." AgBiome.

32 "Howler Fungicide for Better Crops by AgBiome Innovations." Howler.

Interestingly, on a per capita basis, Americans only drink 4.2 kilograms worth of coffee beans per person every year. Switzerland (7.9), the Netherlands (8.4), and the Nordic countries (Sweden: 8.2, Denmark: 8.7, Iceland: 9, Norway: 9.9, Finland: 12) all consume almost or more than double that amount per person annually![33]

Most of the coffee the world sips on is produced in countries like Brazil, Vietnam, Colombia, Honduras, Ethiopia, and Indonesia.[34] These places have the best environments for growing the beans, but the ideal locales for coffee production also have unwanted pests that increasingly pose a destructive threat to the industry.

Throughout coffee-producing countries around the world, insects ferociously feed on coffee beans, which in severe cases can decimate up to 80 percent of the crop.[35] The aptly named coffee borer beetle bores its way through the coffee berry and into the two coffee beans encased inside.

The beetle survives on the beans, all the while being exposed to such incredibly high levels of caffeine for its size that proportionally equivalent concentrations would kill any other creature. It's basically comparable to a 150-pound human chugging 500 espresso shots, which obviously would result in death for us, but these coffee borer beetles can handle the heat because of their unique gut microbiomes.[36]

The bacteria that live inside the beetles' digestive tracts allow them to break down enormous amounts of caffeine in their systems. Scientists in a USDA-led project analyzed the microbiomes of coffee borer beetles from around the world and found several varieties of microbes containing caffeine-degrading enzymes. Cleverly, the researchers also began to think that these enzymes could make good targets for synthetic biology to step in and fight back against these beetles. If scientists could engineer a molecule that would inhibit these caffeine-degrading enzymes and make the beetles just as

33   Bernard, Kristine. "Top 10 Coffee Consuming Nations." WorldAtlas. January 5, 2018.

34   Walton, Justin. "The 5 Countries That Produce the Most Coffee." Investopedia. March 12, 2019.

35   Krotz, Dan. "Gut Microbes Enable Coffee Pest to Withstand Extremely Toxic Concentrations of Caffeine." News Center. July 19, 2015.

36   Ibid.

vulnerable to high caffeine concentrations as all of us, they would surely not be able to decimate coffee plants around the world to the degree they do now.[37] It would be akin to removing Superman's powers with kryptonite.

One way to accomplish this task would be to create a highly specialized, target-specific pesticide that could inhibit these caffeine-degrading enzymes in the coffee borer beetles. It could be applied to the surface of coffee berries to act against the female beetles before they burrowed safely into the encased beans to lay their eggs. Another possibility would be to genetically engineer coffee plants to produce a molecule in their berries or beans that would also inhibit the beetles' key enzymes, effectively allowing the plants to protect themselves. An added financial benefit for coffee farmers with this second self-defense approach would be not having to continually purchase this theoretical specialized pesticide or take on the labor cost to apply it.

Snapshot Observation:
It's a case of giving somebody a fish to feed them momentarily or teaching somebody to fish to feed themselves in perpetuity. You can keep applying pesticides, which provides short-term protection, almost like giving plants a disappearing suit of armor. The other option is you can essentially teach the plants microbial kung fu and other self-defense mechanisms so they can protect themselves without consistent pesticide application.

∞

Overall, climate change and pests are going to roast the coffee industry, as well as the crop industry as a whole, if nothing is done to curb the current rate of warming temperatures and if we don't find a more efficient way to deal with plant pests and diseases.

Synthetic biology can definitely provide some solutions to help, and companies like Joyn Bio, Pivot Bio, Indigo Ag, AgBiome, and many others are leading the charge to enhance soil and crops as a whole with microbes rather than with chemicals.

---

37   (n 174)

Microbes are really powerful tools in crop tech as we've now learned, but they also offer a wealth of opportunities to create ingredients for the protein, cosmetics, and energy industries to name a few. I like to call it microbe-managing our future...

CHAPTER 6

MICROBE-MANAGING AND SPIDER-MAN

One of my favorite and most applicable courses during my undergrad was a biotech class I completed senior year. Like most entrepreneurship courses, we had a semester-long project with a goal to come up with an idea, develop a business plan for commercialization, and deliver a presentation. I was just learning about the concept of utilizing microbes to produce ingredients for industry and ultimately landed on the idea of using yeast to produce the highly coveted East Indian sandalwood oil (EISO for short). EISO made a great choice for the project because of the high price it sells for (recall the lesson from Finless Foods about tying your name to a luxury good), as well as its potential to be more beneficial for the environment than current natural-harvesting methods.

The tree EISO comes from, East Indian sandalwood, is a species native to India that is often used in the cosmetics and fragrance industries for its anti-inflammatory, moisturizing, soothing, and sweet-smelling properties.[1] It also sells for upward of three thousand dollars per kilogram![2] Additionally, due to the high price that can be fetched on the market, many areas have been over-harvested and illegally logged throughout the decades while natural disasters and climate change compounded on top of that to further threaten the species.[3]

To meet demand, make a buck, and take pressure off of wild populations, more sustainable operations in the form of sandalwood plantations sprouted up pretty quickly in places like Australia. These

---

1   "Santalum album." Wikipedia. April 28, 2019.

2   Keenan, Rebecca, and Pratik Parija. "This Sandalwood Plantation Is About to Make Its Owners a Lot of Money." Bloomberg.com. February 21, 2017.

3   "Santalum album." Wikipedia. April 28, 2019.

plantations take up thousands of acres with millions of trees grown on the land.[4] While the farmed East Indian sandalwood trees are more sustainable than wild logging, they still take fifteen to thirty years to mature (depending on how long farmers want to wait before harvesting—more years equals higher-quality oil).[5]

Once at the desired maturity, the trees are cut down and their inner heartwood is harvested. The heartwood is where the main chemical constituents of EISO are found in their highest concentrations. Brewing EISO with microbes makes for a better choice, though, because substantial amounts of oil can be made in a matter of weeks rather than fifteen to thirty years. Biofabricated EISO can also be made nearer to factory locations where it's needed rather than on remote plantations requiring long-distance shipping (always good to simplify the supply chain when possible).

If done efficiently, microbially synthesizing EISO can become more cost-effective for companies instead of paying higher prices for the plantation-grown product (plus shipping), not to mention being better for the environment. A lot of companies are moving in this direction as the ability to engineer microbes to synthesize valuable biomolecules opens up with gene sequencing, automation, and scalability.

∞

Now might be a good time for us to quickly run through the basics of the biofabrication process we discovered with our EISO project as the principles relate well to our next profiled company, Ginkgo Bioworks, which is at the leading edge of biofabricated products.

The first step for us was identifying the chemical components of East Indian sandalwood oil. We found four main chemicals make up roughly 90 percent of the oil:

1. alpha-santalol
2. beta-santalol

---

4   Keenan, Rebecca, and Pratik Parija. "This Sandalwood Plantation Is About to Make Its Owners a Lot of Money." Bloomberg.com. February 21, 2017.

5   Pallavi, Aparna. "Return of Scented Wood." DownToEarth. September 19, 2018.

3. epi-beta-santalol
4. alpha-exo-bergamotol[6]

Other commercialized oils, or even products like coffee, can have hundreds if not thousands of constituent molecules.[7] EISO was chosen in part because attaining 90 percent of the characteristic sandalwood scent with only four components seemed like a pretty sweet-smelling deal.

The next step was to learn the pathway by which East Indian sandalwood trees naturally produce their EISO chemical components. To put it simply, multiple enzymes are required in succession to convert certain key substrates (ingredients basically) into the desired end products. However, not all versions of the end products come out the same. Two issues came up.

The first challenge: stereoisomers are molecules that have the same chemical formula and sequence of atoms but ultimately have different structures in 3D space (perhaps think of it like having a shoe for the right foot and a shoe for the left foot). These varying arrangements of atoms can lead to the molecules exhibiting different properties. With EISO, an enzyme in the pathway produces the two santalols (alpha and beta) in both the E and Z stereoisomer formations. The Z is preferred because the Z formation produces a more fragrant scent. To be most efficient, a version of the enzyme would have to be found (or engineered) that only produces the Z stereoisomer formation.[8]

The second problem: the enzymes could not be guaranteed to produce the four components in the same concentrations found in natural EISO. If you were cooking spaghetti, you wouldn't want it to come out 99 percent sauce and 1 percent noodle, right? If the ratio of the four molecules in the natural solution was supposed to be 1:2:2:3 for example, one strain of yeast with the genes for all four biomolecules could not make them precisely in that required ratio.

6 Diaz-Chavez, Maria L., et al. "Biosynthesis of Sandalwood Oil: Santalum Album CYP76F Cytochromes P450 Produce Santalols and Bergamotol." PLOS ONE. September 18, 2013.

7 Davies, Emma. "Chemistry in Every Cup." Chemistry World. April 28, 2011.

8 Celedon, Jose M., et al. "Heartwood specific Transcriptome and Metabolite Signatures of Tropical Sandalwood (Santalum Album) Reveal the Final Step of (Z) santalol Fragrance Biosynthesis." The Plant Journal. April 15, 2016.

The resulting EISO fermentation product would just not match the natural EISO characteristics very closely at all. To get around this, the genes responsible for producing the various components would have to be engineered into separate strains of yeast. This would allow for the individual molecules to be produced and collected separately and then combined in the correct proportions at the end to create the perfect, well-balanced EISO product (voila, your spaghetti is served).

Aside from these issues, all efforts in microbially producing ingredients have to deal with other details as well:

- Ideally, you want the microbes to have a high density in the container you are growing them in. This allows for them to synthesize a lot of the product in the least amount of space.
- Additionally, you want to engineer the microbes to be highly efficient in converting "X" amount of substrate into the maximum amount of product in the fastest amount of time.
- Once made, the desired molecules need to be separated from the other components in the solution (the yeast and by-products), which is usually done by steam distillation or solvent extraction.
  - Chemical-based solvent extractions are not the best for the environment if the wastewater is not treated and properly disposed of.
- There is also the matter of volume of water used throughout the fermentation process. However, if you can find a way to purify the water from the spent yeast cells, by-products, and chemical solvents (if used), you can recycle that water into your next fermentation batch.
  - Re-using the water is not only much better for the environment, but it can also help save money when the water recycling process costs less than pumping in new, clean water.

Many companies in the biofabricated ingredient sector of synthetic biology currently face these considerations. And today, with the advantage of new tech, research, and improving fermentation methods, companies are starting to become really adept at engineering microbes for high efficiency and scalability.

"The Organism Company" and De-extincting Scents

One of the most exciting, up-and-coming companies in the synthetic biology space today is Ginkgo Bioworks, that is if being valued at over one billion dollars can still be considered up-and-coming. Founded in 2008 by four bioengineering PhD students and their mentor at MIT, Ginkgo is referred to as "the organism company" because they are not pigeonholed into one facet of synthetic biology. They simply deal in organisms—whether that is enhancing existing strains for more efficacy or even creating new ones!

To get into more detail, Ginkgo is a world leader in biofabrication. They engineer microbes to produce ingredients for the food, fragrance, cosmetics, pharmaceutical, materials, and fuel industries. Their genetically modified organisms are having an extraordinary impact on the future of these spaces because of their commercial advantages over incumbent manufacturing methods. Ginkgo is able to produce desired molecules at a much faster rate and for a much lower price. This attracts the attention of big businesses. In many cases, Ginkgo also has the considerable benefit of being much better for the environment than the natural collection of these same ingredients, which is a win for the industries, Mother Nature, and Ginkgo!

I was able to speak with two of Ginkgo's co-founders, Austin Che and Barry Canton, to learn more about their struggles and successes while founding the company, as well as what they hope Ginkgo can become in the future. Their founder stories are incredibly insightful, exciting, and optimistic for where microbial-production can go.

∞

It all started in 2002, when four of the five co-founders were working in two separate bioengineering labs (those of Dr. Drew Endy and Dr. Tom Knight). These two MIT labs worked very closely together, and this is how they all originally met. In 2005, the five co-founders created their first entrepreneurial endeavor together—a wiki called OpenWetWare that served to connect the two labs as a platform to openly share and discuss research. It has vastly expanded since then to over one hundred research labs both domestically and internationally. But the co-founders ceased involvement after a couple of years to turn their focus in a more globally impactful and profitable direction.

As the four students in the group were all finishing their last year before finally attaining their PhDs, they had this concept incubating in their minds of programming microbes to make things. After all, microbes can be like little manufacturing machines. It was a very broad idea at first with no specific direction, but they knew that microbes were too difficult and slow to engineer at the time, which was negatively affecting the funding opportunities in biotech. With the end of their studies quickly approaching, they began throwing around some ideas and taking action on their mission to make engineering biology easier.

The four entered a one-hundred-thousand-dollar MIT startup competition, and although they did not win, they realized that this broad microbial-production concept had some really incredible potential. They approached Tom Knight to see if he would join them to pursue this endeavor outside of MIT, and fortunately for them he did. Knight provided an initial investment of $100,000, and off to the races they went.[9] Investment aside, Knight's involvement gave the team an incredible amount of credibility as the man who is sometimes referred to as the "godfather of synthetic biology" was now helping co-found this promising venture.[10] In addition to his knowledge of synbio, Tom Knight also had skills with computer science and a vast network of respected connections.

Main Takeaways:

Startup competitions are incredibly beneficial.
- You can obtain feedback on your idea, gain insight into other startups in your space, and meet other startup founders and like-minded individuals with the entrepreneurial mindset.
- Connections are everything in entrepreneurship because building a company requires an army of people by your side supporting you.

---

9   Feldman, Amy. "The Life Factory: Synthetic Organisms From This $1.4 Billion Startup Will Revolutionize Manufacturing." Forbes. Forbes Magazine, August 2, 2019.

10   "Tom Knight (scientist)." Wikipedia. December 22, 2017.

In biotech especially, it's absolutely vital to have trusted advisors you can go to, and not just when you get stuck on a problem.
- If you want to seek investment from angels, accelerators, or venture capitalists, you need to have a well-developed team that includes someone with credibility in the industry, preferably someone with past startup success.
- This is particularly important if you are a young founder because while investors tend to look favorably upon the vigor of youth, they also want to see the support of an individual who guides from a position of experience as an accomplished scientist, programmer, business leader, etc.
- A team with youthful enthusiasm for innovation / a pulse on the habits, problems, and needs of younger generations, plus some experiential wisdom and past credibility from a seasoned professional is a killer combo for attracting investments and ultimately, success.

Coming out of MIT, the now five Ginkgo co-founders bootstrapped like crazy to acquire lab equipment. Founding a biotech startup can be very difficult in this way because in order to complete anything, all of the proper equipment for a functioning lab must be sourced.

Both Che and Canton told me funny stories about how initially they were extremely scrappy and constantly going onto Craigslist to find second-hand refrigerators. They would then go to shady basements and try to move the heavy machines back to their lab.

The team also snatched up any of the older lab equipment that MIT was discarding. This sourcing and setting up of the scientific operations was difficult, but at least Che, Canton, and the rest of the team were all well-versed in working in a laboratory environment and knew exactly what they needed to create their facility. However, none of the five co-founders had extensive business experience, so this presented a challenge and made them learn a lot on the go!

Interestingly, they also worked with a film student to create exciting videos for pitches and learn the art of crafting a brand for themselves. They took what they learned and approached several venture capital firms pretty early on. These interactions with VCs actually turned them off from pursuing venture capital investment. Looking back, Che stated that Ginkgo was nowhere near ready to accept VC funding that early in the company's development. Instead, the team acquired grants from government agencies to fund their platform, ultimately allowing them to have a five-year streak where they did not have to raise any money from angels or VCs.

Snapshot Lesson:

You should never take money from someone if you don't have to. There are other ways of getting funds, such as utilizing crowdfunding resources like Kickstarter, IndieGoGo, Patreon, etc., or arranging terms with people you owe money to. This would be like getting ninety days to pay them back so you can use that money for something else to generate funds. Boom, free loan!

Some of Ginkgo's initial grants came from the Department of Energy (DOE), and the team worked on using microbes to create electrofuels (storing energy from renewable resources in chemical bonds of liquid fuels like alcohols or gas fuels such as methane) as well as completed some DNA assembly work.[11] Other grants came from the Defense Advanced Research Projects Agency (DARPA) to tackle antibiotic-resistant bacteria by creating probiotics that target and remove harmful microbes in the gut. Additionally, they began looking into using microbes to produce scents and flavors since they had worked on an iGEM project while at MIT years prior to transform the foul smell of *E. coli* into fragrant freshness.[12]

The Ginkgo team utilized their momentum and in 2014, after meeting Y Combinator (YC) president Sam Altman, they became the first biotech company to become backed by YC—quite an accomplishment.

This really changed everything for the co-founders as they began gaining large investments and growing quite rapidly. With their newfound funds, they steered away from electrofuels and probiotics and began concentrating on ingredients for the food, fragrance, and cosmetics industries. The new direction also had the added benefit of higher profit margins if they could draw in clients. And this is exactly what they did with a great business model.

---

11 "Electrofuel." Wikipedia. November 29, 2018.

12 Feldman, Amy. "The Life Factory: Synthetic Organisms From This $1.4 Billion Startup Will Revolutionize Manufacturing." Forbes. Forbes Magazine, August 2, 2019.

∞

We can use rose oil as an example to delve into why Ginkgo has been so successful (which was also at the center of Ginkgo's first big deal when they were hired by French fragrance, cosmetics, and flavor company Robertet to produce a biofabricated rose scent).[13]

The business side of Ginkgo stems initially from a company like Robertet who approaches them seeking a microbially produced product, which in this case is rose oil to be used for fragrance. But why would a company want rose oil brewed by yeast to begin with?

Naturally sourced rose oil is extremely expensive and requires vast amounts of rose petals to produce very small quantities of the oil. It can take three thousand kilograms of rose petals to produce just one kilogram of rose otto oil via steam distillation.[14] Ginkgo can offer a vastly cheaper way for companies to source ingredients like rose oil (sometimes at one-fifth the cost of sourcing naturally) and in a much faster timetable with predictable yields. Clients are all over this because they subsequently have much lower manufacturing costs—more money in their pockets.

The fortunate by-product of all this is that biofabrication helps the environment by reducing the harmful practices of natural sourcing operations. For example, perhaps all the land used for growing countless roses by a company and its suppliers can now be used for another company's rose petal needs, harvesting something else, or become re-wilded so more of nature can remain undeveloped. It really follows the same premise as clean and plant-based meats. You cannot force people to make a switch solely based on what is best for the environment, so you have to make that choice for them by offering an alternative that is not only the same or better quality but is also available at a lower price.

The powerhouses behind Ginkgo's incredible capabilities are their foundries. The foundries are the high-tech, largely automated laboratories in which all of the microbes are genetically engineered and optimized for high fermentation efficiency and product yield. Ginkgo

---

13   Ibid.

14   Parry, Ernest John. "The Chemistry of Essential Oils and Artificial Perfumes." Google Books.

currently has four foundries that employ automation and machine learning to design the best microbe strains possible, and they really are the key to the company's rising success.

After the microbes are created for the client's needs, Ginkgo Bioworks will most often license the designed microbes to the client company so the client can brew the ingredient, like rose oil, by themselves. I was curious about how Ginkgo deals with the varying component ratios of their oils, and just as with my project for EISO, Canton explained that they and their clients mostly employ the same method of piecing out the genes into separate strains and later combining the harvested molecules into the appropriate amounts. It is just easier and quicker to blend them after the fact.

When you take into account the length of time for roses (a couple months) or sandalwood trees (more than fifteen years) to grow, as well as the amount of land, water, labor, transportation costs, etc. for these growing plantations, the natural-sourcing costs and detrimental effects on the environment really start to add up. This is why biofabricated products are becoming the better alternative in every way for businesses to acquire their ingredient needs for scents, flavors, cosmetics, pharmaceuticals, and so much more.

∞

But Ginkgo isn't stopping there. When you think about how many molecular compounds are required by countless companies across the globe, and at what high volumes, there are an extraordinary number of possibilities. Trying to tackle them all or even figure out which ones are most worthwhile to balance financial costs with environmental impacts is completely overwhelming. Ginkgo is big (well over one billion dollars) and expanding, but just like with Wild Earth's scaling strategy for example, how can Ginkgo most effectively achieve ten times the impact soonest? And how can they continue being a fast fish as they continue to grow?

Smartly, Ginkgo has already began creating spin-off companies like Joyn Bio (previously mentioned in chapter 5 for alternative to fertilizers) and Motif FoodWorks for food ingredients and alternative proteins. In fact, CEO Jason Kelly stated in a *Forbes* interview that this mode of building spin-off companies is a way for Gingko Bio-works to become "... a Berkshire [Hathaway] for biotech."[15] Ginkgo will ultimately scale up by becoming a company-creator and investor, whether that's through partnering with other companies like Bayer to create Joyn Bio or investing in ambitious Gene-trepreneurs who can start their own biofabrication endeavors on Ginkgo's discovery platform.

This means that in the near future, you as a Gene-trepreneur may be able to take advantage of Ginkgo's huge library of genetic data and engineering capabilities to build a startup with the potential to disrupt an array of unsustainable ingredient sourcing practices (whether they are sourcing unsustainably from biological sources or chemically synthesizing and treating ingredients).

∞

One last thought-provoking note about Ginkgo: quite intriguingly, just as alternative meats will eventually be able to develop completely novel proteins or potentially bring the taste of an extinct species to your plate, Ginkgo will be able to engineer novel flavors, scents, etc. as they have already exemplified with an extinct flower project. The company helped bring back the potential fragrance of a Hawaiian hibiscus plant, "*Hibiscadelphus wilderianus Rock* or *Maui hau kuahiwi* in Hawaiian" that went extinct in 1912 due to cattle ranching.[16]

With a sample taken from a museum, Ginkgo scientists and partnering paleogeneticists were able to piece together the genomic fragments, print the sequence for suspected enzymes and compounds contributing to scent, and brew those constituents with yeast.[17] While it's possible to know what molecules were made by the plant, it's impossible to figure out in which proportions they were produced. A scent artist then created eleven combinations of possible fragrance profiles by varying compounds and proportions to give options that

---

15   Feldman, Amy. "The Life Factory: Synthetic Organisms From This $1.4 Billion Startup Will Revolutionize Manufacturing." Forbes. Forbes Magazine, August 2, 2019.

16   Agapakis, Christina. "Reviving the Smell of Extinct Plants." Ginkgo Bioworks, May 7, 2019.

17   Chakravarti, Deboki. "Resurrecting the Genes of Extinct Plants." Scientific American, January 18, 2019.

one could elucidate the smell this extinct plant could have had. The project has since been featured as an installation in several museums in Europe and the US where museum-goers caught a whiff of the past.

This isn't de-extinction as we will discuss in chapters 9 and 10. Rather, it's simply a sensory glimpse into a bygone era. While very cool, this project also sheds light on what's at stake. Museums are typically about seeing, so by appealing to another sense, this could make future projects like this a helpful and effective tool in public education.

Potentially, if parts of plant genomes from much older samples, say from the last Ice Age, were available since the DNA has been preserved beneath the ice for over ten thousand years, it would be possible to recreate the potential fragrances of extinct Ice Age flowers too. It is completely feasible for Ginkgo to bring to life many more scents, flavors, and conceivably valuable biomolecules lost to time and human activities given relatively well-preserved genes from museum specimens and other sources.

Ultimately, Ginkgo's founders view their platform as applicable to all potential projects involving programming microorganisms. With that frame of mind, the potential for Ginkgo Bioworks and YOU to be a part of microbe-managing the future into increased sustainability looks quite promising.

Main Takeaways:

Youth and experience are a powerful and wise partnership for attracting investment and credibility.

- Young founders can bring on experienced advisors who can help the company avoid previously made mistakes.
- Older founders can bring on young advisors who can help the company have a pulse on the mindset and needs of younger segments of the market.
- Also, just in general having diversity amongst teams produces better odds that a company will succeed.

Be careful who you take money from, and if you can, don't take money at all (unless for partnership reasons).

Sometimes the best scaling strategy isn't creating more products.
- You and your team can only manage "X" amount at a time, so you won't be getting a more exponential growth rate.

Sometimes, if your business provides an amazing platform, the best way to scale is to build and invest in companies to use it.
- You can become a Berkshire Hathaway for biotech and remain a fast fish even as you grow larger.

Bolt Threads and Ecovative Design

You may have heard about past raves over spider silk for its high tensile strength. It's stronger by weight than steel and six times tougher than Kevlar. If you've ever seen the hit cinematic comedy *Get Smart* starring Steve Carell and Anne Hathaway, you may also recall Carell's character accidently shooting himself with the swiss army knife crossbow that had spider silk thread attached to it in an airplane lavatory.[18]

In the film, they say that the spiders have to be individually milked, but that's just not an efficient way to obtain spider silk. Bolt Threads will tell you that it takes too long, as well as the fact that spiders tend to cannibalize each other when in the same space. It would be an abysmal undertaking to set up a spider farm for silk harvesting; it would be a spider *Hunger Games* in there. "May the odds be ever in your favor."[19]

The better method of making spider silk is to transfer the genes responsible for the silk protein production into another organism. One wacky way this has been done is by implanting silk genes into the mammary glands of goats. The spider silk protein is expressed in the glands and comes out when the goats are milked. [20] *Don't tell anybody, but I heard that if you drink the milk you can gain some incredible abilities—the next Spider-Man origin story.*

---

18   *Get Smart*. Directed by Peter Segal. Performed by Steve Carell and Anne Hathaway. Get Smart. June 20, 2008.

19   *The Hunger Games*, Directed by Gary Ross. Performed by Jennifer Lawrence, Josh Hutcher-son, and Liam Hemsworth. 2012.

20   Hanson, Joe. "20 MILLION Year-Old Spider and the Science of Spider Silk." It's Okay To Be Smart. December 12, 2017.

A company called Bolt Threads is employing a goat-free method, though. Much like Ginkgo and many other synbio companies, they brew their product in a fermentation process.

Established in 2009 with $213 million in funding to date as of late-2019, this synbio venture was created by three co-founders with PhDs in chemical biology, bioengineering, and biophysics from UC San Francisco: Dan Widmaier (CEO), David Breslauer (CSO), and Ethan Mirsky (VP Operations).[21] Combining their research experience, the three were able to spin out their expertise into the company and have since made substantial progress engineering silk genes into microorganisms.

Bolt Threads' initial product is called Microsilk, a biofabricated spider silk they are utilizing in apparel through partnerships, such as with outdoor lifestyle company Patagonia. Bolt Threads also strategically acquired a clothing, gear, and accessories company, Best Made, through which they can also commercialize their Microsilk products. Furthermore, the startup smartly linked with the fashion space through working with world-renowned, cruelty-free designer Stella McCartney.[22]

Spider silk is a little different than our rose oil example with Ginkgo though, right? Rose oil has many different scent compounds that are combined in the end to make a product. How do microbes make strands of usable spider silk? Well, microbes aren't exactly slinging webs out of sugar at Bolt Threads' facility. It actually works very similarly to our first Gene-trepreneur's startup, Dr. Molly Morse's Mango Materials, which we learned about in the preface. Perhaps you recall microbes transforming methane into carbon polymers that can then be extruded into filaments for apparel?

This is a similar premise, except Bolt Threads is recreating part of what spiders do naturally.

Bolt Threads' yeast generate silk proteins, which are subsequently isolated and dried into a powder. All of the polymers in this powder are then made into a thick solution with the consistency of molasses.

---

21 Bolt Threads. Crunchbase.

22 Feldman, Amy. "Clothes From A Petri Dish: $700 Million Bolt Threads May Have Cracked The Code On Spider Silk." Forbes. August 15, 2018.

But why would you want a syrupy solution? Interestingly, if you look inside the silk glands of spiders, they create their silk out of a thick, viscous substance; there isn't a tightly wound spool in their abdomen just waiting to be unraveled as some might be inclined to believe. By forming a viscous concoction with the silk proteins dissolved in it, Bolt Threads can replicate what the spiders do innately and extrude out those polymers into long, strong threads of spider silk.[23] The individual threads get wound into spools, and the fibers can then be dyed and implemented into products like ties, shirts, dresses, you name it.

It was not easy to figure out how to make this long-sought-after material, however. Bolt Threads cracked the case of producing their Microsilk by first studying how spiders create their fibers naturally. There are around forty-six thousand species of spiders in the world, and many of them can make up to seven or eight different kinds of silk.[24] The type that most closely aligns with the one Bolt Threads produces is called *major ampullate*, which is used by spiders for rappelling, ballooning (essentially spider parasailing), and as the structural outer rim of their webs.[25] And again, much like Mango Materials, which can formulate their biopolymer based on end use (apparel, packaging, etc.), Bolt Threads too can tweak their formulation for more strength or stretch depending on the intended end use of the filament.

This is far beyond the capabilities of the traditional silk industry, which is built off of silkworms. Silkworms are actually believed to be extinct in the wild and today only grown on farms.[26] To harvest their silk, the worms are typically boiled alive in their cocoons so that they won't damage the precious fibers boring their way out to emerge as moths. There is also a no-kill method, which is just letting them emerge from the cocoons naturally and boiling the silk casing afterward to loosen the threads. But this takes extra time that many

23   Hanson, Joe. "20 MILLION Year-Old Spider and the Science of Spider Silk." It's Okay To Be Smart. December 12, 2017.

24   Ibid.

25   Arthur, Rachel. "Bolt Threads Is Launching Its First Bioengineered Spider Silk Product At SXSW - A Necktie." Forbes. March 10, 2017.

26   "Saint Louis Zoo." Silkworm | Saint Louis Zoo.

operations aren't willing to spend, as well as damages the silk threads themselves.[27] So in addition to having more expansive applications and better fiber characteristics, fermenting spider silk with microbes simply supersedes traditional silkworm farming from sustainability and ethical perspectives.

Beyond being a great material for apparel, spider silk is also being developed for the skincare sector. Bolt Threads already has a mixture called B-silk that they've used to spin out a skincare company called Eighteen B. Spider silk is additionally being explored in the medical field for use in cancer therapies, detecting biomarkers, and serving as scaffolding for cell growth.[28] These healthcare applications are all opportunities that Bolt Threads can certainly expand into by integrating anti-microbial, water-resistant, and UV-resistant qualities into their brewed fibers.

The ability to biofabricate spider silk makes entering a whole host of industries feasible because with microbes, Bolt Threads can make alterations and progress very quickly, thereby giving the company a major leg (or eight) up on the incumbent silk industry.

∞

In addition to spider silk, Bolt Threads also licensed in a technology from a startup called Ecovative Design to spin themselves a wider web of commercialization influence. Bolt is using Ecovative's mycelium technology (mycelium makes up the root structure of multicellular fungi like mushrooms) to produce a new leather-like material called Mylo.

This mycelium fabrication technology was originally created by Ecovative, which is based in New York, with the initial intent to use it as a replacement for Styrofoam packaging.[29] However, this proved somewhat difficult from a cost-competitive standpoint as Styrofoam packaging manufacturers have had decades to squeeze out every

27   "Bombyx Mori." Wikipedia. May 19, 2019.

28   "New Way to Form Bioactive Spider Silk for Medical Use." ScienceDaily. December 04, 2017.

29   Feldman, Amy. "Bolt Threads Debuts New 'Leather' Made From Mushroom Roots." Forbes. May 31, 2018.

nickel and dime from the process. Luckily, Dan Widmaier of Bolt Threads ended up connecting with Ecovative's co-founder and CEO Eben Bayer, and a bargain was struck.

You see, Ecovative is really strong in research and development and is more of a platform for crafting innovative mycelium-based designs rather than a company focused on commercializing lines of Ecovative-branded products. In this way, Ecovative and Ginkgo Bioworks are very similar. Both recognize that the quickest way to scale and derive impact is to be the R&D platform and investor that enables others to make the commercialized products.[30] And just as with Ginkgo, Ecovative has a world of possibilities.

For example, Ecovative CEO Eben Bayer has been looking into producing a bacon substitute with mycelium, which will hopefully join the ranks of plant-based proteins helping to disrupt animal agriculture in the food system. Ecovative intends to find an expert partner in the food space soon and carry on from there.

The company is also working with NASA and DARPA on structural applications for mycelium, such as creating origami-like and inflatable-built environments with the capabilities of self-forming into specific shapes and completing self-repair.[31] Not only could this help in situations of humanitarian disaster relief, but it turns out that mycelium could also be a big deal in the future of space travel and making humans an interplanetary species!

Bayer mentioned in an interview with SynBioBeta that fungi have been found at Chernobyl. These fungi contain melanin which allows them to feed and grow on radiation, which is very unique.[32] This immediately made me think of a fantastic sci-fi show called *Stargate Atlantis* (which actually stars Jason Momoa—the actor who plays Aquaman in the DC Universe, as well as Khal Drogo in *Game of Thrones*).

---

30   Feldman, Amy. "Bioengineered Bacon? The Entrepreneur Behind Mushroom-Root Packaging Says His Test Version Is Tasty." Forbes. Forbes Magazine, December 17, 2018.

31   Mischel, Fiona. "How Fungi Will Give Form to the Future of Food: A Conversation with Ecovatives Eben Bayer." SynBioBeta, August 12, 2019.

32   Ledford, Heidi. "Hungry Fungi Chomp on Radiation." Nature News. Nature Publishing Group, May 23, 2007.

In the show, which takes place in a distant galaxy called Pegasus, there is a life-sucking alien race called the wraith. Their spaceships are actually biological; they are grown, self-repairing, and conceivably protect the wraith inside from space radiation. If you can imagine self-assembling human spaceships that can do the same and can be integrated with electronic machinery, that may sound like science fiction (and it completely is right now), but what if that were actually possible in the bio-based future? It's something fun to think about.

Anyway, also notice that all of these projects are non-branded and R&D-focused.

Snapshot Lesson:
If you're strong in research and development and that's your passion, don't waste your personal and company resources trying to build brands and lines of products to follow. You can license your work out and focus on what you're best at to extract maximum value.

The partnership between Ecovative and Bolt Threads has shown to be a really wise move because Bolt Threads used Ecovative's research to create the trademarked material Mylo. They are also set up well to commercialize Mylo as they can integrate the leather-like material into Best Made's products, which is the apparel company Bolt Threads strategically acquired. The licensing partnership between Bolt and Ecovative is a win for both companies.

The way the mycelium is cultivated is really cool as well. Ecovative grows it in corn stalks, after which it can be compressed into very dense blocks that can be cut just like leather into specific widths and shapes. The traditional industry employs excruciatingly harmful chemicals to treat leather, but Mylo is dyed naturally with tea bags.[33]

Additionally, Mylo can be produced in just ten days as opposed to the year(s) it takes an animal to grow large, be harvested, and have its hide undergo the harsh leather treatment process. Plus, remember how cattle are the bane of the environment as methane-producing

---

33   Canales, Katie. "I Went inside the Bolt Threads Factory, Where Synthetic Spider Silk and Mushroom Root-derived Leather Materials Are Produced for the Fashion Industry." Business Insider. May 19, 2018.

machines? If plant-based and clean meats work out, there should be less of them and therefore less leather to boot. Mylo can pick up the slack, and it is even better than faux leather because imitations are usually petroleum-based.[34] Mylo is all natural and much more sustainable.

The possibilities for this material are absolutely endless, and it can replace real and faux leather in products including handbags, automobile seats, wallets, belts, shoes, 80s-style leather jackets, whatever you desire. And if leather pants make a comeback, well, we're set.

∞

Overall, between Bolt Threads' original spider silk tech (Microsilk, B-silk) and their mycelium tech licensed in from Ecovative (Mylo), the commercialization strategy for these and any future novel materials will have to start by selling at a premium—no different than cell-based meats, right? The great thing is that silk and leather goods are generally very high-end to begin with. Widmaier notes in a Hello Tomorrow talk that he often advises young entrepreneurs to shoot for 50 percent profit margins on products because that's what VCs want to see. In fact, he says that even before creating a product, you want to make sure that your space has at least two orders of magnitude in price range. This means there should be at least a hundred-fold increase from the lowest-priced products to the highest.

Widmaier states fashion is a great industry for this because there are four orders of magnitude, thereby leaving plenty of room for Bolt Threads to start their products out as luxury and subsequently descend the value curve.[35] Mycelium-base fashion will be a fair bit quicker than spider-based fashion to commercialize, however. Whereas mycelium is relatively easy to grow and can actually be produced at a similar price point to real leather (opens up the market widely), the spider silk biofabrication process will take a bit longer to figure out. Synthesis on a large scale at an affordable cost is a big

34   Feldman, Amy. "Bolt Threads Debuts New 'Leather' Made From Mushroom Roots." Forbes. May 31, 2018.

35   Widmaier, Dan. "How Nature Inspires Us to Build New Materials | Panel | HT Summit." Hello Tomorrow. March 19, 2018.

challenge, but hopefully Bolt Threads will get there so we can all afford some cool and sustainable spider silk apparel.

Speaking about scaling, Widmaier also noted in his Hello Tomorrow talk that young biotech entrepreneurs tend to think the science is the most challenging part, which *it is until* the science is nailed down and these young Gene-trepreneurs find out that the next step of scaling up is even more difficult. Just because something works on a small-scale in the lab does not mean it translates well to large-scale manufacturing. (Widmaier) That is a whole other wall to climb. Luckily, spiders are great at climbing walls. But this is an important lesson to note. Scaling is a challenge, so bring on advisors, investors, and team members who can help you do this efficiently without making big mistakes.

One last thing: Widmaier was also very insightful in this talk about team-building. He stated that sometimes the right person for the job doesn't exist yet, so they have to be built. At Bolt Threads, he finds that the most successful people are the ones who seek out those who are very different from themselves and learn from them. This is great to hear for those who aren't experts yet but are willing to throw themselves fully into the mission at these synthetic biology companies. The synbio projects being worked on today and tomorrow haven't been done yet, and so there are ripe opportunities for you to build yourself into the person to do it. Gene-trepreneurs are built, not born.

Main Takeaways:
Invest your company's time into what you're best at.
- If you're great at R&D, be the R&D platform for you, corporate and government partners, and fellow Gene-trepreneurs to use.
- Don't waste your time building lines of branded products if you can get ten times the impact elsewhere.

In the small scale, your manufacturing process might work great; in the large scale, maybe not so much.
- Bring on co-founders, employees, advisors, investors, etc. who can help you scale effectively.

Get into a field where there is at least two orders of magnitude so you can start luxury (with high profit margins) and ride the value curve down as you scale.

All of these amazing biotech projects are new with no one having cracked the long-term code for the science, scaling, business development, etc. before.

- It's okay if you don't know how to do something right now, but don't let that limit you (recall Bethencourt's quote from chapter 3 about giving yourself permission).
- Seek out others from completely different areas and learn from them because this is how you build yourself into the right person for the job.

Chapter 7

Species Conservation Part I: Genetic Tools and Guardians of the Galaxy

Back in 2015, Dr. Jennifer Doudna came to speak at my university. Several of my professors mentioned how big of a deal her work was although at the time I had little notion of just how massive her research was becoming. Doudna's progress on clustered regularly interspaced short palindromic repeats (a.k.a. CRISPR) was allowing researchers to take any desired genes in an organism and edit them as they pleased, effectively giving people new and unprecedented power over the genetic code. It's a true landmark in science, and CRISPR is certainly a tool that we are currently using, as well as will increasingly continue to use in the future to unlock all sorts of amazing advancements in medicine, agriculture, and wildlife conservation among many other areas.

After multiple professors encouraged students to attend Doudna's lecture, I decided that I would regret missing it if I didn't go. In the late afternoon on a brisk November day, I made the trek to listen to Dr. Doudna's lecture on this groundbreaking technology.

When Doudna came in and began getting into the specifics behind how CRISPR works, the biochemical mechanisms went far above what I had learned from my introductory courses at the time. I began to see why so many professors, grad students, and post-docs had shown up. That same year I saw Dr. Doudna speak, she was named into the 2015 *TIME 100*.[1]

Even though I didn't fully comprehend the entire lecture on CRISPR technology at the time, I am so glad I attended because it

---

1   "Jennifer Doudna Named to 2015 "TIME 100"." Jennifer Doudna Named to 2015 "TIME 100" - Innovative Genomics Institute (IGI). April 26, 2015.

felt like seeing a part of scientific history. What if you were present at a speech from Watson and Crick about discovering the structure of DNA? Having gone through many more specialized biochem and biotech courses later on and doing some research of my own, I understand much more now, and it's some pretty thrilling stuff...

∞

CRISPR has so many world-benefiting applications. One example is disease treatment. But it has to be done the right way.

Recently, outrage was sparked when a Chinese scientist used CRISPR to genetically engineer embryos to be HIV-resistant and then allowed them to develop into newborn twins.[2] Such applications are currently very restricted because many scientists and bio-ethicists argue that experimentation on humans is extremely premature and too risky at this stage.

The general consensus is that genetically editing humans should only be allowed when no successful alternatives are available. Preventing the children of an HIV-positive parent from contracting HIV has successful alternatives available and thus doesn't supersede that consensus. However, many scientists agree that more widespread genomic alteration is inevitable and that we must set up policies to protect against threats in the future.

Stephen Hawking even mentioned that "... there is no time to wait for Darwinian evolution to make us more intelligent and better natured."[3] He also elaborated that:

> *"Once such superhumans appear, there are going to be significant political problems with the unimproved humans, who won't be able to compete. Presumably, they will die out, or become unimportant. Instead, there will be a race of self-designing beings who are improving themselves at an ever-increasing rate. If the human race*

2   Rana, Preetika. "How a Chinese Scientist Broke the Rules to Create the First Gene-Edited Babies." The Wall Street Journal. May 10, 2019.

3   Hale, Tom. "These Are Stephen Hawking's Last Messages To Humanity." IFLScience. October 16, 2018.

manages to redesign itself, it will probably spread out and colonise other planets and stars."[4]

Fantastic shows and films like *GATTACA, The Crossing, Almost Human,* and many others all address societies wherein there are varying levels of conflict derived from those with designer genes and those without. It will be exciting to see what designing humans looks like moving forward, but genetically engineering other creatures with CRISPR can actually really aid wildlife today if used correctly. Gene-trepreneurs can assist in the tough battles we are facing with species conservation. Although, it should be noted that this marks a change in the possibilities available for these Gene-trepreneurs because to make businesses out of species conservation is highly difficult. This is why the bulk of species conservation as it relates to biotech is typically done by non-profit organizations and academic research labs, which are primarily funded by a mixture of government, industry, and private foundation grants.

Chapters 7 (this chapter) through 10 represent a look into transferring novel biotechnologies into impactful research endeavors in environmental sustainability. But there are still some for-profit business applications as well.

Biodiversity and Vortexes

To reiterate what we touched upon in chapter 3, according to the World Wildlife Fund, the average size of wild animal populations (mammals, reptiles, fish, birds, and amphibians) left on Earth has declined by 60 percent of what it was forty years ago.[5] For some, this is attributable to hunting and overfishing (as with bluefin tuna for example). But in many cases, wild animals are simply running out of space due to habitat loss at the hands of urban expansion, forest destruction for agriculture and mining, and of course, climate change.

Individuals are unable to breed due to segmentation of habitat that remains livable for them, and having isolated pockets of animals

---

4   Ibid.

5   Carrington, Damian. "Earth Has Lost Half of Its Wildlife in the past 40 Years, Says WWF." The Guardian. September 30, 2014.

leads to dilution of the gene pool from inbreeding populations.[6] This has a snowball effect because a lack of genetic diversity can be seriously harmful to any group as it places them at more risk of succumbing to new diseases. How do you think human societies were able to avoid being completely wiped out by wide-spread illnesses like the Black Death, the plague that killed between 30 to 50 percent of Europe's population in the mid-1300s?[7] If humans in Europe had low genetic diversity, well, it would have been far more apocalyptic.

Diluted gene pools can also hinder species' ability to adapt to climate change. In the case of polar bears for example, their loss of habitat is concentrating them further North where many bears may inbreed due to lower numbers and closer proximity.[8] This is effectively leading them into what is called a "polar vortex"... sorry, I meant "extinction vortex" wherein gene pools with fewer allele variants cause the fitness of the whole species population to collapse (can't adapt, they have less offspring, just generally not able to survive as well).[9] Genetic diversity is obviously a very important key to the longevity and success of any species, yet human expansion for crops and meat is coming at a cost of genetic diversity for wildlife.

What's promising is that advancing capabilities in genetic sequencing have already helped many groups come back from these ominous vortexes. Experts can determine which individuals are genetically distinct enough to breed, thereby allowing diversity to be re-introduced into isolated gene pools through offspring of specifically chosen mates.[10] This is referred to as "genetic rescue" and can be achieved through moving individual animals around so they will naturally breed. It can also be done more deliberately via artificial insemination.

---

6   Hanski, Ilkka. "Habitat Loss, the Dynamics of Biodiversity, and a Perspective on Conservation." Ambio. May 18, 2011.

7   Berezow, Alex. "Black Death: The Upside To The Plague Killing Half Of Europe." Forbes. May 12, 2014.

8   Gammon, Katharine. "Climate Change Is Forcing Polar Bears North-Here's Why That's Bad News." TakePart. January 09, 2015.

9   "Extinction Vortex." Wikipedia. May 22, 2019.

10   Flinders University. "DNA Match-making for Endangered Animals in Captivity." Phys.org. November 11, 2016.

Another option is employing CRISPR to accomplish what is called "facilitated adaptation" wherein alleles from an already adapted population, from previous organisms in museum collections, or from an entirely different species are genetically edited into organisms to speed up their acclimation to changing global conditions.[11]

Coral is a perfect example of a target organism for facilitated adaptation. Along with rainforests, coral reefs are super high-density regions of biodiversity on the planet, so there's a lot to lose. While we're not clearing coral reefs for cattle farms, they are still very much at risk from cascades of cause and effect reactions (ranging from fertilizers to animal agriculture contributing to climate change). A lot of carbon humans create doesn't just float out into the atmosphere but is actually absorbed by the oceans in the form of carbonic acid. Corals are made up of calcium carbonate, which is basic on the pH scale, so you see where there might be a problem having acids and bases mix. Ocean acidification from increasing amounts of carbonic acid is essentially dissolving corals, as well as the shells of other sea-dwelling creatures who rely on extracting calcium carbonate out of the sea water to create their homes.[12]

Carbon retains heat rather well too, so increasing levels of absorbed marine carbon are contributing to the rising ocean temperatures. Just like grapes require specific growing conditions as we discussed in chapter 5, corals are quite delicate too. The warming ocean is disagreeing with coral like a bad crunch wrap supreme from Taco Bell, and it's causing coral to expel their mutualistic algae called *zooxanthellae*. These microorganisms provide the coral with nutrients and give them their unique colors. It'd be as if trees lost all their green leaves (which contain the chloroplasts of course) and couldn't photosynthesize. When the *zooxanthellae* are expelled, the coral turns white. This "coral bleaching" makes corals much more likely to perish since they are no longer being provided nutrients from the photosynthetic algae.

---

11   Brand, Stewart. "2017 : WHAT SCIENTIFIC TERM OR CONCEPT OUGHT TO BE MORE WIDELY KNOWN?" Edge.org. 2017.

12   Cornwall, Warren. "Researchers Embrace a Radical Idea: Engineering Coral to Cope with Climate Change." Science. March 21, 2019.

The good news is that scientists are now seeing how genetically modifying corals can help save them. Researchers are compiling a database of coral genes and their functions by disrupting certain genes in coral embryos and observing the resulting phenotypic (observable) alterations.[13] This better understanding of coral DNA will eventually allow scientists to genetically engineer both embryos and existing corals to be more resistant to climate change. Scientists are also looking at employing the *zooxanthellae* in a solution.[14]

Certain varieties of these coral-inhabiting microorganisms are able to withstand higher temperatures. The genes that allow them to survive and not be expelled could be copied into the microorganisms that live in other corals, thereby making reefs around the world less susceptible to bleaching. This same premise of influencing microorganism species and qualities is also being used in crop technology as we talked about in chapter 3.

One really tragic thing about climate change affecting biodiversity is how it deals a heavy blow to the advancement of biotechnology. Not only are changing habitats killing off species that are a part of a healthy ecosystem, ones that have traditionally been around for millions of years and survived multiple past extinction events, but climate change is also wiping out potential biotechnology marvels.

Continually, pharmaceutical companies are going out to do what is called "bioprospecting" in places like rainforests and marine environments. Their purpose is to find novel enzymes and other proteins with valuable commercialization potential. They research these biomolecules and some are successfully implemented into their pipeline of drugs. There's BIG money to be had in it too! But all of that potential is being lost when the rainforests and coral reefs are suffering. Earth's natural biodiversity is like the famed Library of Alexandria in Egypt that burned around 48 BC (supposedly burned by Julius Caesar's fleet).[15] All that knowledge lost... we can't let that

---

13   Park, Alice. "How CRISPR Gene Editing Could Save Coral Reefs." Time. April 23, 2018.

14   Jones, Nicola. "As Ocean Waters Heat Up, A Quest to Create 'Super Corals'." Yale E360. August 4, 2015. Jones, Nicola. "As Ocean Waters Heat Up, A Quest to Create 'Super Corals'." Yale E360. August 4, 2015.

15   "The Burning of the Library of Alexandria." eHISTORY, n.d.

happen with reefs and rainforests. We must try to save what we have left to discover.

So many species are left to discover, and we can still learn much more both biochemically for medicines and structurally/functionally for biomimicry (modeling wind turbine blades after whale fins, structuring bullet trains after the beaks of woodpeckers, etc.).[16] However, with the current rate of species loss that we are observing on a global scale, we just don't know what we're losing at this point. We haven't uncovered it all yet! Without doubt, some big technologies have been lost forever because species that otherwise would not have gone extinct have now disappeared because of human-driven activity.

All hope is not lost though...

Corwin and Rhino Tinder

If you watched Steve Irwin's *The Crocodile Hunter* growing up like I did, you may have also seen a show called *The Jeff Corwin Experience*. I was lucky enough to see Jeff Corwin, the renowned biologist, environmentalist, and goofy TV show host, give a lecture about his travels and the importance of conservation several years ago while attending Penn State University. If you want some laughs, I highly recommend watching Jeff Corwin bloopers on YouTube. It was such an amazing experience to be in the presence of one of my childhood heroes. (I was also lucky enough to see Bill Nye speak on another occasion ... "Science Rules.") Corwin brought up some really great points regarding the situation we're currently in. He stated that amphibians have been around for 350 million years, survived five major extinction events, and now we are expected to lose half of amphibian species on the planet within just the next three to four decades.[17] That's crazy, right!

Corwin likens amphibians to canaries in the coal mine because their lives are so connected to the environment. As you may know, canaries were historically used in coal mines because they are more sensitive to carbon monoxide than humans, thus served well as early

---

16   "What Is Biomimicry?—Biomimicry Institute." Biomimicry Institute.

17   Herdell, Josette, Maureen Cavanaugh, and Jeff Corwin. "Biologist Jeff Corwin Draws Attention To The Earth's Most Endangered Species." KPBS Public Media. November 10, 2009.

warning systems for miners (hence the expression "canary in a coal mine"). Carbon monoxide has no scent and by the time you start feeling its effects it's too late to escape the underground. So you may have also heard the expression "sing like a canary" in crime shows. When miners noticed the eerie silence of no canary chirping, checked on the bird, and found it keeled over in its cage, well, that meant get out now! Today, we have sensitive machinery to test air quality and detect dangerous levels of carbon monoxide, so canaries can rest easy.

Amphibians, in a more grandiose sense, serve the past function of canaries in coal mines but as early warning systems for the planet. They are much more sensitive to changes in the environment than humans as they breathe through their skin. This makes them extremely sensitive to humidity, temperature, and the chemistry of their surroundings. When amphibians start dying off, it signifies a serious problem![18] And right now, amphibians are being affected everywhere. The alarms are sounding!

Following up on bioprospecting, Corwin often mentions in his talks how 40 percent of medicines we use come from the rainforest, many of which are found in amphibians' skin. He says that ... "we now know with the extinction of a number of species by examining the remaining preserved tissue that we've lost very valuable medicines that we'll never be able to reproduce."[19] It really puts things into perspective and makes you imagine what we could have lost.

Advancements in CRISPR beg the question: can we use the tech to engineer more hardy amphibians and save many at-risk species like we hope to for coral?

I think the answer is undoubtedly yes. However, it will take a lot of funding to conduct research and time-intensive environmental impact studies before any actual steps are taken. Right now, it's a lot of genetic rescue efforts (selecting breeding pairs and doing artificial insemination) and not as much facilitated adaptation (using CRISPR) because risks must be managed with genetically engineering animals intended to eventually be released into the wild. Also, it's especially precarious with endangered species who are already few in number.

---

18   Ibid.

19   (n 229)

Personally, I think it would be worth it to genetically engineer not only for the sake of morality (since humans are why many amphibian species are collapsing), but also in regard to the lost biotechnological potential.[20] As stated though, employing such techniques must be handled carefully because once altered organisms are released into the wild and breed, it's kind of hard to undo things; such is the case with gene drives as we'll talk about shortly.

∞

This is one reason why zoos serve an important purpose. Although people often condemn zoos for keeping animals in captivity, zoos strategically manage breeding programs to sustain and enhance genetic diversity within endangered species.[21] They have the knowledge and resources to house animals and study them before any would be released into the wild to restore dwindling populations, that is if there are even any populations left.

Corwin actually went to Panama and found the last wild Panamanian golden frog, a male. This species was once the symbol of Panama, but it is now extinct in the wild. That last male is in a breeding facility alongside captive females in the hope that the species can be kept alive and genetically diverse enough to be introduced back into the wild if and when the habitat can support them again.[22]

Another huge success story, and one of Corwin's favorites, is the black-footed ferret. Corwin recalls the whole tale in his own book, *100 Heartbeats: The Race to Save Earth's Most Endangered Species.* The condensed version is that in the 1970s, the black-footed ferret was thought to be completely extinct until Rex, the dog of a rancher in Wyoming, came back home with a dead ferret in his mouth. The rancher, who I guess wanted to get it mounted or at least identified, brought it to a taxidermist who recognized the different-looking animal as the

20 Fogel, Dave, and Jennifer Fogel. "Reptiles And Amphibians In Pharmaceutical Research." Reptiles Magazine.

21 Taronga Conservation Society Australia. "10 Endangered Species Saved from Extinction by Zoos." Medium. May 19, 2017.

22 Herdell, Josette, Maureen Cavanaugh, and Jeff Corwin. "Biologist Jeff Corwin Draws Attention To The Earth's Most Endangered Species." KPBS Public Media. November 10, 2009.

supposedly extinct species. The pair then informed the US Fish and Wildlife Service who sent officials out to the ranch. There, with much surprise, they found the last colony of black-footed ferrets. The last colony was comprised of about one hundred individuals.

Unfortunately, plague quickly took that number down to just eleven. Not wanting to risk losing the species forever, the remaining ferrets were captured, cared for, and introduced into a breeding program. Luckily, the eleven individuals had enough genetic diversity to allow the population to build back up. Now there are over two thousand of these animals in preserves around the US![23]

Species like the rhino aren't so lucky in their comeback story ... yet.

∞

Poaching has absolutely decimated rhino numbers (approximately two rhinos are killed every day).[24] If you do some math, rhinos usually only give birth to one baby at a time every three to five years starting at around age six. And white rhinos live somewhere between forty and fifty years.[25] This means that in a lifetime, one white rhino can produce between six and twelve offspring—not many in the scheme of things. These numbers are applicable in the wild. Captive rhinos breed less often, which makes their drastic drop in numbers alarming because even with expert care in zoos and sanctuaries, they can't multiply as quickly as they're being poached.

It's the same situation with certain species of whales and elephants too. They have long pregnancies and, compared to other animals, do not produce many babies over the course of their lives. This makes every animal an important part of conservation efforts to replenish their numbers. Specifically, the northern white rhino subspecies has really taken some hits and become one of the notable symbols for species conservation today.

You may have seen article headlines about the last male northern white rhino, Sudan, passing away in 2018. He was forty-five and

23   Ibid.

24   Markus, Matthew. "Rhino Poaching Stats 101." Pembient. Pembient, February 18, 2019.

25   "White Rhinoceros." Wikipedia. May 19, 2019.

died from health issues related to old age. In 2015, he was even given a Tinder profile to help generate funds and awareness for species conservation—talk about a great marketing strategy! With the passing of Sudan, there are currently only two females still alive: a mother-daughter pair named Najin and Fatu. Sudan was actually the father of Najin and grandfather of Fatu. With only two female northern white rhinos left in the entire world, science is really this subspecies' only hope for survival.[26]

Barbara Durrant, who is the San Diego Zoo Safari Park's director of reproductive sciences, has hope however that their "Frozen Zoo"—a collection of over ten thousand genetic samples from various species—can help bring back northern white rhinos, as well as help save many other species from ultimate extinction. In this frozen collection, the zoo has twelve northern white rhino cell lines that together contain enough genetic diversity to bring back a successfully self-sustaining population.[27] The hope is to artificially inseminate the two northern white rhinos, along with using southern white rhino surrogates, to bolster the northerns back up to a healthy number.

The San Diego Zoo also hopes to use a very cool and cutting-edge technology called in vitro gametogenesis (IVG) that will allow regular rhino skin cells to be converted into stem cells and subsequently into sperm and eggs.[28] Although IVG studies have mainly focused on mice as of yet, scientists say that it is only a matter of time before they will be able to accomplish this with other species (as is being worked on for Sumatran tigers for example).[29] With successful research efforts and sufficient funds, the Frozen Zoo could create eggs and sperm from any of their twelve viable northern white rhino samples and use in vitro fertilization (IVF) to raise the next generation of northerns from southern white rhino surrogate mothers!

26 Berlinger, Joshua. "World's Last Male Northern White Rhino Dies." CNN. March 20, 2018.

27 CBS News. "Scientists Hope "Frozen Zoo" Will Help save Endangered Species." CBS News. February 27, 2015.

28 Lewin, Tamar. "Babies From Skin Cells? Prospect Is Unsettling to Some Experts." The New York Times. May 16, 2017.

29 Great Big Story. "Four Stories About Saving Endangered Species." YouTube. October 15, 2018.

IVG is truly an exciting beacon of hope for the northern white rhino subspecies and many other animal species as well who are struggling to survive as a direct result of humans.

∞

As an aside, IVG could theoretically allow for same-sex couples to have a baby together once the mechanisms are figured out for human applications. The missing sperm or egg, depending on the sex of the couple, could be created from the cells of one partner, combined together with the available sperm or egg, and result in a baby that is genetically half of each.[30]

IVG could also help men and women who suffer from fertility problems. Many people out there are either naturally infertile or become infertile after undergoing chemotherapy. One of my past professors once told a TMI (too much information) story about looking at his sperm under a microscope when he was younger. He considered letting students do this as well in the name of science, BUT he quickly realized that it might be upsetting news if someone were to discover the life-changing fact that they were infertile. Probably best to avoid that situation, right? Although, IVG could get around that one day so those who were infertile could know it isn't the end of the road for their family line if that's important to them.

Thought-provokingly, IVG could also effectively let one person clone themselves or result in not needing sexual reproduction at all in the future.[31] Humans could end up like that race of genetically engineered golden people, the Sovereign, that chase around Star-Lord and the gang in *Guardians of the Galaxy Volume 2*. We could create our own Adam Warlock![32] You can even imagine a dysfunctional sci-fi story about some lunatic harvesting skin cells from unsuspecting people, maybe even celebrities or Nobel laureates, and creating babies with the genetic material without the cell donor even knowing it. You

---

30   Pontin, Jason. "Science Is Getting Us Closer to the End of Infertility." Wired. March 28, 2018.

31   Ibid.

32   *Guardians of the Galaxy Vol. 2*. Directed by James Gunn. Performed by Chris Pratt and Zoe Saldana. Guardians of the Galaxy Vol. 2. May 5, 2017.

can imagine how crazy that could become. If it doesn't already exist, please don't make a *Black Mirror* episode out of this scenario though, I beg of you.

∞

Overall, this discussion about genetically engineering species to keep up with changing environments and using IVG eventually on humans requires healthy debates about bioethics (although recall how in vitro fertilization creating "test tube babies" was once highly controversial and has since become commonplace). Regardless, these topics must be discussed by everyone so the public is at least mostly in agreement and prepared about the use of genetic engineering. It will be tough with the ever-quickening rate of scientific innovation.

So what do you think about facilitated adaptation? Should we let species who can't keep up with anthropogenic climate change fall by the wayside, basically letting our natural Library of Alexandria burn to see what organisms are tough enough to survive the inferno? Or should we actively take measures in genetic engineering to give species a renewed chance? And who's going to do it: wealthy pharma companies, non-profits funded by donations, public and private university labs, zoos? Would you be okay with tax-payer dollars going to fund facilitated adaptation? Would you like to see IVG become available to humans one day? These are all things to take note of and have conversations about together. It affects the world around all of us, and so all of us should consider each other's viewpoints.

I will say, though, all of the technological progress that is opening up these doors is creating a universe of potential projects for hungry Gene-trepreneurs to sink their teeth into. If you're in academia, you can operate research endeavors funded by grants out of a university. Others passionate about conservation (scientists, business execs, serial Gene-trepreneurs) can partner with or create a non-profit such as Revive & Restore (which is featured in chapter 10). Or perhaps you can eventually spin out your skills into a profitable biotech startup like our next Gene-trepreneur, Matthew Markus, has done with his company Pembient.

Main Takeaways:

Many wildlife conservation technologies are also being used in the medical sector.

- You can therefore spin out your skillsets into either field (medical or conservation), become adept at technology transfer, and create impactful businesses and research endeavors when opportunities present themselves.
- Ask yourself what skills you have and technologies you know of that could be transferred to make an impact; they don't even have to be especially technical as this story (see footnote)[33] proves when a prop designer set out to catch turtle egg poachers.

---

33 Birnbaum, Sarah. "What I Learned from 'Breaking Bad' about Saving Sea Turtles." Public Radio International, June 5, 2017.

CHAPTER 8

SPECIES CONSERVATION PART II: CLEVER STRATEGIES AND MIDDLE-EARTH

Poaching is a huge problem across much of species conservation. As stated before, an example is that two rhinos are killed every day, which drastically hampers efforts to rebuild their numbers. There are two sides to poaching: the side that kills the animals for products and the side that captures them for the pet trade. Both are exceedingly horrible.

On the killing side, lemurs in Madagascar are snared for their meat. Elephants, typically the tusky African variety, are taken down by locals desperate to gain a huge payday from the ivory trade. Other animals often affected are sea turtles for their shells, gorillas for their meat, whales for their meat, tigers for their skin, bones, and meat, manta rays for their gill plates, pangolins for their scales, sharks for their fins, and the list goes on and on.[1]

One way to help prevent poaching for animal products is to educate locals about the value their wildlife can bring to them through eco-tourism. An example of this is teaching locals in the Philippines how whale sharks, the world's largest fish, can bring them booming tourism rather than killing them to sell their fins, meat, and skin to Asian markets.[2] There is also another approach, although controversial, which is creating biofabricated animal materials. Rhino horn is a great case of this synthetic approach, and a company called Pembient is leading the charge to disrupt the rhino poaching industry with 3D-printed horns.

1   Phelan, Jessica. "6 Endangered Animals That Poaching Might Take from Us Forever." Public Radio International. July 20, 2015.

2   Summers, Hannah. "How Whale Sharks Saved a Philippine Fishing Town and Its Sea Life." The Guardian. December 10, 2018.

Animal Poaching Part I: Pembient and Michelangelo

I was able to speak with the founder and CEO of Pembient, Matthew Markus. I will admit that I was rather skeptical of the company before our interview due to reading some articles saying conservationists are condemning the synthetic approach. But this also made me highly interested in hearing Markus' point of view.

Some believe that flooding markets with biofabricated product will increase the demand for rhino horn based on past precedents.[3] However, after speaking with Markus, I began to understand a bigger picture. I could see how knowledgeable he was about these concerns and the horn market as a whole, as well as how much he cared about addressing the rhino horn trade responsibly. Pembient's mission is the same as the conservationists, after all—to stop rhino poaching and save the species.

∞

Markus had the idea to create biofabricated rhino horn back in the 90s, but the technology to accomplish this didn't exist yet. When there was an uptick in rhino poaching in the late-2000s, he familiarly recalled his idea and kept a vigilant eye on advancing technologies that could be used to address the issue. Years later, when tissue culture and biofabrication research were at a stage to make his vision a possible reality, Markus asked George Bonaci who had a background with keratin in the cosmetics industry (the same material that makes up your hair and fingernails, as well as rhino horn), if he would like to go after the issue of rhino poaching together. The two partnered up.

---

3   Neme, Laurel. "Petition Seeks Ban on Trade in Fake Rhino Horn." National Geographic. February 10, 2016.

Snapshot Lesson:
Don't discount your ideas simply because they aren't possible yet. Take a note from Markus's long wait that you can keep an idea in the back of your mind to execute on later, even if it's more than a decade down the line. This is actually something I'm currently doing with a seafood innovation concept that isn't currently feasible. However, I have done a decent amount of groundwork on the subject, including visiting an expert University of Pennsylvania professor, to be ready when the opportunity arises.

Markus, being an experienced serial entrepreneur who founded three companies prior to Pembient, did what any good entrepreneur would do. He went to Vietnam to learn about the rhino horn market, talk to the people who use it, and validate his value proposition with customers. And it turns out that Markus found a specific pain point driving the demand for rhino horn that isn't what you might think.

By physically speaking with rhino horn users and craftsmen, Markus importantly discovered that a lot of horn is actually not used for medicinal purposes as we are so often led to believe in Western culture. Instead, the horn is often used as a functional material for art and furniture.

He shared with me the story of an experience he had with a Vietnamese family who had been working with horn for generations. Markus first saw how they were creating tiles from water buffalo horn and topping a desk with it. Then, one man gestured to a couple of others to go get something. The two men went off on a motorbike and returned with a huge conglomerate of solid buffalo horn they had tried to piece together from many smaller pieces. Markus said that it looked like a mess, all bubbly from the process of heating and unraveling the hollow buffalo horn into manageable pieces.

But why would they want to put all the pieces together into a solid chunk, you might wonder? It's about having a large block of material to sculpt out an artistic masterpiece with. Water buffalo horn, being hollow, is creatively limiting. However, if you have a large, solid piece of horn, you can sculpt it into a sturdy work of art that is going to be more valuable for the craftsmen.

You can picture rhino horn as the beautiful block of white marble every stone sculptor would love to carve their own statue of David out of. Yet Markus said that with other forms of horn like that of water buffalo, "It's like Michelangelo trying to work with pebbles."

Markus elaborated that this is really why some families go rogue and use rhino horn instead. Rhino horn is the single largest piece of solid keratin you can get. Seeing this pain point, Markus realized that he could develop synthetic rhino horn to be used by artisans and craftsmen who want to work with a unique material while simultaneously combating rhino poaching.

Biofabricated horn can be sold at an eighth of the price of the real thing. If this cheaper synthetic horn flooded the market, arguably, it would de-incentivize the poaching of rhinos because the enormous black-market payday wouldn't be there anymore for poachers to cash out on. Markus and Bonaci realized they really had identified an opportunity, and the two co-founders then began applying to accelerators. They were accepted into the very first class of IndieBio in 2015.

∞

The two initially began working to create a powder because forming the keratin into a structured horn is a lot more complex (similar to how creating structured beef steaks, pork loins, and fish fillets is a lot more difficult than creating processed meat like sausages). They engineered yeast to brew a special mix of keratin and then added real rhino genetic material to it so that if tested by any suspicious parties, it would identify as coming from real horn.[4] Eventually, they turned this powder into a sort of filament for a 3D-printing process that resulted in chunks of synthetic rhino horn. Conceivably, the limit on the size of their biofabricated horn would just be the size of the printer, which would solve the big pain point for horn craftsmen. Pretty amazing, right?

As mentioned, however, there have been concerns about whether offering commercialized rhino horn would succeed in its mission to help prevent poaching. There are previous cases in the animal trade, for instance, where species bred in captivity have stoked demand and

---

4   Neme, Laurel. "Petition Seeks Ban on Trade in Fake Rhino Horn." National Geographic. February 10, 2016.

caused a rise in stealing animals from the wild (i.e., tiger farms).[5] There is also a litany of other reasons some conservationists oppose synthetic animal products being introduced into the market (one being they see it potentially undoing their expensive consumer education).[6] Markus stated that this is attributable to skeptics adhering to the "precautionary principle," whereby any new product or process whose effects are not yet known should be resisted. This principle is often applied to much of the biotech market (here with horns, facilitated adaptation, etc.) as many synbio founders will tell you, and it slows down their progress.[7]

Safety is paramount, of course, but sometimes people can use the precautionary principal and fear-mongering with the public for their own selfish agendas.

To satiate those who are steadfast in the opposition and build their case for a regulated synthetic horn market, Markus stated that Pembient is trying to amass a great deal of evidence to support their intervention, which other cases may have lacked in the past. Pembient is also staying well clear of rhino horn as medicine (which is in powder form). People already have water buffalo horn and others for consumption. Pembient's focus is solely on artisanal use of large pieces of solid, biofabricated horn because that is where the pain point truly lies. Personally, I think Markus is working on this incredibly carefully and responsibly. If he can disrupt rhino poaching and provide better options for artisans, carvers, and designer, I believe Pembient has a real shot at making a sizeable difference in the conservation of rhinos.

5   Warfield, Kristen. "People Are Farming Tigers For This Bizarre Wine." The Dodo. July 27, 2018.

6   Neme, Laurel. "Petition Seeks Ban on Trade in Fake Rhino Horn." National Geographic. February 10, 2016.

7   "Precautionary Principle." Precautionary Principle - an Overview | ScienceDirect Topics.

∞

As an extra bit of info, I was also under the impression that all of the horns are taken from wild rhinos, but Markus informed me that a third of South Africa's rhinos are actually privately owned. A man named John Hume (who sounds like a cross between John Locke and Desmond Hume on *Lost*—do you like rhinos, brotha?)[8] has a place called Buffalo Dream Ranch where he protects his 1,600 southern white rhinos with heavy security on an eight-thousand-hectare plot. On this ranch, every now and then the rhinos are tranquilized and their horns are removed to de-incentivize poaching. The rhinos come out of the ordeal just fine, albeit a little lighter on the front end. While this is ultimately a conservation endeavor, the rhino horns are actually a means of funding the extremely expensive operation whose main mission is the protection of the species.

Kind of a clever idea how these rhinos can pay for their own security team and ultimately help the survival of their species, right?

Under current South African law, however, Hume can only sell rhino horns domestically and not internationally, which has put his operation on the brink of collapse.[9] So this ethical "farming" of rhinos is not currently sustainable, and it opens the door for Pembient to biofabricate the horns to quell international demand for using it as a sort of bioplastic in sculpture pieces and furniture.

---

8   *Lost*. Directed by J.J. Abrams. Performed by Matthew Fox and Evangeline Lilly. Lost. September 22, 2004.

9   Neme, Laurel. "Petition Seeks Ban on Trade in Fake Rhino Horn." National Geographic. February 10, 2016.

If the international demand can be met with the cheaper synthetic approach, we might see rhino poaching activity plummet. In the future, Markus said they will hopefully expand into materials like elephant ivory and tiger bone although these are more difficult because they are living tissue unlike horns made of keratin, which are akin to our fingernails or hair. I am certainly rooting for Markus and Pembient to succeed. We need all the help we can get to ward off those who would destroy entire species for a tusk or a horn.

Main Takeaways:
Don't give up on ideas if they aren't currently feasible with today's technology.
- If you are technical, you can try to create the tech.
- If you aren't technical, you can partner with somebody who is and could help develop the tech.
- Or you can wait for the tech that would make your concept viable; you just have to be willing to wait a few years and keep the idea in the back of your mind.

Even in a space dominated by non-profits like species conservation, you can still find a way to create a business to achieve conservation goals (but it is definitely tough to do so).
- Businesses can probably be more successful in the long run because they don't have to rely on donations or federal grants to continue operating.
- But there is a lot of regulation and red tape to manage when your business is dealing with synthetic products whose natural predecessors come from endangered and highly poached species.

Animal Poaching Part II: Invasive Species and Lions of the Sea
On the other side of poaching, we have the capture of wildlife for the exotic animal trade. Popular species for this include slow lorises, lemurs, squirrel monkeys, blue macaws (as featured in the popular film *Rio*), sloths, kinkajous, galagos (a.k.a. "bush babies"), amongst many more.[10]

---

10 Actman, Jani. "Exotic Pet Trade, Explained." National Geographic. February 20, 2019.

The fish trade is also a part of this and can be extremely harmful to the environment when fish are released willy-nilly into habitats where they have no natural predators. This is when you see headlines about fishermen catching piranhas in the Delaware River, or pacu in Lake Michigan![11] The piranha and pacu are warmwater fish, though. They don't survive the winter in these areas meaning they can't set up breeding populations. However, invasive fish species do become a problem in more tropical places like Florida (of course, right! everything happens in Florida). For instance, snakeheads are carnivorous fish native to Africa and Asia, which can breathe air for a day as they crawl on land between watering holes. They can also reach up to three feet long, so they're nothing to sneeze at.

Unfortunately, Florida's canals are now littered with snakeheads. When most anglers catch them, they destroy the fish right on the spot because it's illegal to be in possession of a live one. The state can't force you to kill, though, so catch-and-release is permitted.[12] If you do release a caught fish, however, it's not great for the environment as snakeheads absolutely decimate small fish populations. It's like releasing a serial killer into a city. Snakeheads have even been known to attack humans when protecting their nest and fry. You can watch an episode of Jeremy Wade's *River Monsters* to learn all about them.[13]

Lionfish are also an immense problem in the Atlantic Ocean. They are native to the Indian Ocean, but the exotic pet trade has led them to be released into places where they don't belong. Lionfish can be found along the east coast of the US and into the Caribbean and are bottomless pits that devour innumerable smaller fish species. For this one, you might relate it to releasing prides of lions in Yellowstone. Reefs are annihilated by hordes of them feeding on anything that will fit into their mouths.[14] The small fry of grouper are even on the menu, which means that fewer members of large fish species live

11   Weisberger, Mindy. ""Vegetarian Piranhas" with Human-like Teeth Found in Michigan Lakes." CBS News. August 15, 2016.

12   "Bullseye Snakehead." Florida Fish And Wildlife Conservation Commission.

13   "The Giant Snakehead - River Monsters | Animal Planet." Animal Planet - Full Episodes and Exclusive Videos.

14   National Geographic. "Divers Fight the Invasive Lionfish | National Geographic." YouTube. July 24, 2015.

long enough to grow to their full sizes in areas infested with lionfish. I was shocked when I actually saw one of these lionfish for myself on a reef in Roatan, Honduras. Their numbers are obviously growing.

Currently, the only way to deal with lionfish is by catching them, usually with a spearing rig. Many spear fishermen and people who go lobstering down in Florida will nab them whenever they see any swimming around nearby. In fact, in Florida they are so dedicated to tackling the lionfish issue that they have whole competitions called Lionfish Derbies. Competing teams will spend one to a couple of days hunting lionfish on the reefs. Prizes are awarded to teams that catch the biggest, smallest, and most lionfish. These fun competitions have helped to remove thousands of lionfish from the Caribbean and areas off the Florida Keys. Specifically, REEF Derbies have taken out 23,322 lionfish since they began in 2010.[15] Imagine how many native reef fish those removed lionfish would have consumed—many multiples of twenty thousand for sure. Additionally, conceptualize how many more those twenty thousand-plus lionfish could have multiplied into if they were still out there breeding.

The fish caught in these derbies help researchers and are also sold or given to restaurants. An emerging commercial market for lionfish has sprouted up in the hopes of incentivizing people to catch them (and I hear they taste delicious). You just have to be careful in their preparation because they have some venomous spines (not poisonous, because poison means that the harmful effects come from ingestion, whereas venom must be injected into the bloodstream via a bite or sting). Someone even created a robot that can be steered down to depths that traditional divers can't reach. The robot sucks up the lionfish like a vacuum.[16] Sounds kind of fun, right? Maybe it could become a real-world video game one day.

Gene Drives and New Zealand Kiwis
In addition to lionfish and snakeheads, various other invasive species are brought about by the exotic animal trade. Anacondas and Burmese pythons are decimating the Florida Everglades by eating

---

15   "Lionfish Derbies." Lionfish Derbies | Reef Environmental Education Foundation.
16   Vocativ. "This Robot Hunts Invasive Lionfish." YouTube. April 21, 2017.

all of the small mammals, birds, and even alligators. A 2012 study in the Everglades concluded that pythons had a hand in diminishing raccoons by 99.3 percent, opossums by 98.9 percent, and bobcats by 87.5 percent (because bobcats are left with scarce prey items).[17]

People are actually getting paid to hunt pythons due to this crisis: $8.10 an hour to look for snakes, $50 per snake collected four feet and under, an extra $25 dollars per every foot over four feet in length, and an extra $200 for finding a snake with a nest of eggs.[18]

Fascinatingly, one clever method used by staff members of Big Cypress National Preserve in Florida (an area larger than Rhode Island) to locate and remove pythons is called the Judas Snake Program. Scientists attach radio transmitters to male snakes, the "Judas snakes," which then lead them to breeding females, clutches of fifty to one hundred eggs, and other males in the vicinity looking to bolster their numbers. Over two years, the pilot program has allowed staff to catch seventeen pythons. There are estimated to be over ten thousand in the preserve, though, so this Judas program, although cool, is ultimately unscalable. It has still been valuable for learning about the python expansion in this habitat for future management efforts.[19]

∞

On the other hand, some invasive species are not the result of escaped or intentionally released former pets. Some are stowaways or are actually brought in by the government.

The cane toad was introduced into Australia in 1935 by the Bureau of Sugar Experiment Stations as a means of pest control. It was hoped that the toads would eat beetles ravaging the sugar cane fields.[20] In retrospect, this was a very bad decision, which has since

---

17   Killer, Ed. "Can Burmese Pythons Be Eradicated from the Everglades? Judas Snake Program Shows Promise." TCPalm. Treasure Coast Newspapers, June 13, 2019.

18   Fleshler, David. "Easy Money? Not for Python Hunters Who Grapple with Everglades Giants for $8.10 an Hour." Sun Sentinel. December 29, 2017.

19   Killer, Ed. "Can Burmese Pythons Be Eradicated from the Everglades? Judas Snake Program Shows Promise." TCPalm. Treasure Coast Newspapers, June 13, 2019.

20   Morris, Lulu. "Quolls Trained to Stay Away from Poisonous Cane Toads." National Geographic. May 22, 2017.

resulted in thousands of animal deaths. The toads didn't eat animals like snakes, but animals ate the toads, which happen to be poisonous.

In an innovative turn of events, conservationists are employing a training program with quolls (a small, carnivorous marsupial) that is equivalent to making your child smoke a whole pack of cigarettes so they never smoke again. Quolls often think the increasingly abundant cane toads are ripe for the picking, but this has been a harmful miscalculation for the species. Researchers were in Queensland, an area long inhabited by cane toads, and happened to observe Queensland quolls had learned not to prey on the toads. Obviously, the Queensland quolls had stumbled upon something and proved the behavior was transferable to other members.

The researchers are now teaching this cautionary lesson to quolls in the Northern Territory, an area more recently inhabited by cane toads, to speed up the collective learning curve of the local population and avoid some preventable casualties. They capture these Northern Territory quolls and feed them a small amount of cane toad (with an added special ingredient—a bit of thiabendazole that will make them feel sick for several hours but will not kill them).[21] In this manner of aversion therapy, researchers have found success in teaching Northern Territory quolls not to consume those pesky cane toads. Lives have been saved, and the quolls can pass on this teachable behavior to their offspring.

∞

Another example of an introduced species wreaking havoc can be seen in the beautiful country of New Zealand, home of kiwi fruits, kiwi birds, and Kiwi people, as well as the location of J.R.R. Tolkien's Middle Earth in *The Lord of the Rings* and *The Hobbit* film trilogies.

Although inadvertently, merchant ships brought rats onto the island. These critters, along with other introduced species (weasels, possums, cats, etc.), are crushing endemic bird populations by eating their eggs and chicks alive. For birds as a whole on the island, over twenty-six million eggs and chicks are consumed every year;

21   Ibid.

25 percent of New Zealand's unique birds have already been eaten away, literally![22]

One extremely adorable, unique, and flightless bird in New Zealand is the kakapo parrot. It is plump, green, and the heaviest parrot in the world. In 2014, there were just 123 of these magnificent parrots left climbing trees and adorably scampering across the forest floors of New Zealand.[23] Unlike posh quolls, kakapos and other birds can't go to therapy to help save them. They're not doing the eating; they're being eaten.

Many Kiwis, the people of New Zealand, have gotten behind a plan to eradicate non-native predators from the island by 2050 to protect their native birds like the kakapos.[24] It is no easy feat though, as the largest island ever cleared of rats was Australia's fifty-square-mile Macquarie Island. New Zealand is two thousand times that size. Smaller islands off of New Zealand have been cleared of rats via poisoning, which sometimes requires multiple rounds of poisoning to clear the rodents, and this is where many kakapo parrots have been rehomed in efforts to boost their numbers.[25]

So far it has worked as in 2016, thirty-three kakapo babies survived their first few months of life![26] However, these paradisal islands free from predatory mammals are now reaching their kakapo capacity. There is no more room left to keep placing birds in these isolated safe havens.[27] Conservationists will soon have to re-home birds in areas of the mainland where mammal predators still pose a risk to their eggs and young. But this is where an up-and-coming synthetic biology tool could be used to tackle invasive and pervasive

22 Yong, Ed. "New Zealand's War on Rats Could Change the World." The Atlantic. November 16, 2017.

23 Valentine, Katie. "The Critically Endangered Kakapo Parrot Is Having One Fantastic Year." Audubon. August 5, 2016.

24 Regalado, Antonio. "Can CRISPR Restore New Zealand's Ecosystem to the Way It Was?" MIT Technology Review. February 10, 2017.

25 Yong, Ed. "New Zealand's War on Rats Could Change the World." The Atlantic. November 16, 2017.

26 Valentine, Katie. "The Critically Endangered Kakapo Parrot Is Having One Fantastic Year." Audubon. August 5, 2016.

27 Yong, Ed. "New Zealand's War on Rats Could Change the World." The Atlantic. November 16, 2017.

species on the island for good. It is futuristically called a hyperdrive. No, no, sorry, that's spaceship science fiction. It's called a gene drive!

∞

Gene drives are selfish genetic elements, which are inherited more often than they should be and can be exploited through genetic engineering to modify isolated populations and even entire species.[28] For a simple example, if you have two alleles, one for green eyes and one for brown eyes, then statistically you should have a fifty-fifty chance of passing on one gene variant versus the other to your offspring. However, a gene drive changes the odds so that you would have more than a 50 percent chance of passing on one specific allele, green or brown, over the other. Now in reality, eye color is actually affected by multiple genes, but you get the gist.

Selfish elements have been around for a while as they can be found in wild populations, such as in field mice for example.[29] However, some of these naturally occurring gene drives are more effective than others. One gene drive may tip the balance to pass on a genetic element to 60 percent of the offspring while another may boost the odds to 70 percent. The goal is of course to hit that magic 100 percent when building them to tackle invasive species. And humans are finding ways to ensure desired components get inherited almost indefinitely by the next generation.

Researchers are using a whole CRISPR system called CRISPR/Cas9 to edit genomes. Along with the desired edited gene variant you wish to have higher chances of passing on to offspring, genes encoding for the Cas9 enzyme and some guide RNAs are incorporated. The guide RNAs tell the Cas9 enzyme exactly where to cut the unwanted genetic component out of the genome. Then, the desired gene variant is built into its place through DNA repair. We can end up with two

---

28   Ibid.

29   Regalado, Antonio. "Can CRISPR Restore New Zealand's Ecosystem to the Way It Was?" MIT Technology Review. February 10, 2017.

copies of our desired DNA construct and thus likely ensure that a trait will be passed on to any progeny.[30]

But then, how can we ensure the progeny of the progeny and those continuing down the family line inherit the same genetic construct? We might want to engineer in some longevity so our work isn't diluted out through generations of breeding. Instead of using CRISPR/Cas9 as a one-and-done tool, we can actually put the whole CRISPR/Cas9 system itself into the organism so it will get passed along as well to repeat the cut and repair process. This way, any offspring will end up with not just the one copy from the engineered parent, but two copies of the desired genetic variant too. This is how we can consistently turn all progeny from heterozygous individuals into homozygous ones for the desired trait.

If we apply this concept of gene drives with rats in New Zealand, it is possible to engineer rodents so that their offspring, regardless of having the male XY or female XX sex chromosomes, all end up developing as male rats.

A study published in 2017 bred mice in a ratio of 90 percent male to 10 percent female.[31] If mostly male rats were produced as offspring, the rat population would quickly collapse due to lack of breeding females. The researchers in the study used the *Sry* gene (traditionally on the Y sex chromosome and responsible for encouraging male development) and engineered it to be on the autosomes (not sex chromosomes). More specifically, within the mice they engineered *Sry* to be implemented within a naturally existing gene drive element on chromosome seventeen called the t-complex.[32] Attaining 90 percent male offspring isn't bad for the beginnings of gene drive technology, and being that mice and rats are so strongly related evolutionarily, a similar approach could be employed with invasive, bird-devouring rats.

When it comes to wild rats, 95 percent do not reach one year old due to predation and conflict with each other. However, they

30   "CRISPR." Wikipedia. May 21, 2019.

31   Leitschuh, Carolina M., et al. "Developing Gene Drive Technologies to Eradicate Invasive Rodents from Islands." Taylor & Francis. December 19, 2017.

32   Ibid.

also multiply like crazy (can go from two to fifteen thousand in one year)![33] This fast reproduction cycle and short lifespan are perfect for seeing quick results through a gene drive in a population.

This male-dominant gene drive is also being worked on for mosquitoes. Only the females have the mouth-structure to bite, which means the females are spreading diseases like malaria. So if we lessen the number of females, we lessen the overall bites and egg-laying. And if we make female mosquitoes have mouths more like the males, mosquito populations of the varieties that pose a real danger to humans could collapse over a small number of generations.[34]

We could also engineer a gene drive to make mosquitoes resistant to the malaria parasite.[35] In this way, instead of killing the middle-man, we make them resistant to the real source of the problem, the parasite responsible for malaria in the first place. So as you can see, gene drives can be set up in many configurations. Before actual employment of gene drives, the different configurations will be considered, and hopefully the best one for the environment ultimately used. We don't want a cane toad situation where the solution to one problem creates an even bigger one.

For example, there are concerns that these gene drive rodents and mosquitoes could spread across the world rather easily, whether as unintended cargo or intentionally by humans looking for a permanent extermination solution of their own. In regard to rats, some experts say that one or a couple vermin would find it very difficult to set up shop and infiltrate the international rat gene pool if they were brought to a place that already had a rat population established. One New Zealand ecologist said that "... rats have a strong incumbent advantage" and that you would "... really have to introduce a lot of individuals."[36]

---

33 "Brown Rat." Wikipedia. April 24, 2019.

34 Akst, Jef. "Gene Drive–Equipped Mosquitoes Released into Lab Environment." The Scientist Magazine®. February 20, 2019.

35 Regalado, Antonio. "Releasing CRISPR into the Wild Means No Turning Back." MIT Technology Review. December 08, 2015.

36 Yong, Ed. "New Zealand's War on Rats Could Change the World." The Atlantic. November 16, 2017.

Then again, it's not impossible because animal trafficking is not uncommon around the world, and through sheer human will we wiped out the passenger pigeon even though there used to be millions of them in the forests of North America. It wouldn't be difficult to envision humans accidentally or even purposefully making certain rat species extinct too by getting ahold of rats with gene drives and smuggling them to their own little corner of the world.

So is it possible to protect against such outcomes? Can we build in safeguards before releasing gene-drive-carrying organisms out into the wild?

This is where gene drives can become more elevated as a protective measure and be engineered to only last for a certain length of time. Kevin Esvelt, a biologist at MIT, refers to the splitting up of the essential components of a gene drive onto multiple chromosomes as a "daisy drive" because like a daisy chain, if one part fails the whole chain falls apart.

Basically, if the genes for the RNA guides, desired genetic component, and Cas9 enzyme are all placed into separate chromosomes, eventually they will become distanced and the gene drive machine will stop working.[37] It will be interesting to see whether scientists can come up with reliable ways to time out gene drives at various intervals or by approximate generation numbers depending on placement of the CRISPR/Cas9 components in the genome. There are also many other concerns with biosecurity, like gene drives accidentally finding their ways into other species, but more safeguards will be thought out as the technology is studied and proven more in the lab. It's always better to be safe than sorry!

Overall, many are definitely hopeful that gene drives can be a winning tool in the ongoing battle for wildlife conservation. Humans can't go out and capture all the pythons from the Everglades, all the cane toads from Australia, all the lionfish from the Atlantic Ocean, and so on.

Sixty percent of vertebrates on islands around the world have disappeared, mainly due to invasive species.[38] If New Zealand can

---

37   Ibid.

38   (n 281)

successfully set an example on an unprecedented scale with gene drive technology, they will help change the world for the better and hopefully show other island-owning nations how they can best protect their native wildlife humanely and sustainably without harmful poisons, which often have unintended casualties.

Eventually, once we have a stable hold on all aspects of the tech, meaning both creating gene drives and destroying them, we could also utilize them in countries that aren't geographically isolated to contain invasive and nuisance species. The problem of invasive species is spreading like a disease and is responsible for killing millions of native and unique animals every year. The longer we wait, the higher the death toll and destruction. We must be cautious before acting, but we must act before it's too late.

Main Takeaways:

Traditional conservation vs. Biotech conservation:

- Traditional conservation work is very important and certainly makes a huge difference to individual animals, their potential and future family lines, and the survival of the species.
- But synthetic biology can help make a 10x, 50x, 100x, or even greater impact in the future of conservation.
- How can you help develop or even simply support species conservation through synbio? (lab research, class projects, funding grants, corporate or government partnerships, having conversations with others, etc.)

Gene drives can be set up in many different ways depending on the characteristics of the species targeted (breeding interval, lifespan, habitat, etc.), so there's a lot of building options to think through.

- Just as important as building options are destruction options if you need to stop a gene drive in its tracks.
- Entrepreneurially speaking, if a group of scientists become such experts at implementing gene drives, they may be able to form a company and be contracted by governments around the world to deal with invasive species.

Bioethics is a conversation for all of us to join because it can be incredibly powerful in saving species or wiping them out if things go wrong.

- There is much more to learn about conservation tech in controlled lab settings, as well as much to discuss between governments and the public before employing gene drives as the silver bullet for tackling specific cases of invasive species.
- We don't want another cane toad situation, so we must be appropriately cautious, yet still swift, before more animals become extinct at the hands, fins, claws, poison glands, teeth, etc. of invasive species.

CHAPTER 9

DE-EXTINCTION PART I: WHERE TO
BEGIN AND NOT JURASSIC PARK

On the opposite side of eradicating invasive species is bringing native animals back. I'm not just talking about reintroducing wolves into Yellowstone; I'm referring to full-on de-extinction where we can bring back entire species that have no current members left alive on Earth. While we are lucky that some animals like the Panamanian golden frog and black-footed ferret are still around, other species are actually gone for good, or at least for the time being...

But as you can imagine, there is a great deal of controversy and questions about bioethics surrounding de-extinction. The great debates about it are things like:

1. Do we as humans have the moral responsibility to resurrect species that humans caused to go extinct?
2. Is there still a spot remaining in the ecosystem for the species in question to successfully inhabit?
3. What safety concerns would we have for humanity and wildlife living today (such as potentially resurrecting ancient viruses)?

In fact, you can watch an infatuating debate between four top scientists and conservationists on the topic (see footnote).[1] *You can imagine this next part as the beginning of an *Epic Rap Battles of History* video or the announcement before a heavyweight bout...

On the side arguing for resurrecting species:
· Dr. George Church of Harvard University, the Personal Genome Project, and Veritas Genetics, and...

---

1   Brand, Stewart, George Church, Lynn J. Rothschild, and Ross MacPhee. "Don't Bring Extinct Creatures Back to Life." IQ2US Debates. January 31, 2019.

- Stewart Brand, co-founder of the esteemed non-profit Revive & Restore and publisher of the *Whole Earth Catalog*

  On the opposing side, arguing against de-extinction:
- Dr. Ross MacPhee, curator in the Department of Mammalogy, Division of Vertebrate Zoology at the American Museum of Natural History, and...
- Dr. Lynn J. Rothschild, evolutionary biologist and astrobiologist

It's a completely fascinating discussion that you will be absolutely enthralled listening to. I promise it's worth checking out.[2]

Anyway, good candidates for resurrection are species like the passenger pigeon, dodo bird, and great auk (which fun fact: great auks are in the same family classification as puffins, the bird that the porgs are modeled after in *Star Wars: The Last Jedi*).[3] All three of these bird species were hunted to extinction because of humans' demand for meat.[4] There are other species, many also birds, whose habitats were destroyed or were severely affected by pesticides, invasive species, demand for feathers, etc. rather than consumed by humans.

We also often hear about the thylacine, commonly referred to as the Tasmanian tiger, which was hunted by farmers for killing sheep in Australia and Tasmania. Videos do come out every so often depicting blurry striped marsupials running about the bush, although no definitive DNA evidence has been collected as of yet to definitively prove that they're still around.[5]

Some of my favorite TV show hosts, Josh Gates of *Expedition Unknown* and Forrest Galante of *Extinct or Alive*, have taken on the search for the thylacine in their respective series with promising results. Galante even has a return trip planned to continue his search in North Queensland, Australia twelve hundred miles deep into the

---

2 Ibid.

3 Meslow, Scott. "The Last Jedi's Porgs Are Actually... Puffins?" GQ. December 21, 2017.

4 Strauss, Bob. "These 10 Birds Went Extinct Thanks to Humans - and Cats." ThoughtCo. February 23, 2019.

5 JRE Clips. "Searching for the Tasmanian Tiger | Joe Rogan & Forrest Galante." YouTube. February 06, 2019.

bush where he's traveled before. Sightings have occurred, and ongoing university-funded research expeditions are still progressing.[6]

Galante's show is specifically amazing for species conservation because the objective of *Extinct or Alive* is to seek out species, which many have written off but that Galante believes could still be, well, alive. Galante has shown that there is hope for some of the species he has searched for, with a major highlight being when he and his team caught the Zanzibar leopard on camera.[7] It is a subspecies of African leopard found in Tanzania that was declared extinct in 2008 due to hunting.[8]

Now with video evidence in hand, Galante and others can dedicate further efforts to obtaining DNA evidence, the ultimate confirmation of species identification, so they can fight for policies and funding to determine if a viable population still exists. If so, we can protect the remaining animals of this very endangered subspecies from extinction. You can only fight to protect something if you know and prove it's there, at least when it comes to convincing government action and funding on behalf of wildlife.

Woolly Mammoths and Mammoth Mozzies
The main species at the forefront of so many discussions about de-extinction is the woolly mammoth. Josh Gates completed a two-episode expedition where he traveled with a team in search of genetic samples from mammoth blood found in mosquitos frozen in amber. Just kidding! This isn't *Jurassic Park*, and that's not even possible—still a great movie, though.

Gates and the team journeyed to Siberia to collect genetic material from mammoth tusk and bone marrow locked away in permafrost during a two-episode special (season four, episodes five and six respectively: *Cloning the Woolly Mammoth* and *Journey to the Ice Age*).[9,10] DNA typically breaks down rather quickly, but

---

6   Ibid.

7   Animal Planet. "Has The 'Extinct' Zanzibar Leopard Been Found Once More? | Extinct or Alive." YouTube. September 30, 2018.

8   "Zanzibar Leopard." Wikipedia. April 26, 2019.

9   Expedition Unknown. "Cloning the Woolly Mammoth." Discovery.

10   Expedition Unknown. "Journey to the Ice Age." Discovery.

the extreme cold temperatures of frozen soil can preserve genetic material fairly well for hundreds of thousands into the millions of years range. However, genetic material continues to degrade over this time as its half-life is 521 years, meaning you can expect half of all remaining bonds to degrade per 521-year time interval.[11]

Now, 25 percent of the Northern Hemisphere is composed of permafrost (so lots of great genetic samples still left to be found there), but this percentage is quickly melting away as global temperatures rise.[12]

Along with the valuable DNA of extinct creatures and plants, billions of tons of CO_2 from millennia of decaying biological matter are trapped in permafrost. There are also ancient bacteria, once dormant but now coming back to life, that the world has not been exposed to for thousands of years. Bacteria drastically contribute to the generation of CO_2 from these areas by consuming the organic matter rapidly once thawed.[13]

It's easy to see that climate change is setting off a very detrimental chain reaction here. Permafrost melts away fast, thereby thawing out microbes that degrade the likewise thawed organic matter, which vastly increases the amounts of CO_2 in the atmosphere and oceans. This isn't a daisy chain that can be easily broken. The scale of this compounding cycle is just too gargantuan to tackle with anything but biotech.

From an archeological and biological perspective, the unprecedented amount of permafrost thawing out around the world is also causing the loss of artifacts from human settlements and biologics (animal and plant remains) that have been securely locked away in the frozen ground for millennia.[14] Many priceless discoveries are now becoming exposed in areas that humans simply do not occupy—incredibly vast areas of wilderness that scientists cannot cover. And to compensate, researchers are increasing their work speed so they

11   Kaplan, Matt. "DNA Has a 521-year Half-life." Nature News. October 10, 2012.

12   Resnick, Brian. "Melting Permafrost in the Arctic Is Unlocking Diseases and Warping the Landscape." Vox. February 06, 2018.

13   Ibid.

14   Shankman, Sabrina. "In Alaska's Thawing Permafrost, Humanity's 'Library Is on Fire'." Inside-Climate News. November 30, 2017.

can lose an acceptable amount of data on every discovery but increase the rate at which they make new discoveries, as well as save already-known artifacts still in the ground which have yet to be collected under the accelerating time crunch.

Similarly to how we related Earth's biodiversity (especially rainforests and coral reefs) in chapter 7 to the Library of Alexandria (which burned in history's greatest loss of knowledge), an archaeologist stated that her colleagues who work in the Arctic also liken the melting of Earth's ice and permafrost to the Library of Alexandria's demise.[15] I suppose Earth itself is a library all on its own, and the living biodiversity and the preserved remains of extinct biodiversity are just two separate wings of the library. Both are burning in different ways, but the fact is their information is still vanishing.

Our frozen library with millions of years' worth of biological history is decaying away as it continues to thaw out—microbes and oxidation being the big enemies here.[16] Occasionally you'll see an exciting article about hikers or locals stumbling upon some ancient bones. Other times you may see an attention-grabbing headline about scientists finding rare extinct baby animals like horses, cave lions, wooly rhinos, wolves, and of course all those mammoths! But for the most part, we can expect that for every item found serendipitously or otherwise, many more are lost.

There are pockets of wilderness today where it's like the wild frontier, and instead of California gold, people are venturing out into the middle of nowhere to seek riches in valuable biological artifacts like mammoth ivory...

∞

Josh Gates and his team accompanied scientists from Sooam Biotech, a South Korean organization known for cloning your canine best friend to the tune of $100,000, to help in their more futuristic

---

15   "Library of Alexandria." Wikipedia. May 29, 2019.

16   Shankman, Sabrina. "In Alaska's Thawing Permafrost, Humanity's 'Library Is on Fire'." Inside-Climate News. November 30, 2017.

endeavor of trying to resurrect the woolly mammoth.[17] Together, they went deep into the Siberian wilderness and gained access to a frontier camp in the hopes they could collect some genetic material fresh from the permafrost.[18] The fresher the better because the delicate DNA wouldn't be exposed to any degrading warmth.

But how do the frontiersmen find the preserved specimens? They couldn't possibly get anywhere trying to dig through solid permafrost with hand tools, and the areas are way too remote to bring in heavy machinery. The mammoth miners actually pump bone-chilling water from the nearby river into huge hoses and shoot it into towering banks of permafrost. This creates unstable caves of frozen dirt that are literally collapsing around them, but it's an effective way of boring into the rock-solid ground. If they're lucky, the dirt washes out and leaves the heavier bones, tusks, or even mammoth dung for them to find!

Gates and the team were allowed to take several samples from a newly uncovered tusk, which they brought to a nearby lab in Siberia to be isolated and sequenced. They also brought a sample from the inner marrow of a bone they found in a separate Siberian location (Batagaika crater), as well as from a whole baby mammoth specimen housed at the lab.

The mammoth ivory mine samples from the tusk only yielded segments around three hundred to five hundred base pairs of DNA in length (very small segments), but there was a very high concentration of that DNA. High concentrations are great because it means more genetic data for scientists to work with.

The crater sample from the inner bone marrow yielded similarly sized segments to the mammoth ivory sample, although not nearly as high in concentration.[19]

And lastly, the sample from the baby mammoth at the lab tested surprisingly well! It yielded segments of more than two thousand base pairs in length and at a very high concentration. This beat

17   Duncan, David Ewing. "Inside the Very Big, Very Controversial Business of Dog Cloning." Vanities. August 07, 2018.

18   Expedition Unknown. "Journey to the Ice Age." Discovery.

19   Expedition Unknown. "Journey to the Ice Age." Discovery.

Sooam's previous best segment lengths which were about 1,200—1,300 base pairs.[20] But this is still a drop in the bucket of the entire mammoth genome.

For comparison, we know that the African elephant genome contains approximately 3.1 billion base pairs.[21] Sooam Biotech will be continuing their search for the one treasured specimen that will fill in the vast majority of missing pieces. However unlikely, they only need to get lucky once in order to solve the puzzle.

While Sooam's approach represents one strategy for de-extinction of the mammoth and other fallen species, there is another.

George Church at Harvard University is also working on bringing back the woolly mammoth. Church is employing a very different method than Sooam Biotech as Church's approach is more like *part* of what was shown in *Jurassic Park*. Instead of splicing together an array of genes from various birds, reptiles, amphibians, and mosquito-derived dino DNA to create living dinosaurs (which for the record, is really not feasible because dinosaur DNA has long degraded over millions of years), Church's lab is simply looking to swap some key mammoth genes into the elephant genome for endurance in a cold habitat (like having long hair). It wouldn't be full-on mammoth, but it would be mammoth-like.

Church could also engineer resistance to the herpes virus that plagues many elephants today and which some believe may have contributed to the decline in mammoth populations millennia ago.[22] Overall, this approach of building off an established base and yielding a mammoth-like animal will likely be much faster than Sooam Biotech's approach, which is kind of like the search for the Holy Grail. Obviously, the goal with both is to get as close to the real thing as possible.

∞

---

20 Ibid.

21 "Loxafr3.0 - LoxArf3 - Genome - Assembly - NCBI." National Center for Biotechnology Information.

22 Begley, Sharon. "Scientists Reconstruct the Genome of a Moa, a Bird Extinct for 700 Years." STAT. February 27, 2018.

Just as with CRISPR and gene drives, there are of course risks to be assessed before we actually take the next steps to resurrect any species into a self-sustaining population. One of these considerations is whether there is still a suitable environment for the animals to inhabit once they return. Some animals went extinct long ago, and there may not be a place for them to inhabit anymore. But others were around much more recently than you might think.

Believe it or not, mammoths were still roaming the Earth during the construction of the Great Pyramid of Giza in 2560 BCE and for several centuries thereafter. To make the math easy for you, this means the Great Pyramid was built almost forty-six hundred years ago.[23] The last mammoth refuge was on Wrangel Island, which in modern times is a Russian island in the Arctic Ocean. This last stronghold didn't see its last mammoth inhabitants die out until around four thousand years ago.[24] Crazy imagining mammoths still walking around during the time of the Egyptians, right?

While we're at it and just for fun, here are some other things that will alter your perception of time:

- Buzz Aldrin and Neil Armstrong landed on the moon in 1969, just sixty-six years after the Wright brothers invented powered flight in 1903.[25]
- People were still traveling along the Oregon Trail in wagons when the first preliminary fax machine was granted a British patent in 1843 as an "Electric Printing Telegraph."[26], [27] (Golder) (Fax)
- Cleopatra lives closer in time to the invention of Snapchat than to the construction of the Great Pyramid of Giza since she was born in 69 BCE.[28]

23   "Great Pyramid of Giza." Wikipedia. May 17, 2019.

24   "Woolly Mammoth." Wikipedia. May 31, 2019.

25   Golder, Andy. "23 Facts That Will Totally Fuck With Your Perception Of Time." BuzzFeed. December 11, 2016.

26   Ibid.

27   "Fax." Wikipedia. May 23, 2019.

28   Golder, Andy. "23 Facts That Will Totally Fuck With Your Perception Of Time." BuzzFeed. December 11, 2016.

For mammoths, the ideal habitat would be in Siberia. The thought is that the mammoths would prevent trees from growing (which absorb more heat than grassy plains) and also trample the fluffy snow cover that traps heat into the ground during the winter. The unpacked snow, acting as insulation, lets the trapped heat melt away the permafrost below. If it were compacted by herds of mammoths and other grazing animals, the ground would be exposed to the bitter Siberian cold and stay frozen as it should be.[29] There is already an effort to reintroduce grazing mammals into this mammoth steppe habitat called Pleistocene Park. Reintroductions began in 1988, and the sixteen-square-kilometer park in Siberia is now home to five species of mammals: bison, moose, musk ox, reindeer, and horses. Things are going great, and the next step is to bring back the woolly mammoths.[30]

Perhaps the best example of habitat transformation via reintroduction of species to date, although not de-extinction itself, was when wolves were released into Yellowstone National Park in 1995. The places that the wolves roamed in the park were drastically changed for the better. They hunted deer and elk, which in turn allowed more juvenile trees and plant life to flourish. More bugs and birds came back because of the increased vegetation, and the increased plant growth along the river banks prevented soil erosion. This led to the beaver, which hadn't been seen in the park for some time, to return, along with an increase in many more species like foxes. Yellowstone is a healthier ecosystem now than it ever was before the return of the wolves, and this is a fantastic example to look toward for what species reintroduction can do for a habitat.[31]

Despite the environmental benefits that grazing mammoths would have roaming the Arctic tundra, there is also a matter of ethics about how to bring this animal into the world. Woolly mammoths are more closely related to Asian elephants than African elephants.[32]

29   "Woolly Mammoth Revival." Revive & Restore. April 18, 2018.

30   "Pleistocene Park." Wikipedia. April 17, 2019.

31   MacNeil, Caeleigh. "How Wolves Saved the Foxes, Mice and Rivers of Yellowstone National Park." Earthjustice. October 26, 2016.

32   Handwerk, Brian. "Woolly Mammoth DNA Reveals Elephant Family Tree." National Geographic. December 20, 2005.

But would it be ethical to have an Asian elephant carry the woolly mammoth baby? Would elephants even be biologically equipped to give birth to a live mammoth as they're still different species? Well, it depends on how much the mammoth is mammoth-like. Is it the Sooam Biotech mammoth that has as much of the mammoth genome as possible, or is it developed more from the George Church method as an Asian elephant with cold-adapted genes?

If it's the first case of "gimme as much mammoth as possible," we must consider that though the Asian elephant and mammoth are similar in size, we just don't know 100 percent if things would work out safely for the surrogate elephant mother. Asian elephants giving birth to mammoth babies has never been attempted before. The circumventing solution in this case would be to use an artificial womb partially through the pregnancy, but the research to do so with a mammoth is conceivably still many years away.

In 2017, a groundbreaking achievement was made when scientists developed artificial wombs, called biobags, and finished the development of prematurely born lambs in them.[33] The lambs started out growing in mother sheep because currently, starting at embryogenesis and going all the way to fully formed organisms within artificial wombs is not possible.[34] All of the interactions between the mother and early embryo are too important and complex to be successfully replicated. Hopefully, someday in the future it will be possible like we see in plenty of science fiction features with forms of artificial wombs: *Avatar* with the blue people, *Oblivion* with Tom Cruise, *Altered Carbon* on Netflix, and I think even *Star Wars: Episode II—Attack of the Clones?*

A few of the lambs survived after continuing their development within and subsequently being birthed out of the biobags. Scientists have been monitoring them for any long-term effects ever since to compare against other normally birthed animals' health. We will most likely see biobags having human trials within the next few years

---

33   Couzin-Frankel, Jennifer. "Fluid-filled 'biobag' Allows Premature Lambs to Develop outside the Womb." Science. April 25, 2017.

34   CTV News. "Baby Sheep Successfully Grown in Artificial 'biobag' Womb." YouTube. April 26, 2017.

as this technology could help babies born prematurely on the edge of viability to have a much higher chance of survival.

Furthermore, this artificial womb tech could be a way to bring a baby woolly mammoth into the world by first placing the embryo in an elephant, doing a premature C-section, and then utilizing the biobag to complete the baby's development. It's going to take a pretty big bag and a lot of artificially produced amniotic fluid, though! And of course, there would also be concerns about unnecessarily putting the mother elephant through this process, same with the baby, and the risks that come with it.

The second method of adapting an Asian elephant for cold climates using mammoth genes would more than likely mean that the Asian elephant would still be able to naturally and safely give birth to a baby that is basically an Asian elephant sparing some of those cold-adapted alterations like hair, increased fat stores, etc. The resulting mammoth-like animal could then be genetically engineered, have its sperm or eggs engineered, or be selectively bred with others to achieve various features like more cold-adapted genes. This is all still in the realm of science fiction for now, but with skilled scientists working on it, it comes closer to a potential reality every day.

There are many other considerations about bringing mammoths back to life too, such as the danger of resurrecting an ancient virus since viruses encode their DNA into the host's, being able to bring back multiple mammoths simultaneously so that they can live in a herd as they would naturally (first in a controlled and protected zoo environment before being introduced into the mammoth steppe habitat of Pleistocene Park), and having enough genetic diversity to bring back a self-sustaining and healthy population. De-extinction of mammoths is very exciting to talk about, but there are a lot of complex nuances to take into account for safety, conservation, and ethics. Nevertheless, I am hopeful that with the exponential technological advancement happening in the world today, we'll see mammoths begin their revitalization within the twenty-first century.

Several other species will likely see their resurgence a bit before though...

Main Takeaways:

Even though this chapter is less about entrepreneurship and more about sustainability (as is the nature of species conservation and de-extinction), the tech discussed, like artificial wombs, have the potential to be commercialized for human applications.

- Enterprising Gene-trepreneurs in academia and non-profit work can apply artificial wombs being developed for humans to species conservation, for example. This is technology transfer—the same thing as medical-grade tissue culturing being transferred to the food sector (i.e., cell-based meats).

De-extinction is a delicate matter as the purpose would be to increase biodiversity and benefit the climate.

- We don't want a de-extincted species becoming akin to an invasive species in its former native habitat or in a new habitat, which would result in the loss of biodiversity.
- It's not just a moral debate; we must balance the cost of de-extinction (which takes funds away from conservation of alive species) with the net impact and return on investment (ROI) the species would create.
- Nobody has cracked the code on making de-extinction profitable, which debatably, would help mitigate the argument that de-extinction takes away funding from more important conservation efforts needed to support the creatures we still have around for the time being.

Just as bioprospecting Earth's living biodiversity leads to the discovery of valuable biomolecules, our other wing of the biodiversity library frozen in the permafrost is also important to save before all that knowledge thaws and degrades away.

CHAPTER 10

DE-EXTINCTION PART II: RESTORING BALANCE AND LAL NOT LOL

As mentioned, other animals are deserving of second chances aside from mammoths, and endeavors akin to Sooam Biotech's or George Church's lab will see that those species receive them.

The Lazarus Project, Brooding Frogs, and Big Birds

The Lazarus Project is one of those endeavors.

An effort by Australian scientists, they have almost resurrected the bizarre yet amazing southern gastric-brooding frog—a species that only recently went extinct in the early 1980s.[1] The female frogs literally ate their eggs, turning their stomachs into a kind of "brooding" chamber for their tadpoles to develop. Around six weeks later, baby frogs would be regurgitated out into the world. It's kind of like the aliens from the *Predator* movie series, except the baby frogs aren't aliens burrowing out of your abdomen.[2] Actually, it's more like in *Harry Potter and the Chamber of Secrets* when Ron Weasley tries to curse Draco Malfoy, but the spell backfires due to his broken wand so Ron ends up regurgitating slugs.[3]

Anyway, as amazing as this frog was, it was unfortunately discovered just eleven years before it went extinct, leaving little time to study it.[4] But eleven years is definitely better than never discovering it at all because now we can help bring it back.

---

1   Thomson, Craig. The Lazarus Project- to Bring Back Australia's Southern Gastric-brooding Frog. March 29, 2017.

2   "Alien (franchise)." Wikipedia. June 02, 2019.

3   "Slug-vomiting Charm." Harry Potter Wiki.

4   "Gastric-brooding Frog." Wikipedia. May 31, 2019.

In 2013, researchers were able to take nuclei from a frozen frog specimen and implant them into enucleated eggs from another frog species. Although southern gastric-brooding frog embryos were formed, they only divided for three days and no living specimens resulted from the experiment.[5] The researchers were able to preserve the dividing cells for future experiments, though, which is an amazing step forward.[6]

The reason why no embryos survived is because viable embryos do not seem to develop 100 percent correctly when the implanted nucleus comes from a different species. This is most likely due to the signals for successful cell division and differentiation getting all messed up due to some species-specific differences. Developmental biology is very complex because so many unique signals and pathways are triggered in the nucleus and extracellular environment, which must happen at precisely the right times.

This method of implanting a nucleus into an egg of a closely related species exemplifies a potential way to clone an animal. The de-extinction work around the gastric-brooding frog is also especially important research for living amphibian conservation because, as you may recall from Jeff Corwin's section in chapter 7, Corwin likens amphibians to Earth's canaries in the coal mine. We're losing them at an alarming rate, and the loss isn't just a moral one, but a loss of valuable biomolecules since amphibians are a source of pharmaceutical discovery.

For example, if we were to resurrect the southern gastric-brooding frog, it could be studied for the eggs' and tadpoles' ability to shut off the mother's stomach acid production during development. This could lead to potential medical applications for helping humans with gastrointestinal issues.[7]

By perfecting the de-extinction process of a recently extinct frog like the gastric-brooding variety, we can be better prepared to save other endangered amphibians that will inevitably become extinct due

5   Phillips, Nicky. "Extinct Frog Hops Back into the Gene Pool." The Sydney Morning Herald. March 15, 2013.

6   "Lazarus Project: Extinct Frog Brought Back To Life, What Next." nexpected, n.d.

7   Gross Science. "Meet The Frog That Barfs Up Its Babies." YouTube. May 08, 2017.

to humanity's influence—some of which we probably haven't even discovered yet. Time is truly of the essence because it's easier to do this research before it's absolutely required. Populations are decreasing, members of species are becoming harder to find, old museum specimens can easily get mis-labeled or misplaced in large collections, and DNA from those preserved specimens degrades over time, leaving gaps in the genome (a complete genome is needed for this nuclei replacement method to succeed). So there isn't any time to waste in perfecting this de-extinction and cloning technology.

Snapshot Lesson:
The return-on-investment argument for putting resources into mammoth de-extinction is largely centered around trapping CO_2 in the Siberian permafrost and reflecting more heat away from Earth. Other herding animals in Pleistocene Park can do this, though maybe not to the same extent as mammoths. The argument for de-extincting amphibians is that not only are they much more present in modern history (recently extinct or prepping for possible extinction in coming decades), but they are also very valuable to pharmaceutical discovery. Plus, investing in de-extinction methods for one species, like the southern gastric-brooding frog, can be applicable to so many others. There are an estimated eight thousand species of amphibians, of which at least two thousand are threatened.[8]

∞

The same method of nucleus-replacement cloning the Lazarus Project used for the gastric brooding-frog was also implemented with the Pyrenean ibex—a sub-species of Iberian ibex (basically a mountain ram, the Pyrenean variety being native to the Pyrenees Mountains between France and Spain). The last Pyrenean ibex was killed in 2000. You might imagine a hunter shot the last one, but it was actually killed by a falling tree. Freak accidents happen in nature too. In 2003, with the preserved genome in hand, a Pyrenean ibex embryo

---

8   "Even More Amphibians Are Endangered than We Thought." ScienceDaily. ScienceDaily,
      May 6, 2019.

was created via this cloning method, was carried to term, and then born.[9] This marked the first de-extinction event in history! Sadly, the animal died from a lung complication soon after. However, scientists are confident that if given funding they could remedy the lung issue and deliver a healthy Pyrenean ibex into the world.[10]

So in addition to the de-extinction method like George Church is working on for mammoths (building off something like an elephant genome and piecing together a mammoth-like creature), cloning is yet another way to resurrect a species if intact cells are available. De-extinction isn't some science fiction dream; it's already here.

The other option of de-extinction is back-breeding like the Nazis were trying to do with the auroch, the great super-cow of its time that went extinct in 1627.[11] Since the Nazi era was in the 1930s into the 1940s, meaning this was before the discovery of the double helix in 1953 or any genetic engineering tools,[12] the best the Third Reich could do was try to breed current cattle for the desired physical and behavioral traits (like big horns and aggressive dispositions).

It's similar to how dogs have been selectively mated into breeds for specific purposes, except instead of honing new traits, the Nazis were trying to sire creatures resembling their extinct ancestors. Why would they do this, though? Well, during World War II, the Nazis were trying to build an ancient forest filled with fantastical beasts for canned hunting. It's really intriguing, and there are some great videos online if you are interested in learning more about it.[13, 14]

The Lazarus Project could also help bring back the moa, a flightless bird similar to ostriches and emus, which was native to New Zealand. The largest of the nine moa species could reach twelve feet

9   "Pyrenean Ibex." Wikipedia. May 24, 2019.

10 Rincon, Paul. "Fresh Effort to Clone Extinct Animal." BBC News. November 22, 2013.

11 Boissoneault, Lorraine. "When the Nazis Tried to Bring Animals Back From Extinction." Smithsonian.com. March 31, 2017.

12 "The Francis Crick Papers: The Discovery of the Double Helix, 1951-1953." U.S. National Library of Medicine.

13 "Nazi Nature." National Geographic - Videos, TV Shows & Photos - International.

14 National Geographic. "NG Hitler's Jurassic Monsters - Video Dailymotion." Dailymotion. June 16, 2015.

tall.[15] For reference, ostriches reach a maximum of just over nine feet, so some moas were a 33 percent taller than them—huge for a bird![16] They went extinct six hundred years ago, their decline coinciding with the arrival of humans on the island. (They were quite delicious apparently.) Their genes confirm too that the species began to wane after humans arrived. The low genetic diversity in later organisms exhibit that humans had a direct impact on moa species. This is especially driven home by the fact that the genetic evidence also displays that moa populations were stable for the previous four thousand years.[17] Humans arrived and boom, there were no more moas within a couple of centuries. Humans ate em' all up.

Luckily, researchers at Harvard have put together a nearly complete genome of one of the nine species of moas called the little bush moa. They accomplished this using a toe bone from a museum specimen at the Royal Ontario Museum in Canada.[18] The team had nine million nucleotides of sequence split amongst millions of DNA segments and were able to piece them together like a puzzle by comparing with the emu genome. 85 percent of the little bush moa genome is complete. The remaining 15 percent is tougher to match with the emu, so it awaits assembly into the rest.[19] Nevertheless, this accomplishment paves the way for reconstructing other extinct bird species like the dodo, great auk, eight additional moa species, as well as the passenger pigeon, which we'll now discuss in this next section.

---

15   "Moa." Wikipedia. June 04, 2019.

16   Bradford, Alina. "Ostrich Facts: The World's Largest Bird." LiveScience. September 17, 2014.

17   Morell, Virginia. "Why Did New Zealand's Moas Go Extinct?" Science. March 17, 2014.

18   Begley, Sharon. "Scientists Reconstruct the Genome of a Moa, a Bird Extinct for 700 Years." STAT. February 27, 2018.

19   Ibid.

Main Takeaways:

Developing the tools for de-extinction is about more than just bringing back long-gone species from the past.

- It can also be about restoring recently extinct species like the southern gastric-brooding frog and the Pyrenean ibex, as well as preparing to bring back species that will inevitably go extinct in the coming decades due to human activities.
- Conservation won't work for all the endangered species currently out there, so we are perfecting the tools for de-extinction before they are severely needed.

Researchers and conservationists with the entrepreneurial mindset can use the methods and tools available to them for one species and apply them to other recognized opportunities to aid related species (amphibians → amphibians, birds → birds, mammals → mammals).

Revive & Restore and Blue Bloods

Now that we have a larger understanding of both species conservation and de-extinction from this chapter and the previous few, I want to introduce you to a non-profit aiding Dr. George Church as well as supporting many other unique endeavors to prevent future extinctions called Revive & Restore. I was fortunate to have the opportunity to interview founder and executive director Ryan Phelan to learn more about her entrepreneurial journey and the successes of the non-profit project thus far. Phelan and her latest organization are the embodiment of employing biotech to achieve high impact in wildlife conservation.

Having previously built two companies in the medical sector, Ryan Phelan already had an impressive résumé as a Gene-trepreneur before founding and directing Revive & Restore.[20] Phelan's entrepreneurial history displays how she is absolutely mission-driven with her heart in the best of places as her previous ventures were also positioned to help underserved groups.

Direct Medical Knowledge was the first comprehensive consumer health website to open a vast array of medical information to

---

20 "Ryan Phelan." Ryan Phelan | Edge.org.

individuals for assessing their ailments. It was essentially the precursor to WebMD, which it was later acquired by. Yes, the huge site that all of us hypochondriacs use to dangerously diagnose ourselves with life-threatening illnesses.

Phelan's second medical startup was DNA Direct, which opened the doors for more people to have their genes tested and analyzed. Both companies sought to give patients a more level playing field when it came to their personal health.

And now, her lifelong mission to create opportunities for groups that aren't served well enough has been transferred from people over to endangered species in her third big endeavor. Phelan's Revive & Restore is a beacon of hope helping to lead the charge for wildlife conservation and restoration via biotech.

The non-profit organization was founded in 2013 when Phelan looked at where her expertise in understanding the role of genetics and technologies in making medical decisions could be applied to benefit wildlife. This led to building Revive & Restore, which now drives the conservation field of genetic rescue as we previously touched upon in Chapter 7. The org supports endeavors to prevent further extinctions, as well as to revive species that have been wiped out at the hands of humans. Just like Jon Snow in *Game of Thrones* though, fighting for the living takes precedent.[21] But both groups, endangered species and the presently extinct ones, are benefitting from the organization's activities.

Revive & Restore is building what they call "the Twenty-First Century genetic rescue toolkit," and this deals with sequencing the genomes of alive and extinct creatures, storing cell lines (like the Frozen Zoo is doing), working on reproductive technologies (like IVG—recall turning regular cells into sperm and eggs), advising gene drive developments, and supporting de-extinction efforts (like George Church's project with woolly mammoths).

The non-profit also recently launched their Catalyst Science Fund wherein they provide grants to jumpstart projects with the potential to make enormous positive impacts in conservation. Phelan noted that one of the main challenges in this line of work is fragmented

---

21   "Jon Snow." Game of Thrones Wiki.

funding because there aren't enough success stories being shared along with the saddening headlines about more species edging closer to extinction. Additionally, since it's mainly non-profit work, financial support isn't being dedicated toward conservation groups steadily because people fail to see how they'll directly benefit from their investments.

The Catalyst Science Fund is Revive & Restore's opportunity to see that new projects and technology developments that can benefit conservation receive important financial support to get off the ground and make a difference. The first grant was given out recently to a Stanford University marine biologist, Steve Palumbi, studying the genetic stress triggers that cause corals to bleach.[22]

Revive & Restore has many other notable involvements as well. You may recall the tale of the black-footed ferret from Jeff Corwin in chapter 7,[23] and of course, as mentioned in the last chapter, the advancements to resurrect the woolly mammoth.[24] But Revive & Restore's flagship project deals with a species of extinct wild bird— the passenger pigeon. Phelan stated that while a lot is known about farmed birds like chickens, not nearly as much research has been done on wild bird populations. This makes it a bit more difficult to facilitate genetic rescue amongst native bird species around the world. Extinct bird species are even more difficult to work on, but Revive & Restore is really on the cusp of bringing the passenger pigeon back to the skies and forests of North America once more.

The passenger pigeon project is led by researcher Ben Novak. He began collecting DNA from some of the fifteen hundred passenger pigeon specimens stored away in museums.[25] Today, Novak has earned his way up to working as the lead scientist at Revive & Restore, and he is employing a method that is a mixture of breeding and genome editing to see "The Great Passenger Pigeon Comeback" project successfully through.[26]

22   "First Catalyst Fund Grant Awarded." Revive & Restore. October 25, 2018.

23   "Black-Footed Ferret." Revive & Restore. April 30, 2019.

24   "Woolly Mammoth Revival." Revive & Restore. April 18, 2018.

25   Servick, Kelly. "The Plan to Bring the Iconic Passenger Pigeon Back From Extinction." Wired. June 4, 2017.

26   "About the Passenger Pigeon." Revive & Restore, July 10, 2018

The CRISPR/Cas9 system allowed him to edit the primordial germ cells (precursors to sperm and eggs) of the band-tailed pigeon, a very close relative of the passenger pigeon. By implanting genes for the passenger pigeon into the band-tailed pigeons, Novak created what are called chimeras. They have DNA from two distinct species within them. The hope is that through the creation and breeding of chimeras, the passenger pigeon genes will become inherited in subsequent generations and lead to a pretty much genetically identical species to the known genome of the passenger pigeon over the coming years. It's kind of like back-breeding (recall attempts for aurochs), but the passenger pigeons have a genetic head start. Revive & Restore has set hatching their first chicks of the new passenger pigeon line by 2025 as their ambitious goal.

You might be wondering what will happen once the genome is successfully recreated through breeding over the coming years (hopefully hitting that goal before 2025). I mean, captive animals can't just be released back into the wild. Right? Plus, we would want to see proof on some scale that passenger pigeons would have a positive effect on biodiversity and the environment too—not overrun it.

The plan is that the flock will be placed into a netted woodland area and monitored. This is called a "soft release" and has been used for the restoration of the pink pigeon in Mauritius for example.[27] The birds would breed and raise their offspring exposed to the natural elements. Other species could be introduced to the aviary to monitor interactions between the passenger pigeons and current native species.

Around 2034, Revive & Restore would then begin re-wilding the soft release birds and continue supplementing the population with soft release birds until the numbers reached a goal of ten thousand. With that quantity of birds free, passenger pigeons would be easily on their way to recovering their former population (into the millions) and resuming their important ecological roles as disruptors of North American forest canopies as they did before their extinction in 1914.[28] Disturbing tree canopies serves an important role in nature as it

---

27 "Progress to Date." Revive & Restore, October 19, 2018.

28 Yeoman, Barry. "Why the Passenger Pigeon Went Extinct." Audubon, April 13, 2016.

allows opportunities for new plant growth. The current method of disturbance is done by humans deforesting huge patches of woods so that all the trees don't age out at the same time. Passenger pigeons could restore the natural balance.

If all goes well with the project, the success of passenger pigeon restoration can serve as a model for the revival of other bird species in the future such as the heath hen, a type of prairie chicken found in the Northeast US until its demise in 1932.[29]

∞

Aside from The Great Passenger Pigeon Comeback, another extremely interesting project Phelan is helping to pioneer is centered around horseshoe crabs. Although not de-extinction, it is certainly helping prevent one.

These living fossils have been around for 450 million years, but they are being wiped out for their blood. Horseshoe crabs have blue blood which humans make into an ingredient called Limulus Amebocyte Lysate (a.k.a. LAL). LAL is very useful for detecting bacterial contaminations in vaccines, which is vital if you don't want bacterial infections injected straight into your bloodstream.[30]

Before LAL, scientists would inject vaccines into tons of rabbits to see if they would become infected with bacteria like E. coli and die—not a great time to be a rabbit. Since 1970, scientists can put a drop of LAL into a vaccine and see if any clusters appear. If any do, it's because LAL is clotting around gram-negative bacteria, thereby serving as an early indicator that the vaccine may end up becoming deadly to a patient if given.[31] Seems like a fantastic improvement on inefficiently injecting hordes of rabbits. Right? Well, we've just swapped one species for another, and it turns out it's been a pretty rough fifty years for horseshoe crabs.

---

29 "About the Heath Hen Project." Revive & Restore, August 20, 2019.

30 "Horseshoe Crab." Revive & Restore, June 5, 2019.

31 Business Insider. "Why Horseshoe Crab Blood Is So Expensive | So Expensive." YouTube. September 01, 2018.

Approximately six hundred thousand of these crabs are caught in the US every year to be inverted and drained of their blood. They are only drained about 30 percent max—at least that's the goal. With a room full of bleeding horseshoe crabs of various sizes, this doesn't always happen. And up to 30 percent of the crabs die.[32] The remaining ones are released back into the wild to hopefully be caught again the following year, but nobody knows exactly how many of them actually recover and survive the process after release. With a third of their blood gone, the crabs are quite weak and disoriented, so perhaps they cannot fend for themselves. It's also thought the whole ordeal may affect the females during spawning. Over the years, we've seen horseshoe crab numbers decline substantially as a result of LAL demand. And this is also further exacerbated by the use of horseshoe crabs as bait in the eel and conch industries.

Progress is being made to provide a synthetic solution, though.

Over twenty years ago, two scientists at the National University of Singapore developed recombinant factor C (rFC). The patent for this has since been held by one manufacturer, and the industry has been wary of adopting the alternative until it can be supplied by more than just one company. [33] Additionally, the FDA has been slow to give rFC the green light as a replacement of LAL. Now, the first drug tested with rFC has been approved by the FDA and that barrier-to-entry patent is expired in the US, so more manufacturers will be able to competitively produce rFC and in turn, hopefully incentivize pharmaceutical companies to make the switch.[34]

Revive & Restore has conducted and published a study confirming that rFC is equal to or even more efficacious in some cases than LAL when it comes to detecting bacteria in vaccines.[35] The synthetic

---

32   Ibid.

33   Maloney, Tom, et al. "Saving the Horseshoe Crab: A Synthetic Alternative to Horseshoe Crab Blood for Endotoxin Detection." PLOS Biology. Public Library of Science, October 12, 2018.

34   "FDA Approves First Drug Using the Recombinant Factor C Assay for Endotoxin Testing." FDA Approves First Drug Using the Recombinant Factor C Assay for Endotoxin Testing, November 8, 2018.

35   Maloney, Tom, et al. "Saving the Horseshoe Crab: A Synthetic Alternative to Horseshoe Crab Blood for Endotoxin Detection." PLOS Biology. Public Library of Science, October 12, 2018.

rFC also has less false positives, so hopefully a more rampant adoption of the synthetic version will drastically lessen our reliance on horseshoe crab blood for LAL in the coming few years.

There is no time to waste as several Asian species are on the brink of collapse. And declines in horseshoe crab populations are negatively affecting other species as well. Sea turtles eat the crabs, and many sea birds rely on consuming horseshoe crab eggs in order to make it up to the Arctic Circle during their northward migration.[36] It goes beyond just horseshoe crabs because everything above them on the food chain suffers along with them as they disappear. Hopefully rFC will help prevent that from happening. Things are looking optimistic, and Revive & Restore is helping drive the cause.

∞

One final point I wish to share: I always like to ask the founders if they have any advice for those who are just starting out. After all, trying to recognize opportunities and develop early stage ventures out of them is no easy feat, and Phelan has been so successful at it. She gave some incredible insight about this, saying you really have to step back and ask yourself how profound is your solution. How impactful will it be?

If the world needs your solution, then absolutely go for it. If it's just incremental improvement, it's not worth the hassle to start it from scratch. It will end up being a waste of time with no fruits from your labor except for some increased knowledge about a subject and experience of how not to do something. These lessons are valuable too, but it's not what you set out to accomplish. So, whatever you decide to do, it needs to warrant the commitment.

For Phelan, Revive & Restore is a necessary leader in the field pushing conservation advancements more quickly and to higher levels—a catalyst of conservation, if you will. And it's worth putting everything she has into it. All of the endeavors may not pan out exactly as planned, just like you may not find success with the first things you do. Revive & Restore's largest impact may end up being the

---

36 "Horseshoe Crab." Revive & Restore, June 5, 2019.

support of bleaching trigger research in corals, resurrecting the passenger pigeon, or driving adoption of rFC to save horseshoe crabs. But all of these have big impacts associated with their potential success.

Whatever you decide to work on, no matter if it's in synthetic biology or another field, you need to make sure your product, startup, or non-profit will carry you through the inevitable tough times you'll have when creating it and that it is achieving a high net impact.

Main Takeaways:
Like Phelan, you can transfer your business-world experience into the realm of non-profits to cultivate your impact.
- It's all about transferable skillsets, opportunity recognition, and taking action.

When you recognize many different opportunities, as there are so many in species conservation and de-extinction, you must ask yourself how deep the problem is you want to help solve.
- Incremental improvements will not yield success in developing an early stage venture.
- So ask, "How can I use biotech to make ten times the improvements?" and chase your answers to that.

Culturing Change and Building More Gene-trepreneurs

Gene-trepreneur is at its core a knowledge-builder that conglomerates information for you, threading the needle to display how many of our top sustainability challenges are interconnected, how they affect you, and what's being done to solve them. Additionally, I hope this book highlights how no matter your age, location, or background, you too can get involved in the changes happening today and the many more to come. And you know what? There is no better way to see an improved future for yourself, your family, all animals, and the planet than to be a part of shaping it.

This also hits on the two key components required to become a great Gene-trepreneur, and it's really the same as with any dedicated endeavor: 1) knowledge and 2) action.

To acquire the knowledge means we must constantly be soaking in widespread information about what scientific and sustainability problems are out there and which varieties of tech we can combine from diverse fields to meet big challenges in more efficient ways. We must observe, read, and speak about the ventures of others and how they strategically approach new markets, such as cellular agriculture (real meat without animals is entirely new, having just sprouted up vigorously within the past decade). And we must have our ears to the ground listening, analyzing trends, and learning from the past and present to best predict the future.

The good thing today is that the scales of knowledge are tipped well into our favor.

As previously mentioned at *Gene-trepreneur*'s outset, the rise of synthetic biology is akin to the rise of the internet in the 1980s and 90s. In those decades, however, people still relied heavily upon encyclopedias, newspaper articles, person-to-person information exchanges, and so on for research. In the present day, we have massive amounts of information readily at our fingertips. We have more power to learn new material quicker than ever before—how new biotechnology works, ways to market it, how to invest in it, what software programs are needed for its growth, and more. We can learn at unprecedented rates.

Following the knowledge comes action. We went through this earlier in the preface, but to reiterate: Bill Gates in a Twitter thread to his now nearly fifty million followers stated that younger generations "...know more than I did when I was your age," and that those coming into their own paths today "...can start fighting inequity, whether down the street or around the world, sooner."[1]

If you don't know exactly where to start, well, a good place to begin is by asking yourself what inequity you still see in the world that deeply upsets you, that you would do anything to see change. Then, let that pain point become your purpose. Once you've got those seeds of knowledge about the subject, it's about taking action and following the rabbit hole. To help you accomplish this, here are the seven top takeaways I hope you can apply to your actionable path forward—toward becoming a Gene-trepreneur to create *your greatest impact*.

Seven Lessons and A Few More References

1. Ideas alone don't mean anything. Execution on those ideas means everything.
Building your knowledge base and accumulating the forthcoming ideas is worthless if you don't try to activate those ideas into something tangible. It'd be like expanding your root system without growing the tree. Doesn't do much good, does it? A way to begin taking actionable steps is by sharing your concepts with others. Bounce ideas off everyone you can. By doing so, you are breathing more life

---

1   Gates, Bill. "New College Grads Often Ask Me for Career Advice. At the Risk of Sounding like This Guy..." Twitter. May 15, 2017.

into them, sowing seeds that may have the potential to turn into something worthwhile.

A lot of people are so worried about sharing their ideas because they're afraid someone will steal them. That's just about the most unproductive thing you can do. You *need* to speak with others (and not just friends and family) to get their valuable, unbiased feedback. With new insights, you can hone your concept and pivot as needed (including discarding the bad ones—check out Google's company called X, commonly referred to as "the moonshot factory," and how they try to shoot down all their new ideas).[2] You should only be worried about sharing your ideas if the person you speak with will actually *do something* about them. A successful prospect isn't just the initial "aha moment." It's everything you do after in order to turn your idea into a reality.

The point is, you'll find that good ideas can be valued, but execution on them is a revered attribute above simply clever thinking. So Share. Adapt. Execute. It's incredibly more helpful and efficient than sitting on your concepts like a chicken on its eggs. Plus, we don't want more chickens. Do we? They're becoming an obsolete technology.

This quote from George R.R. Martin, the author of the popular book series *A Song of Ice and Fire* that has been adapted into the award-winning series *Game of Thrones*, sums up this first lesson perfectly and leads nicely into the next one:

> *"Ideas are cheap. I have more ideas now than I could ever write up. To my mind, it's the execution that is all-important. I'm proud of my work, but I don't know if I'd ever claim it's enormously original. You look at Shakespeare, who borrowed all of his plots. In A Song of Ice and Fire, I take stuff from the Wars of the Roses and other fantasy things, and all these things work around in my head and somehow they jell into what I hope is uniquely my own."[3]*

---

2   Thompson, Derek. "Google X and the Science of Radical Creativity." The Atlantic. November 16, 2017.

3   Mochari, Ilan. "'Game of Thrones' Author George R. R. Martin on What Makes Ideas Work." Inc.com. May 02, 2014.

2. Opportunity recognition isn't about creating something entirely new. It's about bringing together things that have never been combined in that way before.

Every great idea is simply a combination of others, whether it's basing your world-famed book series on a combination of real-life events and fictional works or creating a company that is the amalgamation of seemingly disparate technologies brought together for a new purpose.

For example, as we've delved into cellular agriculture with start-ups like Finless Foods and New Age Meats, these companies are taking tissue-culturing technology from the medical sector and applying it to the food sector. Medical technology is put to use when making real meat without animals in a very similar manner to brewing beer. New protein companies like these are also implementing 3D printing and using it to structure the cultured muscle, fat, and connective tissue into steaks, fish fillets, pork loins, and more.[4] So just as with every other field, cellular agriculture starts by drawing upon technologies transferred from other areas and then can begin developing its own.

Typically, standout technologies change the game for many different markets. To name some popular ones:

- 3D printing
  - creating plant and cell-based meats
  - fighting black market trade in rhino horn as we've learned with Pembient [5]
  - duplicating masterpiece paintings, brush strokes and all, for museums and personal art collections [6]
  - crafting prosthetic limbs for humans and our four-legged friends [7]
- Drones

---

4   Khazan, Olga. "The Coming Obsolescence of Animal Meat." The Atlantic. April 16, 2019.

5   "Pembient." Pembient.

6   "3-D Printed Copies of Famous Paintings Recreate Brush Strokes, Cracks." CBCnews. June 12, 2016.

7   Van Zeijderveld, Jessica. "3D Printed Prosthetics: 8 Incredible Animal Prostheses." Sculpteo. May 02, 2018.

- delivering organs for transplants [8]
- fighting animal poaching on African nature reserves [9]
- hunting for treasure [10]
- delivering Amazon packages [11]
- Genetic sequencing
  - helping solve crimes as with the case of the Golden State Killer[12]
  - tracing ancestral roots like with 23andMe [13]
  - assessing risks of certain diseases like Parkinson's and late-onset Alzheimer's for personal healthcare [14]
- Genetic engineering
  - aiding immensely in species conservation like crafting corals that can withstand climate change [15]
  - protecting against mosquito-borne illnesses like malaria [16]
  - engineering humans to eventually be impervious to certain conditions and more effectively fight off diseases (various forms of cancer, sickle cell anemia, an inherited type of blindness, etc.) [17]

You may want to ask yourself if some of these blockbuster technologies can be applied to your pain point of choice to achieve a valuable solution.

∞

8   Scutti, Susan. "First Drone Delivery of a Donated Kidney Ends with Transplant." CNN. May 01, 2019.

9   Worland, Justin. "How Air Shepherd Is Fighting Poachers With Drones." Time. May 31, 2018.

10 Auvsi News. "PrecisionHawk Uses Drone Technology to Hunt for Buried Treasure in the Philippines." Association for Unmanned Vehicle Systems International. March 26, 2019.

11 "Prime Air." Amazon.

12 Molteni, Megan. "The Future of Crime-Fighting Is Family Tree Forensics." Wired. December 26, 2018.

13 "DNA Genetic Testing & Analysis." 23andMe.

14 Boddy, Jessica. "FDA Approves Marketing Of Consumer Genetic Tests For Some Conditions." NPR. April 07, 2017.

15 Cornwall, Warren. "Researchers Embrace a Radical Idea: Engineering Coral to Cope with Climate Change." Science. March 21, 2019.

16 Swetlitz, Ike. "Researchers to Release First-ever Genetically Engineered Mosquitoes in Africa." STAT. September 04, 2018.

17 Stein, Rob. "First U.S. Patients Treated With CRISPR As Human Gene-Editing Trials Get Underway." NPR. April 16, 2019.

Just as there are all these game-changing technologies to be on the lookout for, there are also widely applicable business models that can be adapted to potentially fit your needs.

If you look at the gig economy for instance,[18] people have tried creating a version of Uber for every industry (Uber for massages, food, alcohol, healthcare).[19] Another example is subscription boxes: whether for monthly beauty products, meals (like Blue Apron), book genres, movie-lovers (*Harry Potter, Game of Thrones*, Marvel, etc.), tea enthusiasts, grooming supplies (Harry's Razors and Dollar Shave Club), pet toys and food (Chewy.com), and for whatever additional industries you can think of. And although not a subscription box model itself, companies like 23andMe have done a great job at making the process of receiving a package, giving a sample of your DNA from the comfort of home, and shipping the package back off to the lab incredibly customer-friendly.

You get the point. Everything is just a combination of different ideas, technologies, and business models. It all truly boils down to finding unique connections that solve a problem and meet a demand.

Overall, the fact is that if you can become a great problem-solver, you can be successful in any industry. I enjoy thinking of opportunity recognition (OR) like being a chef. A professional chef typically doesn't work to create new base ingredients (new fruits, vegetables, or spices), but rather finds new ways of combining existing ones into delicious dishes. That's what brings people into their restaurants and gets them hired to cater for private events. It's about being an actionable dot-connector and serving up something great!

Also, please keep in mind, the more ingredients and ways of preparing them you know about, the more possible dishes you can make. It comes back again to building that knowledge base (studying both the industry you're in as well as the ones you're not), strengthening your mindset for creative combinations, and sustaining the will to experiment and see your ideas through.

---

18   Roe, David. "What Gig Workers Bring to Forward-Looking Companies." CMSWire.com. April 18, 2019.

19   Fowler, Geoffrey A. "There's an Uber for Everything Now." The Wall Street Journal. May 05, 2015.

3. Only work on something if you'd still do it for little to no money. Money is a by-product of mission-driven endeavors.

The financial rewards and accolades these Gene-trepreneurs receive is not sought out. As stated, it's a by-product.

Financial success is in no way guaranteed in startups as evidenced by the slew of unsuccessful ones. In fact, 75 percent of venture-backed startups ultimately fail.[20] The only thing that is guaranteed is the blood, sweat, and tears you will put into building something that you and hopefully many others find meaningful. If you ask most successful people in the world, regardless of the space they're in, they will tell you it's not about chasing money; that's a fool's errand. It's more so about chasing purpose and sharing that purpose with those around you (but that's getting a bit ahead into the next lesson).

Here is a quote from Tom Bilyeu, an entrepreneur who founded the second-fastest-growing company (Quest Nutrition) in the US on Inc. Magazine's 2014 list.[21] He says in one of his articles that "...the game I thought I should play was getting rich ... Despite how powerful money is, though, it can't change the way you feel about yourself ... If you're not proud of who you are, money won't change that. If you don't believe in yourself, money will fail you there, too."[22]

This is why to give yourself the best chance of becoming a successful Gene-trepreneur, you should choose to work on endeavors that will carry you through both the happy highs and energy-sapping lows. These endeavors should also embody some of the effective altruism philosophy we talked about in chapter 3—the creation of the greatest possible impact in others' lives and the world at large with a set amount of skills and resources at your disposal.

This way, when you have the money, you'll be able to feel good about yourself beyond the short term because the work you're doing is making a visible difference in a cause you care about. And when you're gone someday, the best way to be remembered is not by the amount of money you made but by the impact you made in others'

20   Henry, Patrick. "Why Some Startups Succeed (and Why Most Fail)." Entrepreneur. February 18, 2017.

21   "Thomas Bilyeu." Wikipedia. March 25, 2019.

22   Bilyeu, Tom. "I Stopped Chasing Money-Here's What Happened." SUCCESS. August 1, 2017.

lives. Right? You'll find more success by adding value to others' lives than by chasing financial gains any day. This is the proven winning method.[23]

I like to relate this notion of chasing something (like money) for the wrong reasons to a scene in *Harry Potter and the Sorcerer's Stone* (or *Philosopher's Stone*, depending on what country you're in). Professor Quirrell desperately desired to give the sorcerer's stone to Voldemort, who could use it to achieve immortality. However, he was unable to retrieve it from the Mirror of Erised. Harry did not wish for the stone to use it, yet it was given to him as his mission-driven purpose was to keep the stone out of Quirrell's and thereby Voldemort's hands.[24]

It's also very similar to Red Skull's plot in the Marvel cinematic universe wherein Red Skull so desperately sought to obtain and abuse the power of the space stone, which was inside the tesseract. Unlike Quirrell though, Red Skull got it. And when he was holding it at the end of *Captain America: The First Avenger*, it teleported him to Vormir where he became guardian to the soul stone—a treasure he was forced to guide others to but could never claim for himself.[25] Danaerys's storyline and character transformation in *Game of Thrones* is another great example.[26] I'll stop there.

To sum up this whole sentiment, as Jeff Hoffman, renowned business leader, motivational speaker, and serial entrepreneur (notably founding Priceline) says: "Don't chase money. Chase excellence."[27] If you do, the money will follow because chances are if it's important to you, it's important to other people as well... and that leads us into the next lesson.

---

23 Carmody, Bill. "How Can I Help? Why 'Adding Value First' Is the Winning Formula for Growth." Inc.com. October 14, 2014.

24 *Harry Potter and the Sorcerer's Stone*. Directed by Chris Columbus. Performed by Daniel Radcliffe, Emma Watson, Rupert Grint. Harry Potter and the Sorcerer's Stone. November 14, 2001.

25 *Captain America: The First Avenger*. Directed by Joe Johnston. Performed by Chris Evans, Hugo Weaving, Hayley Atwell. Captain America: The First Avenger. July 19, 2011.

26 *Game of Thrones*. Directed by David Benioff, D. B. Weiss, and George R. R. Martin. Performed by Emilia Clarke, Kit Harrington, Lena Headey, Peter Dinklage. Game of Thrones. May 19, 2019.

27 By Jeff Hoffman. Next Gen Summit, New York City, June 10, 2018.

4. Operate with 100 percent transparency. People support causes (and people) they care about.

While chasing purpose is important, the true power lies in opening up and sharing that purpose with others. Following up with another quote from Tom Bilyeu: "There doesn't need to be a conflict between who you are at your most honest and vulnerable and building a big business. We're living in a time when the kingmaker traits are authenticity and transparency."[28] This works on both personal and commercial levels.

On a personal level, you are building the brand for your mission-driven endeavor to get people behind it. But the smaller the brand, the more its image is reflected in its founders, which is why building your personal brand as a Gene-trepreneur is a critical component too. So how do you do this? You have to be open. Lay it all to bare. Not only tell people but show them why you are working on your undertaking. What is driving you? Illustrate vivid imagery of your story and the stories of those you are trying to help in others' minds because connecting emotionally is incredibly efficient and powerful. To humans, pathos (the appeal to emotion) beats out logos (the appeal to logic) almost every time in storytelling—whether that's in a movie, commercial, or during public speaking.

There's a quote from author Neil Gaiman, famous crafter of many popular stories (*Neverwhere, Stardust, Good Omens, Coraline, American Gods*, a couple of episodes of *Doctor Who,* and so much more), about the importance of being transparent with others in regard to yourself: "The moment you feel, just possibly, you are walking down the street naked, exposing too much of your heart and your mind, and what exists on the inside, showing too much of yourself... That is the moment, you might be starting to get it right." [29]

On the other hand, with transparency on the commercial level, especially in regard to synthetic biology and sustainability, it is more about sharing information openly with others, having conversations about it, and listening to the responses to help shape the field you're in and your company within it.

---

28 Bilyeu, Tom. "I Stopped Chasing Money-Here's What Happened." SUCCESS. August 1, 2017.

29 Gaiman, Neil. "Neil Gaiman: Keynote Address 2012." University of the Arts. May 17, 2012.

For example, startups in genetic engineering, biofabrication, and cellular agriculture are having many conversations with regulatory bodies, with each other, and with the public about safety, ethics, and the direction of their technologies and businesses going forward. They are cultivating trust within their own company as well as outside of it because when something like gene drives to get rid of invasive species (chapter 8—Gene Drives and New Zealand Kiwis) has the potential to affect many others on a global scale, the risks and rewards need to be put out in the open. Everyone should have their voice heard. And those conversations should help dictate how and when such tech will be used. Any mistakes made by one company can be detrimental to all the rest, which is why education and communication in decision-making is so vital, especially in the realm of biotech.

Furthermore, brands and their subsequent failures or successes increasingly come from consumers deciding what they stand for and whether or not they support that cause too.[30] The bigger a company gets, the more the brand is shaped by and belongs to its consumers, which can be a great thing. They'll become your best marketers and biggest supporters when they believe in the same world you're trying to create.

Overall for this lesson, just remember that being open with yourself and your endeavor is paramount, especially as a Gene-trepreneur. Good will come from doing so because transparency builds trust, and trust is key in biotechnology. In building any business, transforming lives, whether human or other fellow animal, is what brings in support and marketshare.

5. Fast fish eat slow fish, so build the most agile, adaptable teams.

Klaus Schwab, founder and executive chairman of the World Economic Forum, stated that "...in the new world, it's not the big fish that eats the small fish. It's the fast fish that eats the slow fish."[31] This is reinforced by what Ryan Bethencourt (co-founder of IndieBio and Wild Earth) stated to me in our interview: "Speed is safety." Today, the

---

30   Hesse, Jason. "Consumers Are Defining Brands." Raconteur. 2012.

31   Casadiego, Dulce. "BE AGILE! In Today's Economy, the Fast Fish Eats the Slow Fish!" LinkedIn. September 11, 2017.

most successful companies are the ones that can adapt the quickest to compete most effectively in the marketplace.

For startups, being the fast fish does two things:

1. increases their odds of survival (They must avoid being squashed like bugs by the big guys of the industry.)
2. gives them a greater chance at eventually ousting some of those incumbent players

According to an analysis of S&P 500 companies (which measures stocks of five hundred large-cap companies that influence America's market),[32] big corporations today can only expect their S&P 500 reign to last for twelve years by 2027. This is down from a twenty-four-year average length in 2016 and a thirty-three-year average in 1964.[33] For currently growing startups to overtake incumbent companies on the list, these smaller operations (especially in synbio and sustainability due to costly barriers to entry) often need investment and partnerships to see beneficial change happen as quickly as possible. This gives rise to a symbiotic relationship between resource-hungry startups and forward-thinking corporations looking to extend their stay at the top of the market.

Many startups receive investment from, partner with, or get acquired by big corporations because betting on these small startup teams can lead to an established company's biggest sources of innovation in new product and brand development. It's large companies' strategy for corporate longevity—their version of rich people buying young people's blood because they think it might help them live longer (which startups are really cashing in on by the way).[34] The food and beverage industries are capitalizing on this fountain of youth big time—the investment, partnerships, and acquirements part, not the blood-selling.

32 Amadeo, Kimberly. "What the S&P 500 Tells You About America's Health." The Balance. December 21, 2018.

33 Anthony, Scott D., S. Partrick Viguerie, Evan I. Schwartz, and John Van Landeghem. "Corporate Longevity Forecast: Creative Destruction Is Accelerating." Innosight. 2018.

34 Robbins, Rebecca. "Young-Blood Transfusions Are on the Menu at Society Gala." Scientific American. March 2, 2018.

Examples of avid corporate partners are PepsiCo, Mondelez, General Mills, Nestle, Mars, Whole Foods, Chobani, and more, some of which even have their own accelerator and incubator programs.[35] The startups benefit from partnering with big companies by gaining investment, expert mentorship, access to manufacturing and distribution channels, credibility of a big-name brand behind them, and so on. It can also lead to profitable exits for the startups via eventual acquisition.

∞

Even though startups are huge sources of innovation for larger companies, it's no secret that sometimes startup acquisitions happen more to absorb the startup team themselves and not as much for the startup's manufacturing infrastructure, brand identity, or intellectual property (IP). Why do you think this is? Skilled workers who collaborate efficiently as a team are very valuable to investors and companies because they cut down on headhunting resources spent, as well as the fact that it takes time for teams to get in the groove (if they ever do). To acquire a team that's already killer is something corporations are willing to pay a premium for.

Why do you think the sharks on *Shark Tank* will sometimes invest in startups with shaky numbers or rather, choose not to invest in other companies with great numbers? It's because the true investment and greatest foreteller of success is the team and entrepreneurs leading the endeavors. Are they highly adaptable fast fish that you can bet your money on?

So how do startups, and *you*, build one of these strong, cohesive, and sought-after teams?

I've found through both research and personal experience that it comes from:

1. sharing a common mission
2. having diverse and complementary skillsets when it comes to the team's individual members

---

35   Cabane, Olivia Fox. "The Landscapes." The Alternative Protein Show.

Just as in nature, a monoculture for an ecosystem is absolute death while high biodiversity is a winner. The best teams are made up of people in different specialties with aligning missions—people who bring their own special tool to the table and figure out how to combine it with someone else's to find a better way to fix a problem. It's the recipe for success and agile swimming.

Because it's truly a case of "adapt or die" in the business world today, these diverse teams and the startups they build are big companies' way of stocking their large corporate ponds with fast fish.

Management expert Gary Hamel stated that "...you can't build an adaptable organization without adaptable people, and individuals change only when they have to, or when they want to."[36] So in summary for this lesson, be an adept, fast fish on a fast-fish team in a fast-fish company because then, you've got a good shot at owning a piece of the ocean.

6. Think BIGGER. Don't limit yourself to what others think is possible.
If you don't consider yourself proficient at thinking big just yet, know that it goes hand in hand with building up your knowledge base, opportunity recognition, and taking action. You will become better at it if you read about, listen to, and surround yourself with others who think big too. You will absorb some inspiration passively, like water entering a cell through osmosis, but other things simply need active transport. They require energy.

Thinking big and coming up with an ambitious goal can be absolutely energy-draining. It's like looking up at a mountain and anticipating the climb to come. Many people are intimidated and choose to back down. Some aren't willing to put forth the energy at all. An example is that many people want to write a book (80 percent of Americans feel they have a story in them to tell)[37], start a podcast, or create a YouTube channel, but what percentage of these do you think actually get completed? The same notion goes for industry-disrupting

---

36   Kerpen, Dave. "11 Powerful Quotes to Inspire Your Team to Embrace Change." Inc.com. February 26, 2014.

37   Dietrich, William. "The Writer's Odds of Success." HuffPost. May 04, 2013.

synbio and sustainability startups as well, or really any big dream you have.

Let's return to Jeff Hoffman from the end of lesson 3. When I heard him speak at an entrepreneurship conference called Next Gen Summit, he presented a hack to staring up at the mountain.[38] He said to imagine you're already at the top and work out all the small steps you would have had to take in order to get there. Work from the top down. Broken into smaller pieces, the roadmap toward your vision becomes a lot clearer and more manageable. Then, with your course charted step by step, you can begin the climb.

It's also important to remember that in a way, you are your biggest and foremost project since you will continually be building yourself into the person capable of taking those next steps. As long as you don't limit yourself and don't let others limit you, your goals can be as big as you want them to be. Plus, if you're going to spend your life climbing a mountain, you might as well make it one worth the trip and become a terrific climber along the way. As you find yourself ascending and closer to reaching the top, you may just discover that you're making an impact that is greater than you had ever previously imagined.

One last thing: I also heard Jeff Hoffman say, "It's easier to act your way into thinking than think your way into acting."[39] I've found this to be very true in my own life as well. Act like the person you want to become.

The bottom line is to think BIG, plan your goals backward, and start your climb. Don't be afraid to adapt and change course when necessary either. If you shoot for the stars and hit the moon, that's not so bad is it? Along the way, you will act your way into thinking big, and that will fundamentally change you. The key to start is having the vision and beginning your trek.

People are constantly backing down from their mountains. Will you?

---

38   By Jeff Hoffman. Next Gen Summit, New York City, June 10, 2018.

39   Ibid.

7. Give yourself permission. Sometimes nobody else will, but you absolutely must.

I will keep this last lesson short and sweet, and it's another fantastic message from Ryan Bethencourt. Nobody told him he was allowed to be the co-founder of the world's leading life sciences accelerator, IndieBio. And nobody gave him permission to co-found Wild Earth, a company disrupting the entire pet food industry. He gave himself the permission to do those things. He gave himself permission to climb his own mountains.

Likewise, nobody gave Bill Gates the go-ahead to invent Microsoft, nor did anyone tell Stephen King he was allowed to write horror and supernatural fiction stories that would sell over 350 million copies worldwide.[40] The same can be said of Shark Tank's Barbara Corcoran building her real estate empire. The list goes on and on. Permission comes from your sense of self, your ambition, and your willingness to become the person you think the world needs at the moment.

It's certainly important to surround yourself with supportive friends, family, and fellow change-drivers because they can help and cheer you on. After all, absolutely nothing worthwhile in entrepreneurship, or life, is done completely alone. The best and most impactful things are built together. But the one person's permission you always need to start with is your own.

Give yourself the green light to chase your highest purpose, pursue your most impactful project, and ascend your highest peak.

∞

And so you have all the valuable lessons from this chapter in one nice list:

1. Ideas alone don't mean anything. Execution on those ideas means everything.
2. Opportunity recognition isn't about creating something entirely new. It's about bringing together things that have never been combined in that way before.

---

40   "Stephen King." Wikipedia. May 15, 2019.

3. Only work on something if you'd still do it for little to no money. Money is a by-product of mission-driven endeavors.
4. Operate with 100 percent transparency. People support causes (and people) they care about.
5. Fast fish eat slow fish, so build the most agile, adaptable teams.
6. Think BIGGER. Don't limit yourself to what others think is possible.
7. And give yourself permission. Sometimes nobody else will, but you absolutely must.

∞

Building Your Next Steps

If you take the above lessons to heart, they are the most valuable takeaways I can ever hope to share with you as you move forward on your journey toward becoming a Gene-trepreneur in whatever unique way that looks like for you. Remember though, "It's easier to act your way into thinking than think your way into acting."[41] These lessons will only serve you well if you apply them. Luckily, there are countless ways to do so.

In synthetic biology and sustainability, you can invest, build software, write an article or book, create a podcast or videos, make artwork, work in a lab doing research, share content on social media, discuss with your friends and family, start a club, do a school project, and so much more. There are heaps of opportunities to be actionable in these exciting spaces. And while building out your root system to begin with is absolutely vital, your end goal is to grow the tree.

Years ago, I heard a lecture from an industrial engineer who was recruited into venture capital to help make decisions on technical investments. His whole transformative life story was enthralling to listen to, but the one main takeaway I retained from his talk was not to sit around and cut bait when you can put a line in the water.[42]

---

41 By Jeff Hoffman. Next Gen Summit, New York City, June 10, 2018.

42 The Pennsylvania State University College of Engineering, University Park, Pennsylvania, 2018.

You'll learn a lot more about how to catch fish by fishing rather than always preparing to catch fish.

Aside from becoming more knowledgeable and using your knowledge to connect dots and take action, you mustn't forget that building your community is also critically important. It's like enlarging the body of water you fish in. Just make sure you're putting fish into the water before you're taking any out. Paying it forward by adding value to others' lives and endeavors will get you far.

Of note here is that it's also better to build your network than buy one. I learned this from Eric Koester, the entrepreneurship professor and Next Gen speaker who originally inspired me to write this book. For example, my undergraduate alma mater and many other universities often use the size of their alumni networks as big selling points (currently living: about seven hundred thousand alums of Penn State University).[43] That's great! But what percentage of people do you think actually take advantage of these networks? Not many. Networks don't passively work to your benefit. You must use them to gain anything consequential out of them. Build your network based off of meaningful, personal interactions and shared purpose turns that network into a community. A community is infinitely more valuable than a network full of almost seven hundred thousand people you've never interacted with. It's a stronger foundation that runs deeper.

As a Gene-trepreneur specifically, you may be pursuing a project that is all about saving animals, but without a community of people supporting you and your mission, you won't get very far at all no matter how valiant your endeavor is. Although somewhat of a popular quote (especially in tech and politics), the first time I saw these words they were written on a wall in the Irish startup accelerator I worked at in Dublin: "If you want to go fast, go alone. If you want to go far, go together."[44] So spend time building a community. It's an investment that pays off more than you may realize and will continue to do so for a lifetime.

---

43 Penn State Alumni Association.

44 Goldberg, Joel. "It Takes A Village To Determine The Origins Of An African Proverb." NPR. July 30, 2016.

∞

Moving on from the importance of people to expectations, sometimes the results of being a Gene-trepreneur won't be as quickly seen as in other lines of work. If you're a doctor, you can often see the direct impact you have on your patients. If you're a trial lawyer, you can often see the immediate results of your representation in the court's verdict. For a Gene-trepreneur, those outcomes will be more distant:

It will be helping save thousands of animals who weren't demanded on the meat market and thus were never brought into lives not worth living.

It will be saving some sea turtles and birds who would have choked on plastics had you decided not to recycle them or offer an alternative.

It will be sparing trees that, when combined with those saved by others, are equivalent to a whole biodiverse forest that didn't need to be cut down to keep up with supply.

It will be bringing attention to sustainability issues that matter most and inspiring others to take action, thereby multiplying your effects.

And on the human level, it will be improving the lives of people who would have otherwise had chronic diseases and illness. Perhaps they will avoid extra hospitable stays, save money and years of their life. Maybe now they'll live long enough to see a grandchild graduate from college or get married, to travel to the places they've always dreamed of visiting but haven't gotten to experience yet, simply living a longer and healthier life to enjoy more of the things they love.

You won't know these people or the animals you've affected, but they'll be out there and better off because of the work you've done. So as a Gene-trepreneur, you can achieve a 10x impact, but you won't always see the results immediately. They'll happen over the long term because that's the game we wish to play—the one in the big picture. Collectively, that's where the biggest impact lies. And as Tony Stark said: "That's the endgame."[45]

---

45 Avengers: Age of Ultron. Directed by Josh Whedon. Performed by Robert Downey Jr., Chris Evans, Scarlett Johanssen. Avengers: Age of Ultron. May 1, 2015.

Please also be mindful that pursuing entrepreneurship and becoming a Gene-trepreneur is a means to an end goal, not a glorified end goal in and of itself. It's a tool to be wielded to achieve vast and meaningful outcomes.

I don't want to romanticize this dream for you because it's going to take a lot of effort. But if you can accomplish it, or even come close, perhaps you will be able to look back on your life one day and be proud of the work you've done, of the relationships you've made, and of the lives you've improved.

Of course, everything won't happen overnight because for all of us, including the most successful Gene-trepreneurs we've highlighted in this book, it's a long journey toward and up the mountain. But the journey continues as long as you maintain your will to keep taking those next few steps further. If and when you get to your peak, or even a significant milestone along the way, the best any of us can hope for is that we'll be able to feel a sense of pride and know the journey has been worth it.

On a parting note for this section, I once saw a young media entrepreneur named Jahleel Coleman speak at a conference, and I loved Coleman's quote: "If you're a little different and a little smart, everything can be yours."[46] For Gene-trepreneurs, having everything be yours is not in regard to fame or fortune. Instead, it means that you've been able to give so much back and to make the impact you initially set out to make. And that's pretty inspiring, isn't it?

Your Starfish Problem, Becoming a Gene-trepreneur, and a New Hope

For us to conclude and move from knowledge to action, I now wish to share with you a parable that has always lived in the back of my mind since first hearing it. Perhaps it will live in yours too when you think about your power to influence beneficial change in the world at large:

One day, an old man was walking along a beach that was littered with thousands of starfish that had been washed ashore by the high

---

46   By Jahleel Coleman. Next Gen Summit, New York City, June 9, 2018.

tide. As he walked, he came upon a young child who was eagerly throwing the starfish back into the ocean, one by one.

Puzzled, the man looked at the child and asked what he was doing. Without looking up from the task, the child simply replied, "I'm saving these starfish."

The old man chuckled aloud, "Kid, there are thousands of starfish and only one of you. What difference can you make?"

The child picked up a starfish, gently tossed it into the water, and turning to the man, said, "It made a difference to that one!"[47]

Synthetic biology means to me the possibility of throwing every starfish back into the ocean all at once. It offers that level of hope and that level of impact. What you can do now is find your own starfish problem. You can elevate it with your growing skillsets and the power of biotechnology. You can find others who are passionate about it too and together work toward building a solution through STEM and the entrepreneurial mindset.

There has never been a time in human history with as much hope as there is today to change the world for the better. I ask you now to seek out your starfish problem, become a Gene-trepreneur in your own right, and add to the hope.

~~End~~

Begin

47   "The Parable." Starfish Project.

ABOUT THE AUTHOR

Brett Cotten is a writer in the realm of popular science and a Gene-trepreneur on a mission to culture sustainability through biotech and the entrepreneurial mindset.

Having studied biochemistry and technology-based entrepreneurship at The Pennsylvania State University and bioscience enterprise at the University of Cambridge in the United Kingdom, Brett cares deeply about bridging the gap between science, business, and actionable storytelling to cultivate positive impacts for animals (humans included) and the environment. He has worked on endeavors in telemedicine, apparel sustainability, and food innovation. Brett has also experienced the Dublin, Ireland startup scene in one of Europe's top accelerators, NDRC, right across from the Guinness Storehouse (very entertaining for people-watching, by the way).

Gene-trepreneur is Brett's first book. He hopes it will serve as a catalyst not only to educate but also to motivate others to turn their pain points into purposes. We need all hands on deck to change the world for the better, and everyone can be a part of that change.

Brett loves *MythBusters*, cactuses, and pizza-making—sometimes simultaneously. If you'd like to get in touch about the book or any of the former, please find him on LinkedIn or contact him via email: brett.a.cotten@gmail.com.

Selected References

Preface

Weller, Chris. "Bill Gates Reveals What He'd Study If He Were a College Freshman Today." Business Insider. May 15, 2017. https://www.businessinsider.com/bill-gates-what-college-freshman-should-study-2017-5.

"Fifty Years Hence (Popular Mechanics, 1932)." New Harvest. January 15, 2016. https://www.new-harvest.org/fifty_years_hence.

Introduction

4ocean. "4ocean Is Actively Cleaning Our Oceans and Coastlines." 4ocean, 4ocean.com/.

Avengers: Age of Ultron. Directed by Josh Whedon. Performed by Robert Downey Jr., Chris Evans, Scarlett Johanssen. Marvel Studios. May 1, 2015.

Biello, David. "Did the Anthropocene Begin in 1950 or 50,000 Years Ago?" Scientific American, April 2, 2015. www.scientificamerican.com/article/did-the-anthropocene-begin-in-1950-or-50-000-years-ago/.

Carrington, Damian. "The Anthropocene Epoch: Scientists Declare Dawn of Human-Influenced Age." The Guardian, Guardian News and Media. August 29, 2016. www.theguardian.com/environment/2016/aug/29/declare-anthropocene-epoch-experts-urge-geological-congress-human-impact-earth.

Chiorando, Maria. "UK Government Announces Plans To Ban Single-Use Plastics." RSS, 26 Oct. 2018. www.plantbasednews.org/post/uk-government-ban-single-use-plastics.

Gaiman, Neil. "Neil Gaiman: Keynote Address 2012." University of the Arts. May 17, 2012. https://www.uarts.edu/neil-gaiman-keynote-address-2012.

Hyde, Embriette. "Building Synthetic Biology Companies at Scale: Practical Advice from Seasoned Investors and Entrepreneurs." SynBioBeta, September 19, 2018. synbiobeta.com/building-synthetic-biology-companies-at-scale/.

Joyce, Christopher. "Replacing Plastic: Can Bacteria Help Us Break The Habit?" NPR. NPR, June 17, 2019. https://www.npr.org/2019/06/17/728599455/replacing-plastic-can-bacteria-help-us-break-the-habit.

Lewis, Simon L, and Maslin, Mark A. "A Transparent Framework for Defining the Anthropocene Epoch." The Anthropocene Review, vol. 2, no. 2, 2015, pp. 128–146., doi:10.1177/2053019615588792.

Liu, Marian. "Great Pacific Garbage Patch Now Three Times the Size of France." CNN, Cable News Network, March 23, 2018. www.cnn.com/2018/03/23/world/plastic-great-pacific-garbage-patch-intl/index.html.

Ocean Cleanup. "The World's First Ocean Cleanup System Launched from San Francisco." The Ocean Cleanup, September 8, 2018. www.theoceancleanup.com/press/the-worlds-first-ocean-cleanup-system-launched-from-san-francisco/.

Quilty-Harper, Conrad. "The World's Fattest Countries: How Do You Compare?" The Telegraph, June 2012. www.telegraph.co.uk/news/earth/earthnews/9345086/The-worlds-fattest-countries-how-do-you-compare.html.

Steffen, Will, et al. "The Anthropocene:" Environment and Society. December, 2007, pp. 12–31., doi:10.2307/j.ctt1ht4vw6.7.

Stromberg, Joseph. "What Is the Anthropocene and Are We in It?" Smithsonian.com, Smithsonian Institution. January 1, 2013. www.smithsonianmag.com/science-nature/what-is-the-anthropocene-and-are-we-in-it-164801414/.

Treat, Jason, et al. "We Depend On Plastic. Now, We're Drowning in It." We Depend on Plastic. Now We're Drowning in It., May 16, 2018. www.nationalgeographic.com/magazine/2018/06/plastic-planet-waste-pollution-trash-crisis/.

Webb, Jonathan. "Famous Peppered Moth's Dark Secret Revealed." BBC News, BBC. June, 2016. www.bbc.com/news/science-environment-36424768.

"Applications." Mango Materials. mangomaterials.com/applications/.

"Finding Nemo." Directed by Andrew Stanton. Performed by Ellen Degeneres and Alexander Gould. Pixar Animation Studios. May 30, 2003.

"The NCES Fast Facts Tool Provides Quick Answers to Many Education Questions (National Center for Education Statistics)." National Center for Education Statistics (NCES) Home Page, a Part of the U.S. Department of Education. nces.ed.gov/fastfacts/display.asp?id=372 (http://nces.ed.gov/fastfacts/display.asp?id=372).

"Tidying Up with Marie Kondo." Netflix, 2019.

Chapter 1

Back to the Future Part II. Directed by Robert Zemeckis. Performed by Michael J. Fox and Christopher Lloyd. Universal Pictures. November 22, 1989.

Binging with Babish. YouTube. https://www.youtube.com/channel/UCJHA_jMf-CvEnv-3kRjTCQXw.

Bowie, David. David Bowie: Space Oddity. 1969.

Brown, Mary Jane. "Should You Avoid Fish Because of Mercury?" Healthline. September 14, 2016. www.healthline.com/nutrition/mercury-content-of-fish.

"Deep Sea Fish Farming in Geodesic Domes: Upgrade." YouTube, Motherboard, December 18, 2014. www.youtube.com/watch?v=WpPZUGIJ2Mo.

EarthSky. "The Aquapod: A Free-Floating Fish Farm." Fast Company, Fast Company, July 24, 2012. www.fastcompany.com/1680239/the-aquapod-a-free-floating-fish-farm.

"Fifty Years Hence (Popular Mechanics, 1932)." New Harvest. January 15, 2016. https://www.new-harvest.org/fifty_years_hence.

Friedrich, Bruce. "Why Clean Meat Is Kosher." The Good Food Institute. June 22, 2017. www.gfi.org/why-clean-meat-is-kosher.

Greenberg, Paul. "The Four Fish We're Overeating — and What to Eat Instead | Paul Greenberg." YouTube, YouTube, January 13, 2016. www.youtube.com/watch?time_continue=172&v=_jaWs87t5UM.

Harbage, Claire. "In Korean DMZ, Wildlife Thrives. Some Conservationists Worry Peace Could Disrupt It." NPR. NPR, April 20, 2019. https://www.npr.org/2019/04/20/710054899/in-korean-dmz-wildlife-thrives-some-conservationists-worry-peace-could-disrupt-i.

Keledjian, Amanda, Gib Brogan, Beth Lowell, Jon Warrenchuk, et al. "Wasted Catch: Unsolved Problem in US Fisheries." Oceana, March 2014. https://oceana.org/sites/default/files/reports/Bycatch_Report_FINAL.pdf.

Kentish, Benjamin. "Fish and Chips Are Being Replaced by Something Much More Disgusting." The Independent, Independent Digital News and Media, December 12, 2016. www.independent.co.uk/news/uk/home-news/fish-and-chips-squid-cod-haddock-global-warming-warmer-seawater-chip-shops-a7469836.html.

Komar, Cedric, et al. "Understanding Fish Vaccination." The Fish Site, March, 21 2019. thefishsite.com/articles/understanding-fish-vaccination.

"MicroSynbiotiX." Microsynbiotix. www.microsynbiotix.com/.

Morgan, Rick. "Bill Gates and Richard Branson Are Betting Lab-Grown Meat May Be the Food of the Future." CNBC. March 23, 2018. www.cnbc.com/2018/03/23/bill-gates-and-richard-branson-bet-on-lab-grown-meat-startup.html.

NOAA. "Bluefin Tuna Angling Category Daily Retention Limit Adjustment." NOAA Fisheries, April 23, 2018. www.fisheries.noaa.gov/bulletin/bluefin-tuna-angling-category-daily-retention-limit-adjustment.

Parker, Laura. "Ocean Life Eats Tons of Plastic-Here's Why That Matters." National Geographic. August 18, 2017. news.nationalgeographic.com/2017/08/ocean-life-eats-plastic-larvaceans-anchovy-environment/.

Pennsylvania, University of. "Delivering Medicine Through Lettuce, World Altering Medical Advancements." YouTube, YouTube, April 10, 2014. www.youtube.com/watch?v=6z7qwwtHQTY.

"The Future Of 'Wild Fish,' The Last Wild Food." NPR, NPR, July 1, 2011. www.npr.org/templates/transcript/transcript.php?storyId=137524798.

Thompson, Andrea. "From Fish to Humans, A Microplastic Invasion May Be Taking a Toll." Scientific American. September 4, 2018. www.scientificamerican.com/article/from-fish-to-humans-a-microplastic-invasion-may-be-taking-a-toll/.

Uusi-Heikkila, Silva, et al. "The Evolutionary Legacy of Size-Selective Harvesting Extends from Genes to Populations." Evolutionary Applications, John Wiley & Sons, Ltd (10.1111), 27 May 2015. onlinelibrary.wiley.com/doi/full/10.1111/eva.12268.

Wells, Sarah. "Project Loon and Project Wing Graduate from X." TechCrunch, TechCrunch, July 12, 2018. techcrunch.com/2018/07/12/project-loon-and-project-wing-graduate-from-google-x/.

You, Jia. "Mercury Levels in Surface Ocean Have Tripled." Science. December 10, 2017. www.sciencemag.org/news/2014/08/mercury-levels-surface-ocean-have-tripled.

"Ghost Nets, among the Greatest Killers in Our Oceans..." Mission Blue, May 23, 2013. mission-blue.org/2013/05/ghost-nets-among-the-greatest-killers-in-our-oceans/.

Chapter 2

"Climate One." Climate One - The New Surf and Turf, 2018. www.facebook.com/climateone/videos/10151147444469987/.

"Explore Our Library of up-to-Date Resources." The Good Food Institute, January 6, 2016. www.gfi.org/essentials.

Fletcher, Rob. "The (Finless) Future of Fish Production." The Fish Site, March 21, 2019. thefishsite.com/articles/the-finless-future-of-fish-production.

Kasireddy, Preethi. "What I Wish I Knew about Fundraising as a First-Time Founder." Medium, Medium, May 31, 2018. medium.com/@preethikasireddy/what-i-wish-i-knew-about-fundraising-as-a-first-time-founder-243644968567.

Khan, Ahmed. "Finless Foods Raises $3.5 Million in Seed Funding To Grow Cultured Fish." Medium, CellAgri, June 21, 2018. medium.com/cellagri/finless-foods-raises-3-5-million-in-seed-funding-to-grow-cultured-fish-9c27c27d1585.

Kirby, David. "One More Reason the World Should Stop Eating Whale Meat: It's Filled With Pesticides." TakePart, Mar 13, 2015. www.takepart.com/article/2015/03/13/one-more-reason-world-should-stop-eating-whale-meat-it-filled-pesticides.

Kopelyan, Alex. "FAQ." IndieBio. IndieBio, January 24, 2017. https://indiebio.co/faq/.

Portfolio | DFJ Venture Capital. dfj.com/portfolio/index.php.

Press, Associated. "Bluefin Goes for $3 Million at 1st 2019 Sale at Tokyo Market." NBCNews.com, NBCUniversal News Group, 5 Jan. 2019. www.nbcnews.com/news/world/bluefin-goes-3-million-1st-2019-sale-tokyo-market-n955101.

Selden, Michael. "Making Sustainable, Lab-Grown Fish Meat a Reality | Finless Foods | HT Summit 2017." YouTube, Hello Tomorrow, March 8, 2018. www.youtube.com/watch?v=1_22OYyE7D4.

Shapiro, Paul. "Making Mastodon Gummies, Geltor Is Recreating a Truly Paleo Diet." TechCrunch, TechCrunch, March 12, 2018. techcrunch.com/2018/03/12/making-mastodon-gummies-geltor-is-recreating-a-truly-paleo-diet/.

Specht, Liz, et al. "An Ocean of Opportunity Action Paper." The Good Food Institute, 2018. www.gfi.org/seafood.

"The Office: Gossip." The Office, September 17, 2009.

Willy Wonka & the Chocolate Factory, Directed by Mel Stuart. Performed by Gene Wilder. 1971.

Chapter 3

Andrew Grantham, and Talking Animals. "Ultimate Dog Tease." YouTube. YouTube, May 1, 2011. https://www.youtube.com/watch?v=nGeKSiCQkPw.

Bain, Jennifer, and Amanda Woods. "Rogue Goat May Have Helped Dozens of Farm Animals Escape." New York Post, New York Post, August 10, 2018. nypost.com/2018/08/09/rogue-goat-may-have-helped-dozens-of-farm-animals-escape/.

Berger, Sarah. "Mark Cuban Just Invested $550,000 in a Vegan Dog Treats Company on 'Shark Tank'." CNBC. CNBC, March 18, 2019. https://www.cnbc.com/2019/03/18/billionaire-shark-tank-just-mark-cuban-just-invested-half-milion-dollars-in-a-vegan-dog-treats-startup.html.

Bethencourt, Ryan. "5 Lessons I Learned from Going on ABC's Shark Tank." Wild Earth. Wild Earth, March 22, 2019. https://wildearth.com/blogs/news/5-lessons-i-learned-from-going-on-abcs-shark-tank.

Brodwin, Erin. "'Cat Parents Think It's Cool': A Peter Thiel-backed Startup Pursuing Mouse Meat for Dogs Has Begun Selling Its First Products." Business Insider. October 1, 2018. https://www.businessinsider.com/vegan-pet-food-startup-peter-thiel-mouse-meat-now-selling-treats-2018-9.

"Burger King—Impossible Foods." Impossible Foods. https://impossiblefoods.com/burgerking/.

Canal, Emily. "This 'Shark Tank' Founder Valued His Company at $11 Million With No Sales. Here's Why Mark Cuban Invested $550,000." Inc.com. March 18, 2019. https://www.inc.com/emily-canal/shark-tank-season-10-episode-16-wild-earth-mark-cuban.html.

Carrington, Damian. "Earth Has Lost Half of Its Wildlife in the Past 40 Years, Says WWF." The Guardian, Guardian News and Media, September 30, 2014. www.theguardian.com/environment/2014/sep/29/earth-lost-50-wildlife-in-40-years-wwf.

CBS This Morning. "Natalie Portman on 'Eating Animals,' Rise of Factory Farming, and Harvey Weinstein." YouTube, YouTube, June 15, 2018. www.youtube.com/watch?v=Dm96uLZfDcg.

"Climate One." Climate One - The New Surf and Turf. 2018. www.facebook.com/climateone/videos/10151147444469987/.

Dvm, Nigel Caulkett. "Do Cattle Feel Pain the Same Way We Do?" Canadian Cattlemen, April 3, 2017. www.canadiancattlemen.ca/2017/04/03/do-cattle-feel-pain-the-same-way-we-do/.

Fox, Katrina. "Why Wild Earth Cofounder Ryan Bethencourt Is Applying The Science Of 'Vegan Biohacking' To Pet Food." Forbes. March 16, 2018. https://www.forbes.com/sites/katrinafox/2018/03/15/this-vegan-biohacker-is-set-to-launch-the-first-cultured-protein-foods-for-pets/#21d9332f5fe7.

"Francis Bacon." Wikipedia. Wikimedia Foundation, September 4, 2019. https://en.wikipedia.org/wiki/Francis_Bacon.

"Galileo Is Convicted of Heresy." History.com, A&E Television Networks, November 13, 2009. www.history.com/this-day-in-history/galileo-is-convicted-of-heresy.

"Game of Thrones: Mother's Mercy," June 14, 2015.

Gibbs, David, et al. "By the Numbers: The Value of Tropical Forests in the Climate Change Equation." By the Numbers: The Value of Tropical Forests in the Climate Change Equation | World Resources Institute, October 4, 2018. www.wri.org/blog/2018/10/numbers-value-tropical-forests-climate-change-equation.

Grefski, Lorie. "Is Your Pet's Food Tested on Animals?" One Green Planet. February 10, 2015. https://www.onegreenplanet.org/animalsandnature/is-your-pets-food-tested-on-animals/.

Grooten, M., and R.E.A. Almond. "Living Planet Report 2018." WWF. World Wildlife Fund, 2018. https://www.worldwildlife.org/pages/living-planet-report-2018.

"Intensive Animal Farming." Wikipedia. Wikimedia Foundation, September 4, 2019. https://en.wikipedia.org/wiki/Intensive_animal_farming.

Kubala, Jillian. "Essential Amino Acids: Definition, Benefits and Food Sources." Healthline, June 12, 2018. www.healthline.com/nutrition/essential-amino-acids.

"Life Cycle of a Market Pig." Pork Checkoff. www.pork.org/facts/pig-farming/life-cycle-of-a-market-pig/.

Loria, Joe. "Forbes: Millennials Driving Force Behind Global Vegan Movement." Mercy For Animals, March 27, 2018. mercyforanimals.org/forbes-millennials-driving-force-behind-global.

MacDonald, Fiona. "Goats Are as Smart And Loving as Dogs, According to Science." ScienceAlert, June 30, 2018. www.sciencealert.com/goats-are-just-as-smart-and-loving-as-dogs-say-scientists.

Webber, Jemima. "Can Dogs Be Vegan? 5 Meat-Free Foods to Try." LIVEKINDLY. Publisher Name LIVEKINDLY Publisher Logo, June 8, 2019. https://www.livekindly.co/vegan-dog-food-brand-keep-hound-healthy-happy/.

Martin, Glen. "Should Our Pets Be Vegans, Too?" Cal Alumni Association. July 11, 2018. https://alumni.berkeley.edu/california-magazine/just-in/2018-07-11/should-our-pets-be-vegans-too.

New Age Meats. "New Age Meats Pork Sausage Tasting Event." YouTube, YouTube, October 19, 2018. www.youtube.com/watch?v=2P2zOHJmQMY.

Peters, Adele. "This Lab-Grown Beef Will Be in Restaurants in 3 Years." Fast Company, Fast Company, July 27, 2018. www.fastcompany.com/90203024/this-lab-grown-beef-will-be-in-restaurants-in-3-years.

"Pork Facts." National Pork Producers Council. nppc.org/pork-facts/.

Portman, Natalie, producer. Quinn, Christopher, director. Eating Animals. Eating Animals, June 2018.

Purdy, Chase. "The Average American Will Eat the Equivalent of 800 Hamburgers in 2018." Quartz, Quartz, January 4, 2018. qz.com/1171669/the-average-american-will-eat-the-equivalent-of-800-hamburgers-in-2018/.

Shapiro, Paul. "Making Mastodon Gummies, Geltor Is Recreating a Truly Paleo Diet." TechCrunch, TechCrunch, March 12, 2018. techcrunch.com/2018/03/12/making-mastodon-gummies-geltor-is-recreating-a-truly-paleo-diet/.

Simon, Matt. "Inside the Strange Science of the Fake Meat That 'Bleeds'." Wired, Conde Nast, September 21, 2017. www.wired.com/story/the-impossible-burger/.

"Six Degrees of Kevin Bacon." Wikipedia. Wikimedia Foundation, August 30, 2019. https://en.wikipedia.org/wiki/Six_Degrees_of_Kevin_Bacon.

Solomon, Ari. "USA Today: Meat-Eaters Consume 7,000 Animals in a Lifetime." Mercy For Animals, March 13, 2015. mercyforanimals.org/usa-today-meat-eaters-consume-7000-animals.

Spears, Brian, and Alex Shirazi. "Brian Spears of New Age Meats - Clean Meat Founders Series - Live Recording." Cultured Meat Future Food , YouTube, August 5, 2018. www.youtube.com/watch?v=4yXeNJCuH8I.

Watson, Elaine. "Impossible Foods Replaces Wheat with Soy Protein Concentrate in Its Plant-Based Burger; Says Color Additive Petition Won't Delay Retail Launch." Foodnavigator, January, 2018. www.foodnavigator-usa.com/Article/2019/01/08/Impossible-Foods-replaces-wheat-with-soy-protein-concentrate-in-its-plant-based-Impossible-burger.

"Why Are Cats Called "Obligate Carnivores?"" CANIDAE®. https://www.canidae.com/blog/2017/10/why-are-cats-called-obligate-carnivores/.

Wright, Edgar, director. Scott Pilgrim vs. the World. Universal, 2010.

Yong, Ed. "Wait, Have We Really Wiped Out 60 Percent of Animals?" The Atlantic. Atlantic Media Company, November 1, 2018. https://www.theatlantic.com/science/archive/2018/10/have-we-really-killed-60-percent-animals-1970/574549/.

Chapter 4

Cabane, Olivia Fox. "The Landscapes." The Alternative Protein Show. www.newprotein.org/maps.

Cardello, Hank. "How the Milk Industry Went Sour, and What Every Business Can Learn From It." Forbes. January 04, 2013. https://www.forbes.com/sites/forbesleadershipforum/2013/01/04/how-the-milk-industry-went-sour-and-what-every-business-can-learn-from-it/#44e9fc0c7127.

Choi, Candice. "FDA May Force Soy and Almond 'milk' Companies to Change Labeling." USA Today. July 19, 2018. https://www.usatoday.com/story/money/2018/07/18/soy-milk-makers-may-need-find-alternative-description/795981002/.

"Count Your Chickens Before They Hatch." EggXYt. https://www.eggxyt.com/.

Ettinger, Jill. "Experts Predict Dairy Industry Could Disappear in 10 Years." LIVEKINDLY. April 07, 2019. https://www.livekindly.co/dairy-industry-disappear-decade/.

"Factory Farms." A Well-Fed World. https://awfw.org/factory-farms/.

Flora, Carlin. "IVF and Gender Selection: What You Need to Know." Parents. https://www.parents.com/getting-pregnant/gender/selection/ivf-and-gender-selection-what-you-need-to-know/.

Howard, Lisa. "How a Genetic Mutation From 1 Bull Caused the Loss of Half a Million Calves Worldwide." UC Davis. October 13, 2016. https://www.ucdavis.edu/news/how-genetic-mutation-1-bull-caused-loss-half-million-calves-worldwide/.

"IVF Process | IVF Information." Monash IVF. https://monashivf.com/fertility-treatments/fertility-treatments/the-ivf-process/.

Leone, Brad. "It's Alive with Brad." Bon Appétit Videos, n.d. https://video.bonappetit.com/series/it-s-alive-with-brad.

Levitt, Tom. "Dairy's 'dirty Secret': It's Still Cheaper to Kill Male Calves than to Rear Them." The Guardian. March 26, 2018. https://www.theguardian.com/environment/2018/mar/26/dairy-dirty-secret-its-still-cheaper-to-kill-male-calves-than-to-rear-them.

Meet the Parents. Directed by Joe Roach. Performed by Robert De Niro and Ben Stiller. October 6, 2000.

"Milk." Merriam-Webster. Merriam-Webster, n.d. https://www.merriam-webster.com/dictionary/milk?utm_campaign=sd&utm_medium=serp&utm_source=jsonld.

Murray-Ragg, Nadia. "'Vegan' Milk Brand Perfect Day Secures $24.7 Million to 'Disrupt the Dairy Industry'." LIVEKINDLY. February 28, 2018. https://www.livekindly.co/vegan-milk-brand-24-7-million-disrupt-dairy-industry/.

"Our Story." Perfect Day. https://www.perfectdayfoods.com/our-story/.

Perfect Day. Crunchbase. https://www.crunchbase.com/organization/perfectday#-section-overview

Pirates of the Caribbean: At World's End. Directed by Gore Verbinski. Performed by Johnny Depp, Keira Knightley, and Orlando Bloom. May 25, 2007.

Popper, Nathaniel. "You Call That Meat? Not So Fast, Cattle Ranchers Say." The New York Times. February 09, 2019. https://www.nytimes.com/2019/02/09/technology/meat-veggie-burgers-lab-produced.html.

Rhinehart, Justin. "How It Works: Sex Sorted Semen." AgWeb. January 21, 2016. https://www.agweb.com/article/how-it-works-sex-sorted-semen-naa-university-news-release/.

Sanders, Laura. "40 Years after the First IVF Baby, a Look Back at the Birth of a New Era." Science News, July 25, 2018. https://www.sciencenews.org/blog/growth-curve/40-years-ivf-baby-louise-brown.

Scipioni, Jade. "This $20 Ice Cream Is Made with Dairy Grown in Lab-and It Sold out Immediately." CNBC. CNBC, July 16, 2019. https://www.cnbc.com/2019/07/16/perfect-day-foods-made-ice-cream-from-real-dairy-grown-in-lab.html.

Sibilla, Nick. "FDA Crackdown On Calling Almond Milk 'Milk' Could Violate The First Amendment." Forbes. Forbes Magazine, February 1, 2019. https://www.forbes.

com/sites/nicksibilla/2019/01/31/fda-crackdown-on-calling-almond-milk-milk-could-violate-the-first-amendment/#6c98c6b77b70.

Stauffer, Krista. "Average Age of a Dairy Cow." The Farmer's Wifee. June 21, 2014. https://www.thefarmerswifee.com/average-age-of-a-dairy-cow/.

Chapter 5

"10 Reasons Why Monsanto Is Corrupt from Its Core." Seattle Organic Restaurants. http://www.seattleorganicrestaurants.com/vegan-whole-food/Monsanto-corruption-gmo.php.

Bayer. "Bayer and Ginkgo Bioworks Unveil Joint Venture, Joyn Bio, and Establish Operations in Boston and West Sacramento." PR Newswire: Press Release Distribution, Targeting, Monitoring and Marketing. June 27, 2018. https://www.prnewswire.com/news-releases/bayer-and-ginkgo-bioworks-unveil-joint-venture-joyn-bio-and-establish-operations-in-boston-and-west-sacramento-300616544.html.

Bernard, Kristine. "Top 10 Coffee Consuming Nations." WorldAtlas. January 5, 2018. https://www.worldatlas.com/articles/top-10-coffee-consuming-nations.html.

Caldwell, Tommy. "GMOs Aren't That Bad, But Monsanto Is the Worst." Vice. June 06, 2013. https://www.vice.com/en_ca/article/nnkqn7/mutant-food-and-the-march-against-monsanto.

"Climate Change Will Cut Crop Yields: Study." Phys.org. August 15, 2017. https://phys.org/news/2017-08-climate-crop-yields.html.

Diane Wu. "Unlocking the Power of Our Soil I Diane Wu, CEO of Trace Genomics." Hello Tomorrow. April 16, 2019. https://www.youtube.com/watch?v=OHzLCjys2HI.

Heikkinen, Niina. "Genetically Engineered Crops Are Safe and Possibly Good for Climate Change." Scientific American. May 18, 2016. https://www.scientificamerican.com/article/genetically-engineered-crops-are-safe-and-possibly-good-for-climate-change/.

"Howler Fungicide for Better Crops by AgBiome Innovations." Howler. https://agbiome.com/howler/.

Indigo Ag. "For Growers." Indigo Ag. https://www.indigoag.com/for-growers.

Indigo Ag. Crunchbase. https://www.crunchbase.com/organization/indigoag

Joyn Bio. Crunchbase. https://www.crunchbase.com/organization/joyn-bio

"Joyn Bio." Joyn Bio. https://joynbio.com/.

Krotz, Dan. "Gut Microbes Enable Coffee Pest to Withstand Extremely Toxic Concentrations of Caffeine." News Center. July 19, 2015. https://newscenter.lbl.gov/2015/07/14/microbes-coffee-pest/.

Oshima, Marc. "How Vertical Can Farms Get? | Marc Oshima | HT Summit 2017." Hello Tomorrow. December 01, 2017. https://www.youtube.com/watch?v=7WDGk-knaRaU.

Perry, David, and Signe Brewster. "Indigo Bets on Microbes to Boost Plants." YouTube. July 21, 2016. https://www.youtube.com/watch?v=flw7fb11kOU.

Pivot Bio. "Pivot Bio, Bayer Announce Research Collaboration." Pivot Bio, Bayer Announce Research Collaboration. November 8, 2018. https://blog.pivotbio.com/press-releases/pivot-bio-bayer-announce-research-collaboration.

Pivot Bio. "Pivot Bio Advances Toward Commercial Launch of First Sustainable Nitrogen Product." PR Newswire: Press Release Distribution, Targeting, Monitoring and Marketing. August 06, 2018. https://www.prnewswire.com/news-releases/pivot-bio-advances-toward-commercial-launch-of-first-sustainable-nitrogen-product-300692236.html.

Pivot Bio. "Pivot Bio PROVEN Outperforms Chemical Fertilizer." Pivot Bio PROVEN Outperforms Chemical Fertilizer. February 6, 2019. https://blog.pivotbio.com/press-releases/pivot-bio-proven-outperforms-chemical-fertilizer.

Pivot Bio. Crunchbase. https://www.crunchbase.com/organization/pivot-bio

"Platform." AgBiome. https://agbiome.com/platform/.

Rathi, Akshat. "The Improbable New Wine Countries That Climate Change Is Creating." Quartzy. November 10, 2017. https://qz.com/quartzy/1108814/the-improbable-new-wine-countries-that-climate-change-is-creating/.

Samuel, Henry. "France Becomes First Country in Europe to Ban All Five Pesticides Killing Bees ." The Telegraph. August 31, 2018. https://www.telegraph.co.uk/news/2018/08/31/france-first-ban-five-pesticides-killing-bees/.

Splitter, Jenny. "Pivot Bio Secures $70M Investment For Nitrogen-Producing Microbes." Forbes. October 03, 2018. https://www.forbes.com/sites/jennysplitter/2018/10/03/pivot-bio-secures-70-million-investment-for-nitrogen-producing-microbes/#-41fabbea3d4b.

Splitter, Jenny. "These Super-Microbes Could Fix Agriculture's Nitrogen Problem." Forbes. September 21, 2018. https://www.forbes.com/sites/jennysplitter/2018/09/20/these-super-microbes-could-fix-agricultures-nitrogen-problem/#36b3214743db.

TechCrunch. "Indigo Bets on Microbes to Boost Plants." July 21, 2016. https://www.youtube.com/watch?v=flw7fb11kOU.

Temme, Karsten. "Pivot Bio: The Crop Microbiome Is the Future of Fertilizer." World AgriTech USA. March 13, 2018. https://worldagritechusa.com/pivotbio-crop-microbiome/.

Temme, Karsten. "Pivot Bio Nearing Launch of First Sustainable Nitrogen Product."
Pivot Bio Nearing Launch of First Sustainable Nitrogen Product. August 6, 2018.
https://blog.pivotbio.com/press-releases/pivot-bio-nearing-launch-of-first-sus-
tainable-nitrogen-product.

Walton, Justin. "The 5 Countries That Produce the Most Coffee." Investopedia. March
12, 2019. https://www.investopedia.com/articles/investing/091415/5-countries-pro-
duce-most-coffee.asp.

"World Population Projected to Reach 9.8 Billion in 2050, and 11.2 Billion in 2100 |
UN DESA Department of Economic and Social Affairs." United Nations. June 21,
2017. https://www.un.org/development/desa/en/news/population/world-popu-
lation-prospects-2017.html.

Chapter 6

Agapakis, Christina. "Reviving the Smell of Extinct Plants." Ginkgo Bioworks, May
7, 2019. https://www.ginkgobioworks.com/2019/05/03/reviving-the-smell-of-ex-
tinct-plants/.

Arthur, Rachel. "Bolt Threads Is Launching Its First Bioengineered Spider Silk Product At SXSW - A Necktie." Forbes. March 10, 2017. https://www.forbes.com/sites/
rachelarthur/2017/03/10/bolt-threads-is-launching-its-first-bioengineered-spi-
der-silk-product-at-sxsw-a-necktie/#6bb82c714d13.

Bolt Threads. Crunchbase. https://www.crunchbase.com/organization/bolt-threads

"Bombyx Mori." Wikipedia. May 19, 2019. https://en.wikipedia.org/wiki/Bombyx_mori.

Canales, Katie. "I Went inside the Bolt Threads Factory, Where Synthetic Spider Silk
and Mushroom Root-derived Leather Materials Are Produced for the Fashion
Industry." Business Insider. May 19, 2018. https://www.businessinsider.com/
bolt-threads-microsilk-mylo-spider-silk-sustainable-technology-fashion-2018-
5#as-far-as-smell-goes-widmaier-said-the-material-smells-like-a-funky-mush-
room-when-it-comes-right-out-of-the-incubator-but-once-its-treated-it-takes-
on-a-neutral-scent-18.

Celedon, Jose M., Angela Chiang, Macaire M.S. Yuen, Maria L. Diaz-Chavez, Lufiani L.
Madilao, Patrick M. Finnegan, Elizabeth L. Barbour, and Jörg Bohlmann. "Heart-
wood-specific Transcriptome and Metabolite Signatures of Tropical Sandalwood
(Santalum Album) Reveal the Final Step of (Z)-santalol Fragrance Biosynthesis."
The Plant Journal. April 15, 2016. https://onlinelibrary.wiley.com/doi/full/10.1111/
tpj.13162.

Chakravarti, Deboki. "Resurrecting the Genes of Extinct Plants." Scientific American, January 18, 2019. https://www.scientificamerican.com/video/resurrecting-the-genes-of-extinct-plants/.

Davies, Emma. "Chemistry in Every Cup." Chemistry World. April 28, 2011. https://www.chemistryworld.com/features/chemistry-in-every-cup/3004537.article.

Diaz-Chavez, Maria L., Jessie Moniodis, Lufiani L. Madilao, Sharon Jancsik, Christopher I. Keeling, Elizabeth L. Barbour, Emilio L. Ghisalberti, Julie A. Plummer, Christopher G. Jones, and Jörg Bohlmann. "Biosynthesis of Sandalwood Oil: Santalum Album CYP76F Cytochromes P450 Produce Santalols and Bergamotol." PLOS ONE. September 18, 2013. https://journals.plos.org/plosone/article?id=10.1371/journal.pone.0075053.

"Electrofuel." Wikipedia. November 29, 2018. https://en.wikipedia.org/wiki/Electrofuel.

Feldman, Amy. "Bolt Threads Debuts New 'Leather' Made From Mushroom Roots." Forbes. May 31, 2018. https://www.forbes.com/sites/amyfeldman/2018/04/16/synthetic-spider-silk-maker-bolt-threads-debuts-new-bio-material-leather-made-from-mushroom-roots/#3642d8121837.

Feldman, Amy. "Clothes From A Petri Dish: $700 Million Bolt Threads May Have Cracked The Code On Spider Silk." Forbes. August 15, 2018. https://www.forbes.com/sites/amyfeldman/2018/08/14/clothes-from-a-petri-dish-700-million-bolt-threads-may-have-cracked-the-code-on-spider-silk/#64d2d02dbda1.

Feldman, Amy. "Bioengineered Bacon? The Entrepreneur Behind Mushroom-Root Packaging Says His Test Version Is Tasty." Forbes. Forbes Magazine, December 17, 2018. https://www.forbes.com/sites/amyfeldman/2018/12/16/bioengineered-bacon-the-entrepreneur-behind-mushroom-root-packaging-says-his-test-version-is-tasty/#6f28b33c4fb4.

Feldman, Amy. "The Life Factory: Synthetic Organisms From This $1.4 Billion Startup Will Revolutionize Manufacturing." Forbes. Forbes Magazine, August 2, 2019. https://www.forbes.com/sites/amyfeldman/2019/08/05/the-life-factory-synthetic-organisms-from-startup-ginkgo-bioworks-unicorn-will-revolutionize-manufacturing/#7072363e145e.

Get Smart. Directed by Peter Segal. Performed by Steve Carell and Anne Hathaway. Get Smart. June 20, 2008.

Hanson, Joe. "20 MILLION Year-Old Spider and the Science of Spider Silk." It's Okay To Be Smart. December 12, 2017. https://www.youtube.com/watch?v=QQOxB_ylkvs.

Keenan, Rebecca, and Pratik Parija. "This Sandalwood Plantation Is About to Make Its Owners a Lot of Money." Bloomberg.com. February 21, 2017. https://www.

bloomberg.com/news/features/2017-02-21/australian-sandalwood-plantation-is-about-to-make-its-owners-a-lot-of-money.

Ledford, Heidi. "Hungry Fungi Chomp on Radiation." Nature News. Nature Publishing Group, May 23, 2007. https://www.nature.com/news/2007/070521/full/news070521-5.html.

Mischel, Fiona. "How Fungi Will Give Form to the Future of Food: A Conversation with Ecovatives Eben Bayer." SynBioBeta, August 12, 2019. https://synbiobeta.com/how-fungi-will-give-form-to-the-future-of-food-a-conversation-with-ecovatives-eben-bayer/.

"New Way to Form Bioactive Spider Silk for Medical Use." ScienceDaily. December 04, 2017. https://www.sciencedaily.com/releases/2017/12/171204091427.htm.

Pallavi, Aparna. "Return of Scented Wood." DownToEarth. September 19, 2018. https://www.downtoearth.org.in/coverage/forests/return-of-scented-wood-48569.

Parry, Ernest John. "The Chemistry of Essential Oils and Artificial Perfumes." Google Books. https://books.google.com/books?id=PspLAAAAYAAJ&pg=PA288#v=onepage&q&f=false.

"Saint Louis Zoo." Silkworm | Saint Louis Zoo. https://www.stlzoo.org/animals/about-theanimals/invertebrates/insects/butterfliesandmoths/silkworm.

"Santalum album." Wikipedia. April 28, 2019. https://en.wikipedia.org/wiki/Santalum_album.

"Tom Knight (scientist)." Wikipedia. December 22, 2017. https://en.wikipedia.org/wiki/Tom_Knight_(scientist).

The Hunger Games, Directed by Gary Ross. Performed by Jennifer Lawrence, Josh Hutcherson, and Liam Hemsworth. 2012.

Widmaier, Dan. "How Nature Inspires Us to Build New Materials | Panel | HT Summit." Hello Tomorrow. March 19, 2018. https://www.youtube.com/watch?v=ObvQ2jUvoGU.

Chapter 7

Berezow, Alex. "Black Death: The Upside To The Plague Killing Half Of Europe." Forbes. May 12, 2014. https://www.forbes.com/sites/alexberezow/2014/05/12/black-death-the-upside-to-the-plague-killing-half-of-europe/#411323a70d32.

Berlinger, Joshua. "World's Last Male Northern White Rhino Dies." CNN. March 20, 2018. https://www.cnn.com/2018/03/20/africa/last-male-white-rhino-dies-intl/index.html.

Birnbaum, Sarah. "What I Learned from 'Breaking Bad' about Saving Sea Turtles." Public Radio International, June 5, 2017. https://www.pri.org/stories/2017-06-05/what-i-learned-breaking-bad-about-saving-sea-turtles.

Brand, Stewart. "2017 : WHAT SCIENTIFIC TERM OR CONCEPT OUGHT TO BE MORE WIDELY KNOWN?" Edge.org. 2017. https://www.edge.org/response-detail/27232.

Carrington, Damian. "Earth Has Lost Half of Its Wildlife in the past 40 Years, Says WWF." The Guardian. September 30, 2014. https://www.theguardian.com/environment/2014/sep/29/earth-lost-50-wildlife-in-40-years-wwf.

CBS News. "Scientists Hope "Frozen Zoo" Will Help save Endangered Species." CBS News. February 27, 2015. https://www.cbsnews.com/news/san-diego-frozen-zoo-safari-park-hopes-genetic-bank-will-help-save-endangered-species/.

Cornwall, Warren. "Researchers Embrace a Radical Idea: Engineering Coral to Cope with Climate Change." Science. March 21, 2019. https://www.sciencemag.org/news/2019/03/researchers-embrace-radical-idea-engineering-coral-cope-climate-change.

"Extinction Vortex." Wikipedia. May 22, 2019. https://en.wikipedia.org/wiki/Extinction_vortex.

Flinders University. "DNA Match-making for Endangered Animals in Captivity." Phys.org. November 11, 2016. https://phys.org/news/2016-11-dna-match-making-endangered-animals-captivity.html.

Fogel, Dave, and Jennifer Fogel. "Reptiles And Amphibians In Pharmaceutical Research." Reptiles Magazine. http://www.reptilesmagazine.com/Reptiles-And-Amphibians-In-Pharmaceutical-Research/.

Gammon, Katharine. "Climate Change Is Forcing Polar Bears North-Here's Why That's Bad News." TakePart. January 09, 2015. http://www.takepart.com/article/2015/01/09/polar-bears-canada-genetic-diversity-climate-change.

Great Big Story. "Four Stories About Saving Endangered Species." YouTube. October 15, 2018. https://www.youtube.com/watch?v=5xQsyOvjOqw.

Guardians of the Galaxy Vol. 2. Directed by James Gunn. Performed by Chris Pratt and Zoe Saldana. Guardians of the Galaxy Vol. 2. May 5, 2017.

Hale, Tom. "These Are Stephen Hawking's Last Messages To Humanity." IFLScience. October 16, 2018. https://www.iflscience.com/physics/these-are-stephen-hawkings-last-messages-to-humanity/.

Hanski, Ilkka. "Habitat Loss, the Dynamics of Biodiversity, and a Perspective on Conservation." Ambio. May 18, 2011. https://www.ncbi.nlm.nih.gov/pmc/articles/PMC3357798/.

Herdell, Josette, Maureen Cavanaugh, and Jeff Corwin. "Biologist Jeff Corwin Draws Attention To The Earth's Most Endangered Species." KPBS Public Media. November 10, 2009. https://www.kpbs.org/news/2009/nov/10/biologist-jeff-corwin-draws-attention-earths-most-/.

"Jennifer Doudna Named to 2015 "TIME 100"." Jennifer Doudna Named to 2015 "TIME 100" - Innovative Genomics Institute (IGI). April 26, 2015. https://innovativegenomics.org/news/jennifer-doudna-named-to-2015-time-100-time-magazines-annual-list-of-the-100-most-influential-people-in-the-world/.

Jones, Nicola. "As Ocean Waters Heat Up, A Quest to Create 'Super Corals'." Yale E360. August 4, 2015. https://e360.yale.edu/features/as_ocean_waters_heat_up_a_quest_to_create_super_corals.

Lewin, Tamar. "Babies From Skin Cells? Prospect Is Unsettling to Some Experts." The New York Times. May 16, 2017. https://www.nytimes.com/2017/05/16/health/ivg-reproductive-technology.html.

Markus, Matthew. "Rhino Poaching Stats 101." Pembient. Pembient, February 18, 2019. https://www.pembient.com/blog/2018/10/23/rhino-poaching-stats-101.

Park, Alice. "How CRISPR Gene Editing Could Save Coral Reefs." Time. April 23, 2018. http://time.com/5250927/crispr-gene-editing-coral-reefs/.

Pontin, Jason. "Science Is Getting Us Closer to the End of Infertility." Wired. March 28, 2018. https://www.wired.com/story/reverse-infertility/.

Rana, Preetika. "How a Chinese Scientist Broke the Rules to Create the First Gene-Edited Babies." The Wall Street Journal. May 10, 2019. https://www.wsj.com/articles/how-a-chinese-scientist-broke-the-rules-to-create-the-first-gene-edited-babies-11557506697.

Taronga Conservation Society Australia. "10 Endangered Species Saved from Extinction by Zoos." Medium. May 19, 2017. https://medium.com/taronga-conservation-society-australia/10-endangered-species-saved-from-extinction-by-zoos-682c454d0125.

"The Burning of the Library of Alexandria." eHISTORY, n.d. https://ehistory.osu.edu/articles/burning-library-alexandria.

"What Is Biomimicry?—Biomimicry Institute." Biomimicry Institute. https://biomimicry.org/what-is-biomimicry/.

"White Rhinoceros." Wikipedia. May 19, 2019. https://en.wikipedia.org/wiki/White_rhinoceros.

Chapter 8

Actman, Jani. "Exotic Pet Trade, Explained." National Geographic. February 20, 2019. https://www.nationalgeographic.com/animals/reference/exotic-pet-trade/.

Akst, Jef. "Gene Drive–Equipped Mosquitoes Released into Lab Environment." The Scientist Magazine®. February 20, 2019. https://www.the-scientist.com/news-opinion/gene-driveequipped-mosquitoes-released-into-lab-environment-65493.

"Brown Rat." Wikipedia. April 24, 2019. https://en.wikipedia.org/wiki/Brown_rat.

"Bullseye Snakehead." Florida Fish And Wildlife Conservation Commission. https://myfwc.com/wildlifehabitats/profiles/freshwater/bullseye-snakehead/.

"CRISPR." Wikipedia. May 21, 2019. https://en.wikipedia.org/wiki/CRISPR.

Fleshler, David. "Easy Money? Not for Python Hunters Who Grapple with Everglades Giants for $8.10 an Hour." Sun Sentinel. December 29, 2017. https://www.sun-sentinel.com/news/florida/fl-reg-python-hunter-results-20171227-story.html.

Killer, Ed. "Can Burmese Pythons Be Eradicated from the Everglades? Judas Snake Program Shows Promise." TCPalm. Treasure Coast Newspapers, June 13, 2019. https://www.tcpalm.com/story/news/2019/06/13/judas-snake-program-removes-burmese-pythons-from-everglades/1407502001/.

Leitschuh, Carolina M., et al. "Developing Gene Drive Technologies to Eradicate Invasive Rodents from Islands." Taylor & Francis. December 19, 2017. https://www.tandfonline.com/doi/full/10.1080/23299460.2017.1365232.

"Lionfish Derbies." Lionfish Derbies | Reef Environmental Education Foundation. https://www.reef.org/lionfish-derbies.

Lost. Directed by J.J. Abrams. Performed by Matthew Fox and Evangeline Lilly. Lost. September 22, 2004.

Morris, Lulu. "Quolls Trained to Stay Away from Poisonous Cane Toads." National Geographic. May 22, 2017. https://www.nationalgeographic.com.au/australia/quolls-trained-to-stay-away-from-poisonous-cane-toads.aspx.

National Geographic. "Divers Fight the Invasive Lionfish | National Geographic." YouTube. July 24, 2015. https://www.youtube.com/watch?v=GzaeYzAC8Ro.

Neme, Laurel. "Petition Seeks Ban on Trade in Fake Rhino Horn." National Geographic. February 10, 2016. https://news.nationalgeographic.com/2016/02/160210-rhino-horn-wildlife-trafficking-pembient-poaching-conservation/.

Phelan, Jessica. "6 Endangered Animals That Poaching Might Take from Us Forever." Public Radio International. July 20, 2015. https://www.pri.org/stories/2015-07-30/6-endangered-animals-poaching-might-take-us-forever.

"Precautionary Principle." Precautionary Principle - an Overview | ScienceDirect Topics. https://www.sciencedirect.com/topics/earth-and-planetary-sciences/precautionary-principle.

Regalado, Antonio. "Can CRISPR Restore New Zealand's Ecosystem to the Way It Was?" MIT Technology Review. February 10, 2017. https://www.technologyreview.com/s/603533/first-gene-drive-in-mammals-could-aid-vast-new-zealand-eradication-plan/.

Regalado, Antonio. "Releasing CRISPR into the Wild Means No Turning Back." MIT Technology Review. December 08, 2015. https://www.technologyreview.com/s/543721/with-this-genetic-engineering-technology-theres-no-turning-back/.

Summers, Hannah. "How Whale Sharks Saved a Philippine Fishing Town and Its Sea Life." The Guardian. December 10, 2018. https://www.theguardian.com/environment/2018/dec/10/how-whale-sharks-saved-a-filippino-fishing-town-and-its-sea-life.

"The Giant Snakehead - River Monsters | Animal Planet." Animal Planet - Full Episodes and Exclusive Videos. https://www.animalplanet.com/tv-shows/river-monsters/videos/the-giant-snakehead.

Valentine, Katie. "The Critically Endangered Kakapo Parrot Is Having One Fantastic Year." Audubon. August 5, 2016. https://www.audubon.org/news/the-critically-endangered-kakapo-parrot-having-one-fantastic-year.

Vocativ. "This Robot Hunts Invasive Lionfish." YouTube. April 21, 2017. https://www.youtube.com/watch?v=V1CT2prWVtc.

Warfield, Kristen. "People Are Farming Tigers For This Bizarre Wine." The Dodo. July 27, 2018. https://www.thedodo.com/in-the-wild/tiger-farm-asia.

Weisberger, Mindy. ""Vegetarian Piranhas" with Human-like Teeth Found in Michigan Lakes." CBS News. August 15, 2016. https://www.cbsnews.com/news/vegetarian-piranhas-with-human-like-teeth-found-in-michigan-lakes/.

Yong, Ed. "New Zealand's War on Rats Could Change the World." The Atlantic. November 16, 2017. https://www.theatlantic.com/science/archive/2017/11/new-zealand-predator-free-2050-rats-gene-drive-ruh-roh/546011/.

Chapter 9

Animal Planet. "Has The 'Extinct' Zanzibar Leopard Been Found Once More? | Extinct or Alive." YouTube. September 30, 2018. https://www.youtube.com/watch?v=WUt-F642eegs.

Begley, Sharon. "Scientists Reconstruct the Genome of a Moa, a Bird Extinct for 700 Years." STAT. February 27, 2018. https://www.statnews.com/2018/02/27/moa-extinct-bird-genome/.

Brand, Stewart, George Church, Lynn J. Rothschild, and Ross MacPhee. "Don't Bring Extinct Creatures Back to Life." IQ2US Debates. January 31, 2019. https://www.intelligencesquaredus.org/debates/dont-bring-extinct-creatures-back-life?fbclid=IwAR1UBW8aRV2aoH-Ef7UHSnXWgeiPnknYmv9jQhUSW2f8SEW4deb-FLHQpmWA.

Couzin-Frankel, Jennifer. "Fluid-filled 'biobag' Allows Premature Lambs to Develop outside the Womb." Science. April 25, 2017. https://www.sciencemag.org/news/2017/04/fluid-filled-biobag-allows-premature-lambs-develop-outside-womb.

CTV News. "Baby Sheep Successfully Grown in Artificial 'biobag' Womb." YouTube. April 26, 2017. https://www.youtube.com/watch?v=LWpsJIFbdIo.

Duncan, David Ewing. "Inside the Very Big, Very Controversial Business of Dog Cloning." Vanities. August 07, 2018. https://www.vanityfair.com/style/2018/08/dog-cloning-animal-sooam-hwang.

Expedition Unknown. "Cloning the Woolly Mammoth." Discovery. https://www.discovery.com/tv-shows/expedition-unknown/full-episodes/cloning-the-woolly-mammoth.

Expedition Unknown. "Journey to the Ice Age." Discovery. https://www.discovery.com/tv-shows/expedition-unknown/full-episodes/journey-to-the-ice-age

"Fax." Wikipedia. May 23, 2019. https://en.wikipedia.org/wiki/Fax.

Golder, Andy. "23 Facts That Will Totally Fuck With Your Perception Of Time." BuzzFeed. December 11, 2016. https://www.buzzfeed.com/andyneuenschwander/23-mind-blowing-facts-about-time-thatll-make-you-say-whoa.

"Great Pyramid of Giza." Wikipedia. May 17, 2019. https://en.wikipedia.org/wiki/Great_Pyramid_of_Giza.

Handwerk, Brian. "Woolly Mammoth DNA Reveals Elephant Family Tree." National Geographic. December 20, 2005. https://www.nationalgeographic.com/animals/2005/12/woolly-mammoth-evolution/.

JRE Clips. "Searching for the Tasmanian Tiger | Joe Rogan & Forrest Galante." YouTube. February 06, 2019. https://www.youtube.com/watch?v=xob8uPXgcIA.

Kaplan, Matt. "DNA Has a 521-year Half-life." Nature News. October 10, 2012. https://www.nature.com/news/dna-has-a-521-year-half-life-1.11555.

"Library of Alexandria." Wikipedia. May 29, 2019. https://en.wikipedia.org/wiki/Library_of_Alexandria.

"Loxafr3.0 - LoxArf3 - Genome - Assembly - NCBI." National Center for Biotechnology Information. https://www.ncbi.nlm.nih.gov/assembly/GCF_000001905.1/.

MacNeil, Caeleigh. "How Wolves Saved the Foxes, Mice and Rivers of Yellowstone National Park." Earthjustice. October 26, 2016. https://earthjustice.org/blog/2015-july/how-wolves-saved-the-foxes-mice-and-rivers-of-yellowstone-national-park.

Meslow, Scott. "The Last Jedi's Porgs Are Actually... Puffins?" GQ. December 21, 2017. https://www.gq.com/story/porgs-only-exist-because-star-wars-the-last-jedi-couldnt-get-rid-of-puffins.

"Pleistocene Park." Wikipedia. April 17, 2019. https://en.wikipedia.org/wiki/Pleistocene_Park.

Resnick, Brian. "Melting Permafrost in the Arctic Is Unlocking Diseases and Warping the Landscape." Vox. February 06, 2018. https://www.vox.com/2017/9/6/16062174/permafrost-melting.

Shankman, Sabrina. "In Alaska's Thawing Permafrost, Humanity's 'Library Is on Fire'." InsideClimate News. November 30, 2017. https://insideclimatenews.org/news/30112017/alaska-global-warming-archaeology-permafrost-history-artifacts-sea-ice-hunting-whaling-traditions.

Strauss, Bob. "These 10 Birds Went Extinct Thanks to Humans - and Cats." ThoughtCo. February 23, 2019. https://www.thoughtco.com/recently-extinct-birds-1093727.

"Woolly Mammoth." Wikipedia. May 31, 2019. https://en.wikipedia.org/wiki/Woolly_mammoth.

"Woolly Mammoth Revival." Revive & Restore. April 18, 2018. https://reviverestore.org/projects/woolly-mammoth/.

"Zanzibar Leopard." Wikipedia. April 26, 2019. https://en.wikipedia.org/wiki/Zanzibar_leopard.

Chapter 10

"About the Heath Hen Project." Revive & Restore, August 20, 2019. https://reviverestore.org/projects/heath-hen-project/.

"About the Passenger Pigeon." Revive & Restore, July 10, 2018. https://reviverestore.org/about-the-passenger-pigeon/.

"Alien (franchise)." Wikipedia. June 02, 2019. https://en.wikipedia.org/wiki/Alien_(franchise).

Begley, Sharon. "Scientists Reconstruct the Genome of a Moa, a Bird Extinct for 700 Years." STAT. February 27, 2018. https://www.statnews.com/2018/02/27/moa-extinct-bird-genome/.

"Black-Footed Ferret." Revive & Restore. April 30, 2019. https://reviverestore.org/projects/black-footed-ferret/.

Boissoneault, Lorraine. "When the Nazis Tried to Bring Animals Back From Extinction." Smithsonian.com. March 31, 2017. https://www.smithsonianmag.com/history/when-nazis-tried-bring-animals-back-extinction-180962739/.

Bradford, Alina. "Ostrich Facts: The World's Largest Bird." LiveScience. September 17, 2014. https://www.livescience.com/27433-ostriches.html.

Business Insider. "Why Horseshoe Crab Blood Is So Expensive | So Expensive." YouTube. September 01, 2018. https://www.youtube.com/watch?v=LgQZWSlLBnA.

"Even More Amphibians Are Endangered than We Thought." ScienceDaily. ScienceDaily, May 6, 2019. https://www.sciencedaily.com/releases/2019/05/190506124115.htm.

"First Catalyst Fund Grant Awarded." Revive & Restore. October 25, 2018. https://reviverestore.org/first-catalyst-fund-grant-awarded/.

"Gastric-brooding Frog." Wikipedia. May 31, 2019. https://en.wikipedia.org/wiki/Gastric-brooding_frog.

Gross Science. "Meet The Frog That Barfs Up Its Babies." YouTube. May 08, 2017. https://www.youtube.com/watch?v=9xfX_NTrFRM.

"Horseshoe Crab." Revive & Restore, June 5, 2019. https://reviverestore.org/horseshoe-crab/.

"Jon Snow." Game of Thrones Wiki. https://gameofthrones.fandom.com/wiki/Jon_Snow.

"Lazarus Project: Extinct Frog Brought Back To Life, What Next." nexpected, n.d. https://www.nexpected.com/2019/03/lazarus-project-extinct-frog-brought.html.

Maloney, Tom, Ryan Phelan, and Naira Simmons. "Saving the Horseshoe Crab: A Synthetic Alternative to Horseshoe Crab Blood for Endotoxin Detection." PLOS Biology. Public Library of Science, October 12, 2018. https://journals.plos.org/plosbiology/article?id=10.1371/journal.pbio.2006607.

"Moa." Wikipedia. June 04, 2019. https://en.wikipedia.org/wiki/Moa.

Morell, Virginia. "Why Did New Zealand's Moas Go Extinct?" Science. March 17, 2014. https://www.sciencemag.org/news/2014/03/why-did-new-zealands-moas-go-extinct.

National Geographic. "NG Hitler's Jurassic Monsters - Video Dailymotion." Dailymotion. June 16, 2015. https://www.dailymotion.com/video/x2u49p5.

"Nazi Nature." National Geographic - Videos, TV Shows & Photos - International. http://www.natgeotv.com/int/hitlers-jurassic-monsters/videos/nazi-nature.

Phillips, Nicky. "Extinct Frog Hops Back into the Gene Pool." The Sydney Morning Herald. March 15, 2013. https://www.smh.com.au/environment/conservation/extinct-frog-hops-back-into-the-gene-pool-20130315-2g68x.html.

"Progress to Date." Revive & Restore, October 19, 2018. https://reviverestore.org/projects/the-great-passenger-pigeon-comeback/progress-to-date/.

"Pyrenean Ibex." Wikipedia. May 24, 2019. https://en.wikipedia.org/wiki/Pyrenean_ibex.

Rincon, Paul. "Fresh Effort to Clone Extinct Animal." BBC News. November 22, 2013. https://www.bbc.com/news/science-environment-25052233.

"Ryan Phelan." Ryan Phelan | Edge.org. https://www.edge.org/memberbio/ryan_phelan.

Servick, Kelly. "The Plan to Bring the Iconic Passenger Pigeon Back From Extinction." Wired. June 4, 2017. https://www.wired.com/2013/03/passenger-pigeon-de-extinction/.

"Slug-vomiting Charm." Harry Potter Wiki. https://harrypotter.fandom.com/wiki/Slug-vomiting_Charm.

Thomson, Craig. The Lazarus Project- to Bring Back Australia's Southern Gastric-brooding Frog. March 29, 2017. https://awpc.org.au/the-lazarus-project-to-bring-back-australias-southern-gastric-brooding-frog/.

"The Francis Crick Papers: The Discovery of the Double Helix, 1951-1953." U.S. National Library of Medicine. https://profiles.nlm.nih.gov/SC/Views/Exhibit/narrative/doublehelix.html.

"Woolly Mammoth Revival." Revive & Restore. April 18, 2018. https://reviverestore.org/projects/woolly-mammoth/.

Yeoman, Barry. "Why the Passenger Pigeon Went Extinct." Audubon, April 13, 2016. https://www.audubon.org/magazine/may-june-2014/why-passenger-pigeon-went-extinct.

Conclusion

"3-D Printed Copies of Famous Paintings Recreate Brush Strokes, Cracks." CBCnews. June 12, 2016. https://www.cbc.ca/news/canada/british-columbia/3-d-printed-copies-of-famous-paintings-recreate-brush-strokes-cracks-1.3624415.

Amadeo, Kimberly. "What the S&P 500 Tells You About America's Health." The Balance. December 21, 2018. https://www.thebalance.com/what-is-the-sandp-500-3305888.

Anthony, Scott D., S. Partrick Viguerie, Evan I. Schwartz, and John Van Landeghem. "Corporate Longevity Forecast: Creative Destruction Is Accelerating." Innosight. 2018. https://www.innosight.com/insight/creative-destruction/.

Auvsi News. "PrecisionHawk Uses Drone Technology to Hunt for Buried Treasure in the Philippines." Association for Unmanned Vehicle Systems International. March 26, 2019. https://www.auvsi.org/industry-news/precisionhawk-uses-drone-technology-hunt-buried-treasure-philippines.

Avengers: Age of Ultron. Directed by Josh Whedon. Performed by Robert Downey Jr., Chris Evans, Scarlett Johanssen. Avengers: Age of Ultron. May 1, 2015.

Bilyeu, Tom. "I Stopped Chasing Money-Here's What Happened." SUCCESS. August 1, 2017. https://www.success.com/i-stopped-chasing-money-heres-what-happened/.

Boddy, Jessica. "FDA Approves Marketing Of Consumer Genetic Tests For Some Conditions." NPR. April 07, 2017. https://www.npr.org/sections/health-shots/2017/04/07/522897473/fda-approves-marketing-of-consumer-genetic-tests-for-some-conditions.

By Jahleel Coleman. Next Gen Summit, New York City, June 9, 2018.

By Jeff Hoffman. Next Gen Summit, New York City, June 10, 2018.

Cabane, Olivia Fox. "The Landscapes." The Alternative Protein Show. https://www.newprotein.org/maps.

Captain America: The First Avenger. Directed by Joe Johnston. Performed by Chris Evans, Hugo Weaving, Hayley Atwell. Captain America: The First Avenger. July 19, 2011.

Carmody, Bill. "How Can I Help? Why 'Adding Value First' Is the Winning Formula for Growth." Inc.com. October 14, 2014. https://www.inc.com/bill-carmody/how-can-i-help-why-adding-value-first-is-the-winning-formula-for-growth.html.

Casadiego, Dulce. "BE AGILE! In Today's Economy, the Fast Fish Eats the Slow Fish!" LinkedIn. September 11, 2017. https://www.linkedin.com/pulse/agile-todays-economy-fast-fish-eats-slow-dulce-casadiego/.

Cornwall, Warren. "Researchers Embrace a Radical Idea: Engineering Coral to Cope with Climate Change." Science. March 21, 2019. https://www.sciencemag.org/news/2019/03/researchers-embrace-radical-idea-engineering-coral-cope-climate-change.

Dietrich, William. "The Writer's Odds of Success." HuffPost. May 04, 2013. https://www.huffpost.com/entry/the-writers-odds-of-succe_b_2806611.

"DNA Genetic Testing & Analysis." 23andMe. https://www.23andme.com.

Fowler, Geoffrey A. "There's an Uber for Everything Now." The Wall Street Journal. May 05, 2015. https://www.wsj.com/articles/theres-an-uber-for-everything-now-1430845789.

Gaiman, Neil. "Neil Gaiman: Keynote Address 2012." University of the Arts. May 17, 2012. https://www.uarts.edu/neil-gaiman-keynote-address-2012.

Game of Thrones. Directed by David Benioff, D. B. Weiss, and George R. R. Martin. Performed by Emilia Clarke, Kit Harrington, Lena Headey, Peter Dinklage. Game of Thrones. May 19, 2019.

Gates, Bill. "New College Grads Often Ask Me for Career Advice. At the Risk of Sounding like This Guy..." Twitter. May 15, 2017. https://twitter.com/BillGates/status/864100357684609025.

Goldberg, Joel. "It Takes A Village To Determine The Origins Of An African Proverb." NPR. July 30, 2016. https://www.npr.org/sections/goatsand-soda/2016/07/30/487925796/it-takes-a-village-to-determine-the-origins-of-an-african-proverb.

Harry Potter and the Sorcerer's Stone. Directed by Chris Columbus. Performed by Daniel Radcliffe, Emma Watson, Rupert Grint. Harry Potter and the Sorcerer's Stone. November 14, 2001.

Henry, Patrick. "Why Some Startups Succeed (and Why Most Fail)." Entrepreneur. February 18, 2017. https://www.entrepreneur.com/article/288769.

Hesse, Jason. "Consumers Are Defining Brands." Raconteur. 2012. https://www.raconteur.net/business-innovation/consumers-defining-brand-values.

Kerpen, Dave. "11 Powerful Quotes to Inspire Your Team to Embrace Change." Inc.com. February 26, 2014. https://www.inc.com/dave-kerpen/11-powerful-quotes-to-inspire-your-team-to-embrace-change.html.

Khazan, Olga. "The Coming Obsolescence of Animal Meat." The Atlantic. April 16, 2019. https://www.theatlantic.com/health/archive/2019/04/just-finless-foods-lab-grown-meat/587227/.

Mochari, Ilan. "'Game of Thrones' Author George R. R. Martin on What Makes Ideas Work." Inc.com. May 02, 2014. https://www.inc.com/ilan-mochari/game-of-thrones-ideas.html.

Molteni, Megan. "The Future of Crime-Fighting Is Family Tree Forensics." Wired. December 26, 2018. https://www.wired.com/story/the-future-of-crime-fighting-is-family-tree-forensics/.

"Neil Gaiman." Wikipedia. May 12, 2019. https://en.wikipedia.org/wiki/Neil_Gaiman.

"Pembient." Pembient. https://www.pembient.com/.

Penn State Alumni Association. https://www.alumni.psu.edu/news.

"Prime Air." Amazon. https://www.amazon.com/Amazon-Prime-Air/b?ie=UT-F8&node=8037720011.

Robbins, Rebecca. "Young-Blood Transfusions Are on the Menu at Society Gala." Scientific American. March 2, 2018. https://www.scientificamerican.com/article/young-blood-transfusions-are-on-the-menu-at-society-gala/?redirect=1.

Roe, David. "What Gig Workers Bring to Forward-Looking Companies." CMSWire.com. April 18, 2019. https://www.cmswire.com/digital-workplace/what-gig-workers-bring-to-forward-looking-companies/.

Scutti, Susan. "First Drone Delivery of a Donated Kidney Ends with Transplant." CNN. May 01, 2019. https://www.cnn.com/2019/05/01/health/drone-organ-transplant-bn-trnd/index.html.

Stein, Rob. "First U.S. Patients Treated With CRISPR As Human Gene-Editing Trials Get Underway." NPR. April 16, 2019. https://www.npr.org/sections/health-shots/2019/04/16/712402435/first-u-s-patients-treated-with-crispr-as-gene-editing-human-trials-get-underway.

"Stephen King." Wikipedia. May 15, 2019. https://en.wikipedia.org/wiki/Stephen_King.

Swetlitz, Ike. "Researchers to Release First-ever Genetically Engineered Mosquitoes in Africa." STAT. September 04, 2018. https://www.statnews.com/2018/09/05/release-genetically-engineered-mosquitoes-africa/.

The Pennsylvania State University College of Engineering, University Park, Pennsylvania, 2018.

"The Parable." Starfish Project. https://starfishproject.com/the-parable/.

"Thomas Bilyeu." Wikipedia. March 25, 2019. https://en.wikipedia.org/wiki/Thomas_Bilyeu.

Thompson, Derek. "Google X and the Science of Radical Creativity." The Atlantic. November 16, 2017. https://www.theatlantic.com/magazine/archive/2017/11/x-google-moonshot-factory/540648/.

Van Zeijderveld, Jessica. "3D Printed Prosthetics: 8 Incredible Animal Prostheses." Sculpteo. May 02, 2018. https://www.sculpteo.com/blog/2018/05/02/3d-printed-prosthetics-8-incredible-animal-prostheses/.

Worland, Justin. "How Air Shepherd Is Fighting Poachers With Drones." Time. May 31, 2018. http://time.com/5279322/drones-poaching-air-shepherd/.

Made in United States
Orlando, FL
08 January 2022

13163533R00134